Light In The Dark

Light In The Dark
Copyright © 2024 by Lin Stepp
Published by Mountain Hill Press
Email contact: steppcom@aol.com

All rights reserved. No part of this book may be reproduced, stored in a retrieval system or transmitted in any form or by any means—electronic, mechanical photocopying, recording or otherwise—without the prior written consent of the publisher, except in brief quotes used in reviews or as expressly permitted by the 1976 Copyright Act.

This is a work of fiction. Although numerous elements of historical and geographic accuracy are utilized in this and other novels in the Smoky Mountain and SC coastal novels, many other specific environs, place names, characters, and incidents are the product of the author's imagination or used fictitiously.

Scripture used in this book, whether quoted or paraphrased by the characters, is taken from the King James Version of the Bible.

Cover design: Katherine E. Stepp
Interior design: J. L. Stepp, Mountain Hill Press
Editor: Elizabeth S. James
Cover photo and map design: Lin M. Stepp

Library of Congress Cataloging-in-Publication Data

Stepp, Lin
Light In The Dark: Third novel in the Lighthouse Sisters series / Lin Stepp

ISBN: 979-8-9877251-4-6
First Mountain Hill Press Trade Paperback Printing: March 2024

eISBN: 979-8-9877251-5-3
First Mountain Hill Press Electronic Edition: March 2024

1. Women—Southern States—Fiction 2. South Carolina—Coastal—Fiction
3. Contemporary Romance—Inspirational—Fiction. I. Title

Library of Congress Control Number: 2024900971

Light In The Dark

3rd Novel In The
LIGHTHOUSE SISTERS SERIES

LIN STEPP

MOUNTAIN HILL PRESS

DEDICATION

This book is dedicated to all my fans and readers who loved my Edisto Trilogy of books set in the Lowcountry of South Carolina and who asked for more!

ACKNOWLEDGEMENTS

"Always have an attitude of gratitude." – Sterling Brown

Gratitude and thanks to everyone at Edisto Island, South Carolina, who shared their memories and stories, making the island, its people, and its history come alive as I worked on planning my new Lighthouse Sisters novels.

Thanks to the Charleston, SC, Visitors Center on Meeting Street where I picked up wonderful brochures, maps, and other helpful information for the portions of my book set there.

I also appreciate the kindness given to us as we visited in shops and restaurants around Charleston for many of the scenes in this new story— especially in downtown Charleston near King Street where much of this book is set ... like the Elliott House Inn, the Charleston Library Society, Gibbes Museum of Art, Buxton Books, and the many charming restaurants around the area like Millers All Day on King, Poogan's Porch and 82 Queen on Queen, the Basic Kitchen on Wentworth, Pizzeria Di Giovanni and High Cotton on Bay, Fleet Landing on Concord, and many more.

Gratitude also to Wey Camp at Trinity Episcopal Church on Edisto, for allowing me to tour the church and grounds, sharing information, and sending me the church's newsletter to continue adding ideas for my new Edisto books. You will find Trinity featured in my books. Also featured in this book is the historic St. Michael's Anglican Church at Broad and Meeting Streets.

Thanks to Karen Carter at the Edisto Island Bookstore for her help with information, island maps, and for introducing me to Charles Spencer's two books on Edisto's history. These and other historical books, found at the bookstore, greatly helped solidify facts about Edisto and fanned my imagination.

Final thanks to the Lowcountry bookstores carrying my South Carolina titles and many of my other books in their stores—Buxton Books on King Street in Charleston- featured in this book, Barnes & Noble Bookstore at Sam Rittenberg Blvd. in Charleston, Beaufort Books on Boundary Street in Beaufort, The Edisto Island Bookstore, and many others.

Acknowledgements to all those who helped with this book:

_ Elizabeth S. James, copyeditor and editorial adviser
_ J.L. Stepp, production design and proofing
_ Katherine Stepp, cover design and graphics
_ And ongoing gratitude to the Lord, who helps me with all my books.

A BRIEF EDISTO HISTORY

2000 BC	Archaic cultures inhabited the island
1550s	Edistow Indians lived on the island
1663	SC Colony founded by King of England
	Lord Proprietors granted lands from Charles II
1700-1770s	Plantations grew, exporting rice and indigo
1775-1783	Rev War; planters fled; property destroyed
1780s-1860s	Plantations thrived growing cotton
1800s	Edingsville Beach formed for wealthy planters
1861-1865	Civil War years; slaves freed; property destroyed
1870s	Many families returned; cotton still a big crop
1893	Hurricane destroyed Edingsville Beach
1920s	Boll weevil ended cotton production
	Drawbridge to island replaced Dawhoo Ferry
	Intercoastal Waterway dredged, linking rivers
	Truck farming and fishing grew on the island
1925	Resort development on Edisto expanded
	Early cottages built, no electricity or water
1935	Edisto Beach State Park built with CCC help
	Palmetto Boulevard paved for cars
1940	Hurricane destroyed most all homes on Edisto
1941-1945	WWII slowed growth; military patrolled island
	Coast Guard patrolled park; reports of spies
	Edisto S.C. Hwy 174 straightened and paved
1950s	Development on Edisto Beach resumed
1954	Big pier built near park entrance; later burned
1959	Hurricane Gracie did heavy damage
	Groins built to hold sand, stop erosion
1970s	Edisto tourism grew and expanded
1973	Oristo resort and golf course opened
1976	Beach changed fr Charleston to Colleton Co
	Remaining Island stayed in Charleston Co
	Many businesses and beach homes built
1976	Fairfield Resorts bought Oristo Ridge
1993	McKinley Washington replaced drawbridge
2006	Fairfield Resort bought by Wyndham
2008	Botany Bay wildlife preserve opened
	Growth continued with beauty remaining

DEVEAUX BANK
ATLANTIC OCEAN
WATCH ISLAND
MAIN BEACH
CABANA
LIGHTHOUSE
Pavilion
INLAND cottage
GUEST COTTAGES
GIFT SHOP
DEVEAUX INN
STOR
FOG HOUSE
Gazebo
Lighthouse ROAD
The LODGE
NORTH EDISTO RIVER
MARINA (Ferry Pickup)
MARSH AREA
Estuary

MAP for WATCH ISLAND

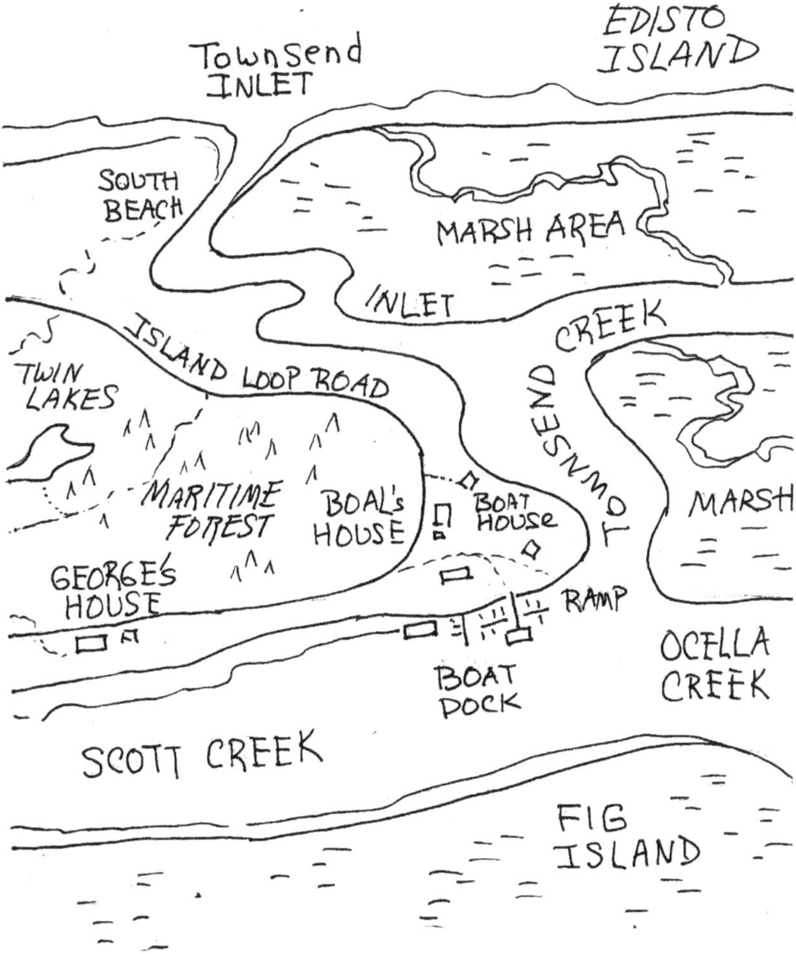

CHAPTER 1

August 2017

The phone woke her. Definitely a little too early. Celeste groaned as she glanced at the clock by the bed while reaching for her cell phone. It was probably her sister Gwen who often called before her school day started.

"Hello," she chimed, trying to sound perkier than she felt. "Is this my wake-up call?"

"Yes, it is," said a deep familiar voice, "and I know where you are."

Celeste sat up in bed, her heart racing.

"Be assured, Celeste Deveaux, I am watching for you to come back and I will find you when you do."

As the line went dead, Celeste dropped the phone as if a snake. How had Dillon found her and gotten her cell number again? She'd changed her phone number after she left Nashville and then again after the divorce finalized. How did he keep finding her? She knew it easy for Dillon to guess she'd come to the island to her family to heal but how did he keep getting her new phone numbers?

Awake now, Celeste headed for the shower, wishing, like the old musical number, she could wash that man right out of her hair, be rid of him and his sick mind forever.

After showering and dressing, she felt especially glad she'd decided to head to Charleston today to take Vanessa to dinner for her birthday. She needed something to get her mind off Dillon's voice echoing in her head. Obviously, she'd also need to stop by her cell service provider in Charleston to switch out the SIM card in her phone and get a new number again.

The smell of hot coffee and breakfast drifted on the air as she made her way through the kitchen toward the Deveaux Inn's dining room. She'd lived at the inn in her old bedroom, in the family apartment, since spring when her sisters Burke and Gwen came to Nashville to find her. Dillon, in one of his senseless rages, had beaten and hospitalized her that time. She hadn't been a pretty picture when her sisters located her, bruised with a broken arm and spirit. But she was grateful they packed her up and brought her home to the island, to her family's home, to rest and heal. She had needed the break and, frankly, it was hard to move on with Dillon still threatening her.

Novaleigh George, the Deveaux Inn's cook and long-time family friend, spotted her as she headed through the kitchen toward the dining room.

"Good morning," she called out, pulling a tray of muffins out of the oven. "Take these with you into the dining room and put them out, would you? They seem popular this morning. Be sure and snag one for yourself too. I put fresh peaches in these muffins and a little vanilla."

Novaleigh tossed the hot muffins into a basket and walked across the kitchen to pass them to Celeste, pausing to study her as she did. "You look upset, sweet thing. What's happened?"

She shrugged. "I got an early wake-up call from Dillon Barlow and not a welcome one."

Novaleigh shook her head. "That man's got a lot of the old devil in him. It sure is a shame with his talent and good looks. I hate that you ever got yourself hooked up with him."

"So do I," she agreed.

"After you take these muffins out for our guests, fix yourself a plate and go join your mother on the screened porch. Waylon, Burke, and Lila are still there, too, going over paperwork."

Celeste hesitated.

"Honey, they all know what you deal with and sharing with them will prove a comfort. They love you, like I do."

"I know. I just hate to upset them."

"They'd be more upset to think you kept this to yourself." Novaleigh paused. "Are you still going into Charleston to take my girl to dinner tonight for her birthday?"

Celeste smiled then. "I am, and I look forward to it."

"It's nice you two girls have gotten back together again. You and Vanessa were such good friends when small, playing around the island here. I know she probably told you we're hosting a family birthday for her at mama and daddy's place after church on Sunday when we're all off work, but I'm glad you could go to Charleston today on her actual birthday."

"I'll take her somewhere special," Celeste promised.

"That would be real nice." Novaleigh's smile slipped a little. "Vanessa's got her own problems right now, too. Maybe you can get her to talk to you about it."

"What's wrong?"

"The job she took at that posh dress shop in downtown Charleston hasn't turned out like she hoped. The hoity-toity store manager, who hired her, promised to train her to be an assistant manager but has back-peddled on her word." Novaleigh made a face. "The woman takes advantage of Vanessa's talents and she steals credit for things Vanessa does, too."

"Like what?"

"Giving her own self credit for things Vanessa does, like arranging clothing in the store real nice, finding and buying items that sell well, and creating pretty window displays. You know Vanessa's always been gifted with that sort of thing."

"I remember. Why doesn't she quit?"

Novaleigh shook her head. "Unlike you, honey child, Vanessa isn't a rich and famous singer with a big bank account to live on. She needs the job, and she left her last job at the mall to take this one downtown in Charleston, thinking it an advancement. She claims job hopping too much doesn't look good on your resume."

"Maybe so, but I don't like to hear she's being treated unfairly."

"Me, neither, but I'm praying over it. Praying for you, too. God will work something out for her and for you. You'll see."

"I hope so."

"Don't you only be hoping-so, that's too much like doubting. Stand in faith, believing that if you ask, God hears and answers." She patted Celeste's cheek. "Go get yourself some breakfast now. I need to make more coffee for all our guests."

Celeste moved into the dining room, putting the fresh muffins on the buffet table and stopping to say hello to a few of the inn's guests. Here at mid-August, they had a full house at the inn with guests staying in two of the rental cottages, too. Summer was always busy at the Deveaux Inn.

After putting a scoop of scrambled eggs, one of Novaleigh's muffins, and some fresh fruit on her plate, Celeste made her way to the big screened porch, more like a cozy sunroom, that spanned the back of the Deveaux Inn. Separate from the inn's porch for their guests, the wide covered room had always been the place where the family ate and shared most of their meals.

"Good morning," her mother said as Celeste made her way out to the porch, sitting her plate on the table and heading to a side buffet to pour herself a mug of hot coffee.

Celeste came back with her coffee and settled into a chair at the table. "Good morning to all of you. I hope I'm not interrupting anything."

"No. We were just looking at the roster of new guests coming in this Friday and talking about plans to put an elevator in the inn this fall when things get quieter." Her mother grinned. "After Rita Jean fell and hurt herself this spring, we started to see the need for an elevator. I admit I wouldn't mind one myself to save running up and down those stairs all day."

Burke laughed. "I wish we could put an elevator in the lighthouse. Then I might not need to climb the 160 stairs to the top every day doing my tours or cleaning."

"You know that's wishful thinking for sure." Waylon winked at her. "But the elevator at the inn is a definite possibility."

Celeste's mother, Etta, passed around pictures and talked more about the elevator plans as Celeste ate her breakfast.

Lila looked across at her in a moment of quiet. "Something's happened," she said. "You look strained."

Celeste sighed. Leave it to Lila to notice.

As they all turned to look her way, Celeste saved any further questions by saying, "Dillon called me this morning and popped off another of his threats."

She saw Waylon's fist clench. "What did he threaten, Celeste? Is he here somewhere nearby?"

"No." She smiled at him, touched at how much like a protective brother he'd become since he married her sister Burke. "He threatened that he'd be looking for me when I came back to Nashville. I keep hoping he'll refocus his attention on someone or something else. He usually does, but all these lawsuits by other women, that he roughed up in the past, seem to keep me on his mind. He blames me for them."

"Why?" Burke put a hand on her hip, annoyed. "You didn't rough those women up. He did. It's his own past catching up to him."

"I know, but someone who is sick like Dillon never sees anything as his own fault. His view is that the publicity I caused created the legal problems for him."

"Excuse me," Burke added sarcastically. "He beat you up and put you in the hospital. You had to get a protective court order served against him. Also, you didn't have anything to do with those hospital pictures, that someone took of you, getting into the tabloids, or with other women he'd hurt deciding to come forward to tell their own stories after seeing what he did to you. I don't see how in the world he can see any of this as your fault."

Celeste shrugged. "Talk to my counselor in Charleston, Burke. He'll explain how a twisted mind like Dillon's works."

"Well, I dearly wish someone would stop him from threatening you," Celeste's mother said. "I admit his threats worry me, especially with your plans to return to Nashville this fall." She paused. "Honey, do you think that's wise?"

Celeste smiled. "Mother, I can't walk away from my life and my career. I have responsibilities."

"I hope your manager and agent will provide some sort of security for you when you go back. Will they?" Waylon asked. "I know Burke told us, after Dillon hospitalized you, that they kept a guard at your apartment."

"They did, and I'm sure they'll see to it I have extra security. They know the threats Dillon has made. I send them any written notes I receive to keep for evidence, and I let them know about any calls I get. People in the entertainment industry often have problems like these," she said, trying to reassure them. "My agency knows how to handle these things."

Celeste turned the conversation in a new direction, reminding them she planned to drive to Charleston to take Vanessa to dinner for her birthday. "I'm also staying over at the Elliott House Inn tonight since I have an appointment with Dr. Conrad early tomorrow. I'll talk some of these things over with him, too."

With a lot on everyone's mind, and a big work day ahead, the family soon returned to their paperwork or left for chores, but Celeste noticed Lila watching her thoughtfully as she finished her breakfast.

She wasn't surprised when Lila walked out with her as she headed back to the family apartment.

"You don't need to remind me to pray, Lila," Celeste said to her. "Novaleigh has already given me that advice."

Her sister smiled, following her into the apartment. "That's good to hear but, actually, I wanted to talk with you about something else. I know you always shop when you go to Charleston. As you walk around, would you check for places I might approach about carrying my paintings? You know one Charleston gallery is keeping some of my work already, but I'd like to find a gift shop that might carry some, too."

"I'll do that." Celeste settled into a corner of the sofa in the apartment. "Do you want to sit down and visit?" She gestured to a chair. "You grew up here at the Inn, like I did, but I understand why you wanted to live in one of the cottages when you came home, to give yourself a more private place of your own."

Lila sat in a chair nearby. "Are you eager to get back to your place in Nashville?"

"Not really, especially with all this mess with Dillon unresolved." She hesitated. "I admit I feel restless and somewhat uncertain about my life right now. Don't you, sometimes, after all the changes from returning home after being in a religious community? It has to feel different for you, too."

"It has been a change, but change isn't always a bad thing. Many people don't have options for change at all in their lives or they are too fearful to take them, even when needed."

"Do you think I'm afraid of change?"

Lila leaned back in the chair and smiled. "No, but I definitely felt timid and reluctant to leave the community when I needed to. I had to be pushed a little. So keep your heart and mind open about your life direction now. Maybe you should explore the idea that a change or changes might be good for you to make."

"Do you think I should give up my career, not sing or write songs again, not entertain?"

"No, and surely you don't think you should. God's given you a fine gift. You know He wants you to use it. But keep your mind open to see if there isn't some other change you might make in your life. I saw shifts and change coming for all of us earlier this year after I came home—for Burke, Gwen, you, and even myself. I've already seen new things come for Burke and Gwen. So have you."

Celeste respected Lila's gift of "knowing" things in the future sometimes. She didn't share the gift, but she respected it in her sister. "Have you seen anything specific I should keep an eye out for?"

"No, but crossroads in our lives often come unexpectedly, so stay alert. There are often opportunities in the midst of problems."

"That's a good thought." Celeste crossed her leg. "Do you want to go to Charleston with me today? I reserved a nice room at the Elliott House Inn. You can go to dinner with Vanessa and me tonight, and we can shop and look for galleries tomorrow."

Lila smiled. "Thank you. That would be fun but I'm needed here right now. The Inn is busy. I run the giftshop. I need to help Burke with the tours, too, and I fill in and work in other places as needed. I also want to paint as much as I can right now. I've connected with a company that can make Giclee prints of my work so I can sell more of each piece. They're also scanning and making greeting cards of my art. Those sell well at the Lighthouse Gift Shop and might sell well in other gift shops I make connection with."

"You have a strong gift yourself, Lila. I'm glad you're finding a way to use it and learning more how to market and promote your work."

"Thanks." Lila glanced at her watch. "And I need to go. Burke has a group tour of the lighthouse coming this morning from St. Christopher's Camp across the river. I don't want those kids unsupervised in the gift shop." She winked at Celeste as she stood. "Stay alert for opportunities."

"I will." Celeste promised.

On her own after Lila left, Celeste answered her emails, made a few necessary business calls, talked to her agent Gary Feinstein in Nashville, and then packed a few clothes for her trip. She'd stop by her cell phone provider in the mall, on Sam Rittenberg Boulevard, as she headed into Charleston, poke around in the Citadel Mall for a while, and then snag a light lunch, before heading downtown to check in at the inn.

Later, at 5:30 and after a full day, Celeste made her way down Queen Street from the Elliott Inn to Thurman's Restaurant. It had been a long time since she'd been in the old restaurant, where she often sang as a young girl, and she thought it would be a nice place to take Vanessa for her birthday dinner.

Thurman's was housed in a historic Victorian mansion, like many of the town's old restaurants. The building's exterior was a soft pinkish buff color with black shutters on the long windows. Three tiers of veranda porches graced the house's side, flanked by a brick walkway and picturesque garden area. It was a beautiful building, but no more so than many other historic homes lining the downtown streets of this old city. Charleston had been named a National Historic Landmark and Celeste had read in a tourist brochure, she picked up at the Elliott, that it had over 2,800 historic buildings in a variety of rich architectural styles. She never tired of walking its streets, taking in the beauty of it.

Celeste arrived at the old restaurant ahead of Vanessa and asked for a quiet table, in her favorite dining room, on the main floor with the piano in it. She looked around the room as she waited for Vanessa, pleased to see the large, high-ceilinged room hadn't changed much, still lavishly furnished, its tables draped in rich crème tablecloths, the chandeliers twinkling overhead in the muted lighting.

At six o'clock, a young Black man, dressed in a tux, settled in at the piano and began to play. The waiters at Thurman's all wore formal attire. It was that sort of place, reeking of elegance and old-world charm. Celeste knew it an old family restaurant and one of the few that only served dinner each day.

She spotted Vanessa coming in the door then, trailing the waiter to their table. She looked good in a blue fitted dress with a sweetheart neck, the soft fabric smoothing over her figure and ending at her knees with a graceful flounce that moved with every step she took. Vanessa had always known how to dress. Her dark hair was sleeked back tonight, caught in some sort of a twist, and her beautiful golden-brown complexion shone in the restaurant's lighting.

Celeste stood to give her a hug. "You look wonderful. Happy birthday."

"Sorry to be a little late," she said. "I had to run home and change before I came. I knew we needed to dress up for Thurman's." Her eyes slid over Celeste as they sat back down. "You look fantastic, too. Red is a great color for you."

Vanessa looked around and then leaned forward to say in a whisper, "You didn't need to bring me to such an elegant place for dinner, Celeste."

"You sound like Gwen," Celeste replied, "always worrying over what a meal will cost. I wanted to come here, Vanessa, so don't worry about the expense. I don't need to think about that in the same way you and Gwen do either. Let me spoil you tonight."

"All right." She gave Celeste a big smile as their waiter came to bring menus. They studied their choices, both deciding on sauteed shrimp and scallops, with parmesan sauce and fettuccine, plus a small house salad with vinaigrette. Handing the menus back to the waiter, Celeste asked Vanessa, "Can I order two glasses of wine for us, maybe a white Zinfandel, to toast your birthday?"

"Yes, for a special occasion I think that would be nice." The waiter jotted down the addition and then left.

"Here, open your present now," Celeste said, handing Vanessa a small wrapped box.

Vanessa pulled the paper away and then her mouth dropped open. "This is a new iPhone, Celeste. This is too expensive for a birthday gift."

"Not for me." Celeste shook her head. "Besides, that old phone of yours is ancient. You needed a new phone. I had to stop by the T-Mobile store at the mall at Rittenberg to get my phone number changed, and this little phone seemed to call, 'Buy me for Vanessa.' Don't you like it?"

Vanessa frowned. "It just doesn't seem right to accept such an expensive gift."

Celeste grinned at her. "It's not like I'm trying to get you to compromise your virtue or anything. I simply wanted to do something special for you. Don't fuss at me unless you don't like it."

"I admit I love it." She turned it over in her hand, examining it. "You even got a case to protect it. Honestly, I don't know what to say."

"Try 'Thank you, Celeste'," she teased.

Vanessa finally laughed and then the two friends chatted and laughed over wine and dinner, enjoying an evening out together.

The waiter came as they finished, bringing a small mini cake, that

Thurman's provided to guests on their birthday. It had a single lit candle on it that Celeste gave to the waiter when she first arrived, telling him about Vanessa's birthday.

Seeing the cake with its lit candle arriving, the pianist began to play a short rendition of "Happy Birthday" on the piano, waving at Vanessa and smiling at her.

"He's been watching you all evening," Celeste told her. "I think you may have an admirer. I saw on the sign in the vestibule that his name is Marcus McClain. He plays here regularly."

Vanessa glanced his way discreetly with a thank you smile. "He is good looking," she whispered to Celeste. "He can really play the piano, too. I've enjoyed it all evening, haven't you?"

"I have. It's one of the things I love about Thurman's. Usually, they only provide entertainment on Friday nights through the year, but during the summer months, they offer it on Wednesdays, too."

The man at the piano moved into a familiar tune then, one of Celeste's well-known numbers, a song she'd also written, as she did most every song she sang. Writing and singing her own songs from the first had been one of the hallmarks that moved her quickly into a coveted best-selling place in the music industry.

Marcus winked at Celeste as she looked his way, scooting down on the piano bench and gesturing to the seat beside him.

With so many memories swirling in her head, of singing here on weekends as a young girl in high school, with her daddy sitting watchfully in the corner, Celeste couldn't resist the appeal. She got up from her seat and started across the room to the piano, sliding onto the bench beside Marcus, picking up the song lyrics at the chorus, and beginning to sing.

CHAPTER 2

Reid Beckett's work day had been a long one. At six, he made his way into Thurman's restaurant and took the elevator to the top floor of the restaurant to his uncle's office. He knew his Uncle Thurman expected him, since he'd talked with him on the phone earlier.

His uncle stood to shake his hand as Reid came in. "Thanks for bringing these papers over, Reid. Your dad said I only needed to read through them, sign where needed, and drop them off tomorrow at the office. Anything else I need to know?"

"No, but Dad said it was a good investment for you to pick up that apartment building while you could, especially since you own the property next door."

Thurman Beckett sat back down, gesturing Reid to a chair. "The building will need some work, but it's in a good location. My son Ryland is going to move into the main floor apartment and manage both rental buildings. I like the idea of having someone on premises, and he's been itching to live downtown since he got back from college."

"Both those buildings are near the College of Charleston and right in the hub of things. They'll rent well." Reid smiled at his uncle, who looked a lot like his dad, both white-headed now in their sixties, but fit and distinguished.

"Well, thank your dad for letting me know about the building going up for sale. I hate to hear the owner died, but I'm glad to get the chance to pick up another property." He paused. "Did you see

Ryland downstairs as you came in?"

"I did, and I know you're glad to have him working in the business with Manny."

"You don't always know if your kids will want to follow in the business when they grow up, but I'm glad they both decided to work with Thurman's and keep the family restaurant going." He grinned at Reid. "I know my brother Heywood was glad you and your brother Charlie wanted to come on board with him in the Beckett Company. He's worked hard to grow the realty business that our Dad started, taking it in several new directions and adding a lot of rental properties downtown."

Reid's uncle paused, as if considering his words. "When you studied in business administration, your dad and grandad weren't sure you'd come into the business, and then, of course, years before I disappointed them and decided to start a restaurant in this old house my wife Emma's grandparents left her. I remember your Grandad was in a huff about that for a while."

"Well, you've made a success of Thurman's and been happy running it. I know Manny has the same passion for it you do. I think you can count on him keeping it going into another generation." He grinned. "Manny's boys T.C. and Harper are already saying they're going to work in the restaurant when they grow old enough, too."

"Well, you know I love to hear those words. You like to think you've built something that will endure, but I've seen a lot of kids just walk away from all their parents and grandparents worked so hard to build."

"Yes, and many have regretted those decisions later. We can all tell some stories about that."

Reid's uncle nodded. "Why don't you go downstairs and have dinner on the house before you start home," he said. "I'm going to head home to Emma. I'll look over these papers tonight and give Heywood a call if I have any questions."

After saying his goodbyes and returning downstairs, Reid stopped for a minute to talk to his cousin Ryland, working at the front desk, and then headed into the main dining room. He settled at a small table in one corner, kept open for family and for Marcus on his breaks from the piano.

Reid could hear Marcus playing familiar contemporary pieces as he talked with one of Thurman's waiters, Tony Abbott, to tell him what he wanted for dinner. Tony was a regular face at the restaurant and a friend to most of the Beckett family.

Reid had been friends with Marcus McClain since their years studying business at the College of Charleston. The McClains owned a graphics and print business downtown, but it had been a surprise to Reid when Marcus sat down one night, at a piano bar they'd dropped in on, and started to play like a pro. Seeing an opportunity for Marcus to make a little extra money on the side, Reid hooked him up with his Uncle Thurman and Marcus had played here ever since.

Glancing up from the piano to see Reid, Marcus nodded at him. Reid would wait around to visit with Marcus on his break later.

In the meantime, he opened a folded newspaper Manny or Ryland had probably left on the table to cruise through it while he waited for his food, enjoying the music, the quiet, and the hushed atmosphere always prevalent at Thurman's. He'd ordered beef tenderloin tonight with a loaded baked potato and sauteed green beans.

He looked up when Marcus moved into a new song. It was a favorite of his, too, and one of Celeste Deveaux's numbers. Reid owned CDs of most of her albums and he'd streamed many of her songs, too. Celeste had sung here as a girl before she moved away and became famous. His Uncle Thurman had pictures of her on the wall from those early years and a few signed photos she'd sent him later.

Marcus scooted over on the piano bench as he played, glancing toward a table across the room, and then Reid saw Celeste Deveaux—walking across the room to the piano. His eyes followed her, such a beautiful woman, dressed in a sleek, red, fitted dress, her blond hair loose on her shoulders and glowing in the lights from the chandelier. He'd know her anywhere, and he knew his heart raced to see her again, exactly as it had all those years ago when she used to come to the restaurant to sing on Friday evenings.

Celeste hadn't been anybody special then, just a local girl from the area with a good voice. But there had been a way about her, even then. Something special, and she'd drawn him in a way no woman had since. He'd found a way to hang out at the restaurant every time he knew she was coming, and one night he'd slipped outside, following her when she took a break. He felt sure she knew he watched her on those nights, that he was always there, sitting at the same corner table.

They'd known a moment in the garden alone that night. One he'd never forgotten. Reid would have pursued her with zeal after that night, until Manny informed him she was barely sixteen years old. She'd looked a lot older, and it certainly explained why her father always came with her. Reid had been twenty-one then and he'd thought Celeste nearly his own age.

He hated backing away from pursuing a further relationship with her, but she was only a girl. So, he decided he'd watch and wait. But when she turned eighteen, she took off and married a man even older than him, a man from Nashville who'd started coming to the restaurant, interested in her voice.

Reid didn't think Celeste saw him at Thurman's tonight, sitting at the same table, and he doubted she would remember or recognize him anyway after all these years. But he certainly knew her.

The room quieted to a hush as Celeste began to sing, everyone knowing they'd lucked into a memorable moment getting to hear Celeste Deveaux perform. Most of her expensive concerts, held anywhere near Charleston, were always sold out.

Reid could see she was enjoying herself, smiling, and relaxed, with that sweet and sultry voice of hers drifting across the room. Near the end of her song, their eyes met. She looked at him for a moment and then as the song ended, she began to play a new melody on the piano herself before Marcus picked up on it and took over the playing.

The song was an old favorite of Reid's, a number on her first album, that had become a runaway best seller. She'd sung the song first here at Thurman's before she left to go to Nashville and Reid remembered that night all too well.

"I see your brown eyes watching me," she sang now. "Across the crowded room. All evening I have seen them, thick with sweetness like perfume." Her voice moved into the chorus. "Your brown eyes make me beautiful, when I see you watching me. You seem to look within my soul, seeing more than I can see."

The verses flowed on, and Reid remembered the first time he'd heard this old song. It had seemed invitational with words like 'bring your feelings to the day' and 'don't let me slip away.' They'd lured him to follow her out of the room later.

Reid foolishly imagined Celeste was singing to him that night. He probably wished it so. He did have brown eyes. He also didn't regret following her that night, until he learned her age. That long-ago night's memory was all he had now. She'd married and left South Carolina, and he'd never seen her again in person, until now.

As Celeste finished her song, Ryland swept in to bring her roses he'd pulled from a vase in the entry, asking to snap her picture. Others crowded around, too, until Celeste whispered quiet words to Ryland and he cleared a way for her, and the friend she'd come with, to slip out a side door and leave.

Did she recognize him tonight? He guessed he'd never know. But Marcus was certainly full of grins as he made his way across the room to join him after Celeste left.

"Man, wasn't that a moment?" he said, sitting down with Reid. "I couldn't believe it when I was playing away and recognized her. She was sitting with this good-looking Black woman I'd been eyeing, but her back was to the room. Probably intentional. Then she turned and I knew it was her."

He paused, now on his break, to drink some coffee and to snag a few bites of Reid's dinner that had just arrived.

"What is she doing here in Charleston?" Reid asked, knowing Marcus kept up with the music scene more than he did.

"Recovering," he answered. "Haven't you been keeping up with the news about her? Her first husband got killed in a wreck and then she married Dillon Barlow not long after, a big-name entertainer she sang with sometimes. Turns out he had some problems she probably didn't know about. I think few people did, but he started beating up on her and put her in the hospital. She began divorce proceedings then."

He winced. "I didn't know that."

"It was bad." He paused, gesturing to Reid's plate. "Can I have part of that baked potato? I had a crazy busy day, barely got here on time and I didn't get a chance to order dinner."

"Sure," Reid said, putting half his potato on a side plate and adding some beef tenderloin and green beans to it. "Enjoy … but finish your story, too."

Marcus ate a few bites and then continued. "During the last bad time when Dillon went after Celeste, he broke her arm, busted some of her ribs and left her black and blue with bruises. Someone from the tabloids got in the hospital and snapped photos that went viral. You know how stuff like that spreads now."

He reached for a piece of bread to butter and ate a little more before moving on. "Evidently other women, that Dillon beat up on in the past, saw some of the photos of Celeste and started coming forward to the police to tell their stories. The whole situation was ripe for lawsuits, and a lot of publicity followed, none of it good for Dillon."

"What happened to Celeste?"

"Her family came and got her, took her home to rest and heal. You know she grew up near here on an island at the end of Edisto down the coast. The big Deveaux Lighthouse is there. You boat a lot on the ocean there, so you probably know where it is."

"I do. My grandparents live at Seabrook across the North Edisto River from the lighthouse."

Marcus paused to eat more, and Reid ate, too, thinking over Marcus's words.

"How long has Celeste been here?" he asked.

"Since spring some time. I imagine she'll be heading back to

Nashville soon." He lifted his eyebrows. "She sure did look good, didn't she? She's one fine-looking woman. I've never gotten to see her this close before."

Reid nodded but didn't answer.

Marcus sat back, drinking a glass of water Tony brought him. "Everybody says Celeste sang here a lot when she was only a teenager. I've seen the group of photos on the restaurant wall. Manny said she cut her teeth performing here, and in a few other local places, before going to Nashville. Has she been back to sing at Thurman's since she left, I mean before tonight?"

"Not that I know of," he answered. In fact, he was sure she hadn't. "But we all got to know her in those days. So gifted and talented. I hate to hear all that's happened to her."

"Life can be hard, even for rich artists in the industry." Marcus glanced at his watch. "Do you think she'll come back? I'd really like to meet that woman who was with her. Wonder if she lives around here?"

Reid grinned. "I don't know. Put the word out to Ryland, Manny, and Uncle Thurman if you're interested. See if they can subtly find out who she is if she comes back again, even on her own."

"I'll do that." He glanced at his watch. "I need to go play again," he added. "You going to head home now?"

"Yes. I have an early meeting in the morning."

"Well, thanks for sharing your dinner," Marcus said as he got up. "Won't we have some sweet dreams tonight remembering that we got to hear an in-person performance by the famous Celeste Deveaux?"

Reid waved him off and then headed toward the door.

Walking home to his house on Clifford Street, only a few blocks away, Reid's mind kept wandering to all that he'd learned about Celeste tonight. She'd certainly led an eventful life since he last saw her. He wondered if he'd see her again before she left? Not as though it would matter if he did. He'd hardly pursue her now. But for a usually sensible man, she certainly gave him some foolish thoughts.

CHAPTER 3

Celeste lay in bed the next morning luxuriating in the beauty of the elegant old bedroom where she'd spent the night at the Elliott House Inn. She often stayed here when she came downtown for her weekly counseling sessions with Dr. Conrad and for the times when she met with her agent. It was easier for Gary Feinstein to fly into Charleston when he was near the area, working with other artists, or when he needed to meet with her individually so she could sign papers or promotional items.

Gary always stayed at the Hyatt near the airport when he came. He liked the convenience, the free breakfast and on-site restaurant, the business meeting areas, the gym, and the more modern environment. He was scheduled to come to Charleston for a meeting with her later this month and Celeste knew decisions lay ahead for her.

A knock at the door brought a staff member carrying one of the Elliott Inn's lovely breakfast trays with a pot of coffee, juice, a cup of mixed fruit, and a bagel with cream cheese and jam as a part of their Complimentary Breakfast. They pampered her a bit here, and she loved them for it. They even offered complimentary bicycles to cruise around Charleston's historic streets, and her bedroom walked out to a lovely balcony looking across the inn's lush, well-landscaped courtyard.

Later in the morning, Celeste walked from the Elliott Inn down Queen Street to Dr. Conrad's office. Since she planned to stroll Charleston's streets and shop after her 9:30 appointment, she wore a pair of navy sandals built for walking comfort, a navy, polka-dot sleeveless dress, the hem dropping to mid-calf, and a navy crossbody shoulder bag draped over one shoulder. She planned to spend the day after her appointment exploring Charleston's charming shops and looking for a gift store that would be ideal for Lila's paintings and cards.

The door to her therapist's office stood near the doorway of the art gallery beside it. Dr. Conrad's door was an inconspicuous one without any signage and with only a street number to identify it. Celeste punched the bell, waiting for his voice to buzz her in.

She'd teased him once, "You have everything set up very unobtrusively here. I imagine you don't draw many new clients, not even putting your name above the door."

He'd looked unconcerned. "My clients come from referrals, Celeste, and my office is located discreetly above this art gallery, so if anyone sees my clients coming or going, the average person would assume them only visiting the gallery. Not everyone wants others to know they are seeing a therapist."

She knew that the truth, and she also knew that many, like herself, might not want to be easily followed. As Dr. Conrad noted, she'd been quietly referred by their family friend, Dean Anderson, the chaplain at St. Christopher Camp across the river from the lighthouse.

Upstairs, Celeste waited briefly in the tasteful sitting room outside Dalton Conrad's office. Her eyes traveled across a group of plaques, giving his counseling credentials, to a sign on the wall that read: *You're always one decision away from a totally different life.*

She smiled at the thought as Dr. Conrad opened his office door, finished with his business call. "Come in, Celeste. It's good to see you again."

"You, too." She pointed to the sign on the wall. "Do you really believe those words?"

He glanced toward the sign. "You should know by now that if I didn't, the sign wouldn't be there. I like my clients to give thought to the idea that no one is locked in to any particular life role, that change is always possible."

She followed him into his office, settling down in her usual chair.

"How have things been going since last week?" he asked, sitting down across from her.

She shared with him about the call from Dillon. "I hate to keep getting these calls from him," she added at the end.

"When you receive a call like that, what do you know about Dillon Barlow that you didn't know before?"

"That he is not a healthy individual." She sent him a small smile. "And that I am not responsible for any of his problems and shouldn't feel guilty that I couldn't help him resolve them. I also understand now that people with Dillon's problems, like narcissism and possibly a dissociative personality disorder, rarely change without some major counseling or divine intervention."

"How would it have affected you if you had stayed with him?"

She stopped to think. "I know now that with a narcissist, the 'self' is always on the throne of their life, not God or the well-being of others. They put their own needs first. They aggrandize and justify themselves in everything they do. They don't feel guilty, as most healthy people do, when they abuse, use, or exploit others, even their own loved ones. They convince themselves instead that whatever they do is justified."

He steepled his fingers. "Knowing that, what would it have meant for you if you had stayed with Dillon?"

"I would have been forced to become what he wanted me to be and not my true self or who God meant for me to be. Any time I resisted my assigned role, Dillon would have grown angry and probably abusive, to punish me for stepping out of line." She hesitated. "In a sense I would have lost myself, as I was doing, trying to cater to and conform to his sickness."

"Those are good words. Do you believe them?"

"I do now, and thank you for helping me these last months to understand what I'd gotten myself into by marrying Dillon Barlow and what it was doing to me."

He changed course. "Did you do your homework this week?"

"Yes, you asked me to list problems facing me and then to list how they could change from actions I might take. I think you said the purpose was so I could see possibilities and not simply limitations."

"Did thinking about that help you?"

She smiled at him. "Yes. Like your sign in the lobby confirmed, I realize I'm in an enviable position in many ways and, as you've helped me to see, I can take ownership of my own life again and I don't have to allow anyone to control me."

He smiled back. "Does it make you feel good to say those words?"

"It does, but I also know that if I make any stands for change in my life, or decide on any new directions, there will always be someone, even if well-meaning, who might try to limit my choices."

"Who will you listen to when those times inevitably happen?" he asked.

She hesitated for a moment. "Not that I would immediately discount the wisdom of others, but, hopefully, I'd seek God's wisdom and counsel first. Like the Bible verse on your wall advises, I'd try to listen to God and not lean simply to my own understanding or to that of others. I do love your signs, Dr. Conrad."

He looked toward the framed scripture. "What does that scripture suggest the outcome will be when we lean to God's understanding and ways first?"

"That He'll direct our paths."

He nodded.

She pointed to another sign on the wall. "Do you believe that scripture, from Psalm 143, is always right, too, that God will help us know the way and the direction where we should walk?"

He laughed softly. "If I didn't, I doubt I would be a Christian counselor. Granted, God doesn't always show us everything we need to know at the exact moment we ask, but I believe He works toward getting the answers to us that we need, if we'll seek and listen."

"What about when we screw up and take the wrong way?"

"Everyone makes mistakes from time to time. You know that, and you should read more in Isaiah this week about how God guides us and shows us the right way to walk, even when we set out on a wrong path."

She grinned at him. "My sister Lila says when you're going down a wrong path, you look around and suddenly realize things aren't going well. The path gets rough and hard to navigate, seems overgrown with weeds and problems. You realize, at that point, that you probably missed the right path back there somewhere. Often you need to backtrack and hunt for it and then get back on the right way again."

"That's a wise analogy."

She and Dr. Conrad talked during the remaining session time about other questions he'd asked her to think about, and then they ended their time together. As always, he'd given her some new things to consider. She'd learned his counseling method was never one to tell her what to do but to always help her see that she had the strength and wisdom to find her own answers, and that she needed to focus on the positives and possibilities ahead rather than the negatives in the past.

"We've had a good session," he said, standing to see her out.

"Yes, we have," she agreed. "I'll see you next week."

Celeste headed for the stores on King Street then and enjoyed a couple of hours shopping. King Street was one of the major shopping corridors in downtown Charleston, and she liked the small boutiques and old family businesses there. While shopping, it seemed like she always spotted some unique and interesting items, clothes, or jewelry she wouldn't find in other places. The charm of the street appealed to her with most all of the shops in historic, colorful buildings with pots of flowers along the sidewalks, cute window displays, and pretty awnings, Even the occasional horse-drawn carriage clattered by now and then, filled with tourists and adding to the ambience.

After popping into Gucci's and Kate Spade's, Celeste walked down Market Street to order a salad at the Sweetwater Café before starting down King Street again to return to the Elliott House Inn. As she passed yet another clothing shop and a small art gallery, she spotted a colorful shop on the left that made her stop right in her tracks. It was called CeeCee's Place, like the nickname her sisters used for her when small. It looked like a cute gift shop that might be a good spot for Lila's paintings and gift cards, so she decided to go in and look around.

The interior made her smile, chocked full of interesting gifts and appealing items of all kinds. An older woman with white, curly hair, glasses, and a warm smile waved at her as she began to browse.

"Let me know if I can help you," she said.

Celeste made her way through two gift areas near the front of the store, both engaging and fun, and then past a collectibles area with tall shelves packed with a potpourri of items that made her want to pick up different ones to examine more closely, like two beautiful glass paperweights and a red enamel cloisonne egg. Overhead, multi-colored lights hung from the ceiling here and there as did wind chimes. An accessories section caught her attention next and she soon got lost looking through delightful hats, purses, colorful flip flops, beach totes, and fun jewelry.

The store was busy, too, even as Celeste looked around. The older woman was surprisingly the only clerk working in the store, cheerfully helping a group of tourists and several shoppers all at once, while ringing up items in-between.

The clothing section at the back drew Celeste's attention next, and she noticed the items weren't only the usual high-priced or high-end selections most stores carried, but also included inexpensive sundresses in fabulous colors, lightweight robes, and lovely casual shirts perfect for coastal vacationers. On the tables were stacks of loose, lightweight sweaters in bright colors, beautiful scarves, and an assortment of T-shirts perfect for a downtown Charleston store with a high tourist clientele.

She moved to the other back section of the store next, behind the main check-out area, where she found local books, puzzles, games, and even cute gift cards. "Lila's cards would be really perfect here," she thought. Celeste had seen local paintings tucked into the shelves and hanging high on the walls around the store, too.

She turned to find the older woman watching her from a stool behind the register. The store had grown quiet now, and Celeste glanced around to see she was the only customer.

"It ebbs and flows how busy we are," the woman said, noticing Celeste looking around. "I waited to say 'Welcome to my store, Celeste Deveaux' until everyone was gone. I didn't want to draw attention to the fact that you were here, but I'm flattered and honored to have you in my little shop."

"Thank you. Is the shop named for you?"

"No, It's not. It's named for my mother who was Cecelia Hathaway but called CeeCee. I'm her daughter Imogene Hathaway."

"Nice to meet you." Celeste smiled at her. "It looks to me like you could use some extra help."

She sighed. "I could, but it wouldn't be fair to hire anyone else right now. The store's for sale."

"Oh, I'm sorry. It seems very successful."

"That isn't the problem, dear. When Mother passed, she left the store to my sister and me. We both loved the store, as Mother did, and we worked here until Erma and her husband Ben were killed in a car wreck this spring. Somehow, Erma never legally wrote anything up about how she wanted her part of the store handled. Foolish of us to not think those things out. The store, as did their estate, went to Erma and Ben's two boys up north, who are busy with their own lives and aren't interested in the store's future. They said they'd be pleased for me to buy out the other half of the store, but the real estate prices here are beyond my means now so I have no choice but to sell."

She paused to look around. "My parents owned this whole building outright, my grandparents before them, but the original property purchase was made in a time before real estate prices here skyrocketed. There's even a lovely apartment right above the store. I lived in it until I moved to live with my mother in her latter years. Erma and I rented the apartment to people we knew and trusted after. Our former store manager lived in it last."

She pointed to the windows near them. "There's a pretty courtyard to the side, good parking in the back with a delivery area and a lot of storage behind the store. Many businesses don't have those assets and, of course, that pushes up the buy-out price I would need to come up with. I simply can't do it."

Celeste had perched on a chair in the book area while Imogene talked. "I'm sure you're simply heartbroken to lose this place. It's so charming and so different from other stores I've seen around the area. You have wonderful taste in buying and decorating."

"Well, that's sweet of you to say. I never married, you know, and running and working CeeCee's has been my life. I admit it will be difficult to say goodbye to the place. My realtor is trying to help me find someone nice to buy it who might let me stay and work here." She shook her head. "But I know the chances of that are slim."

"I'm sure the right person will come along."

Imogene looked around. "I hope so. It's hard for me to run the store alone. I used to have a store manager and a part-time employee to help but now I'm running and working the store by myself. My little high school neighbor comes in to help me on the busy weekends, but I know a buyer could contact my realtor and write a contract on the business and building at any time. When I tell any potential employee the business is for sale they go and look for a more stable job elsewhere. I certainly don't blame them."

"I know someone who would be a wonderful store manager for you," Celeste said, thinking of Vanessa. "She's working in a dress shop now but, in the past, she worked for a gift and garden shop over on James Island on Folly Road. She has a broad retail background and a good education."

"I know that little gift and garden store on Folly Road. It's not far from my house. I go there often." She paused. "I'd be glad to give your friend's name to the owner later, but, honey, who knows when that will be or even if they will keep the store as it is. One buyer, who looked at it earlier, wanted to completely gut it and turn it into a restaurant but he couldn't come up with the financing. I have to admit I was glad."

"I don't blame you for that." The thought made Celeste cringe as she looked around.

As Imogene walked to the door to greet another group of customers, Celeste walked around the store again, an idea beginning to bubble in her mind.

After they left, she said, "Imogene, I think I might know someone who could be interested in this shop. They would want to keep it just like it is, too. Can you give me some contact information of who is handling the sale so I can pass it on to them? I have a feeling they'd really want you to stay, too. After all, who would know the store better than you? If you liked who bought it, would you stay?"

Imogene smiled at Celeste. "I would certainly be interested in doing so. I'm only in my mid-fifties and not ready to retire. I'll need to find some place to keep working, and retail is all I really know."

Celeste saw another group of customers come in and said quickly before Imogene got busy again, "Would you mind if I walk around and see a little more of the store so I'll have more to tell my friend?"

"Honey, I'd be glad for you to do that." She pointed toward the rear of the store. "Go through the back there and feel free to look at the storage area, to walk outside, and to go upstairs to see the apartment. There are stairs to it by the back door, and the apartment door isn't locked right now. It's furnished, somewhat, and the rent from it, like all rents in Charleston, is good. I just rent it to people I know, and I haven't considered renting it since I knew I'd have to sell."

Delighted, Celeste walked through the back door of the store. On her way she passed a small dressing room and a nice bathroom. Across from that a hallway led to several large storage rooms on the other side, all neatly organized.

Climbing the stairs Imogene had mentioned, Celeste let herself into the apartment, a surprisingly large one spanning the entire top of the long store below. It was charming, with beautiful hardwood floors, nice old rugs, built-in shelves everywhere, comfortable furniture, most everything in blues, with the walls a soft blue gray to blend. There were two bedrooms, two baths, a nice kitchen, and a wealth of lovely old windows looking onto the piazza, a long, covered porch spanning the apartment's length on one side.

Celeste let herself out onto the porch and smiled. Old wicker furniture and rockers dotted the porch area, the cushions a little worn, and she spotted paddle fans overhead. Most retail shops in downtown Charleston were sandwiched between two buildings, but Imogene's place held a coveted corner spot by a driveway that lay between her shop and another business to one side. It was a perk to have this much privacy, especially a driveway to one side, with parking at a premium in Charleston, and she loved the patio and courtyard below the piazza.

Stepping back inside, Celeste walked around the apartment again. It needed some updates and more personality, but even as is, it was nice enough. Certainly, nice enough for the buyer she had in mind.

Returning back downstairs, Celeste walked around outside as well, noting the nice area for deliveries, a few pieces of outdoor furniture on the side patio, and the lush array of shrubs and flowers in brick-lined beds. Someone had a green thumb, probably Imogene. And a high stucco wall gave privacy to it all. She was simply charmed.

Back inside the store again, Celeste found Imogene had written down all the information about the shop, including the price, and the realtor contact information. She'd clipped one of her own store business cards to the written note, too.

"With all your contacts, I hope you might know someone who would love this place like I do," Imogene said. "After that restaurant buyer scare, I sure would like someone to buy the store who would keep it going. CeeCee's Place is loved by locals and tourists."

"I imagine it is. It's really special, Imogene."

She reached across to pat Celeste's arm. "You're very kind, with your busy life and all you've been through this year—and yes, I read, dear—to take an interest in me and my little place." She smiled again. "I love your music, and I remember hearing you sing one Friday night at Thurman's when you were a girl. You were pretty and gifted then and you're pretty and gifted now. Don't you let the heartaches of this year get you down. Life will turn around and be sweet again for you."

Celeste felt like crying. "Thank you."

"You're welcome and if you'll be around Charleston for a time, come back to see me."

"I will, Imogene."

"Oh," she added, "and if you're a praying person, offer up a prayer for a good, sweet buyer to pick up this old store and keep it going, and maybe for me to be able to stay on and work a little longer."

"I'll do that, Imogene," she promised.

With Imogene's words on her mind, she walked down King Street, crossed Queen and then turned left on Broad to reach the big St Michael's Church on the corner of Broad and Meeting Street. Right now, she needed a quiet place to think and pray.

St. Michael's Church was an old historic church in Charleston's downtown, built in the 1700s, enduring all these years, and still welcoming parishioners and tourists. It's tall white steeple could be seen for blocks. Celeste walked up the church's front steps, passing between the big pillars and into the main doorway. She scooted into a pew near the back and then sat quietly.

"Dear Lord," she said, not seeing anyone else in the church. "Lila said to be open for new opportunities and Dr. Conrad's sign caught my attention with its words about change. This decision I'm considering, to buy Imogene Hathaway's store, would start me, in many ways, on a totally different life. Not that I would have to give up my music. Imogene could run the store easily with Vanessa's help. I could travel when I needed to, or wanted to, but I could also have the joy of working in the store, living here in Charleston. My heart is simply thrilled to think about it. I've always loved it here, been drawn to this city in a way I've never been able to explain to anyone."

She paused. "What should I do, Lord? I just told Dr. Conrad

earlier that if faced with any new decision I'd lean to You first. I know I'm not close to You in the same way Lila is, but You know I love You and belong to You, and I hope You know I want to live in a way that pleases You. I've made a lot of mistakes these last two years, getting involved with Dillon Barlow after Nolan died, and not leaving when I should have as soon as he began to show his dark side. I almost got killed and now I'm being threatened by this sick man. Singing artists have their stalkers every now and then, but this situation has been grievous, Lord. I know Dillon is dangerous in a way no one else does. It's not a good time for me to return to live in Nashville so accessible to him. I think I would be safer here, and happier, too. Near my family for their support and to be here for them, too."

She looked toward the altar, with the big stained-glass window of an avenging angel above it. "Protect me, Lord, and direct me in Your best way."

She pulled a church Bible from the pew and opened it to Isaiah, that Dr. Conrad had suggested she read. She cruised through the wonderful words in Isaiah 30 while praying quietly, smiling when she came to these words: "And thine ears shall hear a word behind thee, saying, This is the way, walk ye in it, when ye turn to the right hand, and when ye turn to the left."

As if envisioning it, Celeste glanced behind her and then laughed at herself. "I'm sure you'll answer me in Your own way, Lord. But don't wait too long to answer. Imogene needs my help and so does Vanessa. I need help, too, Lord." She got up to leave the church then, hearing others coming in to see the beautiful sanctuary.

A block up Meeting Street, while waiting at the light to cross the road to head back on Queen to the Elliott Inn, Celeste got amused listening to a couple of tourists behind her studying their map of downtown Charleston and arguing over which way to go.

"I think I'm totally turned around, Lois," the man said. "What way are we supposed to go?"

"Well, it's definitely not back the way we came, John. The map clearly shows the way we need to go is straight up King Street."

Celeste stood in place, as they crossed the street and walked on, stunned at their words. "Straight up King Street is the way to go," she whispered to herself and then laughed out loud. "I think I've just had a 'Lila experience,' Lord. Thank you."

CHAPTER 4

Reid's house on Clifford Street was only a block from his family's business, the Beckett Company, on King Street. The business's formal and longer name was Beckett Company: Realty and Brokerage Group, and the building, like many in downtown Charleston, had been converted from an old home. As his Uncle Thurman had mentioned on Wednesday night, the Beckett Company had been in his family for several generations and, unlike many who grew up in Charleston's wealthy families, Reid knew the value of helping to see their well-established and respected business continue on.

The tall three-storied building was a worn, soft cream color with a black railed staircase winding to a porch at the front door. The old structure, an elegant and tasteful one, had tall, black framed windows, many with wrought iron balconies. It also had the added perk of a driveway access on both sides of the building, with a parking area in back.

Shops and galleries lay to the north of the building, and to the south were more parking areas and a garden beside the historic Charleston Library Society. Behind the historic library, paths wound their way to the Gibbes Museum of Art and to the lovely Lenhardt Garden on Meeting Street. Across King Street, opposite the Beckett building, another garden walkway wound through an arched entry leading to the Unitarian Church and cemetery on Archdale. Throughout downtown Charleston lay many quiet, almost hidden, garden walkways like these, and Reid especially enjoyed the ones near his own home and family business.

"Good morning, Mom," Reid said as he entered the main reception area of the business. "Are you filling in for Irina today?" The Beckett Company's office manager, Irina Chen, usually worked the front desk.

"Yes. Her boys have pink eye. I encouraged her not to even think of coming back until they are well. Irina will probably get it, too. It's so contagious."

He grinned. "Well, I hope you wiped down the phone and desk with disinfectant."

She laughed. "You can be sure I did and Herbert, who cleans for us, had already cleaned thoroughly, too, before I got here. Irina called him and put a bug in his ear that he should."

"Do you have any sales appointments I need to cover for you today?" he asked.

"I only had two scheduled. Charlie is covering the outlying one and Heywood will pick up the other downtown. It's a business listing on Bay Street and he knows the owners who are selling." She paused, glancing at an open appointment book. "You have an appointment a little later with a party interested in Imogene Hathaway's store. It still breaks my heart for her that she and her sister didn't get their affairs in order before Erma was killed."

"I'm sorry about that, too," Reid said, sorting through a pile of mail on the desk to look for any he needed to take care of.

"I hope things will work out somehow," she added.

"I think I'll go get some coffee and make some calls, Mom. Let me know if you need me to fill in for you later while you and Dad catch lunch." He knew they often shared their lunch hour together.

"Don't forget we have SueEllen's birthday this Sunday after church. Lori and John are driving in from Summerville to our place at five for dinner and a little birthday party."

Reid listened with one ear while she chatted on about his sister Lori, husband John, and their children Stephen, six, and SueEllen, turning three. Reid's eyes moved to study his mother as she talked. Even in her fifties she was still beautiful and her warm smile drew everyone she encountered. Reid knew, too, that underneath her gracious manner was a strong business woman who had worked with his father since they married to grow the Beckett company.

His mom's hair, like his dad's and Uncle Thurman's was mostly white now. His mother had been a Legare before marriage, and the Becketts and Legares, most with nearly black hair, turned white early. At over thirty now, Reid found himself watching the mirror, wondering when he'd see the first white strands.

"You will come over for the birthday, won't you?" she asked.

"Of course, and what should I get SueEllen?"

"I'd suggest picture books. Pop over to Buxton Books down the street and get Polly or Julian to recommend a few good titles. If they have one of those picture books with the matching dolls or stuffed animals, pick up one of those, too. Books will encourage SueEllen to enjoy reading. We want smart children in the Beckett family."

"Good plan," he said.

She waved a hand. "Go get your coffee now and look through that mail you picked up and the papers on your desk. You'll have time to get some work done before your appointment comes at ten."

Reid was not only a realtor but a real estate broker. Business owners reached out to him, or to his father, to sell their properties. Reid often handled client/buyer interviews, discussions and negotiations, frequently without advertising a property or disclosing the owner, screening each buyer to maintain confidentiality. His job, most of the time, was to act as an intermediary between buyer and seller, assisting and representing both in the transaction process. The Beckett Company also managed business properties for owners, often absentee ones, and they owned properties of their own around Charleston.

Later in the morning he'd just finished a call and was punching in the numbers for another when he heard someone clear her throat. He glanced up to see a woman in the doorway.

"The lady out front said to come on back. I believe you're the one I am scheduled to talk with about buying Imogene Hathaway's store?" She walked toward him and held out a hand. "I'm Celeste Deveaux."

Stunned, Reid stood to take her hand. "I'm Reid Beckett," he said. "Please take a seat and be comfortable."

She did, settling into the chair he indicated and crossing her legs with ease, while Reid let his eyes drift over her discreetly. She wore a chic, professional pants suit today, in a warm ivory color. The short-sleeved suit jacket was cut low, a little tantalizing but buttoned tastefully, the matching pants a perfect fit to her figure, her purse and heeled sandals the same color as her suit. Her hair was pulled back today in a neat twist, rather than loose, and she looked formidable.

Her eyes met his then and her lips twitched in a smile. "I believe we've met before," she said.

"I think we might have," he decided to say. "How did you learn about Imogene Hathaway's property for sale?"

"She told me about it yesterday when I was in the store. We got acquainted and I learned why she was having to sell the business she helped to build and that she loves."

He waited as she paused.

"I do have the means to buy it if there are no difficulties."

"What difficulties would you expect?"

"That Imogene might not be happy to learn of the potential sale. It's important to me that she stays on at the store. If purchasing a half interest in the store ensured that, I would consider that option."

"To save money?" he asked. "I assume Imogene told you the sale price for the business."

A frown touched her face. "Be assured, Mr. Beckett, I can buy the business outright with no problem. I simply want to do the best thing for Imogene, too."

"Most people don't take factors like that into account when they consider buying a property."

She lifted her chin. "I'm not most people."

He couldn't help grinning. "That's certainly true."

She crossed her arms in annoyance, so Reid added, "Look, my job as a real estate broker is to connect buyers and sellers in a transaction good for both. My point is that you are a well-known entertainer. You write songs, sing, record, perform, and travel extensively. I want to be sure this purchase you're considering is going to be the best for both you and Imogene. Could you tell me briefly why you think this is a purchase you want to make at this time?"

"That's a fair question." She grew quiet for a moment. "My life is rather public as an entertainer so perhaps you know I've recently gone through a difficult time and am now divorced. Do you need details about that?"

"No." He waited again.

She sighed before continuing. "Dillon Barlow is a mentally unstable and sick man. He views the publicity that hit over our breakup and the negative impact of it on his career as my fault. He is angry. Evidently other women before me were charmed by him and later abused by him, as well. Many decided to come forward after Dillon hospitalized me. It seems they wanted to tell their stories, too, and frankly I'm sure they saw a ripe opportunity to sue for damages."

"I'm truly sorry you experienced that, Celeste," he said with feeling, dropping the more formal business mode.

"It's caused me to reevaluate my life in many ways." She paused. "I do have other gifts and interests and, fortunately, I'm in a position where I can consider developing some of those. I may not always want to perform to the extent that I do now. The entertainment business is constantly changing. I don't like some aspects of it even now. I like the idea, at this time, of developing a side business to put much of my heart and interest into." She paused again. "Additionally, I don't think I'd feel safe to return to live in Nashville right now. Few people know it but I receive frequent threats about returning."

"From Dillon Barlow?"

She nodded. "Yes. He is a dangerous man, Reid. Most people see only his charming and talented side, but I have seen and experienced his darker side, and it is not pretty."

He thought about her words. "Have you ever run a retail establishment?"

"No, not unless you count my upbringing at the Deveaux Inn and Lighthouse and the work I did there helping with the family business until I left. There are similarities in the endeavors." She leaned forward. "I have no doubt I can learn the business, Reid. I also know a good friend, experienced in retail, who I believe will come on board. If I also have Imogene and her experience, the store will run well, even when I need to travel and be away."

"What if Imogene isn't interested?"

She grinned at him, a Cheshire smile "Then I wouldn't be here talking to you. She was terrified at the idea of her lovely store being gutted to create a trendy restaurant. I know, too, how much she wants to see the store continue. I've felt her out, telling her I knew someone who might be interested in buying. Her response was what I hoped."

He sat, considering her words.

Finally, he said, "Here's what I'd like to do, Celeste. First I'd like to fill out all the needed information to begin the negotiations for a sale. Then I'd like to get input from my father, who is also an attorney, about the best way to handle a possible partnership between you and Imogene. Then I'd like to go and talk to Imogene about what might be the best way to handle this and see if, as you say, she is interested in continuing at the store. Is her staying contingent to your purchasing it?"

"I would certainly prefer it if she stayed, but at the least I'd like her to stay long enough to train me and possibly my friend Vanessa George. Imogene knows the store better than anyone. It would make the transfer easier."

"That sounds reasonable," he said and then added, "Before we get to all the paperwork, would you mind if I pose a few questions?"

"Not at all."

"The commute from Edisto and the Deveaux Inn is at some distance. I know the lighthouse and property well as my grandparents live in a retirement home at Seabrook."

She interrupted him. "Reid, there is an apartment above the store. I think it would be ideal for me. It simply needs a little facelift, so I won't need to commute. I also own a condo in Nashville, paid for, as you'll learn when you look into my assets for this sale."

"Will you be here enough in Charleston to actually work in and help to run the store or do you plan to be an absentee owner?"

"I plan to work at the store whenever I can be here. I want to be an active working owner."

"All right. Final question. Would you consider a trial period, working with Imogene at the store, possibly for two weeks, to be sure this is a purchase you'll both be happy with? We could get all the paperwork ready but delay the final signing until the trial is ended. When two people are merging, this is especially appropriate."

She tapped her nails on the desk, considering it. "I would agree to that, especially if it's what Imogene would like best."

"Well, then I will talk to her. Our family is fond of Imogene, especially since, as you saw, our businesses are next door."

She lifted her eyebrows. "I did notice that."

"Are you staying in the city right now?"

"I stayed over Wednesday night and last night at the Elliott."

He nodded. "With the weekend coming in now, how about if we meet again on Monday morning—possibly with Imogene, to see if you feel the same after thinking this over for a couple of days. Would ten o'clock again on Monday morning work for you?"

"That would be fine."

"Then we'll start all the paperwork now and discuss the legal aspects relating to the sale. It will take a while. Do you have time?"

"I do," she said. "Do you?"

"Yes." He stood. "We have a conference room that will work better for this. Let's move to that location. There's coffee and water there, too."

"Fine. I want to cooperate in every way I can."

And she did, artfully with a professionalism that surprised him. Obviously, Celeste Deveaux had grown and matured in many ways in the years since he first met her. She was no longer a green girl but a highly intelligent woman, seemingly up to any challenge and certainly eager for this new opportunity before her.

After Celeste left, Reid finished finalizing the needed aspects of the sale. As he did her credit and financial checks, he was incredulous at the wealth she'd accumulated. In his experience with entertainers in the past, he'd found most lived lavishly with multiple homes, cars, boats, and a continuing array of opulent vacations and purchases. Celeste lived a surprisingly modest life for an entertainer, with only one condominium in downtown Nashville, one car, and her travels, in most instances, only for business. She was generous, too, from the philanthropic donations listed.

Reid's father glanced over the paperwork after Celeste left. "Her first husband managed her money very well," he commented. "I actually met Nolan Culver, a time or two. His family own a music business here in town, sell pianos, sheet music, and such. Nice people. Not pretentious."

He paused. "I'd say Nolan learned a lot from them about how to be careful. He was certainly prudent in how he managed his money and Celeste's. I heard, as you did from Celeste, how he insisted she keep her own name, took care of her finances, and worked to protect her at every point. He left her all his assets, too, and they were significant. Both lived modestly for people with as much wealth as they had."

"It gives us no reason to stand in the way of Celeste buying Imogene's store then," Reid added.

"No, but if they choose to partner, I'd want to put some very clear legal aspects in their paperwork to protect them both if either decided to leave the partnership or if either died. I certainly think Imogene would understand the wisdom of that after all she's gone through. In some ways it might be easier if Celeste simply buys the store and keeps Imogene on to manage it with a good salary." He paused. "See what Imogene thinks about it all. I'd hate to see her back in this same position later if Celeste decides it's too much for her owning a store and performing, too."

Reid tapped his fingers on the pile of paperwork on the table. "I tend to agree a straight buyout would be better. The store makes good money and has little overhead, with the building belonging to the owner outright. Celeste would be able to pay Imogene a generous salary to manage the store and offer an appealing salary to her friend who she wants to bring on board."

"What was the woman's name again?"

"Vanessa George. Celeste said she had the woman with her at Uncle Thurman's on Wednesday night." He didn't mention to his father that he'd hardly noticed her, his eyes so intent on following Celeste.

His dad grinned. "I heard about that night. I'd say Thurman will be tickled if Celeste Deveaux stays around town, especially if she'll pop in and sing now and again at Thurman's—or simply eat there to draw attention to the restaurant."

He paused. "This will be a good sale for us, Reid. I think you can handle everything else that's involved."

Finally, near the end of the day, Reid went over to Imogene's store at around six to talk with her. He'd called to tell her he had interviewed a potential buyer for the store and she told him she'd close early so they could sit down and talk.

She was watching for him as he made his way next door.

"Come in." She opened the door to him. "I put out my closed sign a little while ago. Working this store alone is simply too hard for me, and I can't stay open late like I used to sometimes in the summertime or at holidays. I plan to go straight home tonight after we have our meeting, put my feet up, and read a good book."

She locked the door and turned. "I visited with a little college girl here earlier today who said she would love to fill in some for me to help out around her class schedule. Sweet girl. But I really need more reliable help, Reid."

"Perhaps you won't need any extra help now," he said, following her to the back of the store to a table in the shop's book area.

Imogene moved a few books off the table and gestured to a chair. "We can sit here. Tell me who's interested this time."

He noticed a break in her voice as she said the words.

"Do you remember when Celeste Deveaux came in your store Wednesday?" he asked.

Her face lit up. "How could I forget? That was a treat. I'm a fan. Are you?"

"Yes, I am," he replied, knowing he was more than that.

"But how did you know she was here?" Imogene asked.

"Do you remember she told you she might know someone interested in the shop?"

"Oh, I do remember that." She leaned forward. "Wasn't that sweet of her to be a help? I'd never met her in person before, but I surely did like her. Smart, nice, and easy to talk with. My kind of person. I hope she stops back by again."

Reid couldn't help grinning at her words. "I think you might get your wish. It was Celeste Deveaux who came to talk with me this morning about buying the store."

Imogene's eyes flew open. "Are you serious?"

"Her biggest hope was that you would stay on to manage the store and keep working here. I think she liked you, too." He paused. "What would you think about that idea?"

"Honey, I'd feel like I died and went to heaven. You have no idea how stressful all this has been for me. And every day when I lock up for the night, I worry about what will happen to my little store. I cried for two days when that contract was in negotiations for that man to buy my place, gut it, and make a restaurant out of CeeCee's. I could just imagine my mother weeping in heaven, too." She paused. "Are you sure Celeste Deveaux really wants to buy the store?"

"That's what she says. She seems sincere about wanting a change and about wanting to work at the store with you. She also knows a friend she thinks would be a good assistant manager. She can afford to pay you both well and she wants to.

"The store has always been profitable. Erma and I both made good money, enough to live comfortably, even after paying full and part-time help as needed. I won't feel Celeste is getting herself into something where she'll have financial problems and regret her decision."

Reid thought it sweet Imogene was worrying about Celeste's finances.

"I don't think the financial end will be a problem for Celeste."

"Well, frankly, I think a change and something new and fun to set her mind to will be good for Celeste. Lord in heaven, do you know all that girl's been through? It would break your heart to read about it."

He avoided that topic. "Celeste thinks she can be hands-on in the business a good part of the time, Imogene, even if she has to travel some. She also wants to live in the apartment upstairs. Will that be a problem for you?"

Imogene grinned. "Honey, why should it be if she owns the store and the building?" She paused then, looking anxious. "She is wanting to keep it as a store, isn't she?"

"Yes, and she told Dad and me that she loves the store name, too, and she doesn't intend to change it. Her sisters used to call her CeeCee when she was small."

"Gracious, I feel like I ought to just get up and do a happy dance. This good news has made my day." She leaned across impulsively to kiss Reid's cheek. "Thank you so much for working with Celeste and me on this. I just have a really good feeling about it all."

"Would you feel better about this if I worked to set up a partnership between you and Celeste for the store—you selling her Erma's half so you could pay off her boys, but retaining half ownership yourself?"

She scratched her chin, thinking about it. "Is that what Celeste wants to do?"

"She wants you to be happy, Imogene, and to stay to run the store for her and train her and then possibly her friend. Her young friend has experienced some betrayals and poor treatment in her current job." He hesitated and then added, "Celeste's friend is African American. Will that matter to you?"

Imogene put a hand on her hip. "I'm about half insulted you'd even ask me that, Reid Beckett, as long as you've known me."

He smiled. "I'm just trying to put everything on the table clearly. This is the time for thought and negotiating—before the paperwork is signed. Think what you want to happen here."

She rubbed her neck, giving his words some thought. "At this time, I think I'd be happy to simply manage the store for Celeste and let her carry the financial responsibility. I feel I can trust you and your father to set up everything right, so the paperwork is all it should be and so I'll be taken care of. It will be a big nest egg for me selling out my half as well as Erma's but still getting the fun of working here." She laughed. "And think how much fun it will be to tell people Celeste Deveaux runs and owns the store. Honey, business will surely pick up! Tell Celeste she'd better get her friend in here working with us quick!"

They talked a little longer about specific points that Reid wanted to be sure Imogene understood. "I'll ask you the same thing I asked of Celeste, to think about all of this over the weekend. I also asked if the two of you would do a trial period of working together, maybe two weeks, to be sure you're going to do well together and both want to move through with the sale. Then we'll sign the final papers. Are you agreeable to that, too?"

"That sounds sensible."

"I've got some papers with me now for you to look over this weekend, explaining things. You'll see a lot of Dad's protective legal clauses in place for both you and Celeste." He passed them to her. "Celeste is coming to my office on Monday morning at ten to give me her thoughts. Perhaps you could let me know yours before then."

He pulled a card from his briefcase to give to her, scribbling his cell phone on the back. "Call and let me know how you're feeling early on Monday. If all is still good with both of you, I'll probably bring Celeste here to the store, since you can't readily leave, so you can both sign the needed paperwork and talk about everything else afterward. Will that work for you?"

"Honey, I'll be on cloud nine all weekend looking forward to seeing that sweet girl again. I've been praying a long time for the right answer to come about my store, but I sure never imagined God would answer my prayers in such a big way, linking me up in business with a bestselling singing artist. Isn't that just something?"

Reid had to agree, and he wondered how he was going to handle being around Celeste Deveaux on a more regular basis, too. She still attracted him as much today as when she was a girl, and he had no idea what he was going to do about it.

CHAPTER 5

Celeste's week had certainly proved eventful. Following her visit to CeeCee's Place, and her experience at the church on Thursday, she set an appointment with the Beckett Company to talk to someone about buying Imogene Hathaway's store. With the appointment early on Friday, she decided to stay over again at the Elliott, and she also persuaded her therapist, Dr. Conrad, to meet with her briefly on Thursday afternoon. She knew she faced a big decision and would inevitably encounter resistance and, possibly, a lack of support from many. As usual Dr. Conrad didn't offer any personal advice, but he buoyed Celeste's confidence that she was eminently capable of making the best decisions for her own life.

Today, after her appointment with Reid Beckett—and hadn't that been a surprise to meet him again—Celeste explored the King Street area around CeeCee's Place, getting a feel for the store's location and competition, and scoping out nearby restaurants. She also spent time in the Pottery Barn on King looking at furniture, bedding, and accessories and planning ways to spruce up her new apartment. Frankly, she needed a little time to calm herself, too, after the morning and before heading home to her family at the island. Shopping was always therapeutic for Celeste.

After driving to Jenkins Landing on Edisto later, Celeste caught the four o'clock ferry to the island, giving her time to rest and change into something more comfortable before dinner at the Inn. Her sister Gwen, husband Alex and the children were driving over from Port Royal for dinner, too, and spending the night, so Celeste knew she'd be facing her entire family with this new venture she'd decided on. She didn't know what response to expect from them, but she felt very calm and assured, for once, about her own direction.

Gwen came to find her at five-thirty, hugging on her and dragging her out to the buffet table in the dining room to fix a plate to take to the porch to eat with the family, before the Inn's guests came at six. She babbled away almost incessantly about her new teaching job at the school, her new students, and happenings in her first weeks at Port Royal Elementary.

"I absolutely love the school," Gwen said with enthusiasm.

Celeste laughed. "That seems obvious." She chatted with others in the family as they filled their plates and headed out to the big dining table on the family porch.

Novaleigh had prepared a seafood casserole, made with shrimp and crabmeat, for the evening. As sides, she'd added a spinach salad with mandarin oranges, a sweet corn saute made with fresh corn cut off the cob, a mixed fruit salad with a light lime and honey dressing, plus golden-topped yeast rolls, and an apple crisp dessert with thick, fresh whipped cream for a topping. It was always an effort, as an entertainer, for Celeste to monitor her eating and keep her weight in line when home at the island.

Gwen's children were excited about sharing their new school experiences, too, so conversation didn't lag at dinner. Everyone just assumed she'd seen her therapist and shopped, as usual, in town, so it gave Celeste time to wait until after the children went outside to play, and Waylon and Alex decided to go fish off the dock, before Celeste felt she had the right time to share.

In a moment of quiet she said, "Mom, remember the other day when you said you worried about me returning to Nashville this fall?"

"I do. Why?" her mother asked, her attention snagged now.

"Well, I've been thinking about that," she said casually, sitting back in her chair and crossing her legs. "I think you might be right that I shouldn't return to Nashville full-time right now. Dillon's threats haven't lessened." She hesitated and then played one of her trump cards. "He attacked one of the women who came forward about being abused by him. There's no proof it was him, of course. It happened in a dark alley at night. A man came up behind her, knocked her out, and beat her. Dillon apparently had an alibi, but the woman's attorney feels sure it was Dillon, since he had warned her to drop her lawsuit and recant."

Her family looked stunned.

"Anyway, the man is dangerous right now, to say the least. He's always had problems but they seem to have escalated."

"Honey, you know you can stay here as long as you like," her mother said, leaning forward with concern.

"I do know that, but I've also been talking with my financial advisor. He thinks it would be wise for me to invest a portion of my money into an enterprise that might be beneficial to me and might also help with my taxes and such."

She waved a hand. "I've been looking into this idea for some time. I do have other interests and talents, you know. Additionally, the entertainment business is not always the most stable career choice. As entertainers age, their appeal sometimes fades and the physical demands of performing and traveling can become challenging. The industry is constantly changing, too. Frankly, you never know when your 'stardom' will fade, so to speak, and when other new sensations will take your place."

She saw Gwen lean forward to dispute this, and jumped in to continue before she could. "I don't expect this to happen to me and I have no problems with my career right now, except for my issues with Dillon, but it's wise to think ahead. At some point I may want another career opportunity to pursue, and many entertainers plan ahead by buying a business they might enjoy later." She smiled. "I think that's what I'm going to do. I discovered a lovely gift shop for sale that I like on King Street while in Charleston and I'm in process of negotiating a contract on it."

"What?" Burke looked shocked. "None of us had any idea you were looking for a business."

She shrugged. "In my line of work you learn to keep your business and personal affairs very quiet. My financial advisor previously informed me about several opportunities in Nashville. That idea seemed the most sensible investment at first, since I lived there. But I believe this will work better for me now."

"I admit I am absolutely stunned." Her mother shook her head. "I assume you have the money to do this or your financial group would never have suggested it."

"What's the name of the store?" Gwen interrupted. "Is it one we know? Where is it?"

Celeste smiled. "It's called CeeCee's Place, so you can imagine why it drew my attention, and it's a delightful gift shop right on King Street with a variety of appealing merchandise. I know you all will love it. It has a nice apartment above where I can live whenever I'm in town—and I expect to do that for a season until my issues with Dillon Barlow diminish."

With the unexpected silence still in the room, she added, "I hoped you would all be pleased. I'll be closer and here more often now."

"Well, of course we are pleased about that, darling," her mother assured her. "We're simply so surprised,"

"Tell us more about the store." Lila beamed at her. "I want to hear everything about it."

Celeste launched into her story then about how she'd stopped into the store while in the city, about meeting Imogene and learning why she was being forced to sell.

"Well, bless her heart," Lila said. "It must have been hard for her to realize she'd need to sell the store her mother started and that had been in her family so long."

She told them about Imogene's scare with a buyer almost purchasing CeeCee's Place to gut it and create a trendy restaurant.

"Oh, that would have been awful." Burke shook her head. "Tell us about Imogene. What is she like, Celeste? Do you like her?"

"I really do like Imogene Hathaway, Burke, or I wouldn't have considered this purchase at all, and I simply love the store." She told them more about Imogene, how she looked and acted.

"She sounds so nice," Lila put in.

"She is, and she said she prayed and hoped she'd get to stay and work at the store with a new buyer. I definitely made it clear I wanted her to stay on. She knows and loves the store, and I know I can safely leave it in her hands to manage whenever I might need to travel. I don't plan to give up my career, but right now I do plan to pull back for a season while I get established with the store."

Her mother leaned across the table to put a hand over hers. "You know, the more I think about it, Celeste, the more I like this idea. You've always been business smart and possess wonderful taste in furnishings and clothes. You're highly creative and good with people, used to being in the public eye. I can't see why this won't work for you, if you want it to, and if you and Imogene Hathaway get along well."

"Thank you, Mother." Celeste felt pleased with her words. "Reid Beckett and his father, at the realty company that is handing the sale, discussed the idea of a partnership with me, but they felt in many ways simply buying the store would be better. Partnerships can often be problematic just as they turned out to be for Imogene and her sister Erma. They're giving both Imogene and me very wise counsel in this sale and seeing all the paperwork is as it should be."

Gwen wrinkled her brow as if thinking and then her eyes popped open wide. "Wait a minute, Celeste. Is this Reid Beckett the same Reid Beckett that ..."

Celeste interrupted and gave Gwen a cautionary look. "Yes, it is. I believe Reid Beckett's uncle, Thurman Beckett, owns Thurman's Restaurant on Queen Street where I used to sing as a girl. I met most of the Beckett family while singing there years ago."

Gwen raised her eyebrows, and Celeste felt certain she hadn't heard the end of this discussion with Gwen.

"Oh, I remember that lovely place," her mother said with a dreamy expression. "Sometimes I'd go with Lloyd to eat dinner and hear you sing when you were in high school. It's where you got your first professional start in the business. And where you met Nolan."

"That's true."

"Have you been to see Nolan's parents since you got back? After all of us got over the shock of you two running off together to get married, Lloyd and I met them on several occasions." Her mother smiled. "They used to like to come to the Inn for dinner now and again, especially when you and Nolan could be here. They are lovely people, very down to earth."

"They are good people, and I haven't been to see them. I should, though." She looked down at her lap. "I guess I felt a little embarrassed to visit them after remarrying so soon after Nolan died and marrying so poorly."

"Honey, you were lonely, and still very young. They won't hold that against you, and I know they'd love to see you."

She nodded. "You're right, and I'll try to get over when I can. That will be easier with me living downtown."

Her sisters bombarded her with questions as they sat and visited on the porch, while keeping an eye on the children playing outside. But eventually everyone dispersed, Gwen, along with Chase, Rose, and Leah, to the Seaside Cottage where they were staying, Lila and Burke to their own places, and Etta to the kitchen to help Novaleigh clean up from dinner so she could head home.

Celeste helped her mother gather the family dishes on the porch, stacking them on a big tray to carry into the kitchen. As she and her mother rounded the corner, Vanessa smiled at her from a stool by the counter where she sat.

"What are you doing here?" Celeste asked, going to hug her.

"I'm off tomorrow at the store and I didn't have to work tonight so I decided to come to the island and spend the night with Mom and Dad." She stood and took the tray from Etta, sitting it on the counter. "Daddy came in his boat to pick me up at Jenkins Landing where I left my car. I thought I'd go to church with the family tomorrow and then enjoy my birthday and the afternoon with everyone before I need to go back to the city."

"And we're delighted to have our girl here," Novaleigh said as she loaded the last of the dishes into the dishwasher. She glanced toward Etta. "I think we're about done now. Maggie Bouls will be here to do breakfast in the morning, as usual, and I made sure I picked up all the groceries she asked for."

"We'll be fine," Etta assured her. "You and Vanessa go on home. I'll check the dining room a last time and unload the dishwasher later."

Celeste interrupted. "Novaleigh, could you spare Vanessa to me for a short time? I have something I really need to talk with her about. It won't take long."

"Sure," she said, pulling off her apron. "You girls go visit and take your time. I'll take a plate of supper home to Clifford and we'll watch that television show we both enjoy while he eats."

Celeste led Vanessa through the kitchen and passageway to the family apartment where she was staying. "Make yourself comfortable. Do you want some hot tea? I have some fancy vanilla chamomile we can enjoy."

"Sounds nice. I'm just happy to be putting my feet up. I worked a long day at the store and it wasn't a good day. That's one reason I came home. I wanted to be with people who loved and appreciated me."

"Tell me what happened," Celeste said as she made the tea.

"You know I told you about my problems with the manager at the store." Vanessa pulled off her shoes and tucked her feet up on the sofa. "The store's owner, Gregory Hendricks, actually recruited me from the mall store and hired me to work at Hendricks. He made it clear to Christina Ventrice, the store's manager, that he was hiring me to train as the assistant store manager once I became fully comfortable in the shop. However, Christina has stalled at every turn about starting my training. In addition, she's trying to find small ways to discredit me to the owner."

"Like what?"

"Anything she can, mostly lies. I admit I've been shocked at that. Gregory Hendricks recruited me because of all the buying I did for the Loft and because he'd learned from the store manager that I'd personally created all their chic and trendy store and window displays. Although I've continued in those roles at Hendricks, Christina takes credit for my ideas. I've also heard her suggest to Mr. Hendricks, when she didn't know I was listening, that she needed to help me with them and that the clientele at Hendricks is obviously a little above what I'm used to."

"What a cat." Celeste brought their tea back and sat down in the chair across from Vanessa. "I'm so sorry to hear that."

"Today, two women came into the store and I began helping them both find cocktail dresses for an upcoming event. I could easily see the best colors for them." She grinned at Celeste. "You helped me a lot in that area, introducing me to color design and how to knew the best colors for different women according to their hair and skin tones."

"And?" Celeste asked.

"I went in the back to get one of the dresses in another color and as I came out, I heard Christina telling them about a clerk she was grooming for management and it wasn't me."

Vanessa shook her head. "Christina leaned toward the two women I'd been working with and said, 'Our little friend Vanessa, that you met, thinks we might move her up, but she's obviously not a good choice. She tries really hard, as an African American girl, and she is certainly sweet but her mother is a cook somewhere. I've been telling our owner, Gregory Hendricks, that we need someone with the right background to work here at Hendricks with women like yourselves.'"

Celeste's mouth flew open. "What a conniving snot and a hateful racist. What did you do?"

"Nothing. I went in the back for a few minutes more and then came back out smiling with the dress. The women acted patronizing to me after that, like I was a second-class citizen or something."

She started to cry a little. "It's been hard to work with Christina all these months but now it's going to be worse. I so wish I'd kept my job at the Loft. They were wonderful to me. I never should have left."

Celeste shook her head. "Sometimes we don't know what we're getting into with people. I'll bet Christina's drawn-on eyebrows would fly off her forehead if she knew your mother, Novaleigh, makes more money than she does as the cook and chef at the Deveaux Inn. She's been written up in gourmet magazines, too."

"What am I going to do, Celeste?"

"Turn in your notice Monday."

"Celeste, I can't go without a job. I moved into a new apartment with a year's lease when I took the job this spring. I have bills to pay and I need to work. My situation isn't like yours." She heaved a sigh. "It hurts your work credentials, too, if you change jobs too often, but if I could find something right now, I'd consider it anyway."

"Good, because I know something perfect for you. Do you know where CeeCee's Place is on King Street?"

Vanessa thought for a minute. "Is it that cute gift shop with a black awning that's close to the old Charleston Library Society?"

"That's it. And the current store manager needs help. She lost her assistant manager and she's basically running the store all by herself right now."

"Why do you think she might consider me for that position?"

Vanessa smiled. "Because I talked to her about you."

"Are you serious? I love that shop, Celeste. It's so charming, a mix of cute, fashionable fun gifts, clothes, and collectibles. It's even closer to my apartment than Hendricks, too. Do you think I might have a chance at the job?"

"I'm sure of it."

"Who should I talk to at the store and when? I'm totally over it with Christina Ventrice and her snotty, dishonest ways."

"What is your work schedule like on Monday?"

"I work late afternoon to close on Monday. Why?"

"Because I want you to meet Imogene Hathaway on Monday, to see if you like her and if she likes you. If you both hit it off, you're hired and you can graciously give your two weeks' notice at your current job if you think they even deserve two weeks' notice. I probably wouldn't even give them one."

"Celeste, you can't know if she'll hire me as easily as that ..."

"Yes, I can," she interrupted. "Because I'm signing papers to buy the store on Monday and I already told Imogene, who's staying on to manage the store, that I wanted to bring you on board. She is tickled about it. She even lives near the little gift and garden store where you used to work on James Island."

Vanessa's mouth flew open. "Oh, my goodness. You're buying the store, just like that? Can you do that, Celeste?"

"I can and I need to do it for myself and as an investment. I really want you to work for me, too. Even though I love Imogene already I want someone else in the store that I love and trust. You know I'll have to travel sometimes and I want to know I'm leaving the store in good hands." She grinned. "If you're hesitating about the money, assistant managers make a lot more than clerks, and whatever you're making now, be assured I'll be paying much more and with better benefits. I'll also be a lot nicer to work for."

"I can't believe this." Vanessa jumped up to hug her. "Thank you. If Imogene will have me, I'll say yes in a heartbeat!"

Moving back to her chair, she asked, "Do you have a place to live in downtown Charleston? It's too far to drive back and forth every day. I only have a one-bedroom apartment but you're welcome to share."

"You sweet thing. That's the kind of friend you are, but actually there is a nice apartment over the store I'm going to move into. You can give me your ideas for fixing it up on Monday. My appointment with the Beckett Company is at ten. We should be finished and ready to talk with Imogene before lunchtime." She giggled then. "Won't this be fun, Vanessa? We're going to have our own store. I can't wait."

Vanessa laughed, too. "When the word gets out that Celeste Deveaux has a store in Charleston, you can count on being busy."

Celeste winked. "More reason for you to come to work with us as soon as possible."

They spent the next hour talking about ideas for the store and laughing together. Celeste had never made many close girlfriends, but Vanessa had been her good friend ever since they met when only seven years old. There was something about old friends that was especially comfortable, too. Celeste knew these friends weren't cozying up to her because they wanted something. Or simply becoming friends with her because of her fame. They just really liked her for who she was.

CHAPTER 6

Reid's father leaned his head into Reid's office early on Monday morning. "Do you have a minute?"

"Sure, come on in Dad."

His father came in to settle in the chair across from Reid's desk. "Do you think the sale of Imogene Hathaway's property will be formally initiated this morning? I know Celeste Deveaux is due here at ten. Have you talked to Imogene yet?"

Reid grinned. "Imogene called and is still, as she says 'over the moon' that Celeste wants to buy her shop and that she can continue to work there. I think you were right in discouraging the idea of a partnership. Imogene will net a big profit with this sale. We can help to see she gets the money from the sale properly invested for her benefit, and she can still work in the shop as she hoped."

"It isn't a bad investment for Celeste, either. A lot of entertainers buy businesses for financial reasons but I sensed Celeste is really excited about working in the store, too. Apparently, she's been through a rough time, causing her some disenchantment with the entertainment business, and it certainly seems wise to me that she stays out of the orbit of her past husband for a time."

"I agree. I expect her to come in today wanting to move forward, but you never know."

His father glanced at the clock on Reid's wall. "On another subject, Annabel Pennyman called me this morning. I know you are acquainted with the Pennyman family since you are good friends with Annabel's son Benson. Is he still in England?"

"Yes, he is. We texted the other day. He's finishing his graduate coursework at the end of this month at the university in Cambridge but hanging around to do a little research in the fall before heading back. What's going on with Annabel? Is she all right?"

"Yes, but she hasn't had an easy time since the wreck five years ago that took her husband Monroe's life and left her in a wheelchair. Your mother Frances says she has good help in the house, though." He hesitated. "She seems to think she might like to move into a smaller place on one level. You know she's still in the big family home on Church Street."

"Yes, and the house isn't far from the Pennyman family's appraisal business on Broad Street." He nodded. "If I remember right her husband's sister Florence, and Florence's son Robert, Annabel's nephew, are running the family business now. They do all our appraisal work."

"Yes, and Annabel's son Clarence is still at the Folly Beach office handling their rental properties there."

Reid wrinkled his nose at the mention of Clarence's name.

His father laughed. "You never did like Clarence much, even as a boy. I seem to remember he and Ben never got along well either."

"That's an understatement."

"Well, anyway, I know you're as fond of Annabel as we are, and she asked if you would come to talk with her about selling one or more of her properties at the beach so she can buy a smaller place outright."

He hesitated. "She made it clear she was looking into this on her own at this point, without talking to either of her sons, Clarence or Benson. She wants you to make inquiries for her confidentially. I saw no reason we shouldn't help her. Despite her physical disability, Annabel's mind is as sharp as a tack. She keeps a hand in at the appraisal business and she knows what's what."

"Wouldn't Charlie be a better choice to help her?" Charlie, or Charles Dean Beckett, was Reid's younger brother, also a major member of their realty and brokerage business. "Charlie works at Folly Beach more than I do and he handles most all our sales out of the city. Wouldn't he be a better option to help Annabel with this? Especially if she wants to move out of the city. Charlie would have the best handle on good locations."

"Probably, but Annabel knows you better and she asked for you. Charlie can help, too, when we know more what Annabel wants." He grinned. "Annabel promised to make you some kind of cookies she said you especially liked."

Reid laughed out loud. "That's worth a trip to Annabel Pennyman's. Ben and I used to love those cookies she made, called Half Moon Cookies—a sweet, buttery cookie with one side dipped in dark chocolate icing and the other in white chocolate. Man, they were to die for."

His dad winked. "Well, see if Annabel will give your mother the recipe, and give her a call and set up a time to go talk with her. If she decides to sell the big house, you know it's worth several million. Also, any of their beach houses at Folly would sell at high price points, too. We won't be hurt giving time to help Annabel Pennyman with whatever she wants to do. But don't pressure her."

"You know I won't, Dad, and if her ideas aren't well thought out, I'll discourage her from buying or selling anything."

Reid finished some needed paperwork after his father left, and then looked up at almost ten to see Celeste Deveaux standing in the doorway. She had a way of making an entrance into a room, and today she leaned casually against the door frame, dressed in a sleeveless sky-blue sundress that complimented the blue of her eyes. The top had little rows of pleats and the skirt was patterned subtly with field flowers—a happy look. Her sandals, as usual, matched the dress, making Reid wonder how many pairs of shoes the woman owned.

"Come on in," he said. "How long have you been there?"

"Only a few minutes." She gave him a smile. "I like watching handsome men work. You looked so dedicated."

He'd always felt Celeste held a flirtatious streak and this certainly confirmed it.

"I suppose it wouldn't be inappropriate on that note to mention that you look beautiful today, as always."

"A woman never tires of words like those, Reid Beckett." She glided across the room and sat down in the chair across from his.

"I wouldn't have thought you'd be interested in adding a man to your life just now, Celeste, after what you've recently passed through."

"You'd be right in that." She crossed her leg casually. "But I am interested in adding a little shop on King Street to my life."

"I'm glad to hear that. Imogene is certainly enthusiastic to see that happen, too."

"What do we need to do today?"

"Sign a few papers here, a few more with Imogene, and then I guess the next negotiations will be between the two of you." He glanced at some notes on his desk. "Will you want to move into the apartment now or wait until the trial period is over to do that?"

She studied a nail. "Imogene decorated the apartment herself. She has excellent taste. It looks nice, and it is certainly nice enough for me to stay in and more convenient right now. When we finalize everything, I'll make changes to personalize the apartment more, of course."

"That sounds sensible."

Celeste frowned. "I really wish the apartment had a piano, though. I've been getting a few songs---you know I write all my own songs, and I like to have a piano at hand so I can write the music." She laughed a little. "At the Deveaux Inn, I often slip downstairs to the piano after midnight to work since, during the day, it's simply impossible to work there. People come in, gushing and wanting to talk or get my autograph or they want to hear me sing. They really don't understand I'm working and need quiet."

"I can see you would need that." He thought for a moment before saying, "I have a piano at my place. My house is about a block from your apartment on Clifford Street. You can come use it until you find one of your own later."

She looked surprised at his offer. "Do you play the piano, Reid Beckett?"

"No, except for a little diddling I do occasionally from my years of forced piano lessons. The piano came with the house. The owner died and the family members, all absentee, wanted to sell all the furnishings except for personal items they came to get. I'd been living in a small apartment, with little furniture. I liked most of the furnishings in the house so I bought them." He shrugged. "The piano looks aesthetically good in the house's bay window, too, and my friend Marcus loves to play it when he comes over."

"Marcus." She said the name thoughtfully. "Is that the same Marcus who plays the piano at Thurman's?"

"Yes, it is. We became fast friends while in school together at the College of Charleston. After I heard Marcus play the first time, I pushed him to audition for Uncle Thurman to play at the restaurant. My uncle only had random people coming in before, so he was glad to get someone to play regularly who lives downtown. Marcus's family owns M&M Sign and Graphics on Wentworth. They do great signs and graphics of all kinds if you ever need anything for the business."

"Thanks." She glanced out the window thinking. "You know, it would be good to have someone to work with to try songs out. I'm used to doing that with a pianist in Nashville, who's in the group that plays for me at my performances."

"I imagine Marcus would be thrilled at that idea. We could set up some times later that would work for both of you. Usually when Marcus comes over to play, I sit, read, and listen. It's relaxing, and I appreciate talent." He paused. "But If you need privacy, I have an office and a den upstairs."

She straightened a ring on her finger. "Well, this is certainly an idea to consider. I really liked Marcus, too."

"He's an easy-going guy." Reid picked up the file on his desk. "Are you ready to go sign some papers or do you have more questions?"

She gave him a big smile. "I don't have more questions now. I think you and your father made everything very clear. I faxed copies of all the papers to my financial advisor after me met on Friday. He was very impressed with the competence and clarity of everything, with the Beckett Company, and with your background."

Reid decided not to reply to that, surprised again at Celeste's competence and that she'd conferred with her financial group and had someone check out his company—and him.

They signed needed papers then and gathered the rest to take to Imogene's shop. She couldn't easily leave the store with no additional help right now.

"Did everything go well?" his father asked as they started to leave. He was leaning on the front desk in the Beckett Company entry, talking to his mother who was still filling in for Irina.

"Yes, and thank you for your help." Celeste sent him one of her charming smiles. "It looks like we're going to be business neighbors."

"Heywood and I are so pleased to meet you, Celeste," his mother put in, "and we're very pleased at your kindness in allowing Imogene to continue managing CeeCee's Place. It's been her love and her heart since she was only a girl. It was her mother's joy, too. We were very fond of her mother, Cecelia Hathaway. She trained her girls—they were twins, you know—to work with her in the store from a young age. Erma married and had a family, but Imogene never did. Her mother said the man she loved dearly and intended to marry was killed in the military, and she simply never met anyone else to take her heart."

Reid felt this was rather a lot of personal information to introduce, but his mother was always a very open person.

"I feel sure Imogene and I will work very well together," Celeste assured her. "Stop by the store to see us sometime."

"Oh, I will," his mother said. "It's my go-to place for gifts I need for most any occasion. CeeCee's Place is very loved in Charleston."

On that rush of goodwill, Reid held the door for them to leave and took Celeste's arm in a gentlemanly manner as they walked down the curved stairway to the sidewalk. However, his feelings certainly weren't gentlemanly as he tucked his arm into hers, snug against his side, and moved close enough on the stairs to catch the soft, sensual hint of a jasmine-tinged perfume in the air.

At Imogene's shop, more hugging than handshaking went on as Imogene and Celeste met again. Around their enthusiasm and a surprising stream of customers, even for a Monday morning, Reid eventually got the two women to sit down at a table in the store's book section to sign the additional paperwork needed and to clarify the legalities of their new relationship. Both agreed to contact him if they had further questions and Reid finally made his way out of the store.

He glanced at his watch as he left. It was nearly noon now and feeling a little restless, Reid decided to head over to Marcus's business, a few streets over, to see if his friend could get away for lunch. Time with Celeste Deveaux had left him feeling edgy and he thought some casual time with Marcus exactly what he needed to erase the lingering feelings of being in close company with her. At least for a time.

He walked up King Street, crossing Market and passing a few side streets, including Beaufain and Hassell, before turning on Wentworth to head down the street to M&M Sign and Graphics, housed in a stately old gray building. Seeing Marcus's car in the small parking area beside the building cheered him, and he sprinted up the steps to the front door and let himself in.

"Well, look who's here," Marcus's mother Aretha McClain said, looking up from the front desk. She got up to hug him, a given any time he stopped by.

"How are you doing, Mrs. McClain?" he asked, stepping back.

"I'm fit and well. Thank you." She glanced at an appointment book on her desk. "Is Marcus expecting you?"

"No. I stopped by on a spur, hoping he might be free to go grab a bite of lunch with me."

"Well, go on back. He's on the computer, creating some graphics for something or other. I'm sure he can run out for lunch."

Reid wandered down the hall past several big print production rooms to Marcus's office near the back. "Hey, brother," he said, stopping at the open door.

"Well, if it isn't my fraternity brother. What brings you here?" he asked, shifting around in his chair.

"Thought you might snag time for lunch."

Marcus glanced at the clock. "I can do that. I don't have an appointment until two, and a man's gotta eat. Where do you want to go?" he asked as he saved his work and shut down the computer.

"Let's walk down the street to the Basic Kitchen. We can get one of their burgers with sweet potato fries and cabbage slaw. I'll treat. You know everything is fresh there."

"Good plan and it isn't far either."

They soon settled into a table in the restaurant's corner and ordered. Marcus, as usual, had been talking away about a project at work, Reid nodding appropriately at the right places.

"What have you been doing today?" he asked Reid.

"I found a buyer for that shop by our business, CeeCee's Place." He grinned at Marcus. "Guess who bought it?"

Marcus named a totally unlikely subject in jest, making Reid laugh.

"No. Celeste Deveaux bought it."

Marcus's mouth dropped open. "You're kidding me, man."

"No, I'm serious. While she was in the city last week she stopped by the store, liked the place, got acquainted with the owner, and then set an appointment with me to write contract. Evidently, her financial advisors have been encouraging her to buy a business for investment, tax reasons, and such. She decided CeeCee's Place just what she was looking for."

He looked confused. "But why Charleston?"

"My guess is because it's far away from Nashville and Dillon Barlow, her ex-husband. You know what happened there. You told me most of it yourself and, evidently, he's still threatening her, warning her not to come back to Nashville."

"Man, I hate that for her. But will she stick around?"

"She says so. Wants to get into a business, likes Charleston and the idea of living closer to her family when not in Nashville. She'll still record and travel, especially after all this mess with the ex-husband settles down, but for now, she'll be around town. The former owner is staying on as manager. They seem to have hit it off. She's going to live in the apartment above the store."

"That isn't far from you, brother." He wiggled his eyebrows. "She's one fine-looking woman and I saw you watching her at Thurman's. Maybe you should go after her."

He laughed. "And why would Celeste Deveaux be interested in me?"

"Hey. You're not exactly ugly, man, and you got a nice house, a fine business, good car, and money of your own, a gentleman's ways. Women like that stuff."

Reid laughed out loud. Marcus always cheered him up like no one else could. "I also own a piano, and she's already told me she's interested in that. She's also interested in possibly getting together with you to try out some new songs she's working on. Her main pianist is back in Nashville, a little far for collaboration right now."

Marcus leaned forward with excitement. "Are you telling the truth about that? Don't you be messing with me about something like that."

"It's true. When Celeste started talking about wishing there was a piano in her apartment, I mentioned having one at my place. I also mentioned you liked to come over and play." He grinned at Marcus. "She remembered your name, posed the idea herself about getting together with you. She said she really liked you."

Marcus crossed his arms and smiled broadly. "Man, that makes my day, and I sure do hope you'll help me make that happen."

"I'll do my best. It's one of the reasons I decided to come take you out to lunch."

Their food came and both settled in to eat.

"Hey," Marcus said after a time, leaning across the table. "That fine-looking woman I saw at Thurman's on Wednesday was with Celeste Deveaux. Wonder if she might know who she is?"

Reid laughed. "You still thinking about that woman?"

"I am. She's hung around in my mind. She did something deep to me. Some women are like that you know. They stay playing around in your mind, making you want to be with them." He grinned.

"You know."

Reid smiled. He did know.

"Well, as it happens," Reid put in, "I actually know who that woman is. Her name is Vanessa George. She's a good friend of Celeste Deveaux's. Celeste says she plans to hire her to work in the store with her and Imogene."

"Well, isn't that flippin' fine." He grinned widely. "There's those two good-looking women working together right here in the city near us. They're friends. We're friends. Put the pieces of the puzzle together, man. We can get something going. I can play a little piano for Celeste. She can sing and practice whatever she's working on. We can all have a little cookout together on your excellent patio at your big house. Get acquainted real nicely. I am picturing it right now and liking it."

Reid laughed. "You may be imagining more than we can work out."

"Well, why not? Nobody ever gets anywhere without trying. You work on it. Follow up on it. Set something up. Tell Celeste it will be a nice way for her to check out your piano and talk to me again. And for her friend to have a nice little evening out, too. Girls like that double-dating thing. They feel safer like that."

"Well, we'll see, Marcus." Reid finished the last of his lunch. "I need to get back to the office. You finished, too?"

"Sure thing, but I'll be riding high all afternoon over this good news." He punched Reid on the arm as they got up. "Thanks a lot, my brother. I owe you one for this."

They split then to head in different directions, but Reid smiled on the way home, thinking about Marcus's idea. It might just fly.

CHAPTER 7

September - A Month Later

Celeste walked downstairs and through the store at 9:30 am to get ready to open CeeCee's Place for the day. Glancing at the calendar by the register, she realized a whole month had passed since the Wednesday when she first walked into Imogene Hathaway's store.

She heard the back door open as Imogene let herself in. "Happy one month anniversary," Imogene called out, coming to set a bouquet of flowers on the check-out counter. "It's been a whole month since the Wednesday when you first came in the store."

"I'd just noticed that on the calendar." Celeste's eyes moved to study the flowers. "These flowers are really pretty."

"I picked them in my yard this morning. They're called star asters." Imogene pointed at the lavender-blue, daisy-like flowers in the vase. "Most everything else in my garden is beginning to fade, but asters love the early fall." She smiled at Celeste as she tucked her purse under the counter. "I do think we've shared a happy first month, don't you?"

"Yes, I do," Celeste replied, giving her a big smile. "I started coffee in the back. It should be ready. Do you want me to bring you a cup?"

"Yes, thank you, dear. I'd love that," Imogene answered, arranging the flowers in the vase to display better.

Celeste brought two mugs back and sat them on the table near the store's book area and then sat down to sip on her own coffee while it was hot.

Imogene joined her, adding the day's newspaper to their table.

She always read the news every morning around customers.

"The weather's sunny and pretty today, so I hope we'll have another good week again." Imogene glanced toward the window. "I often think the tourist traffic picks up for us in September. It's a little cooler in Charleston, and a lot of people, knowing the children are back in school and the Lowcountry area less crowded, love to come to the coast at this time."

"Mother said traffic was continuing strong at the lighthouse and inn, too. The inn is booked solid for this week and next."

Imogene drank some of her coffee, glancing over the newspaper as she did, and then added, "I'm glad you invited me down on Sunday to meet your family and to share dinner with everyone. It was a treat. Your sister Burke even gave me a special tour of the lighthouse."

She glanced across the table to a card display rack. "I'm also pleased at how well your sister Lila's lovely cards are selling. We've sold several of her paintings, too. You're blessed to have such a talented family." She finished her coffee and sighed. "I miss family times with Erma gone."

"Were you close?" Celeste asked.

"Very, as twins often are, and we worked together, too. Our lives were mixed up with each other daily. I miss Erma and my mother."

Celeste grinned. "Well, you can share my family. They're all fond of you."

"Thank you. Vanessa has a big happy family, too. I've met many of them now, as well." She hesitated. "Is Vanessa happy working here? She says so but you know her better than I do."

"She loves it here, and I think she's adding a lot to the store with her talents. Like you, she has a good sense about what products might sell well and has wonderful arrangement skills."

"She's a lovely and gracious girl, too, and she talks to everyone who comes in. I liked that about her from the first. She seems to carry a gift for knowing exactly how to deal with people. That is a big help in retail." She patted Celeste's hand. "You carry that gift, too. I can tell how much you enjoy being in the store."

"It's been more fun than I expected."

Imogene laughed. "It's a good thing we got in a huge selection of your CDs, too. Those have sold like crazy, and everyone loves getting them autographed by you."

Celeste glanced at the section they'd created for her CDs in the book area. "I hope Vanessa and I haven't brought in too many changes. She worries about that."

"What?" Imogene looked shocked. "You two have hardly changed anything major, only an array of small things that bring more sales to the store." She paused. "For example, Vanessa had the wonderful idea of ordering bags for the store that say: *I shopped at CeeCees*. I'd never thought of doing that. Now when anyone buys anything they go out carrying a bag that brings us free advertising. She's a clever girl."

"She is."

"I'm glad you felt good about hiring Loretta Griffey to work part-time with us, too. As I told you, she's the college girl who approached me and offered to work when the store was for sale."

"I like Loretta, and I like how she came seeking a job she thought would be a good fit for her and would give her work experience to enhance the marketing degree she's working on. I like, too, that she came back again; that shows moxie."

"She's a friendly girl, with lots of enthusiasm and initiative. She's always prompt for work and she works hard. A lot of young people I've hired in past didn't work out well." Imogene rolled her eyes. "Most kept pulling out their cellphones to text or checking their social media sites; then they'd suddenly look up and realize someone was standing impatiently at the counter, right in front of them, wanting to make a purchase."

"Well, it's been a help having Loretta. It gives me more free time to work on my songs." Celeste glanced at the clock and added, "Let's look at the schedule for a minute before I open the store. Do the hours agree with everyone?"

"Everyone seems fine with them, Celeste. We've fallen into a pattern that seems to suit each of us best. I love to open, so I open most days, sometimes with you or on my own. Vanessa comes in around eleven. We work together in the busiest part of the day, or you come in to help. She likes working afternoons and doesn't mind closing. Loretta works around her class schedule, which right now puts her in the store mostly late afternoons and on Saturdays. We all pitch in as needed to cover for each other for times when we keep the store open late for events going on downtown that bring in a lot of traffic."

"I admit I was surprised at how few stores stay open late on a daily basis on King Street and in downtown Charleston. Most close at five or at six, like we do."

"Yes. The restaurants all stay busy at night in Charleston, but not the shops. It's always been that way. As you've seen, few stores open on Sunday either. I've always liked that, keeping the Sabbath a day of rest."

Celeste couldn't help grinning. "I've actually liked that myself. In the past, when traveling and on the road, I seldom had a chance to rest on Sunday or go to church."

Imogene stood to gather up their coffee mugs to take to the back. "I hope your meeting this afternoon with your agent goes well. Feel free to leave whenever you want to pick Gary up at the airport. Venessa and I will be here and she'll close the store at six." Imogene glanced toward the door, spotting customers looking in the window. "Well, here come customers for us. It looks like our day is ready to begin."

Actually, Celeste didn't pick Gary up at the airport in Charleston when he flew in. He always used the free airport shuttle to the Hyatt Place instead, preferring to settle in at the hotel before Celeste came to meet with him. He reserved a suite whenever staying at the hotel, too, with sofas and a separate meeting area where they could talk without people recognizing Celeste and interrupting them.

She took the elevator to Gary's room at about two in the afternoon. At her knock he opened the door to her, giving her the usual casual, businesslike hug that was his custom.

"Good to see you finally," he said, emphasizing the last word.

Celeste had postponed their meeting more than once.

She settled into a corner of one of the sofas, getting a bottle of water out of the refrigerator on her way into the room. Overlooking the note of sarcasm in Gary's greeting, she smiled across at him. "It's good to see you, too, Gary. How was the flight?"

He shrugged. "The direct flight is only an hour and a half. I left Nashville about 10:30, got here about 1:00. It's an easy trip compared to some I make. I grabbed a sandwich downstairs when I got in. Do you need something?"

"No, I ate before I came. Thanks."

Gary's phone binged then. He glanced at it in annoyance. "I need to get this. It'll only take a minute."

She studied him as he paced around the room, talking to someone. A dark-haired and good-looking man in his forties, Gary Feinstein was Jewish, his family background originally German. He'd grown up in New York but then moved to Nashville about fifteen years ago to work with her husband Nolan and Al Jenson of Capital Records. Celeste knew, as did Gary, that Nolan had "made" him in the industry, meeting him in New York, where he'd been working, liking him, seeing his potential, and recommending him to Capital. He then mentored and worked with Gary personally, helping to establish him in the entertainment business as a strong agent. Nolan, as Celeste's manager and husband, had linked her to Gary when she arrived in Nashville. As her star rose quickly so did Gary's star and his reputation.

"Is there a problem?" she asked him, as he punched off his phone and sat back down.

He rolled his eyes. "No. Just the usual stuff."

She waited, relaxing against the sofa and crossing her legs.

His eyes moved over her briefly before he shook his head and frowned. "You do know that buying this store and staying out of the business isn't doing anything positive for your career," he said, direct as always.

She shrugged. "I've told you my reasons for doing what I did at this particular time, and I think we've been putting a good spin on things. Entertainers sometimes take breaks from the industry."

"Yes, but you haven't performed since early spring. With your popularity and fan base, you usually do an album every year with a tour after, usually in September or October. People are wondering what's going on with no new songs or new album even being talked about. I fend off calls every day from people wanting to book you and it isn't getting any easier with this new decision of yours to take even more time away."

She listened to Gary rant and rave, listing all the opportunities he'd had to turn down, the questions he'd needed to field about her health and about whether she was finished in the industry. Then he went off on another rant about all the publicity in the tabloids and industry media, continuing to rehash her breakup with Dillon Barlow.

He paused at one point, frowning. "You've stayed quiet through all this, but Dillon has certainly been vocal enough."

Celeste finally interjected. "Gary, you know few people with any sense have sympathy for Dillon in all of this. Especially with the continuing publicity coming his way as these women from his past keep speaking out and getting in the public eye."

"Maybe, but he's still out there, Celeste. Performing. Singing. Pushing on."

Her lips thinned. "I would be deeply disappointed, Gary, if I felt you carried any admiration for Dillon Barlow."

He crossed his arms. "You know that's not what I meant." He leaned back in his chair. "I just wish all this hadn't happened."

"So do I," she agreed. "But I am finally finding my way out of this dark time and healing. Strengthening. And coming back to myself gradually. This change I decided to pursue, that you haven't been very supportive of for me, has been a positive change in my life." She gave him a small smile. "You might be pleased to know I've been writing songs through all of this time and especially lately."

He leaned forward. "You haven't told me that. Can you come to Nashville so we can work on recording them? This would be a good time to get something new out from you. To get your name back out there. To let people see you're still singing, working."

"After I write a few more songs we'll talk about it." She paused and then added. "I almost have enough for a new album, nearly twelve written."

"What?" He sounded shocked.

"I thought you'd be pleased to hear that." She picked at one of her nails. "I thought we might call this new album *The Come Back*. One of the songs reflects that theme. I can envision some great publicity linked to that, can't you?"

He shook his head. "Dang. You've always been a woman to keep things close to her chest. Why didn't you tell me you've been working this much? I had no idea you'd been writing again. You told me it was hard to do anything at the island at the inn, with so many people around, and with healing from your injuries and all."

"Gary, I used to get up in the night, tormented with dreams and bad memories. I'd slip out to the old piano in the downstairs living room of the inn, when everyone was asleep, and I'd play and sing out my hurts, regrets, hopes, and desires. Artistic people vent out their pains in creativity as well as their joys. Surely that shouldn't be a surprise to you. When I was starting out in the business in Nashville, and when someone hurt me or a disappointing event happened to me, Nolan would say, 'Go to the piano and work it out, baby. The good and the bad, they happen to all of us. People relate to both. Put your feelings into words that will touch other people, maybe help other people. It's the way artists impact the world and make a difference.'"

Gary closed his eyes. "I can hear him saying something like that. Gosh, he was such a good, fine man. I hate we lost him so soon. I still miss him every day."

"Me, too," she agreed. "I leaned to his counsel and wisdom so much, probably too much. I often think I didn't learn to be as strong in myself as I should have because of that. It's probably one reason why I got involved with Dillon too soon and too easily."

"Dillon was talented, good looking, seemed like a nice guy." Gary made a face. "One of the women called him the charming snake."

"Yes, he was like that, a Jekyll and Hyde type with two totally different sides."

"He really hurt you, too, didn't he, Celeste?"

"Yes. Through him I got more acquainted with the devil than I ever wanted to, learned more about the evil that can live in people than I ever wanted to know. It's taken me time to heal from that, Gary. Whatever costs to my career, I needed that time."

With honesty out on the table now, they talked about a lot of issues and upcoming decisions with more openness. Gary filled her in about all the legal suits and outcomes going on in Dillon's life. Not all the truth in these disputes hit the media but Gary and Capital had ferreted the details out. It wasn't pretty. Some demonstrations had been held outside Dillon's shows recently, targeting him for abuse. Many women and women's abuse support groups were angry at comments of Dillon's, that had slipped out, showing little remorse on his part. Also, he hadn't garnered any favor by continually blaming his victims, as though they deserved any abuse they had received.

"The ongoing legalities and publicity are hurting him, Celeste, and instead of playing contrite, lying low, and letting it all die down, Dillon keeps confronting the women and the media with anger, tossing out threats, keeping everything stirred up," Gary told her. "A lot of sponsors are pulling out on him. Few people of merit, except for the tabloids, want to interview him and be confronted with his anger and bad attitudes. One woman, another entertainer, is now suing him over stealing one of her songs, "You're My Magic." She says she wrote it and not him. Do you think Dillon wrote it?"

Celeste shook her head. "No, Dillon has a gifted voice but he has no gift for writing songs. I often watched him try in frustration to create a song, angry at me when I'd sit and write one while he couldn't."

She hesitated. "Actually, I wrote his hit song, 'A Man's Ways,' for him after we first married. By the time it was recorded, I wasn't surprised he claimed he'd written it himself."

"Do you have any proof of that?" Gary leaned forward. "I could get our legal people working on it."

"No, let it go. I don't want any more trouble with Dillon Barlow. I just want to move on. I'm not interested in any kind of revenge."

"That song was a huge hit for him. I hope he was grateful."

"Gratitude wasn't a characteristic Dillon ever developed well." She changed the subject. "How is Martina doing?"

"She is well and said to send you her best. Martina certainly understands gratitude." He paused. "You changed her life getting her a new job, settling her and her children into a new home, and helping to keep anyone from knowing where she moved. especially Dillon."

"She was a good housekeeper for Dillon and for me. I worried Dillon would go after her one day, as crazy as he could be sometimes. That's why I had you keep up with her. When I learned he'd hurt her later, roughed her up, I made some contacts with a few entertainer friends in California, found her a new job—actually a better job—and I had you find her a small home nearby for her and her children. She has four children, you know. That has to be hard."

"Honey, you bought the house outright for her and furnished it for her and the kids. It was a fine thing you did."

She hesitated. "Martina called you that night when she found me in the floor unconscious after Dillon had beaten me, and she braved facing Dillon about who had called the ambulance to come to get me. Knowing Dillon, I figured he might eventually get angry at her for that, as he did."

"Well, she's doing well now."

"Thanks. You let me know if she ever needs anything. I don't want to risk contacting her in any way with Dillon still so dangerous."

They talked about Dillon's recent threats to her and the protective steps they were taking at the agency.

Gary got up to get a cola out of the refrigerator. "As I told you in August, after Dillon got your new phone number again, we learned he'd bribed one of the cleaning staff at Capital to steal your phone numbers from our files. The man was fired, of course."

"Well, since I got my last 'new' number in August, I haven't gotten any more calls from him."

"Good." Gary pulled a stack of folders from his briefcase. There were always papers, photos, and other things for her to sign whenever they met.

As she started to put her signature on a pile of promotional photos, Gary said, "The media has picked up on the fact that you've bought a store here in Charleston. I'm sure Dillon will learn of it, Celeste, if he already hasn't."

"Dillon knows I've been here in South Carolina, and he knows my family live here. His threats have been for if I return to Nashville."

Gary pulled more papers from an envelope for her to sign. "The restraining orders in place should keep him from coming around to bother you, especially since you're not convenient for him to get to right now."

"I hope that's true, and I hope he'll egoistically interpret it that I'm purposely staying out of his way here." She gave Gary a hard look. "I don't want anyone knowing right now that I'm writing songs down here, getting ready for a new album. That would be fuel to Dillon at this time, who doesn't want to see anything good happen for me. Keep in mind, he's very vengeful and very competitive."

"In due time, we'll have to start publicity, Celeste, and I'll need to schedule time for you to record soon. If we could get this album out this fall, even if a little later than usual, that would be good. You know a lot of other people are involved in this, depending on you. It isn't only about you, as I'm sure you're aware." He paused. "I hope you'll be ready to tour with the new album, too. You know you'll need to."

"I do."

He grinned at her then. "Are you going to sing one or two of these new songs for me? Give me a sneak preview of what's to come?"

She laughed. "I might. I'm taking you to Thurman's for dinner tonight before you fly back to Nashville early in the morning. They like for me to sing there on Wednesdays or Fridays when I drop in, and the pianist I sometimes practice with, Marcus McClain, is playing tonight. He picks up and memorizes any songs I'm working on so easily, Gary. He has an incredible photographic memory."

"Should I try to hire him? Lure him to Nashville?"

"Don't you dare. I love having him here, and he has a happy life in Charleston, a good family, works in his family's business." She lifted an eyebrow. "He's also been seeing my friend Vanessa George a little, the one I grew up with and who works at CeeCee's with me. These are my people, Gary. I care about them. I don't want them tampered with."

He nodded. "I understand. It's a hard business."

"It can be, but it has its joys. I've been looking back on that."

"You've known some great times. I have, too, working with you."

"Thanks." She paused, drinking some water before continuing. "I went to visit with Nolan's family."

"Did you? They're great people. Do they still own the music store? Seems like I remember they sold pianos, sound equipment, sheet music, instruments, that sort of thing."

"Yes, I went over to their business to visit with them. It's not far from the West Ashley/Old Towne area here. They were really sweet to me, understanding about why I married again and sorry it turned out to be such a tragedy."

"Nolan sure loved them. He talked about them a lot. He told me they really liked you, that they encouraged him to marry you."

"He told me that, too." She laughed. "When Nolan's mom and dad learned I needed a piano, they helped me find a little Yamaha in the store that would be perfect for my apartment. They delivered it practically the next day, their people hauling it up all those steep stairs without a word of complaint."

"I'd say dealing with stairs is a given for them."

"Probably so."

"How's the piano working out?"

"It's exactly what I needed, and with the store rarely open at night, I have lots of time to work on getting the music written down for the songs I'm composing. Marcus has helped me with that, too."

"Well, that's all good news for me."

As she finished signing needed paperwork and promotionals, he tapped the table restlessly with his fingers and then added, "You know I'm thinking we can do something really good with this *The Come Back* album idea. Everyone knows you've been through a rough time; the media certainly saw to it with those hospital pictures floating around everywhere. There's even been speculation as to whether you'd come back at all. I think we can play that up, the idea that "she's back" whenever you're ready."

"You let me be the one to decide when that time is though, Gary." Celeste looked at her watch. "It's nearly four now, I'd like to go home and change before we have dinner at Thurman's. It's a dressy place. Did you bring some sharp clothes?"

"Always." He grinned at her. "You usually want to go to that sort of place whenever we get together. Why don't I get a cab to the city to meet you at this restaurant though? What time is good?"

"About five-thirty, I think. I'd like you to meet Marcus before he starts to play at six. It's nearly four now. Does that give you enough time? If so, I'll call and make a reservation."

"Sure. I'll see you there," he said, winking at her as she left.

Celeste sighed as she made her way back to her car. She'd dreaded this meeting, but things had gone better than she'd thought.

CHAPTER 8

Reid felt a little antsy all day, knowing Celeste was meeting with her agent from Nashville. Marcus told him the man was flying in, and that Celeste wanted to sing a couple of her new songs for him at Thurman's tonight. Marcus was naturally stoked about the meeting, but Reid worried the man would pressure Celeste to get back on the road and tour. He knew about agents. If Celeste didn't work and make money, he wouldn't make money either—or not as much.

When Reid expressed concern about it to Marcus, his friend grinned. "My guess is you're thinking about yourself as much as Celeste in this. You're not ready to see her leave yet, especially since you haven't exactly made any moves on her. I can see you care about her. When you, me, Vanessa, and Celeste get together, it's pretty obvious."

Reid scowled. "She's been through a lot. The timing hasn't seemed right."

"Man, you can't always wait for the perfect time for everything. Life's short. The perfect time might never come. Sometimes you just need to take a risk."

His words annoyed Reid. "Our situations aren't the same, Marcus. Vanessa George hasn't been married twice already and she isn't recovering from abuse."

"Yeah, yeah, I know. And Vanessa isn't a big singing star like Celeste, but Celeste is still a woman, too, and a sweet and pretty one. I'd like to see someone step up and show her that men can be good and honorable and kind, too. It hurts my heart for all she's gone through. Seems like she could use a little love and tenderness."

However, despite Marcus's words, Reid continued to notice a wariness in Celeste's eyes any time he moved in too close, a sort of panicked look that held him back. He'd hesitated, not from a lack of interest or desire, but from concern and caring. And he didn't like the idea of Celeste getting back into Dillon Barlow's orbit right now.

Wanting to meet Celeste's agent, Reid made plans to go to Thurman's for dinner tonight. He often did, anyway, when Marcus played. The two of them usually ate dinner together shortly after five before Marcus was due to start playing at six. A perk of pianists at Thurman's, and at other fine restaurants, was free dinner with any performance. Thurman's was open five to nine for dinner, with many guests arriving near nine and lingering until ten, so Marcus usually played for about four hours from six to ten.

At five, Reid joined Marcus at their usual table, deciding with him to order the flounder tonight with stone ground grits, and a broccoli-cheese side that was one of the restaurant's specialties.

Celeste came in shortly after, dressed in a gorgeous green dress in some sort of shimmery material, the man with her spiffy in a sharp suit. Marcus got up to speak with them, suggesting they join them, and after a moment or two of discussion with the waiter, they did.

As they came to the table, Celeste introduced her agent to them. "Gary Feinstein, you've met Marcus but this is Reid Beckett. He helped me with the purchase of the store and his family owns the restaurant." She hesitated. "We met when younger, too."

Gary shook Reid's hand firmly. "Good to meet you. I saw the photo display of Celeste in her earlier years out in the lobby. Nolan Culver often told me she got her start singing professionally here."

"She did and I still remember those times," Reid replied as they all settled in at the table.

After studying the menu, Celeste and her agent ordered, too. As the waiter left, Reid's Uncle Thurman walked into the restaurant to say hello after introducing himself. Reid listened as his uncle reminisced and told Gary a story or two of Celeste's earlier times at Thurman's before he politely left as their beverages arrived.

Celeste smiled at Gary. "My dad, Lloyd Deveaux, used to sit here at this table every time I performed, keeping a watch over me. He always made sure none of the men approached me or tried to act inappropriately. He was very protective."

"I remember Nolan telling me a few stories from those days." Gary replied. "Nolan said he knew from the first time he heard you sing you had that special something that set you apart, that would make a way for you in the industry."

"It was a huge extra that Celeste writes all her own songs, too," Marcus put in.

"Yes, and I hear you've been helping with that," Gary said. "Thank you. Everyone at the agency and at Capital is grateful for that."

Their dinners arrived soon and they talked as they ate. Gary entertained Marcus with stories from the road, Celeste adding some of her own. Reid made appropriate comments now and then but mostly he listened. He saw Gary exhibit a respect and politeness for Celeste that he liked, taking the edge off his earlier apprehensions.

At six, Marcus went to play the piano and entertain and not long after Celeste joined him, scooting on to the piano bench with him as before, singing as he played. She sang a few favorites the audience would recognize and then began a less familiar song, winking at Gary as she moved into the lyrics.

"It's good," Gary said as they listened.

"Yes, it is," Reid answered.

Gary looked toward him as if surprised at his words. "You know Celeste's work?" he asked. "That this is a new song?"

Reid nodded. "I've followed Celeste since she sang here as a girl and then after she moved to Nashville to start to perform."

They listened for a little longer and then Gary said, "She likes you. I've seen how she keeps looking over here at you. Is it mutual?"

Shocked at his candor, Reid hesitated before replying, "Actually that is none of your business."

Gary grinned, unashamed. "Everything to do with Celeste Deveaux is my business, Mr. Beckett."

Reid shook his head. "No, her private life is her own. And if you really stayed so conscientiously on top of things with Celeste, you'd have kept her from getting linked up with Dillon Barlow."

"Ouch." Gary put a hand to his heart with another grin. "Celeste was distraught after Nolan died. She'd been performing with Dillon, working on a few songs with him, even before Nolan was in that fatal wreck. I knew Dillon, as most people did, as a charming, charismatic man, talented in spades, a rising star in the industry. He had another side none of us saw, but I'll admit now I'm sorry I didn't investigate him, check him out as soon as Celeste started seeing him on the side. Nolan Culver would have done that. I share a piece of the guilt for what happened to Celeste. I don't mind admitting that, Mr. Beckett."

Reid nodded, listening to Celeste, not saying more.

Gary caught his eye after a moment. "Be assured I will investigate you, though, or anyone else Celeste ever gets involved with. Dillon Barlow almost killed Celeste. Not many people know that. If Dillon's housekeeper Martina hadn't been working late, hadn't found her, hadn't called me and then called the hospital, Celeste might not have made it that night. I've ramped up my security around her. You can be sure of that." He hesitated. "Will I find any hidden evils in your background, Reid Beckett?"

"No, but I'm comforted you'll be looking."

Celeste moved back to singing familiar songs then, ones the audience knew and nodded to.

Gary sighed. "You may not think I take good care of Celeste, but I want you to know I love her like a sister. Her husband Nolan trained and mentored me in the business. I was often in their home, loved them both. You don't need to worry that I'm not watching this situation with Dillon Barlow carefully, as is our attorney and others at Capital. We, far more than most, know the man is dangerous. If you ever hear of him being anywhere here and near Celeste, you let me know. I'd like to think we're on the same team in protecting her."

Reid turned to look at the man with new respect. "You can be sure I will do that."

"Good." He nodded. "You seem like a strong, good man. Keep a watch over her here if you care for her."

A little time passed, the two men simply listening to the music. Then Gary said, "See her looking this way at you again? I know her. She only does that if she's interested in someone. She's been through hell with Dillon Barlow. Don't mess with her life if you don't care about her. I don't want her hurt anymore."

Reid smiled at him then. "Seems like we're both sending each other the same memos."

"Yes, it seems we are." Gary Feinstein smiled at him, pulling a card from his pocket to push across the table. "Put this away somewhere and call me if you ever need to."

Celeste finished her ongoing song and then stood, smiling to the applause before making her way back to the table.

Reid listened again quietly while the two of them talked, Gary pulling him into the conversation every now and then. After a time, Gary told Celeste he'd call a cab and head on back to the hotel.

"I need to make some calls, check on a couple of my entertainers, work out the problems related to that earlier phone call I got at the hotel. And I have an early flight in the morning."

"I'll see you out and then drive home myself," Celeste replied. "I brought my car. Are you sure you don't want me to drive you back?"

"No, I'm used to cabs and it's late for you to drive to the hotel. You head on home." He reached out to shake Reid's hand. "Good to meet you tonight, Reid Beckett."

"You, too, Gary Feinstein," Reid replied.

Gary stood, pushing his chair in, turning to take Celeste's arm. "Reid and I learned we have a number of interests in common tonight, Celeste." He winked at Reid as they walked away and Reid almost laughed out loud.

A short time later, Reid decided to head on home himself. He'd waited for a space after Celeste and her agent left. He didn't want it to look like he was following them in case they wanted to talk confidentially as they waited for Gary's cab to arrive.

As he strolled out into the lobby, though, he glanced down the side hallway and saw Celeste leaning against the wall in a darkened area. He moved down the hall toward her, and saw that her eyes were closed, her face white.

"What's happened? Are you all right?"

She jerked at his voice, and then grabbed hold of his coat sleeve. "There's a man out in the parking lot, hanging around my car."

He understood her panic then. "Stay here. We'll check it."

Reid walked to the front lobby, gesturing to his cousin Manny at the front desk, filling him in as they headed out to the parking area. They searched around Celeste's car, in the lot and around the patio and garden area by the restaurant, even walking down the street to see if they saw anyone or anything suspicious.

"I don't see anyone," Manny said. "When Celeste headed back in the restaurant after spotting the man, he probably took off. It might have been a fan, hoping to meet her, or some guy, hoping to attract her interest. It happens, especially with someone well known like Celeste. Word has gotten around that she sings here sometimes." He hesitated. "I don't think we need to call the police, do you?"

"No, but I'll take Celeste home, be sure she gets into her own place safely just in case. I was going to walk home to get a little exercise, but I'll drive Celeste's car now."

Manny nodded. "That's good of you, in case someone would follow her or something. Can I do anything else to help?"

"No," Reid said. "But I'm going to walk her out the back door and around to the car in case anyone is watching." He knew he really wanted to protect anyone from seeing Celeste as upset as she was.

He found her still hiding in a corner in the darkened hallway, almost shaking.

Walking close to her, he pulled her against him and patted her back as he would a frightened child. "Whoever it was is gone now. It was probably only a fan hoping to meet you or some random person in the parking lot. Sometimes people cruise the lot, looking for unlocked cars they can get into. It happens." He tilted her face up. "I'm driving you home, though, because you've had a scare."

She looked as if she might protest, but then didn't.

"I told Manny we would walk out the back and around to your car. I didn't think you needed to go walking through the lobby right now, possibly needing to make conversation with anyone there."

She nodded, taking his arm as he led her down the hallway and around to the back door.

Reid felt her tense as they moved through the parking lot. He helped her into the car and then walked around to climb behind the wheel. She finally leaned her head back against the seat to relax a little as he backed the car out, heading out of the lot and down the street.

She didn't say a single word as they drove back. Reid took an alternate route to the parking lot behind the shop and Celeste's apartment, as an extra precaution.

"All looks quiet here," he said as he parked the car. "But I'll walk up with you."

"You don't have to, but thanks for bringing me home." She tried to smile at him. "My place is closer to your house than Thurman's. You won't have far to walk."

He came around and opened the door for her. "I'm walking you up to your place and seeing you in. Don't argue."

She took his arm again and they made their way to the back entrance. Taking the door key from her as he saw her hand shaking, Reid unlocked the door for her. Inside the back entrance, he put an arm around her waist as they made their way up the stairs to her apartment and then he unlocked the door there, too.

Celeste walked in and settled on the couch, leaning her head back and sighing. "I still experience panic attacks and flashbacks sometimes," she said in a soft voice. "Just when I think I'm finally finished with all the fear, something happens that kicks it back up again." She paused on a sigh. "Thank you for bringing me home, Reid. You can drop my keys in that bowl on the table by the door as you leave."

"I'm staying for a while," he said to her instead. "I'll make some coffee."

She didn't argue and he made his way to the adjoining kitchen area to hunt out what was needed and to get a pot of coffee started.

He came back to find her crying.

"It's all right." He sat down beside her and pulled her into his arms. "Really, it's all right."

She sniffed and pulled away after a time. "I'm so sorry, but these times are difficult. You don't have to stay with me. I'll settle down in a little while."

"And I'll be here until you do." He leaned over then and kissed her, a soft sweet kiss, running a hand soothingly over her back.

She jerked a little at first and then settled into the moment, letting him kiss her, and leaning into him at last.

"Let your mind recall another better time instead, Celeste," he whispered. "Remember the time we kissed out in the dark in the courtyard at Thurman's? How sweet and good it was? I'd wanted to kiss you for so long. You sang that song, about the man with the brown eyes watching you. I knew that man might be me. I was so drawn to you already, so under your spell even from across the room."

A little smile touched her face and she put a hand to his cheek. "I do remember that time."

Feeling her relax some in his arms, he leaned in to kiss her again. Like Marcus had said, she needed some love and tenderness after all the cruelty and sorrows she'd known.

"I've been afraid for any man to touch me, to kiss me," she whispered to him. "I'm sure I've offended a few, jerking back even when they offered their arm to assist me or kissed my hand or cheek with no ill intent. But I always remember what Dillon would make me do when I didn't want to ... how he would hurt me."

"Shhh," he whispered, kissing her face and her eyelids. "Not every man is Dillon. Remember that. You've known me for a long, long time. You know I would never hurt you. I wish I had been there to keep that man from hurting you as he did."

"You are sweet," she said softly after a time.

He curled her up under his arm, letting her relax against him.

"Why did you kiss me?" she asked after a time.

He grinned at her. "I thought you needed a distraction." Reid was happy to see her grin back.

"Well, it has been that." She sounded more like herself now.

"Ready for a cup of coffee?"

"Yes, that would be good," she said.

When he came back with a cup for them both, he found her more relaxed, her shoes off and her pretty legs propped on an ottoman. Mercy, she was beautiful and alluring, even upset and stirring his compassion.

"Ummm." She took a sip of the coffee. "You remembered just how I like it."

"We've spent some time together lately."

She smiled at him. "Trying to chaperone Marcus and Vanessa."

He laughed. "They do seem fond of each other."

"We've probably put a damper on their affections being so formal and proper."

He looked at her over the rim of his coffee cup. "We could change that."

She closed her eyes. "Perhaps we will a little but, Reid, as you can see, I'm still not a healthy choice for a dating companion yet. I'm better, but I'm not well. And a very disturbed man is still out there, unhappy with me." She sighed. "It's probably not even safe for you to spend time with me."

"I'll risk it, and you could use someone in your court, and on your team right now. A good friend."

She studied him. "That time long ago after you kissed me, why did you all but disappear? You hardly ever came to the restaurant any more when I sang. I could tell you were trying to avoid me. I know I didn't have much experience kissing then."

He interrupted her. "It wasn't that, Celeste. Manny told me you were barely sixteen. I was twenty-one, five years older than you. To me you'd always looked so much older. I thought you were probably about my age. I had no idea you were only a girl. Underage. I had to back away because of how attracted to you I was, because of the control I seemed to lose whenever I was around you."

Her eyes twinkled. "Well, that's certainly sweeter to hear than what I imagined back then. It hurt my young heart and ego when you backed away with no explanation."

"It wasn't easy," he said. "You were all I could think about. I kept telling myself I'd wait until you grew up a little, turned eighteen, got out of high school. Then I'd go after you like I wanted to."

"I kept singing at Thurman's until then. I'd see you every now and then and I wondered if you ever thought about that night."

He leaned over to kiss her again. "I never forgot it."

"Well, I'm flattered." She put a hand to his cheek. "Do you know you were the first boy, or should I say man, to ever kiss me with more than a quick peck? Or to hold me like you did, teaching me how men felt when passion flared. I kept wondering if I was doing everything right, acting as I should. Such a blaze of feelings rose up between us. It's the first time I'd ever felt that."

"I never discerned your innocence. I was so overwhelmed, too."

She giggled. "I suppose it's a good thing we heard my dad calling, wondering why I'd been gone so long. I'd told him I was going to walk outside to get a breath of fresh air. It was a warm night and a little stuffy in Thurman's."

"And it got a little warmer," Reid said, running a hand down her arm. "I think we were both caught off guard with that."

They sat for a moment, drinking their coffee and thinking their own thoughts.

"After I turned eighteen, did you still plan to come after me?" she said teasingly.

"I did. I had strong feelings. I thought they might change, but they didn't, and then before I could act on them, I learned you'd run off to Nashville and married that entertainment manager that had been coming to Thurman's so often and watching you sing. I could tell he was taken with you, or with your talent—maybe both—but he was so much older. I didn't see him as a potential rival, with you being so much younger. He came and went often, too, didn't live in the area."

"Well, that's a story for another day how Nolan and I met, grew close, fell in love and married. I did love Nolan, despite our age difference. He was a wonderful man, a kind and thoughtful husband, a brilliant manager. Whatever I've become in the entertainment industry, I owe to Nolan Culver."

"I'm glad to hear that you knew so much happiness before you met sorrows and disillusion with Dillon Barlow."

"Yes, it might have broken me otherwise. I'd always been around only healthy people. I didn't know what to do with someone like Dillon, so different day to day. So kind sometimes and other times so cruel."

She looked at the clock on the wall across the room. "It's late, Reid. I need to get some rest."

He touched her face gently. "Do you want me to stay?"

She leaned in to kiss him. "No, I'm very attracted to you and you've been very kind to me, but despite being in the entertainment business and married twice, I hold strong morals. So, yes, you need to go home, and now I think you know one more thing about me, too."

He winked at her as he got up to leave. "I doubt it will run me off, Celeste. Sleep well. Call me if you need anything."

CHAPTER 9

Celeste had gotten up early this Saturday morning, two days after Gary left, to finish changing out the front windows of CeeCee's. She and Vanessa finished most of the work on Friday while Loretta helped wait on customers, but Celeste still had a few extra ideas she wanted to add.

Seeing so many people riding bikes around Charleston gave Celeste the idea of decorating the windows in a biking theme. She drove to the island on Thursday to borrow two of the Deveaux Inn's faded, worn beach bikes, one yellow and one orange. Stopping at a nursery on the way back she snagged pots of orange and yellow mums.

Not happy earlier with the white, faceless mannequins already in the store windows, Celeste had ordered several new ones that looked almost real. She and Vanessa dressed one in a pair of the store's cute leggings, a "CeeCee's Place" T-shirt, and a yellow rain slicker, all ready for one of Charleston's unexpected rainstorms. They added a bucket of colorful umbrellas in one corner of the window and tucked a bunch of sunflowers wrapped in floral paper into the orange bicycle's basket.

The yellow bike centered the other window, the model standing beside it, wearing Jeans, a pumpkin orange overshirt, and one of the store's cute, straw hats. Tucked in her bike basket was a stack of school books. Vanessa found decorative lamp posts in the storage room to put in both windows, and with the pots of mums stacked around on old crates, both windows looked stunning.

"I love how these windows turned out," Vanessa said, letting herself in the front door and locking it behind her. She was scheduled to work all day today with Loretta's help in the afternoon.

"We did good, don't you think?" Celeste asked.

"We totally did." Vanessa glanced toward the windows. "Imogene wasn't offended that we ordered the new mannequins, was she?"

Celeste laughed. "No, she was tickled with them. She said lifelike mannequins are pricey or she'd have ordered some years ago."

"I do like Imogene. She is so easy to work with and such a warm and fun person. Everyone loves her. Customers often stop by the store just to visit with her."

"They always end up buying something, too. A perk of being a nice person." Celeste climbed into one of the windows again to drape a necklace around one of the model's necks.

"Oh, I love those colorful glass beads, and they look great with that casual shirt." Vanessa walked through the store and came back carrying an ankle bracelet. "Let's put one of these yellow quartz bracelets on the other model's ankle. With her leg up on the bike pedal people will really notice it."

"Yes, and it sparkles, too," Celeste agreed. "Good idea!"

They finished adding a few more touches and then pushed the displays back in place that blocked entry to the windows from the back, satisfied that both looked great for the busy Saturday they expected.

"There might be showers today. That will help our umbrellas sell," Vanessa said as they walked to the register after putting the Open sign out to start their day.

Celeste walked to the back of the store to pour them each a cup of coffee. She brought both back, passing one to Vanessa and setting hers on the table by the register.

"Thanks," Vanessa said, settling onto a tall stool behind the counter where she could watch the front door and the shop.

Celeste sipped her coffee, looking around. "You know, I see small things every day that Imogene has done with this store that bring in sales and make it special and unique. Like always keeping umbrellas to sell and putting a display of them visibly in the window. Every time it rains, people see them and run in to buy one."

"She buys cute umbrellas, too," Vanessa agreed. "I tried to get Christina to order some for Hendricks and she said they were tacky."

Celeste laughed. "The more you tell me about that woman, the more surprised I am that you lasted as long as you did there."

"Well, I'm glad to be gone." She hesitated. "Did you know Gregory Hendricks came in our store the other day?"

"No. What for?"

"He said he stopped by to see how I was getting along. I know he's suspicious about why I left, but he could see I'd become an assistant manager, with our lanyard badges displaying our names and positions in the store."

"What reason did you give Christina for leaving?"

Vanessa shifted her eyes to her mug on the counter. "Just that I had accepted another position. She didn't ask me a lot of questions, but Gregory Hendricks did."

"No kidding? What did he ask?"

"He wanted to know if I'd had any problems at the store. He'd been keen to pick up on Christina's delays in training and moving me up. He also asked if I'd noticed any discrimination issues."

Celeste's mouth dropped open. "Did he, and what did you say?"

"I decided to be evasive and simply said not everyone is comfortable with diversity." She lifted her eyebrows. "I think he got the message. He mentioned it had been an ongoing problem at the store."

Celeste laughed. "One day at the Deveaux Inn, this man asked Novaleigh if she felt discriminated against having to work as a cook. She asked him right out what salary he made. He hesitated but then mentioned a figure proudly. She made a face and said, 'Well, I make more than that, have full benefits, my house provided, and except for having to deal with a few rude people like yourself every now and then, I love this job. My employers are like my own family, too."

Vanessa almost spit her coffee out laughing. "I can just hear mother saying that. She is bolder than I am. I admire that."

"Discrimination is alive and well in our world in many ways. I get gender discrimination issues, too, and I face stereotypes about what people think entertainers are like." She shrugged. "You have to pick your battles about when to deal with those issues and when to just let things go."

"Those are wise words." Vanessa glanced toward the door. "I see a group of women coming in and they look excited to see you here today. Why don't you go talk to them?"

The morning grew busy and the time flew by. Loretta came in later, waving at Celeste where she stood talking with two women looking at sundresses in the back of the store.

"I think I'm buying this pretty red-orange dress," the woman, named Polly, said. "Don't you love it, Susan?"

"I love this chartreuse one best," the other woman said, holding it against herself. She turned to Celeste and asked, "What do you think?"

Celeste searched in the rack for a moment and pulled out the same dress in an emerald green. "Come over to the mirror," she said.

As she did, Celeste added, "You may not know it, but I am also a licensed color consultant. There are colors that are the best for all of us, not necessarily the ones we like to look at best, but ones that are perfect in tone for our individual hair color, eyes, and skin tones."

She held the emerald green sundress up to Susan. "Look at how beautifully this color of green looks on you in comparison to the chartreuse one you like." She swapped the dresses out.

The woman's mouth dropped open. "Well, isn't that something? I never realized chartreuse made me look so sallow and drab."

Celeste held the emerald green sundress up to Susan again. "You're a winter by color season, and dark, cool, clear jewel tones like this are best for you, making you look radiant."

"I simply can't believe the difference," she said.

"What about me?" The other woman edged in. She held out her dress. "Is this a good color for me?"

Celeste went to the rack again. "If you love pink, this deep, rich coral pink would look so much more becoming on you." She held the coral pink dress up to Polly. "See how your face comes to life in this color? You're a Spring. If colors are too pale and washed out, like in this light pink dress, they'll drain the color from your face and won't enhance your skin tones." She exchanged the coral pink dress she held in front of Polly for the pale pink. "See the difference?"

"Oh, my goodness, I really do," she answered.

This started the usual excited exchange about colors to bring out the best in both women's natural beauty. They left the store with not only the new sundresses but with several other purchases and a copy of a color consultant guidebook Celeste stocked and kept in the store.

Vanessa laughed as they left. "Every time you do that we make so many sales." She paused. "You probably should charge a fee for helping women learn about their colors. Certified color consultants don't usually give their advice out for free."

"It gives me pleasure," Celeste said. "And look how happy they were when they left? Both of them had no color sense. You could tell from how they were dressed. Maybe they'll pick more flattering clothes for themselves now. I'm always amazed at some of the outfits that women come into this store wearing, the colors bad for them, the styles unattractive for them."

She folded some sweaters and shirts and stacked them on a table. "I feel like it's my contribution to the beauty of the world when I can help someone like that."

Loretta walked over. "You've helped me with my colors and probably in other ways. I still remember when you sent me to the dressing room to change out of those jeans with the slits and holes up the legs I wore to work one day. You gave me a pair of cute leggings and an overshirt from the store to wear instead." She grinned. "It was an improvement."

"Some clothing fashions that evolve are simply absurd, and I'm sorry, but that look with cut-up jeans is not one I support for CeeCee's Place." She lifted her chin. "And it *is* my store."

"I'm not complaining. If I had my way, I'd ban all those barbaric piercings and weird tattoos." Loretta hesitated. "A girl came in here the other day with a tattoo on her arm that said, 'Proud to be hated' and the boy with her had monsters with blood dripping out of their mouths up his arms. Those things are permanent. Don't people realize they might change over their lives? Feel different? Wish they didn't have that stuff on their bodies?"

Vanessa laughed. "We see some crazy stuff in retail."

Loretta walked to greet several customers coming in the store.

"I see a lot of crazy stuff in the entertainment business too, in looks and actions." Celeste added to Vanessa. "So many people today don't seem to have any moral code about their lives."

"That's the truth," Vanessa agreed.

Celeste leaned against the counter for a moment thinking about it. "Lila says being close to God gives people a moral compass for living right and in a way that will bring them the most happiness and joy. I slipped away from that kind of thinking a little, traveling out in the world so much, but I'm moving solidly back in that direction now."

"We have that in common then," Vanessa said and then grinned. "Marcus has been pushing on those morals of mine a little lately, but I've met his mama and his family now. They're like my own family, good Godly people. I think I can count on Marcus and me being all right together, being mostly alike in our thinking and about how people should live. That's important."

"It is important, Vanessa. I learned the hard way how important it is to know someone well before you link up your life to theirs."

The front door opened again before they could say more and Celeste's sister Gwen walked in waving at them.

"Surprise!" she called out. "I came to see if you could get away for lunch."

She came to hug Celeste and Vanessa, and then let Celeste

introduce her to Loretta Griffey.

"I'm happy to meet you, Loretta," Gwen said. "Celeste has told me only good things about you, and I hope you're enjoying working at CeeCee's Place."

"I am, and it's nice to meet you, too. Celeste has promised to bring me to the lighthouse and inn one day and to meet more of your family."

They chatted for a moment and then both Loretta and Vanessa went to help customers.

"What are you doing here today?" Celeste asked then. "And where are the kids?"

"Chase, Rose, and Leah are enjoying a day with their Trescott grandparents and spending the night with them. Alex is working until late tonight, so I decided on the spur to come to Charleston to see you." She hesitated. "Also, Trescotts is having another Old South Day at the first of October, and I want you to help me to find another dress to wear. I love the red one we found for Old South Day in August, but I don't want to wear the very same dress again. You said the other day you were only working this morning at the store, so I took a chance and came to surprise you."

"Well, you did surprise me, but I'm thrilled to see you. I know it's over an hour and a half drive from Port Royal to Charleston." Celeste leaned forward. "Can you stay over and spend the night? I'd love that. We haven't had time together in ages."

Her sister grinned. "I actually packed a bag with that idea in mind, hoping you'd ask. Alex said it was all right with him, too. He said for us to have fun. If I stay over, he plans to go night fishing with Rudy Bailey."

"Well, that settles it." Celeste gave her another hug. "We'll go shopping, grab a little lunch, maybe go to the City Market and explore, and then go somewhere special for dinner tonight."

"Sounds like fun!"

"Where did you park?"

"In the back, next to your car. Is that all right?"

"Yes, but go put this hang tag on your visor." She pulled one from a desk drawer.

"Okay. I'll do that and I'll get my bag to carry upstairs to your apartment."

With Loretta here now, staying until close with Vanessa, Celeste was free to leave.

"Do you need me to pick up some lunch for you and Loretta before I leave?" Celeste asked Vanessa.

"No, I made chicken salad this morning, chopped up some peaches, and tucked in a packet of crackers—plenty to share with Loretta if she didn't bring something for herself. We'll be fine. You and Gwen go and have a good time."

The day proved to be a happy one. Celeste needed a diversion, some good clean fun, and a few laughs after the last several days. She could always count on that from Gwen.

After leaving CeeCee's Place, Celeste took Gwen to some new stores she'd discovered, and to a cute café for a salad lunch. Then they went to several women's shops to look for a dress for Gwen for Old South Night at Trescotts. After trying on a number of lovely dresses in several stores, Gwen found a gorgeous sequined sapphire blue cocktail dress, with a full skirt that swished just below her knees.

"I love this one," Gwen said, twirling at the mirror. "What do you think, Celeste?"

Celeste walked around her sister, studying the dress. "It's absolutely perfect, a wonderful color for you, fits like a dream, and has that exquisite sequined material to reflect the lights at night. You'll catch a lot of admiring glances in that one, Gwen."

"It's also affordable." Gwen turned to study the back of the dress in the mirror. "I told you I wouldn't let you buy this one for me. Alex insisted, too."

"Well, your garnet red dress was a long and slim fitting one. This one will be a contrast, shorter and glittery. I don't think we need to look at anymore unless you want to find shoes or a purse."

"I have dressy black sandals I love, good for dancing, and a small clutch bag that is glittery, too." She smiled at Celeste. "I felt sure you'd know exactly the stores to take me to. Thanks."

After Gwen purchased her dress, Celeste drove to park near Charleston's historic City Market. They'd decided it would be fun to spend time exploring the market, stretching for over four blocks on Meeting Street and filled with shops.

"I never tire of this market because there's always something new here," Gwen said as they started down the long market corridor. "It has boutique shops, crafters, baked goods, little book shops, and artists."

Celeste looked ahead with excitement. "Help me look for some special things to spruce up my apartment. I'd like a handmade sweetgrass basket or two. They're nice in the bathroom and to tuck books into. I'd also like to find some woven placemats for the table, an outdoor art piece for the porch, and maybe a small painting for the bathroom—something in blues to match the towels I bought. The wall in there is really drab; it needs some art."

They enjoyed wandering through the market and Celeste soon filled a tote bag full of purchases, Gwen laughing and buying things for her classroom and for the kids.

Back at Celeste's place later, they had fun placing Celeste's new purchases around her apartment and then resting for a short time, with a cola, before dressing to head to 82 Queen for dinner. Celeste often ate there when she stayed at the Elliot House Inn, also on Queen, and the restaurant had wonderful food and gracious service. Celeste had reserved a nice table for two upstairs, looking out a picture window across the patio, which would soon twinkle with lights when dark fell.

They both decided to order a small cup of she crab soup to start their meal and for their entrees crab cakes, with bacon fried sweet corn, a roasted red pepper aioli, and two non-alcoholic sangrias. They talked and caught up in the quiet charm of the restaurant, enjoying being together again.

"Are things still going well with Alex?" Celeste asked.

"Yes. I think because of what we went through, almost losing each other, we cherish each other all the more." She wiggled her eyebrows. "Alex is certainly seeing to it that I am a very happy and satisfied wife. One thing I can say is that he always has been a sweet, fun lover."

"No more details." Celeste laughed. "How are the children?"

"Very good. They love Port Royal, their neighborhood, friends, and the school. Alex's Aunt Julia's lovely home, where we live, is so comfortable, too, and easy to live in. It seems in many ways, as Lila would say, that things have worked out for the best. Alex and I are so happy to be back in South Carolina again. It feels more like home to us than Arkansas ever did." She smiled. "Alex's old partner Josh Vines came to visit us recently, too, and he brought his new fiancé. His life has turned around happy, too. I'm glad. We both love Josh and we like his fiancé, Diana."

Finishing her soup, Gwen crossed her arms and looked across at Celeste with that serious schoolteacher face of hers. "Now, tell me about Reid Beckett. No more giving me the eye not to say anything. I remember we used to lie in bed talking about him after you came home from singing at Thurman's. You told me that you thought he might be watching you, might be interested in you, but you couldn't tell for sure. You also told me how attracted to him you were, how there seemed to be something simmering quietly in the air, and that he always came to watch you sing, sitting at a table in one corner."

"Yes, but not sitting where my dad could see him easily." Celeste laughed. "Which is probably a good thing. We did a lot of gazing at each other across a crowded room for a long time before he finally followed me outside one night."

Gwen laughed softly. "You lured him out with that song you wrote about him. You told me that."

"Maybe." She sipped at her drink.

"I remember Reid Beckett finally made a move and kissed you outside in a quiet, dark spot, basically pushing you up against the wall and moving in with passion. Neither you nor I had ever been kissed except with an awkward peck or two after a dance. I still remember how you described it." She paused. "Then Reid all but disappeared. He stopped coming to the restaurant except occasionally, seldom stayed long, didn't talk to you except to be polite. He acted like a stranger to you. I remember you cried about it, never did understand it."

Celeste looked out the window, avoiding Gwen's eyes.

"Have you seen him again, talked to him? What is he like now? How is he acting around you? Do you still feel something around him?"

Celeste gave her a little smirk. "You sure are nosy."

"Yes, I am about Reid Beckett. I have a vested interest in this. First, we swooned over him, then we hated him. We don't get many chances in life to see those old loves that went wrong. I have a right to know what he's like now."

Celeste pulled out her phone, opening to some photos taken at Reid's house when she, Vanessa, and Marcus were sharing dinner and clowning around. A few were also of Reid alone.

Gwen looked through the photos. "Oh, my goodness, he's more handsome than ever now. Don't you think? And check out this shot at how he's looking at you."

She glanced at Celeste and saw her flush. "I can tell by your face something has happened again with him. You're still attracted and it's obvious he is, too." Gwen pointed at the picture.

Their dinner arrived and they talked with the waiter briefly and then started eating.

"Our food is here, and it's marvelous, but I expect to hear every detail when we get back to your place later."

True to her word, Gwen made light dinner conversation as they ate, asking Celeste questions about the store, about Vanessa and Marcus, and telling Celeste funny stories about working with her fourth graders at the elementary school where she taught.

Back at Celeste's apartment, though, after they settled on the sofa to talk, Gwen crossed her arms again and said, "Okay, now catch me up on Reid Beckett, from when you first saw him again, how he acted, and everything that's been going on since."

Celeste did, and when she got to the part about growing fearful about the man in the parking lot and about Reid swooping in to be nice and helping her home, Gwen put a hand to her heart. "Oh my, I may have to revise my opinion of him. That was a sweet thing for him to do, watching out for you and bringing you home after that scare."

Gwen, always astute, saw Celeste avoiding her glance. "Tell me the rest. What happened then?"

Knowing it useless to try lying to Gwen, Celeste told her about Reid kissing her and about all he'd said.

Gwen put a hand to her heart. "That is so romantic and sad, like a movie plot or something. And now those old feelings are kicking up again. What are you going to do about it? You said you didn't want another man in your life, but it looks like one has unexpectedly dropped in your lap anyway." She giggled. "Figuratively speaking, of course. Unless he did lay his head in your lap later."

Annoyed, Celeste glared at her. "This isn't an amusing situation, Gwen. My life is not at a place where anyone should get romantically involved with me. You know what I've been through and what I'm still experiencing."

Gwen put a hand on her arm. "Yet, look at this sweet situation that's opened unexpectantly. I'm loving it, and it isn't even my story. You really need to write a lovely song about all this, if not now then later. I was happy to hear you're writing again and that you've been able to work things out with Gary. I think life is going to turn around for the good for you now. Lila thinks so, too, and you know how she is about knowing things."

Gwen paused, pulling her feet up under her. "Have you told Lila about all this?"

"No, and don't you tell her or Burke or Mother or anyone else. Promise me. If Reid and I start to see each other more, I'll bring him over to meet everyone. But give me some time with this, Gwen, to see how things go, how he feels and how I feel." She sighed. "I haven't even seen Reid Beckett since Wednesday. He may decide to disappear out of my life again like he did before. I wouldn't blame him. Getting involved with someone like me, with so many problems, may send him running once he thinks about it for a while."

Those thoughts skittered through Celeste's mind that night as she settled down to sleep. She hadn't heard from Reid at all since Wednesday. Would he disappear again like before? In many ways she really didn't know Reid Beckett well enough to know.

CHAPTER 10

On Monday, Reid headed over to Church Street for his second appointment with Annabel Pennyman. The first had been in August, but she'd gotten a touch of flu after and been ill for a time, so today he was returning. She said she'd made some decisions based on their first visit.

Reid was met at the front door by Justine Johnson, Annabel's nurse, housekeeper, and fierce protector. The woman was a big, tough Black woman, intimidating in appearance and manner. She looked down her nose at him as she opened the door. "I assume you have an appointment?" she asked.

He nodded.

"Well, then, step inside. I'll check to see if Annabel is ready to see you." Reid watched her walk away.

At his first visit she wouldn't even let him in the house, until she'd checked with Annabel. She made him wait on the front porch. Her son Tyrone had played defense with South Carolina's football team and Reid often thought Justine should have tried out for the team herself.

A few minutes later, Justine ushered Reid into a sunny sitting room where he found Annabel in her wheelchair near one of the windows.

"Isn't it a lovely day?" she asked, gesturing him to a chair nearby. "I'm glad to feel better, too, so I can get out in the garden again to see what's flowering."

She rolled her chair across the room to pick up a neat pile of files, and then back. As she did, Reid's heart wrenched as always to know she'd never walk again or work in the garden she'd always nurtured and loved so much. The wreck had been a harsh tragedy, robbing her of her health and taking her husband Monroe's life. Reid knew the first year had been especially difficult for her, but despite her pretty, somewhat delicate looks and small size, Annabel was plucky. His dad told him to never underestimate her and Reid knew it the truth.

Justine opened the door to roll in a little cart then, replete with a lovely afternoon tea. Annabel had set his appointment at three as before, probably with this in mind. On the cart sat a silver pot of tea, flowered cups in their saucers, and a tiered tray of small sandwiches and treats.

She poured out tea for them and then gestured to a stack of small plates on the tray, saying, "Please help yourself to a plate, Reid."

Afternoon tea was an expected ritual at Annabel's with any business or pleasure visit.

"I made those Moon Cookies you and Benson always liked so much." She pointed to them and then sighed. "I do so hope Benson will come back to the states soon. I miss him."

"I'm sure he misses you, too." Reid loaded an array of sandwiches and treats on his plate. It was a given at Annabel's to sip tea, nibble her treats, and make cordial comments about the weather, family, or other interests before business could begin.

After a time of polite chit-chat, she put her cup back on the cart and picked up the pile of files. "After we talked the last time when you were here, I looked through our properties, as you suggested, and decided on one I think would be best to sell at this time."

She opened one of the folders. "I think the best option of our Folly Beach rentals to sell is this one on Cooper Lane. It's an older home and attractive, but older homes always require more upkeep. Clarence has had people in doing renovations and improvements on this one. It should be in excellent shape to sell." She turned the photo so Reid could see it.

"Like you suggested, I studied the prices of other similar homes that sold nearby, comparable ones." She smiled. "As you know you can hardly find a home at Folly now with any size or near the water for less than a million."

She passed the folder for him to look at as she continued. "I remember when Folly Beach first started to develop. Monroe's father bought a lot of property cheap back then." She giggled in an almost girlish way. "Of course, it didn't seem cheap at the time, but Monroe's father, Hiram, thought the area had potential. He developed it some, building homes there, and as Monroe and I began to see the tourism potential developing, we bought land, too, and built more homes, including our family beach house that Clarence lives in. Our house isn't far from the rental office Monroe set up for Clarence to manage. You may recall he didn't take to the Appraisal business as Benson and his father did."

Reid made no comment, remembering well that Clarence couldn't intellectually handle the coursework related to becoming a certified appraiser with the Pennyman business, Broad Street Appraisal. It was a more difficult field to learn and master than most people understood, and he knew it had been a sorrow to Monroe when Clarence couldn't make the grade to join the family appraisal business.

Benson, brilliant in contrast, had taken to it with ease, but interacting with his brother had never been easy. Clarence held charm in spades but Benson had the brains. Even so, Monroe and Annabel had worked to find Clarence an alternate place in their business concerns.

Reid tuned his thoughts in again as Annabel told him a number of facts about the property she wanted to sell.

"My idea is to pass my house here in Charleston to Benson, since he will work in the business nearby on Broad. I want to will the other home at Folly Beach to Clarence." She hesitated. "With all Benson's additional studies in architectural history and his fervent interest in old homes, he would value this old place and keep it in the family. Clarence loves living at Folly and enjoys the more easygoing life at the beach. I imagine he will be pleased to get our home there. The monetary values of both places are similar."

She passed Reid two more folders. "Go and look at the house at Cooper first and tell me what you think. The other two folders show two more homes that might be good alternate options to sell. One is a monstrosity on the beach front that someone interested in showing off their wealth would snatch up. The other is near town and close to all the restaurants and amusements. Some people especially like that."

"These look like good options," Reid said, looking at the printouts.

"We've put a lot of upkeep money into all three. They should be in excellent shape to sell. You'll see notations in each folder of improvements made. At this point, I simply want you to go check them out and give me an idea of what each will sell for. I still have my set of keys that will get you into the properties, too."

"You told me at our last meeting you want to possibly find a one-level home to buy. Have you given more thought to where you might want to live? I think you mentioned in August you had a place in mind."

She smiled. "Agnes and I have been looking at places. It is essential she moves with me." She hesitated. "Agnes takes care of me and of this house. I think her life, as well as mine, might be easier with a smaller place to manage. Despite improvements we've made, this is a very large home to keep up with. It's sensible for me to find something more manageable for us both." She made a little face. "Neither of us are getting any younger."

Reid waited to see if she would add more.

"One place I found recently, that I like, is on James Island on the water. It has character and charm, all the rooms on one level, lovely views out the back, a little land and privacy with a walkway garden, but not too much property. I think Agnes and I could be comfortable there. It would accommodate my situation and has a suite to give Agnes privacy. However, it isn't one of those hideously modern places."

Annabel passed him a printout showing the house, location, and price. "It's such an advantage for someone in my situation that you can look at most anything online these days."

"It's a help," Reid agreed.

She waved a hand. "Anyway, it's the sort of place I have in mind, outside the city but not far outside, and James Island would put me right between my sons and near Agnes' place where her son Tyrone, his wife, and their little girl live right now. I want to consider both of us in what I do. We have become friends and enjoy each other's company."

Reid well knew Annabel depended on Agnes. His mother told him the story of how they met when Annabel was in rehab after the wreck, how they bonded in an odd way. Agnes had been ready for a change from working in a facility and Annabel needed help for when she was ready to go home.

"The house I'm considering may sell before I sell one or two of the Folly Beach houses, but I'm sure there will be others." She leaned forward. "I think Clarence might be upset about this change for me. Benson might, too. Children don't always like changes for their parents. They get bossy, want to interfere too much. I've dealt with that especially because of my health situation. That's why I want to do this discreetly, present it to both my boys as a done deal."

She tapped her fingers on the table beside her chair. "I know I will need to tell them at some point, but I'd like you to help me to investigate all of this first. Can I be assured I will have your confidence?"

"Dad and I have discussed this, Mrs. Pennyman. He sees no reason why we can't help you sell a property or buy a property. You have the funds to buy most any property you wish without selling one of the rentals anyway."

She rubbed her neck. "Yes, I know, Reid, but all that money is wrapped up in ways that would make it difficult to get to easily. I think this will work much more expediently."

Reid stacked the folders neatly, preparing to leave. "I'll drive out to Folly Beach tomorrow and look at the properties. I'm sure your appraisal company, and Florence and Robert, already have an idea what each is worth, but I'll look at all three, get a sense for which would sell the easiest to give you the funds you need."

Annabel interrupted, putting out a hand in protest. "No. I don't want Florence and Robert, or anyone at Broad Street Appraisal to know what I'm looking into yet either. Please know that privacy is important to me right now. I will be disappointed to learn if you breach it."

He nodded again. "Yes ma'am. I understand."

"Contact me, Reid, after you've seen the properties and we'll have another little meeting."

Agnes appeared at the door as if getting a secret request to see him out. Reid hid a grin as he followed her out to the front door. She'd probably listened to the entire conversation.

After leaving Annabel's place, Reid stopped by the office to make a few calls and to fill his father in on the meeting.

"Are you going down to Folly Beach tomorrow?" he asked.

"I think I will. I might as well look at the properties she wants me to see and get back with her about them. I looked at all three on the Pennyman Rental site. The photos and descriptions match the ones Annabel printed for me. Selling one of them will be all she'd need to do to buy the place she's interested in." He paused. "I might drive by to see it, too. The house is on the Ashley River, nice location, quiet area but not far from the bridge to Charleston. The house she's interested in is on Wampler Drive."

"That's a good location. A lot of fine homes there. I can't say she doesn't have good taste." He glanced at his watch. "Your mom and I are going to head home. Irina is already gone. Lock up when you leave."

A short time later Reid did exactly that, but he found his mind drifting to thoughts of Celeste as he headed to the parking lot between their businesses. Not that he hadn't thought about her 24-7 since Wednesday night when he took her home after that scare. He'd given her space since then though, not wanting to push, and because he knew her sister had come to stay on the weekend.

Reid also knew that just because Celeste responded to him the other night, and no matter how sweet it was for him, didn't mean she wanted to build a relationship with him. As she'd told him before, it wasn't a good time for her to do that. He also knew her divorce had only become final in June, three months ago.

The situation was awkward, and the timing for him to try to build a relationship with Celeste wasn't good. Truthfully, would it ever be? She'd inevitably travel and sing again. What did he know about that world? Would she even stay interested in him when her problems resolved with Dillon and when she felt safe to return to her place in Nashville? He knew from doing all her paperwork that she still owned a nice condo in downtown Nashville, completely paid for, and that she intended to keep it.

As he walked closer to her building, he heard a door open and saw Celeste come out onto the piazza that stretched across the side of the building. It was an attractive open porch room with a patio below and a bit of garden area Imogene had nurtured for years. Reid moved closer to a spot where he could look up to her on the porch.

"*It is my lady,*" he called out, quoting lines from the play Romeo and Juliet. "*Thou art glorious, being o're my head as a winged messenger of heaven.*"

She laughed out loud. "What are you doing down there, Reid?"

"I was getting ready to climb into my car to head home but then I was diverted by a vision on your balcony."

She shook her head at him. "Where did you learn lines from Romeo and Juliet?"

"In a high school drama class." He smiled at her. "Have you had dinner?"

"Why? Are you asking me out?"

"I was leaning toward Poogan's Porch on Queen tonight, and thinking about pickled okra with remoulade as an appetizer and maybe shrimp and grits. They have some of the best in town. It's only a few blocks if you want to walk, too. It's a nice night, Juliet."

"I thought you'd disappeared out of my life again, Romeo."

"I was just giving you some space. I also heard your sister was here this weekend."

"She was. Gwen and I talked about you."

He lifted his eyebrows. "Is that right? Was it good talk?"

"It was an interesting talk," she answered.

"Have I met Gwen?"

"I don't think so but she's heard about you."

He ran a hand through his hair. "What's your decision about dinner?"

"If I can come as is, I'll be right down." She stood and Reid looked up at her in the dimming light, dressed in a yellow sundress that shone softly in the porch lights.

"*It is the east and Juliet is the sun*," he quoted. "You look lovely as always."

"And you are always handsome." She leaned over the rail and blew him a kiss. "I'll be right down."

It was a short walk down King Street to Poogan's Porch on Queen. The restaurant, known for southern cuisine, was in a cute yellow Victorian townhouse with white porches. It wasn't too busy on a Monday night and Reid and Celeste were soon tucked into a cozy table in a corner.

They ordered okra with remoulade for an appetizer and then shrimp and grits for their entrees, as Reid had suggested. He also ordered a romaine salad, which Celeste helped him eat. During dinner they talked about light matters and shared humorous stories from work. Celeste chatted about Gwen's visit on the weekend. and Reid told her about his trip to see his grandparents at Seabrook on Sunday.

When the waiter came to ask about dessert, Celeste said, "I need to skip dessert, but I'll fix coffee back at the apartment," she said. "I have ice cream in the freezer if you want something sweet with it."

Reid knew his mind went immediately in another sweet direction but he kept those thoughts to himself.

They looked in store windows on their way back, laughing and having a good time. The evening taught him a lot about Celeste and how good and easy it was to spend time with her.

In her apartment, she started coffee and fixed him a dish of ice cream, pointing out some of the new items she'd bought for the apartment at the market.

He liked her apartment. It had a long blue sofa and two matching side chairs the very color of her eyes, a relaxing color. The walls were a lighter blue with one wall covered with a long row of bookshelves, filled with books and an array of artfully placed decorative pieces. The kitchen and baths he'd seen on his previous visit and he'd peeked into her bedroom to see another room in blues, the bedspread a lavish quilted one and the bed scattered with throw pillows.

She walked back from the kitchen area to sit down with him on the long sofa, dropping her shoes and propping her feet on a round ottoman.

"I like your apartment with all the blues throughout. It's restful and peaceful somehow," he commented.

"I thought so, too, when I first saw it, so I didn't change much. Imogene decorated it originally for herself and her favorite color is blue. She does have good taste. I saw that from the first time I walked in her store."

"Actually, it's your store now." He grinned at her.

She smiled. 'Only in a way. I rescued it for Imogene. I've put it in my will that if anything happens to me, the store is hers."

He caught something in her tone of voice. "Do you expect something to happen to you, Celeste?'

She picked at a nail. "I have learned well that life is uncertain, Reid Beckett. So many times what you expect of life doesn't happen, and what you'd never expect actually does."

"I hate that you live in fear because of Dillon Barlow. I hope a time will come when that is no longer so."

"So do I, dear friend."

"Is friends all that we can be, Celeste?"

She put a hand on his leg. "Reid Beckett, you know we moved past that point long ago and have now renewed our interest. I see no point in pretending we aren't attracted to each other." She glanced away from him. "I don't know what can come of it, but I'm glad for a little happiness, and romance, in my life right now. Is that honest enough for you?"

"Yes, and I will honestly tell you that you have played through my mind all these years, leaving me oddly dissatisfied with other relationships I formed. I knew that was foolish, of course, and it didn't make sense and yet there it was. My old memories ever haunted me, and when I saw you again that night at the restaurant, my heart smiled as if in recognition. Is that honest enough for you?"

"Ah, I do love a romantic man." She scooted toward him on the couch, her jasmine-scent teasing at him. "I hope that means you're going to kiss me now. I so want you to."

Reid had no trouble complying and their kissing soon progressed to thick, sweet uneven breathing, rapid heartbeats, and rising desire. "You probably need to send me home," he said, pulling back.

She leaned in to touch his cheek. "I should, but this is so lovely. I thank you for reminding me how sweet, good, and right healthy affection can be after all the fearful, twisted times I went through with Dillon."

Celeste got up and walked across the room to settle in the chair across from him. "What are you going to do tomorrow? I have the day off. Can you ever sneak away during the week?"

He hesitated. "I have to drive over to Folly Beach tomorrow to look at some houses for a client. You could go with me. It promises to be a sunny day. We could dress casually and play tourist, maybe take a walk on the beach, stroll out on the long boardwalk, maybe get a pizza or a chili dog for lunch."

"That sounds like fun. I'd like that. What time do you want to leave?"

"About noon. I need to go to the office first. I'll call from there when I finish. Will that work for you?"

"Yes, and I plan to sleep-in a little in the morning." She stood and started toward the door. "I'll let you head home now and lock the door behind you. Thanks for a nice evening."

She stopped him at the door with a hand on his arm. "Give me one more kiss to dream on, Reid Beckett," she asked, her voice low and sultry.

Reid moved in to gather her close and kiss her a last time, which turned into several more heated kisses. Her sweet sighs and warm response nearly drove him crazy, but at last he pulled away and stepped outside the door.

Then he turned to smile at her before he left. *"Good night, good night. Parting is such sweet sorrow,* Juliet."

She giggled, making him glad he'd left her happy. She deserved joy after all she'd known.

CHAPTER 11

Shortly after noon, Reid finally got away from the office to pick up Celeste and head to Folly Beach. Celeste had dressed casually in a periwinkle blue knit shirt over white capri slacks, her feet tucked into slip-on white canvas shoes, her hair tied back neatly.

She tossed a tote bag in the back seat of his car as he held the door open for her. "I brought waters for us, a couple of towels in case we decide to wade in the ocean, and a light sweater for myself. You can never tell about the weather in September."

"Smart idea. I threw a hoodie in the trunk myself."

She glanced across at him as she climbed into his car, noticing he wore khaki slacks, a hunter green golf shirt, and a worn pair of boat shoes.

"Nice car," she said, as she fastened her seat belt. "What kind is it? I've never been good with car makes."

"This is an Audi Cabriolet, V6, a good car for getting around the coastal area and the city."

"And it's a convertible. I hope you're going to put the top down."

He glanced at her as he drove up Calhoun Street toward the bridge to James Island. "It might mess up your hair."

"Reid, I grew up beside a lighthouse on the ocean. I think breezes are something I'm used to. Besides I brought a hat, thinking you might be driving this car." She reached in her tote bag, pulling out a canvas hat with a hole in back that she tucked her ponytail through.

"Cute hat." He grinned. "Why don't you hand me that tan visor from the back, and I'll see what I can do to put the top down." In a few moments the Audi's hard top lifted and folded itself neatly into the back trunk just as they headed up the ramp onto the Robert B. Scarborough Bridge.

Celeste gazed out the window across the Ashley River, enjoying the views. "What's our first stop today?"

"I think I'll drive by a house one of my clients is interested in buying on the river. It's not far." He turned off the main highway, onto Fort Johnson Road.

Noting the road name, Celeste said, "Daddy took us to the site where Fort Johnson used to sit on the Ashley River, and he told us about its history. He loved history. Have you been there?"

"Often." He turned off on a side road. "None of the original buildings still stand except the old magazine, but it's on the National Register of Historic Places. My friend Benson calls the site the 'Forgotten Fort' because so much history happened there. He loves history, too."

"Tell me about Benson." She hadn't met many of his friends except for Marcus and his cousins at Thurman's.

"Benson Pennyman's family lives in downtown Charleston, like ours. He and I went to the same schools and church; our families were friends and in similar businesses. Benson's family owns Broad Street Appraisal and our family businesses intersect on many points."

"Does he still live here?"

"His family does. Ben's been in England at Cambridge doing some doctoral graduate work." He slowed the car, spotting the realty sign. "Here's our house. Since I'm a licensed broker and realtor, we can take a quick look around."

He drove down the driveway toward the picturesque home, sprawled on a scenic lot with views of the Ashley River behind it.

"Pretty place," Celeste said. "I see porches on the back of the house. I imagine there are big windows with nice views of the river."

He stopped at the end of the drive. "There's a boat dock, too. It is a nice property."

She grinned. "It also looks expensive. Does your client have a lot of money?"

He nodded. "Yes, she does. She wants to get out of the city, sell her big historic home downtown, and buy a place on only one level, but also a place with a little charm and scenery."

"Well, this would seem to fit the bill."

"Would you like a place like this, Celeste?"

"Me? Heavens, no, but I'd look at your client's historic home in the city." She laughed. "Whenever I want outdoor scenery, I go home to the island. I've become much more of a city girl now. This wouldn't suit me at all. Do you think your client will like it?"

He glanced around. "She seems to think so."

"Are we going inside? It appears to be empty."

"No, I simply wanted to check out the house today. My client isn't ready to buy yet. This place may be gone before her other place even sells, but at least I have an idea of what she thinks she wants."

"It's certainly different from downtown Charleston here. Has she been out to see the house?"

"No, her health isn't good; she spends her days in a wheelchair. Another reason she wants to downsize."

Celeste glanced at the property once more as Reid turned around in the driveway to leave. "I'd hardly call this place downsizing."

He grinned. "Well, if she buys it, I can come fish off the dock."

"Do you like to fish?"

"I like almost anything related to boats and the water. I keep a boat at the marina. You want to go out on the water some day?"

"Sure. We can boat down to the lighthouse. It's closer by water than driving. You probably already know that, since you said your grandparents own a place at Seabrook."

He winked at her. "I visited the lighthouse as a boy when at St. Christopher's Camp. When you started to sing at Thurman's, I sometimes boated by the lighthouse beach hoping I might see you, too."

"Well, I'm flattered to think you were that smitten." She grinned at him and then, after a minute, began to fiddle with the radio, looking for a station.

Settling back in her seat after locating a popular country station, a new song started in. "Oh, I love this song, don't you?"

"You like Alan Jackson?"

"Absolutely, and this song, "The Older I Get," is one of my favorites." The words filled the car and she soon began to sing along.

"Don't you like Alan Jackson?" she paused to ask.

"I do. I have some of his CDs at the house."

"Which of his songs is your favorite?"

He thought for a minute and then smiled. "I like 'Remember When' and also an older song called 'It Must Be Love.'"

"I like those, too." She smiled at him, and as they continued down the road, she held her hand out the window to catch the air.

A new song kicked in after a few minutes, 'Meant to Be' by Bebe Rexha, and Reid joined Celeste in singing along this time.

"You have a nice voice," she interrupted at one point.

He laughed. "I am a car and shower singer; that's all. But it's a pleasure to hear you sing and to have the fun of singing with you."

"Do you think, like the song says, that if it's meant to be, it always will be in things?"

He considered her question. "I think the idea is too fatalistic for me. I'm more a believer that we make our own lives and history, that we create or help to create our own opportunities. I think we should row our own boats, rather than sitting on the shore hoping someone or some random wind of fate will make the way for us."

"Hmmm, that's thoughtful," she said.

Dylan Scott's voice filled the car next with his song 'My Girl" and they both sang along again. It was a treat to enjoy a relaxing, fun day with Reid today, getting to know him in a new way.

As the road they were on ended, Reid turned left on Folly Beach Road to head to the little barrier island on the coast.

"Are you getting hungry?" he asked. "There's a local restaurant I like not far down the road called Lolo's on Oak Island Creek. It's not a fancy place but they make great flounder sandwiches and good fried green tomatoes. I like to sit on the back porch looking over the marsh."

"Sounds good to me," she answered.

Lolo's was a simple place, not like the fine restaurants Reid usually took Celeste to, that she liked, but she talked happily and easily to the staff, giggled when their iced tea came served in mason jars, and enjoyed the marsh views stretching out beyond the porch where they ate. Trying to cut back her calories, she ordered a Lolo's Salad with grilled shrimp on top, but sampled one of the fried green tomatoes Reid ordered as an appetizer ahead of his flounder sandwich and fries.

"This place reminds me a little of Bowen's Island Restaurant," she said as they left a little later. "Have you been there?"

"Sure, Bowen's is an institution." He opened the car door for her. "Are you sure you don't mind looking at a few rental houses at Folly Beach that one of my clients may want to sell?" he asked.

"No. I'm happy simply to be out on a pretty day like today. When I was in Nashville, it seemed like all I ever did was work all the time. Even when I wasn't performing or traveling, there was always so much to do."

"You've put in your share of hours at CeeCee's Place, too. You haven't exactly been idle here."

"Oh, I know that." She grinned. "But the work has been such a happy change. I'm so glad I made the decision I did."

"So am I," he said, heading out onto the highway again.

A short time later, they crossed over the bridge to Folly Island, soon passing the colorful shops and restaurants on Center Street. After a few blocks, Reid turned onto a side street called Cooper Lane, lined with beach homes tucked on sandy lots with palm trees and yucca plants in the yards. Cooper Lane wasn't a beach front street, but no street on Folly Island lay far from the beach, with the entire barrier island only six miles long from the County Park at one end to Morris Island Lighthouse at the other.

Reid soon spotted the white rental house his client suggested as her first option to sell. He pulled into the short drive and walked around to open the door for Celeste.

"Hmmm," she said studying the house. "It certainly isn't as cute as the others around it, but it might look better if it were fixed up." She glanced toward the print-out in his hand. "It certainly looks better in the picture, doesn't it?"

He frowned. "Yes, it does."

"You sound disappointed. I imagine it will be harder to sell a house that isn't in good shape." She sent him a smile. "But a good coat of white paint, a new front deck, some yard cleanup, new windows, a little power-washing of the driveway and cleaning all that nasty mold off the brick wall would make a world of difference. Can your client afford some repairs?"

Reid glanced through the folder, and Celeste could tell he was upset over the materials in some way, muttering as he looked through them.

"Is everything all right?" she asked.

"Sure." He made an obvious effort to keep his voice light. "Let's walk around back and go inside, also, to see what other changes I might need to suggest, if any."

In back they found a tree down over a side fence, green, slimy moss growing all over the upper deck and patio below it, the back steps loose and somewhat unstable in many places, the yard grown up, and the outdoor furniture in desperate need of cleaning.

Celeste made a face. "Maybe the inside will be better."

It wasn't. The carpeting was dirty, frayed and worn in many places, the appliances outdated, the sofas and chairs sagging in from years of wear. The blinds on many of the windows were obviously broken, the curtains in horrible shape everywhere.

"The bathrooms aren't any better." Celeste wrinkled her nose as she opened the door to look in at one.

She turned to him. "Honestly, I hope they don't have this house on the rental market right now. Anyone who came here would be disappointed, don't you think?"

Noticing how quiet he'd become, she asked, "Is that why they want to unload it, because it's so rundown and they don't want to spend any money to fix it up?"

He was quiet for a few moments, scowling, and then answered, "I don't think the owner, who is a woman, is aware of the house's condition. She's had someone else handling her rentals for her."

"Uh, oh." Celeste put a hand to her mouth. "Looks like she hasn't been dealing with a very reputable agency. At the least, they should have kept her updated on the state of her property."

"Yes, I agree."

As they locked up and left, Celeste asked, "Do the other rental houses we're going to see belong to the same person, and are they being handled by the same agency?"

"Yes, to both of your questions," he answered, opening the car door for her. "I hope we find them in better shape. I think the big beach-front home we're going to next might be a better option for my client to sell anyway. She would get more return for any property directly on the ocean."

With the island small, it didn't take long to drive from Cooper Lane to Artic Avenue and the big home on the beach. However, this house proved to be in poor shape, too. Not as bad as the Cooper house but for a big ocean front home it looked shabby.

Celeste walked around with Reid, helping him note the problems to list. "This is actually a beautiful home," she commented. "What a shame it's being neglected. It needs paint, yard work, and so many repairs."

She pointed to a group of broken slats on the porch railings and then wrinkled her nose in disgust when they walked around to the back of the house to see the swimming pool, filthy and in need of cleaning.

"Ewww," she said. "Don't they get complaints when they try to rent a house like this?"

Reid shook his head, looking around. "I would think they would if they're actively renting it. I guess we'd better go check inside, too."

Celeste paused on the back porch as Reid unlocked the door.

"This could be a stunning home," she said. "The wide porch here, and the one above it, both look directly out on the beach, and it has a private walkway leading to the water and a lovely spacious property."

He snorted. "A lovely property now grown up in weeds, the walkway needing repairs, the pool—as you say—a disgrace, and the outdoor furniture totally neglected." Reid turned to her, his face not hiding his annoyance. "I'm sorry to sound cross but I'm upset. These properties are not what I expected or what I was led to believe they would be like. I'm having a hard time making sense of it."

She watched him scribble down more problems in his folder as they walked around inside.

"This is so sad," she couldn't help saying after a while. "This could be such an appealing place and a high dollar rental." She put a hand on Reid's arm. "I know you dread taking this news to your client. I think someone is dealing with her unethically, don't you?"

He nodded. "Yeah, I'm afraid that's true."

"This house isn't as bad inside as the last one," she commented, "but it still needs work and a good cleaning. I almost dread going to the third house in your folder. I hate to think of that poor woman having to be told that someone is cheating her. Is this the same woman you talked about earlier, who is handicapped?"

"Yes, and a widow now."

"That's sad, Reid. Your job must be difficult sometimes when you have to deal with things like this."

The third house, on Ashley Avenue, nearer to town and the county park, was in terrible shape, as well. It was a blue house with a double carport and a once nice lawn, but everything about it, inside and out, was rundown. Celeste watched Reid glance through notes in his folder again. He heaved a deep sigh.

"This has turned out to be a troubling day for you," Celeste said as he locked the last house to leave.

"I'm sorry if I haven't been good company."

She moved closer to him to give him a hug. "I'd think less of you if you weren't concerned about this and weren't sad to have to bring this news to your client. I know you need to keep your affairs confidential but is this client someone you know?"

"Yes, and it's a family friend." He stood back. "Because of that, I really think I'm going to need to talk to my dad about this. He's an attorney as well a broker. He'll know what to do with possible illegal dealings going on." He hesitated and then added, "I have printouts of renovations that supposedly have already been done to all three of these houses that I saw no evidence of."

"Oh, my." She studied him with concern. "No wonder you've gone so quiet on me."

He gave her a quick kiss before they headed down the stairs to his car. "Thanks for being my comfort today."

"I imagine you don't run into situations like this often."

"No, we work with a generally high-end clientele, but deceit, betrayal, cruelty, and crime don't belong to any one social class."

She snorted. "You can be sure I agree with that statement, and I have certainly seen it to be true."

At the car he said, "Folly Beach County Park is only a short distance down the road from here. Let's go take a walk on the beach before we head back. It's pretty and quieter than at the pier. I think a good walk would do me good right now."

"I'd enjoy that, too." She climbed back in the car. "However, I think you should talk to your dad as soon as possible about the best thing to do in this situation. You don't want to handle this incorrectly, especially with legal issues involved."

Reid glanced at his watch. "I'll still have plenty of time to talk to Dad when I get back."

"Attorneys are good at handling these things." She smiled at him as he got into the car. "I learned the hard way that it's generally best to let them take care of problems that are difficult or of any issues that carry potential legal ramifications. My attorney has often kept me from impulsively doing something I might have regretted later."

"I know you're right, but I feel bad that this pleasant day I'd planned for us to spend together has been somewhat spoiled by these unexpected events. I'd hoped to explore Folly Beach with you after we checked out the houses, and I planned to offer to grill steaks at my house later. But now, this situation has to take first precedence tonight."

He smiled at her. "I hope you don't mind if we take a rain check for another day when things aren't so stressful."

"Not at all. Let's go take that walk and then head back so you can speak with your father." She grinned at him. "However, please know I fully expect you to fill me in on all the details of this situation later on when you can. You know I've kept seeing the shock and concern on your face all afternoon, watched you pour through those files, looking at figures and notes. I haven't been fobbed off with your evasive comments, either. It's like a Poirot mystery unveiling. You know I'll wonder about this until you can tell me more what's really going on."

He laughed then. "I promise I'll share with you as soon as I can."

CHAPTER 12

After dropping Celeste off at her apartment, Reid parked behind the Beckett Company and went to look for his father. He'd seen his dad's car in the parking lot, so he knew he hadn't left yet.

"Got a minute, Dad?" he asked, looking in his father's office.

"Sure." His father gestured to the chair across from his desk and closed his computer screen. "What's up? Did you get out to look at Annabel Pennyman's rental properties at Folly?"

He crossed an ankle over his knee. "Yes, and that's where the problem is."

His dad lifted an eyebrow. "You look upset. Fill me in about this."

Reid did, telling his dad about the shape of the rentals and the discrepancies he'd found between what the houses looked like and the way they were pictured online. He'd snapped photos along the way and passed his phone to his dad to study in comparison to the printouts Annabel gave him.

His dad began to frown as he looked through Reid's pictures. "I can't see how Clarence could rent places with this much neglect to anyone." He paused. "Did Annabel say these houses were being actively rented?"

"She seemed to think so, but I remember once she mentioned something about them not renting much with all the renovations going on." He shook his head. "Bless her heart, she seemed to think, with all the money spent on improvements, that these three houses would be in excellent shape to sell."

"Where did you get these detailed improvement printouts included in this file?"

"Annabel gave them to me to clarify the improvements made on each house, all paid for through the Pennyman company she owns. She thought the printouts, detailing the updates and improvements, might be a help as selling points." He ran a hand through his hair. "Dad, what can I tell her? It's obvious someone is dealing fraudulently with her."

His father studied the improvement listings carefully, then looked through the photos Reid had taken again. "It's hard to imagine Clarence Pennyman is unaware of the condition of these rentals. After all, he manages the Folly Beach rental business. He's done so for years for his father Monroe and now for Annabel since Monroe was killed in the wreck five years ago."

Reid felt relieved his father was the first to voice concerns about Clarence's integrity. "I wondered the same thing."

His dad sighed. "I could imagine some clever contractors fleecing Clarence to some degree, cutting corners on expenses, not doing a thorough job with the renovations."

He paused, thinking again, and then said, "Monroe often candidly remarked to me that Clarence didn't have the business skills he'd hoped for. That's why he set him up down at Folly, giving him the rental business to take care of, partly to keep him out of the Broad Street Appraisal Business, which he was totally inept at."

Reid shook his head agreeing.

His father rubbed his chin. "The Broad Street Appraisal Business is well run. You know Monroe's sister Florence is a cracker jack and she handles that business with efficiency, along with her son Robert helping now that Benson is away. I've worked with Robert. He's a good appraiser, sharp young man. Looks a lot like his grandfather Hiram did. Monroe trained him as he did his sister Florence after her husband John died young."

Reid waited, knowing his father liked to talk his thoughts through.

"But here's the thing, Reid," he finally said. "Folly Beach is a small place. Clarence works there; he lives there. I can't imagine he could be completely ignorant of this situation. Can you?"

"No, sir, and that's what has troubled me the most."

His mother looked in the door. "Heywood, it's time to head home. Are you ready to go?"

"No," he replied. "Reid and I have to talk through a problem he's run into." He glanced toward Reid. "Will you take me home when we finish so Frances can go on to the house?"

"Sure," he answered.

"Do you need my help, too?" she asked.

"No, but I'll fill you in at home later to see if you have any additional input, after we decide what to do."

She glanced at her watch. "Finished or not, you and Reid come on to the house in about an hour. I have an all-day roast in the crock pot and I'll put together some vegetables to go with it. You both need to eat. You can work more at the house afterward if you need to."

Heywood winked at Reid. "See why I married this smart woman? She always takes such good care of me."

She smiled. "I'll expect to hear about all this at the house, too." She left then and headed down the hall.

His dad opened his computer again. "Let's check to see if these houses are listed as active rentals with Pennyman Realty." After searching for a few minutes, he said, "Come look at this."

Reid walked around behind his dad to look over his shoulder.

"Here's the Cooper house, the first one you went to. The appearance online matches the printout picture Annabel gave you, but notice under the rental pricing, it says 'Check with agency about availability.' That means you can't rent this house directly online like most beach rentals."

He hesitated, thinking. "My guess is that if you called about the property, you'd be told it was unavailable because of renovations."

Reid winced. "Check the other two, Dad."

His dad did and found the same notation and the same house photos as in the printouts, probably taken years ago.

"We could probably check through all the Pennyman rental

houses to see if others have similar notes, but, frankly, at this point we need to step away from this situation."

"Do we need to go take this to Annabel?"

"No. She'd immediately call Clarence and alert him to what we've found. If Clarence is involved in this, that could be potentially dangerous to Annabel."

Shocked, Reid asked, "Do you think Clarence would hurt her?"

He shook his head. "Not physically, but we don't know how much access Clarence has into the Pennyman business accounts. As an attorney, I've found that once people justify one illegal action they decide to perpetuate, they'll justify others. If this has been going on for some time and if, for example, Clarence has been diverting funds to an account of his own for whatever reason, he could go in and divert more when he realizes his mother is on to him. Do you see the danger?"

"Yes." Reid sat back down. "He could move more of her money. He would also have time to leave town if he's really involved in more than we're aware of."

"It seems likely to me that Clarence has someone working with him, probably a contractor that knew how to write up bills for work not completed. I don't think Clarence would know how to do that." He pointed at the paperwork again. "There are a lot of terms in all these renovation reports that are over Clarence's head. But someone wrote out checks for these renovations, either Annabel or Florence. And it seems likely that Clarence knew they actually hadn't been completed."

His dad leaned his head back and sighed. "There are just too many factors we don't know in all this."

"What should we do, Dad?"

"The Pennyman's attorney needs to be notified and asked to discretely step in to check into this situation and to advise Annabel in order to protect her interests. This might mean closing any funding Clarence could get his hands on until all this can be looked into."

"Do you know the Pennyman's attorney?"

"I do. His name is Gresham Hillard. Great guy and a partner in an old and reputable firm downtown, Hillard and Blanton."

"Will you call him?"

"Actually, it would be better if Benson did, and, frankly, Benson needs to head home if at all possible. If Clarence is involved in this, as it appears he is, it will be hard on Annabel to handle this. She'll want to believe Clarence innocent, want to accept whatever story he concocts to tell her, whatever justification. You and I both know, if there is one trait Clarence has in spades it's charm. And an inability to see his own fault in anything that happens. "

"When should we try to contact Benson?"

"Let me check something." He typed for a few minutes on the computer and then said, "It's five-thirty here in the U.S. right now, so it's 10:30 pm in Cambridge. Benson should be at home. Do you have his number?"

"Yes, it's in my phone." Reid pulled his iPhone out of his pocket to check through his contacts.

"You call him, Reid. He'll recognize your number and hopefully answer or call us right back. Let him know it's important if you have to leave a message, but when we reach him let me talk to him. I'll give him Gresham Hilliard's business and home cell phone numbers if he doesn't have them and I'll suggest he have Gresham call me, too. I want to stress to Benson and to Gresham how important it is that they not contact either Clarence or Annabel at this point until they begin to look into things more."

"When Benson gets home from Cambridge, assuming he can come directly home, should we meet with him to go and talk to his mother? She'll be expecting a report back from me, knowing I went to look at those houses."

"She won't expect to hear from you immediately. She said she wanted you to look into all this confidentially, so she probably won't say anything to Clarence or anyone else just yet. We'll hope not. I'll stress to Gresham Hilliard that he needs to take quick action to protect Annabel's interests, but he'll know that. He's a brilliant man and he knows the family well. He'll see clearly what needs to be done."

While his dad found Gresham Hillard's business and home cell phone numbers, Reid put his call through to Benson. Ben didn't answer immediately but called back a few minutes later.

The first thing he said was, "Reid, it's Ben. Is it my mother? Is she all right? You said it was important and you never call me on the phone; you just text."

"Your mom's okay, Ben, but there's a problem I need to make you aware of. Because there are legal aspects, Dad said it would be better if he filled you in. Can I put him on?"

With Ben's agreement, Reid passed the phone to his dad, who after a brief greeting, began to lay out the problem to Ben and the importance of him contacting the family's attorney immediately, but without getting in touch with his mother or brother.

Reid sat back in his chair listening, trying to imagine how hard this news was for Benson to hear. He'd never gotten along well with his brother Clarence, so bombastic, egoistic, and a little smarmy to be frank, but even Ben wouldn't imagine his brother fleecing his own mother like this. And how could Clarence imagine someone wouldn't find out about this? How could he justify to himself taking advantage of his mother in any way, with all she'd been through?

Eventually, his dad seemed to finish his conversation and passed the phone back to Reid. "Ben wants to talk with you for a minute."

"Reid, thanks for calling. I'm going to get a flight scheduled as soon as possible, clear out my business here, pack, and head home. Mom is going to need some support."

"I'm glad you can do that, Ben."

"I shouldn't have stayed away this long."

"Don't blame yourself, friend. But I'm glad you can get away to come back now. If you want me to meet you at the airport, let me know when your flight will be in."

"Thanks, I may do that."

"Do you need a place to stay?"

"I might for the first night or two until Gresham Hillard and I can get together. Your dad said it was best Clarence not know I'd come home unexpectantly until our attorney digs into all this. Also, he thought it best that Gresham Hillard talks this through with mother on his own before I get in the picture. Whatever decisions and actions mother needs to make, and to take legally, your dad thought it best she makes on her own. I can show up after that, though, to be a support and I'll stay at the house with her then."

"I'm sorry about all this, Ben."

"Me, too. Clarence has always been a pill, and often a pompous ass, but mercy, I never imagined he would get involved in something like this. This won't be easy for my mother however it goes down."

"Well, let us know any way we can help. Our families have always been friends."

"I'd better go get on the computer to find a flight," Ben said then. "I'll call or text you later."

After talking to Ben, Reid and his dad packed up all Reid's papers and the additional notes his dad had made to carry home to the Beckett house on Legare Street. It didn't take them long to drive down King, turning on Queen and then south on Legare to the Beckett family home. Built in 1904, the house was on old gracious, historic property. Reid had grown up in the house, as had his sister, Lori, and younger brother Charlie.

The house had a clean formal look, like many in downtown Charleston, white with black shutters and neat fencing all around, with a drive on the side leading back to off street parking. Like many old Charleston homes. the long length of the house reached far back on the property with a shaded patio and garden area behind not visible from the street.

The house had four bedrooms—his parents' room, Lori's, his and Charlie's room, and a guest room. The home had comfortable living areas, the usual tall ceilings and ceiling fans expected in old Charleston homes.

Reid knew the property a valuable one now, with the house South of Broad, but to him, Lori, and Charlie, it had always just been home. They'd played in the old gardens and cemeteries nearby, walked to the lake or ridden their bikes down to White Point Gardens and on to Waterfront Park. What visitors in the thousands came to see daily was simply Reid's home neighborhood.

His mother Frances heard them come in the back door and called out, "I'm in the kitchen but dinner's nearly ready. Charlie is here, too, so we're eating in the dining room. I've already set the table."

Frances had always been a working mother, part-time when they were small, full-time later, so she'd become a master at meals she could make ahead and freeze, cook in the electric cooker all day, or put together quickly when she came home. Her all-day pot roast was a favorite of his. While his dad went to put his briefcase in his office, Reid headed to the kitchen to see if he could give his mother a hand.

As he walked in the long kitchen, he spotted the roast on a plate on the sideboard, a big bowl heaped with mashed potatoes, a dish of peas with those mushrooms in it he liked, and a side plate of sliced tomatoes and celery sticks stuffed with pimento cheese.

"Ummm. Everything looks good, Mom. What can I do to help?"

"I sent Charlie into the dining room with glasses of tea for everyone, so start taking those dishes in now. And call your father. I'll be there as soon as I pull these rolls out of the oven."

The smell of them filled the air as she pulled the oven door open, and Reid smiled, realizing he was hungry. He spotted his brother as he walked in the dining room.

"Hey, Charlie. Good to see you."

"You, too." His brother grinned at him. "I ran by to drop off some papers from a sale today. Mom invited me to dinner, said you and Dad were on your way. With the smell of Mom's roast in the air, how could I say no?"

Reid laughed. "That's why I'm here, too."

A few minutes later, they all settled down around the dining room table to eat, his dad saying grace, and all of them starting the plates of food around the table. Charlie was excited to have sold a big home in Mt Pleasant.

"Was that the big house on Lakeview Drive with the large

property and pool?" his mother asked.

"Yes. It's a new house with five bedrooms, over 3000 sq feet," he replied. "It looks like an old farmhouse though. Really pretty place with a pool, big garage. Lots of trees on the property, over a half-acre. A family from Michigan bought it."

"Good sale, son, and I'm sure that family won't miss those harsh Michigan winters," his dad said.

As they finished eating, Reid's mother insisted on hearing about the problem with the Pennymans and Reid's father filled her in.

She put a hand to her heart. "I so hate to hear that for Annabel's sake. She's had enough sorrows losing Monroe and having to learn to live with being crippled and in a wheelchair. I hope this doesn't set her health back. You know it will hurt her to think Clarence would be involved with something like this."

Charlie snorted. "Mom, he might go to prison for this. It's not just a little mistake. Isn't it fraud, Dad, when someone deceives another wrongfully with the intent of financial or personal gain to themselves?"

"Yes," Reid's dad answered. "We don't know all that happened yet, though, Charlie, but it could bring serious repercussions to him."

Charlie, Reid's younger brother, was a handsome, rascally looking young man, almost too handsome for his own good, but since college, he'd settled down and was working hard in the family business. Charlie loved the public side of the business and being out of the office more, working in real estate. He was good at it, too, with his natural charm and good sense about people.

"I saw you leaving the parking lot around lunchtime with Celeste Deveaux. Did you take her down to Folly Beach with you?" Charlie asked, spilling the beans on Reid. With all the problems that occurred at Folly, he'd decided not to mention Celeste had been with him.

His parents passed a look between them.

"I don't think you mentioned Celeste went with you, Reid," his dad said after a moment.

"The plan originally was simply to drive down to check out the houses for Annabel. Celeste was off today so I offered to take her along with me. I didn't expect to run into problems."

His dad grew quiet for a moment. "This was supposed to be a confidential matter for Annabel."

"Dad, I never mentioned Annabel's name or any of the Pennyman's names to Celeste, and she didn't push for details. She noticed the homes were in bad shape and sensed there was a problem, but no confidentiality was breached. She won't mention anything about it to anyone."

"You've been seeing quite a bit of Celeste lately," his mother said, after getting a chess pie from the sideboard to bring to the table to cut and pass around.

Charlie grinned. "Man, that is so cool you're dating Celeste Deveaux. Ryland said you hang out at the restaurant every time she sings and that you two are giving each other some looks."

Reid gave his brother a scowl that caused him to put a hand to his mouth. "Whoops. Sorry, Reid. I guess I thought Mom and Dad knew you guys were going out."

Reid felt like a teenager again in situations like this, and not like a man over thirty with a home and career of his own.

His mother passed a slice of pie to him. "Reid is a grown man, Charlie. He doesn't have to tell us who he goes out with anymore. You certainly don't and you're younger than Reid."

"It isn't any big secret," Reid said, frowning. "I guess it simply hasn't come up."

"We do like Celeste," his father said. "And she's been through some rough times. Frances and I are sorry for that. She seems like a nice girl." He hesitated. "However, keep in mind she has only been divorced since June and is still having problems with her ex-husband, as you well know. Be watchful how serious you get."

Reid bristled at his dad's words. "Doesn't she deserve time with someone who'll be kind and thoughtful to her after all she's been through?" he blurted out without thinking.

He saw his parents pass that look between them again.

His mother smiled then. "Reid, you know we only want your happiness. Our concern is linked to that. Celeste, no matter how nice, is a well-known country singer. Invariably, she will go back on the road once all this difficulty settles down. If I recall, that is one of the reasons she so wanted Imogene to stay on at the store as the manager, so she could leave the shop in good hands when that time came again."

"She did talk clearly about those things to us when she bought the store, Reid," his father added. "I know you remember that."

"And, your point is?" he asked, finding himself annoyed.

"Our point is that it could be hurtful for you later if you get overly involved with Celeste Deveaux," his mother stated. "We know you, Reid. Deep within, I believe you're the sort of man who will want a solid relationship, a warm and close marriage in time, with someone you can share your life with and have a family with. We can see potential problems happening easily if you get overly involved with someone like Celeste, no matter how nice she is. So don't take offense. We're just thinking logically."

Which Reid knew meant that he wasn't thinking logically at all. And even if some of their words were true, he didn't like hearing them. He also didn't like them pushing on him to think that far ahead.

As he and Charlie left later, Charlie caught up with him to say, "Hey, I'm sorry I said anything about Celeste. You've been spending so much time with her, I just thought they knew."

"Well, they know now," he said, still a little annoyed.

CHAPTER 13

Celeste always enjoyed sitting down to play at the shiny black grand piano in Reid Beckett's living room. The house, at this moment, was softly quiet with Reid outside putting steaks on the grill. Since his plan to host her for dinner got interrupted by the problems at Folly Beach yesterday, he called this morning to invite her over tonight.

"You need to come," he insisted, when she hesitated. "I'd already bought the steaks, planning to grill them for us last night."

She grinned at his words. "Well, all right, but you have to promise to catch me up on the Folly Beach mystery."

"I will." He laughed. "At least what I know of it."

Celeste's times with Reid were becoming more frequent, and despite her reservations, she had to admit she enjoyed them. The more time she spent with him, the more comfortable she felt, and she knew their feelings were growing for each other.

Reid came into the dining room then, bringing two plates. "The steaks are ready, Juliet. Come sit down to eat."

She slid off the piano bench to come join him. "Do I need to go get anything else in the kitchen?"

He looked around on the table as he put the plates on the woven placemats already there. "I don't think so. Before I went to grill, we put out the salad, dressing, bread, butter, and sour cream, and I snagged our baked potatoes from the oven on my way in."

Celeste settled into her usual place at the table across from Reid. "Everything looks wonderful," she said.

As they began to eat, Celeste let her gaze drift around the dining room, opening into the living area through an archway. Reid's home had a formal, elegant air with its tall ceilings, long windows, polished hardwood floors, and gracious old rugs. Here in the dining room a chandelier hung over the dining table, and lovely oil landscapes and gold-framed mirrors hung on the walls. The furniture, here and throughout the house, was somewhat modern, giving the rooms a comfortable, sleek charm, with an easy mix of old and new. It suited Reid in some way, that mixture of old and new, and Celeste always found herself at home here, too.

He glanced across at her. "How's your steak?"

"Excellent, and cooked exactly the way I like it, medium-rare."

After a moment, she looked up to see him watching her. "Now, that's a thoughtful look. What are you thinking?"

His voice softened. "I was thinking how much I like looking across my table and seeing you here."

She smiled at him. "Those are romantic words."

He winked at her. "I'm a romantic guy."

"I agree. How many women have a boyfriend who quotes lines to her from Romeo and Juliet?"

"Maybe I should go memorize some more lines."

"Please don't." She laughed. "A little is enough. And, besides, that couple both died in that play."

The room quieted as they ate more of their meal.

"You've been preoccupied about something all evening," Reid said after a time. "Do you want to tell me about it?"

She sighed. "I had a long conference call with Gary today."

"Your agent?"

"Yes."

"Is there another problem with Dillon?"

"Not directly, but I imagine there will be soon. I'm scheduled to fly to Nashville later this week to record the songs for the new album. Capital usually puts out a new album of mine in late summer or early fall every year. I generally tour to promote it in September and October." She paused.

A little frown touched his face. "I thought you were going to postpone this longer, wait until all this problem with Dillon resolved."

She sipped on her iced tea thinking how to answer him. "If you quit your family's company tomorrow, Reid, it wouldn't only impact you. It would impact others who depend on you. That's the way it is for me, too. The livelihood of many others are tied to mine—and not just Gary's or my management team's interests but my band members, my recording team, sound engineers, production and road managers, setup and lighting crews, all the production and tour crew. Capital spaces out how they record and tour to keep all the staff working and to keep everything running smoothly. I usually record and tour in the early fall. I'm already creating scheduling difficulties being behind this year."

He waited, while they both finished up their dinner.

"What is the plan?" he asked after a time.

"Because I write all my own songs and because the songs for this new album are finished, with the score roughed out—thanks in part to Marcus—I can record the album in a day or two. The mixing and mastering take a couple of more weeks after, sometimes less. But the album should be ready to head off for distribution next month. After the lead song releases, a little ahead of the album, to generate excitement, and after publicity kicks in, I can start tour."

"There's a lot more in the background behind an album release than most people realize or think about," he said.

"Yes, there is." She smiled at him, glad that he wasn't trying to argue her out of what she needed to do.

"If I delay much longer in getting the album out, Reid, I wouldn't have time to tour before the holiday period begins in late November. The holidays are a bad time to tour with industry staff and others taking vacations and with the public busy, too." She hesitated. "I could wait until January and February to tour, postponing the release of the album until then, but it would cause scheduling problems for Capital with other entertainers, and, frankly, I hate traveling in the winter. There can be so many weather and logistical problems and road concerns."

"Do you fly on these tours?"

She shook her head. "No, not in the U.S. I have a personal tour bus. The crew have buses, too, and we have a fleet of trucks to carry equipment needed from place to place. Because the tour dates are often tight, a Friday here, then a Saturday at some distance away in another city, our crews split up so one can go ahead to set up while another stays to take down. Few people think about all that, but it's part of the job and the industry."

"I admit I never really thought about it at all. I can see, though, it takes a lot of work on the part of many people to coordinate getting an album out and organizing a tour. Does Gary set all the tour dates?"

"He and others." She smiled. "When Nolan was my manager, he worked extensively with Gary to set up my tours, to coordinate my recording sessions, and to set up publicity. He often traveled with me, too, when he could."

Reid pushed back his chair. "I want to talk about this more, but let's take our dishes to the kitchen, pour a cup of coffee, and get comfortable on the sofa in the living room. I picked up a couple of pieces of cheesecake at the little bakery nearby. Do you want some?"

"A small sliver only." She grinned at him. "I have a lot of slinky, snug dresses I tour in that I can't afford to get too big to fit into."

"You can cut your own piece of cheesecake then," he said, gathering up a stack of plates and dishes.

A short time later, they sat on the big sofa in the living room with dessert and coffee on the low table in front of them.

"How long will your tour last?" he asked, after eating part of his dessert.

"I won't know exactly until Gary gets it all set up but I usually tour about six weeks with about ten to twelve shows. Gary might shorten the time this fall because of the scheduling delays. My shows are usually in concert halls or large auditoriums. I don't do arenas or outside events. They don't suit my style of music, and, frankly, I don't like them either. I usually have a Friday and a Saturday show, and sometimes a Thursday or Sunday one. In between we rest, practice a little if needed, and I do interviews, radio and TV spots in the cities we go to. My tours tend to follow a circular flow-pattern around the U.S., southeast to north, across to the west, and then back toward home."

Reid finished his dessert and settled back on the sofa to get more comfortable.

"I thought you'd be more upset about this," she said, watching him.

"It's your job, Celeste. Your work takes you traveling to meet your public, to share your gift." He hesitated. "You shared with me earlier, when you came to my office to buy Imogene's shop, that you'd have to tour and travel part of the year."

She felt a sweep of relief. "And you're okay about that?"

He grinned at her. "If you're asking if I'll miss you, I hope you know the answer is yes. I also hope we'll be talking many evenings, sharing sweet talk."

She laughed. "I do like that idea."

"Why did you think I'd be upset?"

She twisted her hands in her lap. "I wasn't sure what you wanted of me, what you might expect of me if..." She hesitated.

"If our relationship keeps moving forward," he interrupted. "I hope it does, Celeste."

"Your brother came by the shop today and ..."

"Let me guess. He suggested my parents had concerns about our relationship."

"Do they?"

"Parents always think they know best how your life should run, what you should do, how everything should turn out. I suppose it's their protective instinct."

"And they don't approve of me?"

"No, they just worry that if we marry our relationship might not be as traditional as some."

"Does that not worry you?"

"No. From what you've shared with me, as an entertainer you don't travel all year, you don't work clubs everywhere and are always on the road. You do an album about once a year, then a tour, do appearances here and there at other times but not too many." He gave her a big grin. "I don't see any reason why I couldn't take care of any babies or children we have during those times, with a little help. Fortunately, we are both comfortable financially and should be able to hire help we both like." He paused. "I'm told I have a good, easy way with kids, should you want to have some."

Celeste knew her mouth fell open. "Since when have we been talking about marriage and children?"

"Since you brought up my parents' concerns. Doesn't your mother think about things like that with you any time you get serious about anyone?" He laughed again. "It ticks us off but it's the way parents are."

Celeste couldn't think of a single thing to say.

Reid moved across the sofa closer to her. "Celeste, I don't see any obstacles to us falling in love with each other if we want to. I don't see any problems with spending my life with you, if we decide, in time, that's what we both want. Don't go putting stumbling blocks in our paths that don't belong there. Don't create problems that are easy to resolve and work around. And don't let other people's opinions interfere with what we decide is right for us."

"I don't know what to say, Reid."

"Well, I do. I'm hanging right on the edge of falling head-over-heels in love with you Celeste Deveaux. You're the only woman I've ever felt like I wanted to talk about a future with. That's a first for me. And I don't want anything getting in the way of that."

He put his hands on either side of her face and leaned in and kissed her. She wanted to resist but found she couldn't.

After a few minutes, she pulled away to smile at him. "Even when I was sixteen, you thrilled me down to my toes. You still do. It surprised me then; it still surprises me now how strongly I feel about you."

"Those are good words." He moved back toward the other side

of the sofa. "But if I kiss you much longer, I might misbehave." He gave her a wolfish grin.

She let her eyes travel over him. "I understand the feeling. I think I've forgotten what I planned to say next."

They both laughed.

He crossed his arms and sighed. "In seriousness, I do have some concerns about you getting into Dillon Barlow's orbit again. Will Gary provide good security for you in Nashville? I assume you'll stay at your own place there."

"He's hiring a guard again at the building where I live. Someone will pick me up and take me home from recording sessions. I'll only be there a few days, flying over and then back." She hesitated. "My larger concern is that Dillon's career is in trouble. He won't like it that I'm making a come-back after all that's happened. Narcissists like Dillon piggyback off the success of others, but he can't do that any longer off me. He'll want to sabotage any forward movement I make. He'll be threatened by any success I achieve because it will threaten to take attention off him. He'll be resentful, too, and feel I don't deserve any success or attention, that he is more entitled to it than me."

"You seem to have a good understanding about Dillon and about all his problems. Are these things your therapist helped you see about this man?"

"Yes, and I lived with his jealousies of other entertainers. I listened to the comments he made no one else ever heard. It didn't take me long after we married to realize he saw life in a twisted way." She leaned her head back against the sofa. "I can't keep hiding out and living in fear of him though, Reid. I may run into him sometimes in the company of others and at events, but at least I won't be living in the same town with him. In time, Dillon will link up with someone else and get his focus off me. I doubt he'll ever forgive me for leaving him, regardless of what he did to me, but hopefully we'll both move on."

He reached out a hand to take hers. "You will be careful, won't you? Like knowing there's a shark in the water, don't get too close."

"Good analogy. I admit I feel a little anxious about heading to Nashville after all Dillon's threats, but I need to go there to record."

"And then you'll need to tour, too."

"Yes. Dillon isn't on tour right now. He isn't doing as much performing and, according to Gary, he's sabotaging his own image in many ways by not lying low until all this bad publicity blows over."

Reid looked thoughtful. "You said that Dillon drank and sometimes used drugs when you were married, and you also told me Gary said those habits had grown worse. Do you think that's true?"

"Probably. It was Dillon's way to handle disappointments, whether real or illusory."

"What does your therapist say?"

"Dr. Conrad has helped me to see clearly that Dillon is unhealthy, but I am not. That knowledge is powerful. I know who and what Dillon is now, and I have cut him out of my life." She reached over to take Reid's hands. "You caring for me, after all I experienced with him, has been a blessing to me just now. I do want you to know that."

"It has been nothing but a joy caring for you, Juliet." He grinned at her and moved closer. "As Romeo might say, '*Let lips do what hands do.*'" He pulled her closer to kiss her again.

She giggled. "Where did you learn all those words of Romeo's?"

"I admit, I played Romeo in a high school play. I had to memorize all his lines and they stuck." He leaned over and kissed her forehead. "You will be careful in Nashville, won't you?"

"I will. I promise."

They cleaned up the kitchen then and a short time later returned to talk a little more before Reid took her home.

"You haven't caught me up on the Folly Beach mystery yet," she said, taking her shoes off to tuck her feet under her on the sofa.

"Not a lot has happened since yesterday when I went to talk to my dad." Reid filled her in on what had happened at that meeting, sharing the Pennyman's name this time with Celeste's full assurance to keep all confidential. "Dad talked to Benson in England. I did, too. Benson said he planned to contact their attorney immediately and schedule a flight back to the states. He knows his mother will need him."

"Did he get a flight scheduled?"

"Yes, he did, and I'm picking him up at the airport tomorrow when he gets in. He's going to stay with me a few days. The attorney agreed with my dad that Ben shouldn't go home until he has a chance to look into everything and schedule a private talk with Annabel. The family attorney will work to protect her interests and take any legal actions necessary. Ben can move back into the house with his mother after that."

"How sad that Annabel's own son may be trying to take advantage of her financially. To me, it's especially awful with all that woman has been through. You know this will really hurt her. And your friend Ben."

"I keep hoping we'll learn there is some other explanation than what seems obvious, but it doesn't look good."

"Did the Pennyman's attorney, Gresham Hillard, talk with your dad, too?"

Reid heaved a sigh. "He did talk to dad briefly, and he thanked Dad for reaching out to Ben. He also told my Dad that he and Monroe Pennyman were lifelong friends. He's really angry about this for Annabel's sake, and he's taking steps immediately to safeguard her interests. Dad feels confident he'll handle this well."

She shook her head in sadness. "People can surely surprise and disappoint us in this world, can't they? Did you ever imagine Benson's brother could do something like this? From what you tell me they had a loving family, and it sounds like Clarence's parents have been more than generous to him."

"That's true, and actually, Clarence was the charmer in the family, full of flattery and entertaining, sometimes making him the favorite. Ben was the more serious son—bookish, sound and sensible. Clarence's gregarious nature often put Benson in the shade in the family dynamics. But Monroe and Annabel loved both. I always thought they saw the strengths in both their sons, too."

She raised her eyebrows. "Maybe not the weaknesses though. Those charming types can hide some surprises."

He nodded. "You've certainly learned that, haven't you?"

She nodded and then glanced at her watch. "It's getting late, Reid. I look forward to hearing more about this when I get back, but I'd better head home now. I'm leaving for Nashville early in the morning to start my first recording session at ten. Gary thinks we can finish tomorrow or no later than Thursday so I can fly home on Friday. He's set my return flight to come back then."

"Do you need me to take you to the airport in the morning? I should have asked before."

"No, but thank you. Vanessa is taking me over and picking me up." Celeste tucked her feet back into her shoes. "But maybe we can all go to Thurman's on Friday evening after I get back. That would be fun."

"We'll do that."

She paused. "Reid, pray for me, too, would you? I believe prayers are powerful. I wouldn't mind a little protection coverage."

"You know I'll do that."

CHAPTER 14

Two days later on Thursday evening, Reid sat visiting with Benson Pennyman at his house after dinner. He'd grilled ribs for them both tonight and they'd feasted on them along with slaw, baked beans, and corn on the cob. He'd picked Benson up at the airport yesterday, and his friend had been tied up in meetings with the family attorney Wednesday evening and today.

"That was a good meal. Thanks," Ben said, propping his feet on an old ottoman across from his chair on the porch. With the evening warm, the two men had opted to sit outside on the upper porch, on the side of Reid's house, after finishing their dinner. The wide, open porch had an array of comfortable, outdoor wicker furniture, and Reid had turned the paddle fan on to stir the air.

"You've walked through a couple of rough days," Reid said, snagging another of the homemade cookies he picked up at the little bakery nearby.

Benson reached over to get one, too. "It's been a mess."

"Tell me what's been going on."

He rubbed his neck. "I spent yesterday afternoon and evening, after I got in, with our family attorney, Gresham Hillard. He and Dad were good friends; they grew up together. So I went over to his home for our meeting and I had dinner there, too."

He frowned and reached for his cola on the table. "Gresham had spent the day looking into mom's affairs. Everything with the Broad Street Appraisal company, that dad's sister Florence manages, is on the up and up, no problems. You know I worked there with

Florence, my cousin Robert and my Dad as an appraiser, around going to school. I hesitated accepting the Gates Scholarship two years ago to study architecture at Cambridge and to pick up my doctorate, especially with Dad gone, but Mom pushed on me to go abroad."

"It's a huge honor to win a Gates scholarship, Benson. Your mom knew that and she knew how much you loved historic preservation and the studies you'd be involved in."

"I can't regret going, despite all these problems. I learned and gained so much—knowledge that will help me as an appraiser of historic properties. Additionally, a colleague at the College of Charleston has already put out feelers to me about teaching in the school's program in historic preservation. I'll have a lot to bring to it from my studies at Cambridge."

They sat quietly for a few minutes.

Ben sighed. "I still can't wrap my mind around what Clarence has done, what he's gotten himself involved in. Gresham found he'd gotten hooked up with a couple of contractors with a shady background. I have no doubt they spotted Clarence as a likely candidate to scam, but Gresham says Clarence knowingly participated in the fraud perpetuated to claim monies from the Pennyman company for renovations never completed."

He drank more of his cola. "The contracting company, called Carmichael Contractors, was owned by Ralph Carmichael and Darren Blalock. Gresham said, from what he's been able to learn, Ralph Carmichael is the brains of the operation, Darren the brawn, but both moved around the country often, changing the name of their business, always running just ahead of being prosecuted for a spate of different illegal activities."

"I assume Clarence didn't check them out?"

"No. Evidently ever since Dad died five years ago, Clarence has been pocketing money from the realty business he manages, cutting corners on repairs, letting properties run down, padding expenses. He's been sly about it, too. Mother inherited the business. Dad left some trusts for Clarence and me for later in our lives, but he didn't leave any of the business interests to us at this time. He hadn't expected to die when he did, and we were young."

"I remember that."

"Gresham said both my dad and mom thought it healthier for us to work for a living, to prove ourselves, show we might be ready to take over family interests later. That's the way my Grandfather Pennyman did things, too. I never had any problems with it all, but I remember Clarence being resentful about it when Dad died. So does Gresham. He recalls Clarence threw a somewhat petty scene in his office trying to convince him Dad had wanted to leave him the Pennyman Realty business and the family home on Folly Beach where he lives. He seemed to think he should have received a large portion of Dad's money then, too. Gresham said he tossed out comments about contesting the will that left everything to Mother."

Reid propped his feet on the big ottoman beside Benson's. "Do you think Clarence knew from the get-go that the guys with Carmichael Contractors were a little crooked?"

"No one knows yet. What Gresham does know is that these guys didn't write contracts with timelines for their work. They didn't have insurance and as far as anyone knows Clarence didn't ask for references. Clarence's pattern had been to get the cheapest estimate for work he could find and then to pad the expenses." He shook his head. "Even Mother said she wondered why Clarence never used the same people to do work on the rentals. My dad had always worked with Berle Hanes's contracting business in past. Mother also wondered at the money Clarence was spending on updates, renovations, and office expenses."

"Did she ever talk to Clarence about these things?"

"According to Gresham, Clarence always had explanations and used emotionally manipulative ways of fobbing Mother off about any questions she asked. Stuff like suggesting she didn't trust him or that she didn't have confidence in his abilities."

Reid couldn't help laughing. "Clarence was always a schmoozer. Remember how he used to find all those ways to wheedle extra money out of your mother, making up non-existent school expenses, insisting he needed a certain kind of shoes or clothes?"

Benson frowned. "I guess a little pattern of deceit got its roots started even back then. But, honestly, Reid, our mother nearly died in that wreck. Her life isn't an easy one. You'd think even Clarence would have compassion about that, respect all our mother has been through, her losses, her limitations now. I admit it really makes me angry."

"What will happen?"

"I'm not sure. It isn't my decision to make. However, it can't be ignored that illegal fraud has been going on. The tricky thing is that if Mother goes after and prosecutes the contractors and their company for pocketing money for repairs and renovations never made, she'll have to go after and prosecute Clarence, too. Gresham says fraud convictions differ slightly, but most, to the extent Clarence and Carmichael Contractors have been involved in, would be classified as felony convictions and can lead to multiple years in prison. Their collusive, ongoing activities can hardly be classified as a misdemeanor."

Reid blew out a long breath. "Have you talked to your mother?"

"No, but Gresham Hillard has set up a meeting with Mother in the morning. She knows I'm home and that I've been staying with you. She asked if you would come also, since you've been involved in this."

Surprised, Reid said, "I don't think that's necessary, Ben."

Ben turned toward him. "She specifically asked that you come, according to Gresham. I would be grateful if you would, Reid. It would be good to have a friend there."

"When is the meeting?"

"At ten in the morning."

A little smile twitched at Reid's mouth. "I don't think I've ever met with your mother in the morning. My meetings have always been at three with afternoon tea."

Ben chuckled. "Mom must be really serious to schedule a morning meeting."

"Maybe she'll have tea anyway. I sure love her Half Moon Cookies."

Ben seemed to relax a little at the memory. "I haven't had any of those for a long time."

"I'll rearrange my schedule in the morning to go with you, Ben. I know this is a hard time for you."

"I'm sure I can move out of your place to stay at Mother's now, and I probably should. I know this is going to be a tough time for her."

They watched an old movie later and then Benson, exhausted from the trip and stress of the last days, piled into bed early. Reid stayed up for a time, thinking about all Ben had shared. He texted a few messages back and forth with Celeste, too. Evidently Gary had her safety locked up like Fort Knox while in Nashville. She assured him all was well and said the recording session was going smoothly.

Settling into bed later, he finished one of John Grisham's latest novels about victims of a law school scam. Reading about innocents being duped made him think of Annabel. He didn't look forward to the meeting tomorrow.

At ten the next morning, Justine Johnson opened the door of the Pennyman's home on Church Street to Reid and Ben. She didn't give them more than a nod, even Benson, before leading them back to the sitting room, where Reid had met with Annabel before.

They found Gresham Hillard there and also Florence Alston and her son Robert. A few minutes later, to Reid's surprise, Clarence came bustling in.

"Sorry, I'm late, Mother," he said, coming in the door. "I've had some problems with the bank and my business accounts being locked up. Do you know anything about that?" He stopped in his tracks then, looking around. "What are all these people doing here?"

"Have a seat, Clarence," she said.

He did, and spotting Benson, he added. "Hey, Benson. When did you get home?" Alarmed then at the serious tone in the room, he leaned forward and asked. "Mom, are you all right? Are you dying or something?"

Amazingly, Justine came in at that moment, pushing the tea cart, and Annabel said, "Thank you, Justine. And please everyone, let Justine pour you a cup of tea and please get yourself a small plate of treats. In all times, we can practice civility."

Everyone got up to accommodate Annabel Pennyman's request, and Reid had to admire her poise and composure in this situation. As they resumed to their seats, Annabel also asked Justine to stay.

Clarence glared around the room, as if suddenly sensing this meeting might not be a pleasant one. "I think you need to tell us what's going on here, Mother. All this mystery is a little odd, don't you think?"

She studied him thoughtfully and then shook her head the least bit. "Clarence, you mentioned that your business accounts have been closed. I did that. I have unfortunately learned about the business practices you've chosen to become involved in, beginning unfortunately, from what I've been able to learn, since not long after your father's death."

Clarence's face flushed. "What are you talking about Mother? You've questioned me other times about that and wrongly. I really resent this. You know Daddy trusted me with the realty business at Folly Beach. I don't know why you also haven't. Perhaps it's your lack of understanding about business practices." He gave her a haughty look. "As our attorney will tell you, I questioned Daddy leaving everything in your hands."

Annabel crossed her arms. "You may have a point in that, Clarence. Apparently, I have been entirely too trusting and gullible in handling the business. As a few problems came to my attention recently, I had Gresham Hillard look into every single aspect of the Pennyman business interests. Fortunately, the only problems found were ones with the part of the business you manage, Clarence."

"I don't know who you've been talking to," Clarence blustered. "My business is perfectly fine…."

Annabel interrupted. "The Pennyman Realty company is not your business, Clarence, although you have certainly acted as though it is. The business is in my name. I love you as your mother but right now I also am impelled to face you as a criminal stealing money from my business, lying to me and to others, linking yourself fraudulently with crooked contractors, eager to also engage in illegal activities to defraud me and the Pennyman company."

"Now wait a minute…" Clarence started to say.

"No, Clarence," Annabel interrupted. "You listen and you keep quiet. I expected you would be disagreeable about this, so I also invited all these witnesses here today to hear everything I have to say to you. And be assured, I mean every word I have to say to you."

Clarence opened his mouth again, but Gresham Hillard shook his head at him. "Your mother has the floor now, Clarence. Hear her out."

Annabel sipped her tea and then continued. "Giving some thought to downsizing my life, I contacted the Beckett Company, and spoke to Reid Beckett, asking him to look at a number of our beach properties with the idea of selling one of them. I thought this would be the easiest way, at this time, to get some capital to buy a one level home more manageable for myself and Justine. I asked Reid to look at several properties I'd chosen, mostly because I had all the paperwork showing the extensive updates and renovations done on each of them that I wrote checks to you to cover in the last year."

Reid noticed Clarence was looking a little white in the face now.

"To my surprise, I got a call from Gresham Hillard earlier this week asking for an appointment. I learned from him the condition of the properties Reid had found. The Beckett Company felt like I needed to be the one to handle the discrepancies unexpectedly discovered. So did Gresham, who—loving your father as he did—also urged me to move immediately to close access to you to any Pennyman accounts. Well advised, I did so. On his advice, also, I had him carefully research all aspects of the realty business you manage, and I had him look into every aspect of my business concerns as well. As I mentioned, there were no problems with any aspect of the Pennyman businesses except with the realty business you manage."

She paused. "I would like an explanation from you now about this."

"Those contractors I got involved in were crooked, Mother. I was just looking into that myself. They kept finding reasons for not completing the renovation work I contracted them for. I think I will need to find someone more reliable to work with."

"Clarence, you don't pay contractors in full for work in advance. Surely you know that. You don't work with contractors without checking their backgrounds, getting strong references, and making sure they are insured. You don't continue to give them work when they don't complete the first job they were to do. Nor do you pay them for that work. You paid them for work you knew they had not completed."

"I made a few mistakes with these guys, but I can work that out, Mother. I'll bet I can sue them."

She shook her head sadly. "Clarence, there is so much more. Don't pretend any longer. We know how you've been listing properties on the rental site that are in no shape to rent. I know now that I've been paying for a full-time administrative assistant at the realty business who only works part-time. Additionally, I've found many of the other expenses I have paid, for the business for various needs, have been padded or the money pocketed by you and put into your account. In fact, you have two accounts, our old business account your father set up for the realty and a new one you set up after his death which seems to have grown and grown."

"How do you know about my personal business and accounts? That's private information."

She gave him a steely look. "A lot of people around the island seemed eager to talk, Clarence. Evidently, they were worried about me and are fond of me. Which you don't seem to be."

Clarence, red-faced and sweating now, said, "You know Dad meant to leave me that business and give me the house at Folly Beach. He said he would one day. It should have been in the will."

Annabel blew out a disgusted breath. "And so you decided you had been cheated out of what was rightfully yours and thus could, without any remorse or guilt, turn and cheat me out of what was mine. Is that it, Clarence?"

"Well, you wouldn't make things right after Dad died."

"Your father and I felt you and Benson were still too young for such responsibilities. Obviously, we were right, considering all this." She shook her head sadly. "Surely, you know that all I have would have been divided between Benson and yourself in time."

Seemingly unrepentant, Clarence said, "Well, if you want to be mad at someone, be mad at that Ralph Carmichael and his partner. You should get Grisham Hillard to get them arrested. They owe me money. I've been trying to get in touch with them for two days and they won't answer my calls."

Gresham Hillard cleared his throat then. "Since my name has been mentioned, I would suggest to you, Clarence, that if we get the police involved to arrest and prosecute Ralph Carmichael and his partner, that the police would also have to arrest and prosecute you. Together, you both have knowingly and willfully engaged in fraud for well over a year. This is a felony offense, Clarence, and would involve a felony conviction of probably considerable jail time."

"What?" He stood, shaking a finger at Gresham, angry now. "How dare you threaten me? I'm a Pennyman."

"Sit down, Clarence," Annabel said in a firm voice. "You have been very foolish, crossed the law, betrayed and cheated your own family. I have some options for you. My first option is that I can have you and the owners of Carmichael Construction arrested. I have that right, and legally and morally, it is what I probably should do."

Reid noticed Clarence was looking around with alarm now.

"Here is my second option. Pack your possessions and leave the area, preferably the country for your own welfare. I do not want to know where you go, in case I get questioned or called into court in relation to other aspects of this. It seems the Carmichael group were involved in a variety of problematic activities, not only here but in other places. I don't want to know more about any of this or to be implicated in it in any way. "

"But I'm your son!" Clarence cried out then.

"Yes, I know, and I'm sorry for all you've brought on yourself. But I am firm in these options. You have brought a deep disgrace to our family, jeopardized the well-being, heart, and trust of all these people who know and care for you, including your aunt Florence, your cousin Robert, your own brother Benson, his friend Reid Beckett, our family attorney Gresham Hillard, and my loved helper and friend Justine. Do you have no remorse?"

Clarence glared at her. "I was just trying to see that what Dad wanted would happen. Those monies you say I've stolen should have been rightfully mine."

Reid saw Annabel take a deep breath, and it was evident she was close to tears.

"Well, then, take those monies in your account you feel are rightfully yours. Gresham has some idea of the extent of them, gathered over the years since your father died. Take what you see as your rightful money and establish a new life for yourself somewhere." She paused. "These are the only two options, Clarence. And I would move quickly if you wish to take the second option. The word is out at Folly that you are not what most people assumed. Additionally, I will be closing and locking the Realty office and my home where you are staying later this week, so get what things that are yours out of both locations."

Red-faced, Clarence stood again. "You can't mean all this, Mother. That's my house and my business."

"No, you've been living in our family beach home at Folly Beach that your father and I built, rent free I might add, and you've been managing our family's realty company, which we entrusted to you to handle with integrity and honor for the family. Regardless of what spin you've decided to put on things, Clarence, these are the facts."

"You'll be sorry for this." He started toward Annabel with an angry face, but Justine and Benson both jumped to their feet and got in his path.

"That's enough, Clarence," Benson said. "You need to go now and think about what Mother has said and decide what you want to do."

Clarence looked around at them, glaring. "You're all wrong about me, and you'll all be sorry," he said, and then he turned and stalked out of the room.

Gresham Hillard looked after Clarence with sadness. "I'm sorry he had no regret and that this didn't go better, Annabel. We will talk again later, but I think all of us should go now. I'm sure this has been a strain for you." Nodding at all, he gathered up his papers to leave.

Florence and Robert stood also to leave, going to hug Annabel before they did, offering her murmured words.

Reid followed suit, getting up to leave, too. "I'm so sorry, Mrs. Pennyman," he said quietly, patting her arm. "I know you need to rest now, but Benson will stay on with you."

As Reid left, he glanced back to see Annabel's composure break, the tears beginning to stream down her face.

Benson got down on his knees to lay his head in her lap, both of them weeping.

CHAPTER 15

Celeste's straight flight to Nashville on Wednesday left before seven and arrived in the city by nine. Her agent Gary met her at the airport, and they drove directly to the recording studio. There Celeste soon enjoyed a happy reunion with all the people she usually worked with on any album that Capital created for her—her producer Jack Gorman, her incredible pianist Richard Byerly, her regular sound people Otis Stevens and Darrell Logan. The others in the room included an assortment of technicians she knew well, like Fred Allen, Joe Burns, and Don Fowlkes, plus the guys in her band, Jason Stevens, who played guitar, Levi Hannigan, drums, Morie Allen, bass, and others brought in for this session.

It was a happy, easy-going group and all were warm and solicitous of her, knowing all she'd been through.

"Girl, you sure have been through it, but you are looking fine now. How are you doing?" her producer asked, wrapping her in a hearty hug.

"I'm good, Jack, and better seeing you again." She hugged him back and kissed him on the cheek.

Otis, her favorite sound engineer said, "Baby, we were all shocked to learn of that bad side of Dillon Barlow. I still remember when he came here with you and Nolan in past to record a song with you—gifted man, good voice, charming. He sure did hide a dark side, didn't he?"

"He did, Otis, but here we are, all moving on again." She glanced around. "Sorry to have thrown everyone off schedule, but I'm glad we could work this time in now." She grinned. "What do you think about the new numbers for *The Come Back* album?"

Excitement and comments buzzed around the room then as everyone discussed the pre-production plans, or blueprint, worked out for the songs. They shared ideas about which songs to work on today and in what order, which ones they planned to record with live music and which they'd fill in with more instruments later.

As a solo artist, who wrote her own songs at the piano, most all Celeste's songs were recorded with live piano. It had been a gift connecting with pianist Richard Byerly years ago, a gloriously talented man and so connected to her music and style.

She walked over to where he sat at the piano, already warming up. "What do you think of the new songs, Richard?"

A quiet guy, he answered, "They about broke my heart, and I could feel you releasing all that pain you've been through."

Jack joined them. "Yet her optimism for the future, her hope for better times, showed through, plus that longing for a sweeter love," he added. "Honey, if you throw your heart into these songs today, like on the tapes we've worked with, that you already sent us, we're going to have ourselves a sweet little winner."

They began to talk through plans for the first song to record then.

"Everyone agrees with you and Gary that the lead song should be 'I'll Sing Again.' The public wondered if you'd come back," Jack said, "if you'd perform again, so it's the perfect lead."

They talked about the song then, the lyrics, timing, the beat, and ideas the crew had to enhance the production.

After a time, Darrell asked, "You ready to sing a little, Celeste, as a warm-up and trial so we can get all the sound set?"

"Sure." She went to get a bottle of water to sit on the table by her microphone while Darrell, Otis, and the other sound men settled into their spots in the control room.

When recording, Celeste alternately stood at the mike or sat on a padded stool in front of the microphone, with the crew adjusting the sound equipment before any take. For more lively numbers she liked to stand, with room to be expressive with her hands if she wanted, to lean in or out, but for quieter, softer songs, she liked to sit.

Today, she wore comfortable, well-worn, cotton clothes and soft soled shoes, her hair tied back in a ponytail behind her neck. No one dressed up for recording sessions. When recording, all performers and crew also avoided wearing any clothes, accessories, or shoes that might make any distracting noises during takes. A recording session was a work setting, often lasting all day, sometimes grueling, but rich with the joy and creativity of capturing sound and preserving it for others to love and enjoy.

A big Steinway grand piano sat in the main room for Richard, and this recording studio had several versatile aspects—side orchestra rooms, wall panels that could be adjusted as needed, two isolation booths, the control room, and a lounge area. It was a familiar set-up Celeste was used to, and she loved the camaraderie, excitement, and love for good music her crew always displayed.

Jack and a few other staff scurried around her now, checking and adjusting equipment, getting everything ready for a first take.

"You need anything, baby?" Jack asked her. "You ready?" He pointed to a stand in front of her. "The words for your songs are here right in front of you if you need them. You usually never do, but it's a good back-up."

"I'm fine Jack."

He nodded. There was always that little hum of excitement as everyone settled into a session, all knowing they were a part of creating something special and memorable. Celeste knew her part in this day was to give everyone her absolute best and to bring something special to her songs to touch hearts and minds, and to leave awe and sweetness in their wake. She knew she was blessed with a good voice and blessed to have a great producer who always put her at her ease and helped to get the best performances out of her for every song.

As Celeste started to put her headphones on, Richard looked over and said quietly, "You have a voice that could make angels weep, Celeste. Just pour your soul into this session and these songs. That time of grief and sorrow is past."

A little later, they started the first take of Celeste's new lead song "I'll Sing Again" … and she closed her eyes and began to sing: "I watched a bird once in the snow… huff its feathers in the cold. It made its way through that hard day… but it's song it put on hold."

She moved into the chorus: "When life is hard, when life is sad; when you've lost your joy, and your song's on hold; Be like that bird I saw that day, and know you'll sing another day."

She saw Otis smile and give her a thumb's up.

Smiling back, she continued into the next verse and chorus again, "Hold on to life when things are hard; don't let the downers leave you scarred. Don't hold the bitterness in your heart. Love yourself, pull out those darts." She paused and sang the chorus again.

As she moved into the next verse Celeste knew she was singing her life. "I've known the winter dark and drear; I've known pain, life's hurts and fears; but I've always seen spring comes again, and I ain't gonna' miss it because of him…. When life is hard, when life is sad; when you've lost your joy and your song's on hold; Be like that bird I saw that day, and know you'll sing another day."

With Jack holding his heart and Darrell blowing her a kiss, Celeste finished. "Life will show you its smiles and frowns; take you through those ups and downs. But deep within is the courage you need, to push on through—just look at me." She closed her eyes and sang the chorus again, listening to Richard close out the music on the piano.

"Honey, that was sweet. You did that fine," Jack encouraged. "You know we'll do a few more takes, but that one's going to be a heartbreaker song. Especially with everyone knowing all you've endured. They'll be choking up like Otis back there."

Otis laughed. "I don't think I'll be asking you to put more emotion in that number. But I'd like to play with the timing at the end on that last verse before you sing the chorus a final time." He played back the section adding in a little spacing. "Listen and see how this sounds."

The morning went on, doing several takes of each song on the album, sometimes listening back, deciding on the best one, but most times Jack, and all of them, sensed the best take. No recording session was ever exactly the same, but Celeste's went smoother than many artist's sessions because of her preparation, her gift, and because the songs were her own. Who knew them better?

Before their lunch break, Jack said, "Honey, you are a joy to work with—gracious with that glorious voice and your discipline. You always take it to the next level every time."

They finished most of the songs for the album that day, and then spent some time listening through and editing them—fine tuning them, and talking about the work they'd do tomorrow before they finished the new album.

Celeste's agent, Gary, sat through part of the session, then left and returned. A couple of members from her management team stopped by at the end of the day, too, talking, everyone joking around and relaxing, letting down after a day of hard work.

As Celeste left with Gary, he said, "We had a little altercation outside with Dillon Barlow, trying to get past the guards at the door, acting like he was supposed to be here to see someone. Barron Dodd, the guard down at the front, said Dillon acted all smooth and charming at first, but then got a little nasty and had to be threatened to leave the building."

Celeste glanced around, uncomfortable as they made their way toward the lobby. "Do you think he's still around?"

"No. He was reminded of his restraining order to stay away from you and a couple of policemen popped by to be sure he moved on." Gary paused. "It didn't take the press long to learn you were coming into town for a recording session. We tried to keep it quiet, Celeste, but it's the kind of news that invariably gets out."

Celeste felt herself tense, feeling uneasy.

Gary smiled at her. "Don't get worried. A guard is riding the elevator down to the garage with us, staying until we leave safely." He smiled and spoke to the man as they got to the lobby, before they all walked on to the elevator.

At Gary's car, he picked up the conversation with Celeste again. "Henry will be on duty in the hall at your condo all night with extra security outside. Also, I'm staying at your place tonight."

"What? Is that necessary?"

"Yes. We thought about sending Carmen Yost to stay with you. She travels with you on tour; it would have kept you from being alone. But I'm tougher than Carmen. I'm a better choice, Celeste, and I feel responsible in this to be sure all goes well and that you stay safe."

He grinned as they settled into his car. "Besides I promised Reid Beckett I'd watch after you."

She couldn't help giggling. "And when did this happen?"

"We had a little talk when I was in Charleston, and we had another little talk this morning. I think the man is fond of you. Are you all right about that?"

"He's a good man," she said, not adding more.

"Well, he suggested flying over here to stay with you himself, but I explained to him that the press would have an absolute field day with that."

She couldn't help laughing. "He's still learning how all this works."

Gary changed the subject as he backed the car out of the garage. "I think the recording session went well today though, don't you? There won't be much to do tomorrow to finish up. A few of the bigwigs want to stop by the recording studio to talk with you. They suggested a big dinner out tomorrow night, but I wanted to keep you out of the public eye and out of public places."

"Thanks, Gary. I do think that's best."

As they headed down the highway toward Celeste's condominium in Belle Meade, he added, "I'll call and get dinner delivered for us tonight. Be thinking about what you want."

It felt good a little later to take a hot shower after the long recording day. She knew Gary had ordered dinner and she could hear a medley of country music songs that Gary had found, coming from the main part of the condo.

Celeste found an old pair of jeans in her drawer and pulled a sweatshirt over it. She'd left clothes here for times when she knew she'd need to visit.

She came out to the kitchen to find Gary putting dinner on the table across from the kitchen's island.

"Dinner came. I hope you're hungry."

"I am," she said, joining him. "You know I never eat much when I'm recording."

"Yeah, it can affect your voice." He pushed a salad across to her that he'd transferred to a bowl and a plate with grilled salmon on it. "I helped myself to your dishes in the cabinet. I hate eating out of foam dinnerware."

She watched him dump spaghetti onto a plate for himself along with salad and bread.

"Who did you order from?"

"A little Italian restaurant in the Green Hills Mall not far from here. They do Door Dash Delivery so I didn't need to leave to go pick it up." He glanced at her. "You did say salmon and a salad. Will this be all right?"

She smiled. "It will be fine, Gary."

"I got a bottle or two of beer for myself. I hope you don't mind. I know you don't drink much. I don't think Nolan did, either."

"No. He liked a glass of wine now and then, but that's about it."

They ate for a few minutes, listening to the music Gary had put on in the background. "I used to come here a lot to visit with you and Nolan. He sure was a good man."

"That he was."

They were quiet for a time, and then Celeste asked. "Why have you never married, Gary?"

He shrugged. "It's a crazy life agents live, always traveling, always working." He paused. "I've never really met anyone I wanted to stay with long term either. What you and Nolan had was special. I'm sorry you got hooked up with Dillon after he died. I knew you were grieving and lonely. I watched Dillon zero in on you, knew he saw the advantages of hooking up with you. I should have investigated him, tried to slow you down in getting so involved with him so soon."

"It's hardly your fault, Gary."

He shook his head. "No, it is in part. I always promised Nolan I'd look after you if anything happened to him. He knew he was older than you, and he knew the business and how self-serving people can be. How manipulative and phony, often only looking for a way up the ladder. He would have seen through Dillon right off."

"He probably would have." She finished off her salad. "Do you think Dillon is going to cause more trouble?"

"Celeste, no one knows what's going on with Dillon right now. He isn't acting sensibly in anything. Even his agency is ticked off at him." Gary drummed his fingers on the table.

"I need to give you this," he said after a moment. "It's a letter for you that Dillon left with the guard, when he realized he wasn't going to charm his way into the recording studio. I admit I read it. I was going to put it with all the other stuff he's sent and maybe mention it to you later before you left to go back to South Carolina. But I didn't feel right doing that." He pulled the envelope out of his pocket.

She eyed it like she might a snake. "Why don't you just tell me what it says, Gary."

"It was a request asking you to do a song with him. He had a name for it, 'Forever Friends'—said you'd know it."

She shook her head. "I should. I wrote it."

Gary opened the letter. "Dillon wrote that he'd like you to record this song with him so people would know all was well between the two of you now. He said it would help both your careers, dispel the negative publicity. He said it would be like an olive branch between the two of you, showing people that everything was all right, that neither of you were upset with each other anymore."

"Gary, he's not doing this for us, as he says. He's doing this for him. It would help his career, his image, not mine." She crossed her arms. "I hope you're not suggesting I do this? Because the answer is no. I want no proximity with Dillon Barlow now or in the future.

Can you see any advantage in this?"

"The publicity would be off the wall." He grinned at her. "But it's obvious he's hoping to dispel some of the negative press he's had. And considering all that's happened, no, I agree that you should stay out of the man's orbit as Reid Beckett said."

Her mouth fell open in shock. "You talked to Reid about this?"

"No, no." He waved a hand. "Do you think I'm crazy? The man would have been on the first plane here if he knew Dillon had been causing trouble around you. It was just an expression he used."

She rubbed her arm. "Well, you put that letter with all the other junk of Dillon's you filed away. I have no intention of answering it. Ever."

Gary carried their plates back to the kitchen. "You gotta admit Dillon's a smart guy. He knows you're going to get a big hit of interest and publicity with this new album, *The Come Back*, and that all the favor is in your court right now, so he's trying to muscle in on it."

"If you're finally realizing that everything Dillon does is about Dillon then you're finally figuring him out, Gary."

He nodded. "Yeah, and his last words were: You need to do this one thing for me to make up for all the trouble you caused me."

She snorted. "Sounds like him."

Celeste helped Gary clean up from dinner, and then they went to get comfortable in the big living room of her Nashville condo. It was posh and sleekly decorated, but Celeste found, in many ways, she liked her cozy and comfortable apartment above CeeCee's better now. Life had a way of changing how you looked at things.

She went to the piano to begin playing a couple of the songs they'd be recording tomorrow.

"Is that one of the songs you're doing tomorrow?" Gary asked.

"Yes, we're doing this one, titled 'That Little Girl Is Gone,' plus three others, 'Heartache Goodbyes,' 'The Face in My Dreams,' and a song called 'I'll Leave On the Light.'"

"Sing me a little of the one you've been playing."

"Okay ... I'll do a verse and chorus ... and then a couple more of the verses to give you the idea." She played a few bars on the piano, leading in and then sang, "I've seen too much, I've known too much, while traveling down life's road. I sometimes miss the innocence, of days of long ago." She paused.

"And here's the chorus, Gary, 'That little girl of long ago, Playing jump rope on the lawn, Life took her innocence and dreams, That little girl is gone.'"

"Ahhh, that's sweet," he interrupted. "Everyone can remember how life stole their innocence and idealism little by little. Sing the other verses."

Her fingers drifted over the keyboard. "I want her back, that little girl, Chasing seagulls by the sea, Giggling with her happy smiles, Running, laughing, happy, free." She played the chorus again before moving to the next verse. "It's hard the pain betrayal can bring, The lies that love can tell, How can you learn to trust again, When someone shows you hell?"

"Dang, is there anything happy in there?"

"Yes, it's here at the end, listen. 'When you look across the room at me, With eyes so warm and kind, I want to believe in love again, To give it one more try' ... 'That little girl of long ago, is hopeful, meeting you, You resurrect my dreams and hopes, That love might still be true.'"

"Ah, that's good, Celeste." He put a hand to his heart. "It will touch people. They'll relate to it. You sure have a gift."

She turned on the piano stool. "I want to believe in love again, Gary. I don't want to get jaded and hard and broken. This industry can do that to people if they're not careful." She smiled at him. "Nolan used to say to you, 'Keep looking for that special girl, Gary. She's out there somewhere'. Like in my song 'The Face in My Dreams' keep that hope for love alive, Gary."

She turned back to the piano again to sing him a few lines. "A million times I've seen it, Just how that day will be, When I discover you at last, And you discover me."

Celeste got up to head to bed then. "Keep looking for her, Gary. She's out there looking for you, too."

"Ah, you're a hopeless romantic, Celeste Deveaux."
"Maybe." She grinned. "Good night. I'll see you tomorrow."

CHAPTER 16

Reid had hoped to talk Vanessa into letting him pick up Celeste at the airport on Friday morning, but, of course, he went to the meeting at Annabel Pennyman's instead with Benson. Afterward, he had a pile of work appointments, several postponed from earlier that morning, and a house closing, all making for a busy Friday. Celeste texted him she planned to check in at the store and then crash and rest after her busy days in Nashville, so it wasn't until later that evening, when he came to pick her up to go to Thurman's for dinner, that he got to see her again.

He parked his car behind Beckett's and started across the parking lot to the back door of CeeCee's Place and then stopped as he heard her call out, "Well, if it isn't Romeo and right on time."

Reid glanced up to see her on the balcony highlighted by the light overhead. He always forgot how beautiful she was until she sucked the breath out of him like this. She wore a stunning, satiny, silky dress in a deep aqua blue that swished around, revealing her long legs through a deep slit in the dress's side.

Celeste stood there for a moment, looking down at him from the porch's rail. Despite himself, his eyes couldn't help moving to a tantalizing vee at the top of her dress, where the silky fabric wrapped snuggly around her breasts.

She smiled at him and put a hand to her heart. *"What man art thou who bescreened in night, so stumblest on my counsel?"*

He grinned back at her, knowing she'd been studying lines from the play Romeo and Juliet. *"Ah, it is my lady,"* he replied. *"It is my love. ... O, that I were a glove upon that hand, that I might touch that cheek."*

She blew him a kiss. "You are the most romantic thing. Come up here and kiss more than my cheek. I've missed you."

It didn't take him long to get to her door and take her up on that opportunity. "I've missed you, too, beautiful woman."

She stepped back after a minute, straightening her hair and dress. "Don't kiss me anymore now or we'll look too rumpled to our friends."

Reid straightened his shirt as she studied him.

"You look good yourself," she said, her eyes moving over him. "Gray is an excellent color for winters. You do know you're a winter, don't you, with that very dark hair and that black shirt you've paired with your suit, and the little handkerchief to match in your jacket pocket? It gives you an exceptionally suave look."

"I'm fortunate I dressed to please you." He leaned closer to her, his voice softening. "I do want to please you, Celeste."

"You tempter, let's go to dinner now." She smoothed a hand through his hair. "Vanessa said Marcus can hardly wait to hear how the recording session went."

"How did it go?"

"It went well, but let me wait to share until we join our friends."

Reid had made a reservation for five, to eat early tonight, knowing Marcus would need to play from six to ten.

"You don't mind an early dinner for Marcus's sake, do you?" he asked as they walked to his car.

"No, I skipped lunch, tired after getting back, and then I took a long nap." She climbed into the car as he held the door for her.

"Everything was fine at the store though," she said. "Imogene and Vanessa run everything sweetly. Both are wonderful and they even encouraged me to rest when I got back. I am blessed to have them."

He smiled at her as he backed his car out of the parking lot. "You must have found a little free time this afternoon to look up lines from Romeo and Juliet."

She gave him a saucy look. "I can hardly let you get ahead of me and keep all the advantages in your court."

They laughed and talked about casual things on the drive to the restaurant. Inside they found Vanessa and Marcus already at their usual table. Hugs and greetings ensued, and then they settled down to study the menus and order.

"You look better after your rest," Vanessa said. "Honestly, Imogene and I both thought you looked really worn out earlier."

"I was tired. Recording sessions take a lot out of you."

Marcus leaned forward. "How did that go? Tell me about it."

She did, adding details and stories she knew Marcus would enjoy learning about. The waiter brought their dinner then and they all stopped to eat a little before talking more.

"I agree that song 'I'll Sing Again' is perfect for a lead song," Marcus said. "When will it be out as a single?"

Celeste gave him the projected date they'd given her for the release of the single and for the album next month.

"Are they getting a tour set up already?" Vanessa asked.

"Gary and others at Capital are working on it," she answered. "As I told Reid earlier, I'll probably have ten or twelve performances, starting in the southeast, heading north and then west to eventually work back to Nashville to end the tour before returning home."

"Will you have any shows near here?" Marcus asked.

She smiled at him. "Actually, I learned before I left yesterday that Gary has scheduled my first performance of the tour right here in Charleston. They thought it would make good publicity since the media has already written about me buying a shop here."

Vanessa clapped her hands. 'What awesome news! I'm so excited. Where will it be held?"

"At the Gaillard Center on Calhoun Street," she answered.

"Oh, my gosh." Marcus's mouth flew open. "That place is incredible. It's that big old performing arts center in a huge pillared building. You should see it inside. It's gigantic with big balconies all around, a blue-domed ceiling, and a huge stage. They have world class performances there with global stars and everything."

Reid laughed. "You forget Celeste is a big-name star, Marcus."

"Well, yeah, but the Gaillard. Wow. It can seat nearly two-thousand people. I mean, it's stunning. An amazing place. I went there once to see the symphony perform."

Celeste grinned at him. "Well, you'll be going again. Gary's giving you free tickets for helping me—one for you and one for a date. I also get a number of them for myself to share with friends and family." She gave Reid a teasing look. "Gary said he looked forward to seeing you again there, too, and he said to tell you to offer him any suggestions you might have for good security at the Gaillard."

Refusing to be baited, Reid said, "I'll give some thought to that. Make a few calls."

After more talk about the show and the tour, the conversation shifted to other topics. Reid noticed Celeste often did that, moving talk away from her, to ask questions of others to get them to share about their lives. She artfully got Marcus to tell her about his family's business, suggesting Gary might want to get them to help with programs and signage, and she encouraged Vanessa to tell about a funny incident that happened at the shop when a lady got stuck in a snug shirt in the dressing room and couldn't get the shirt off.

Vanessa laughed. "One of the things CeeCee's Place is popular for is carrying clothing in some larger sizes. Many of the trendy upper-end shops in downtown Charleston don't carry any clothes beyond a medium size. That's hardly realistic with more women wearing large and extra-large sizes today than smaller ones. I read that the average American woman today, twenty years old and up, weights 168 to 170 pounds and most wear a size 16 or 18, not a 4 or a 6."

Their waiter stopped by to pour them more iced tea, before she continued. "A size 12 was the largest size Headricks used to carry in their store. I think fashion designers and retailers seem to be ignoring the facts about women shoppers. No matter what size women are they all need clothes and they all want to look nice. At CeeCee's, we have pretty dresses, tops, and clothing items for women in a wider variety of sizes. A lady today said she comes to our store every time she is in Charleston for that reason."

Celeste nodded. "CeeCee's isn't a clothing-only store, by any means, but I do like that the store carries casual clothes in a variety of sizes."

Marcus laughed. "Well, you know my mama is a good-sized woman, and she loves to come to CeeCee's to find cute sundresses, tops, and sweaters plus gifts and knick-knacks for the house."

Glancing at his watch, Marcus added, "I'd better go get to work and play." He looked at Celeste. "Will you sing a number or two later?"

"Maybe at about seven before Reid and I leave." She turned to Vanessa. "Are you going to stay until ten or do you want us to drive you back to your apartment when we leave?"

She smiled. "I'd appreciate a ride. I'm opening in the morning and probably shouldn't stay out late tonight."

Marcus paused behind Vanessa to lean over and kiss her cheek. "Don't forget we're having a cookout at my mom and dad's tomorrow night. My brother and his wife and their two kids are coming. They're all excited about meeting you."

"I haven't forgotten." She looked toward the piano. "You'd better go play."

After Marcus settled in at the piano, moving into his first song, Celeste gave Vanessa a teasing look. "Umm. Umm. If you're invited to meet all the family, things must be getting serious."

Vanessa swatted at her. "It's only a cookout."

"If you say so." Celeste giggled. "But promise you'll tell me about it on Sunday."

They ate dessert, drank coffee, and visited more over the next hour, Vanessa asking Reid about his work, background, and family. He found Vanessa easy and comfortable to be with and he liked her. Knowing Marcus as he did, Reid knew Celeste was right that taking Vanessa to meet his family was a sign Marcus was getting serious about her. He couldn't remember Marcus ever taking a girl to meet his parents before.

Back at Celeste's apartment, after dropping Vanessa off, Reid made himself comfortable on Celeste's big sofa, propping his feet on an ottoman. "Are you glad to get back?" he asked her, as she joined him, pulling off her dressy sandals to tuck her feet up on the sofa.

"I am."

"What's your place like in Nashville?"

"It's a posh, beautifully decorated place in a gated condominium complex in the Belle Meade area of Nashville. Nolan bought it when we got married—paid to have it furnished and decorated. We added our own touches. It's elegant compared to this apartment but comfortable, too. I was always happy there with Nolan. It was close to everything. Convenient and safe."

She gave him a mischievous look. "Gary told me you were thinking about coming over to check it out."

"I was only concerned about you." He frowned.

She put a hand on his leg. "It was a sweet thought, Reid, but I know Gary told you the tabloids would have had a field day with that if they knew I'd entertained any company other than my people from Capital or the agency. Reporters hang out and watch for stuff like that."

Celeste sighed. "Gary tried to keep it quiet that I was coming to record at all, but that got out, too."

"Did it create a problem?"

She hesitated, and he could tell she was deciding what to tell him.

"I had a small problem with Dillon," she said at last.

He sat forward, tensing. "Did he try to hurt you?"

"No, but he tried to schmooze his way into the recording studio with lies about an appointment. The security men in the building's lobby aren't stupid though. They're used to dealing with all sorts of fans and reporters trying to get in to meet or interview the artists recording there. They'd been alerted to watch for Dillon, too, and not to allow him any access into the building or anywhere near me."

"What happened?"

"Nothing at the time since I was working, but Gary said Dillon got nasty and belligerent and they had to call in the police to be sure he left the area." She got up to get them both a bottle of water from the refrigerator and then sat back down.

"Was that it?" he asked.

"Yes, but Dillon had a specific motive in wanting to see me, not to beat me up this time, but to try to get me to do a recording number with him."

"You've got to be kidding? How did you learn about that?"

"He left a letter for me at the desk, and they gave it to Gary. After we got to my apartment, Gary told me about it, and he read some of it to me." She picked up a cushion to hug it to herself. "Dillon claimed that us recording a song together would calm all the negative press swirling around, that it would show the media, and everyone else, that we'd made up, were getting along, were friends again."

She laughed. "The song he suggested we do is called 'Forever Friends' and I wrote it. Dillon must have found it in some of my stuff at the house and kept it. There are suggestive lines in the song that the singers might want to be more than friends."

"What did Gary say about this?" The very idea of it annoyed him.

"Not much at first, but I made it clear to Gary I had no intention of doing that song, or any song, with Dillon. I also told him the only person to benefit from this idea would be Dillon. As Gary said, Dillon knows I'm doing *The Come Back* album now, that I have new songs coming out. He also knows the public's heart is somewhat sweet toward me because of what I've been through. As self-serving as Dillon is, he hardly wants to see any success coming my way unless he can get in on it somehow. He actually suggested that I owed him this opportunity because of all the trouble I'd caused him."

Reid almost spit out the water he'd just drunk. "What?" He shook his head, stunned. "Is that man crazy?"

"Dillon is certainly mentally unhealthy."

Reid reached over to take her hand. "I'm sorry, Celeste. I'm sorry he's still causing problems for you. Sorry he's such a sick person." He scooted closer to kiss her. "But I'm glad you're living here now, out of his orbit, where he can't get to you easily. Do you think he'll be angry when you don't respond, knowing you won't go along with his plan?"

"I'm sure he will."

"What's the answer?"

"Time and staying away from him. Not letting him manipulate me. Not letting him back into my life in any way."

"You wouldn't want that, would you?"

"No. Dillon's a frightening, unstable, and unpredictable man. The worst life mistake I ever made was getting involved with him." She heaved a sigh. "Gary and I had a good talk about that. He regrets he didn't do more to check out Dillon's past, to slow me down in getting involved. But as one of my sound engineers at the recording session said, Dillon seemed like a nice, charismatic, likeable, and talented man. No one saw that other side of him."

"Now, though, a lot of people do know that other side of him. How will that change things for him?"

She shrugged. "He'll find a way to charm himself back into favor in time, I guess. He's good at manipulation. And he's good-looking, talented, a famous star with a great singing voice. He may turn all this around eventually if he'll quit acting stupid like he's doing now."

"It doesn't seem right somehow that everything might turn around in his favor again."

"It's the way of the world, Reid, especially with the rich and famous. Think about all the entertainment stars, sports and political stars, who have done really awful, criminal things and then later schmoozed, bribed, and lied their way back into public favor again. I've seen it in the industry a lot in the years since I've been working as a singer."

Reid thought about her words. "I guess I've seen it in those arenas and in business myself. But it doesn't make it right."

"No. But there's nothing more I can do."

She glanced at the clock. "It's getting late. I think I should get some sleep so I can help in the store with Vanessa tomorrow. Imogene is off and Saturdays are often busy."

He leaned toward her, running his hands gently down her arms. "You're becoming a vital and needed part of my life, Celeste Deveaux. I want you to know that."

She gave him a soft smile. "I'm glad we reconnected, Reid. At first I wasn't, so fearful, so purposed to avoid any kind of relationship with any man again. But you've shown me not all men are cruel and self-serving, that many are good, decent, and kind."

He wasn't sure he really liked her words. "A real nice guy, huh?"

She giggled. "Mixed with being smart, wise, handsome, thoughtful, and very sexy, it isn't a bad package."

"Well, those are better words." He moved in to kiss her and they were soon moving on to more, reveling in the feelings rolling between them.

"You need to go now," she whispered after a time.

He pulled her closer for one more kiss, breathing in the jasmine scent of her, running his hands one more time over the silky fabric of her dress and the warmth of her skin.

His voice still husky, he murmured, "We're going to need to talk about our future seriously at some time, Celeste."

"You think?" She gave him a teasing look.

He grinned at her. "And I need to take you to meet all my family."

She laughed. "I'd like that, getting to know your family, but it isn't the time to talk about a future as long as these problems with Dillon are so raw and problematic. Besides, I've only been separated from Dillon since last spring and divorced since June." She paused. "I was too impulsive moving into a serious relationship after Nolan died. I want, and really need, to take my time this time. I hope you can understand that."

He stroked a hand down her cheek. "I do understand, at least a part of me does. The other part of me, so sure of my own feelings, is fearful you'll run off and marry your manager or somebody else, like you did last time."

She laughed. "Well, I don't think that will happen."

"Good," he said, pulling her to her feet to kiss her one more time before he headed to the door.

However, Reid knew as he walked to his car that although Celeste feared commitment, he really did fear losing her again.

He quoted some words of Romeo's that floated into his mind, *"For stony limits cannot hold love out."*

Reid glanced back toward CeeCee's balcony, thinking of her standing there earlier. "I suppose I'll just have to keep chipping away at her reluctance and bide my time."

He thought of a scripture then, *Let patience have her perfect work.* "Well, I hope that one is true, Lord. Give me a little help, if You would, to show Celeste I'm a trustworthy man she can safely give her heart to. You know I'd never meaningfully hurt her and that I only want to love and protect her."

CHAPTER 17

Well rested, Celeste enjoyed being back at CeeCee's Place to work with Vanessa on Saturday morning. She wore a vee-necked casual khaki green dress today with buttons down the front and a wide ruffle at the hem. Her tan sandals matched the buttons and the tan shell necklace she wore around her neck.

Later in the morning, Reid called. "What are you doing today after your hours at the store?"

"It's my sister Burke's birthday and Mother is having a little party for her at dinner. I'm driving down for the party and to spend the night. But maybe we can get together when I get back tomorrow."

"I hope you have a good time. I know your family will want to hear about your trip to Nashville and the session." He hesitated. "I think I'll call my friend Benson Pennyman and see if he wants to come over and hang out with me tonight. He's had a rough week, and it might be good for him to have a break."

She giggled. "And you can get the story from him about what's happened with Clarence and tell me about it tomorrow when I get back. I'll bring you back a piece of Burke's birthday cake. Her favorite cake is carrot cake with cream cheese icing, so I'm sure that's what mother or Novaleigh will make for her."

"Sounds like a plan. Have a good time." He laughed. "If you weren't staying over, I'd suggest coming with you."

"You've already met my family and been to the island with me before, but I haven't met your family yet. You must not be as serious as Marcus." She knew she teased him but she hadn't met his family, except his parents through business.

"Hmmm. I'll have to work on that," he said, not letting her ruffle him.

She glanced toward the door where a lady was waving at her. "I have customers coming in now. I need to go, Reid. I might go to church with the family in the morning, too, but I'll be back in the afternoon."

"Maybe I can take you out to eat when you get back. If it's all right with you, we can go casual and have seafood at the Fleet Landing Restaurant on Concord Street near Waterfront Park. We can take a stroll at the park before or after dinner, stop by the Pineapple Fountain and walk out on the pier."

"I think I'd like that. I'll text you when I get back."

Later in the afternoon, when Loretta came to work, Celeste packed a tote bag with the clothes she'd need and headed out of the city toward Edisto. Although she'd enjoyed the recording session in Nashville and was getting excited about the tour to come, she carried an uncomfortable feeling about the incident with Dillon. She felt grateful she hadn't run into him in person, but she didn't like the push Dillon had initiated about recording with him. Oh, the letter sounded gracious in content, but Celeste knew it for the threat it was.

She'd timed her trip to the island to catch the four o'clock ferry to the lighthouse. Several guests staying at the inn were waiting at the Jenkins Landing to ride back, too. The only way to the lighthouse island, surrounded by water, was by boat—either a private craft or the ferry.

She was recognized by one of the men waiting at the landing, which created a rush of excitement and questions, especially when they learned her family owned and operated the Deveaux Inn and Lighthouse where they were staying.

When the ferry came, Celeste took a seat up front in the ferry with her brother-in-law Waylon Jenkins.

"Hey, sweet girl," he said, giving her a kiss on the cheek as he steered the ferry out into the creek to head for the open ocean.

"I'm glad you could come down for Burke's birthday."

Waylon and Burke had married earlier in the summer and had made a happy life together, living at Watch Island's old lodge near the marina dock. Waylon had always loved the lighthouse in past and had taken over many of the old tasks her father once carried, like doing the morning and afternoon ferry runs to and from the lighthouse.

"How's everyone at the island?" Celeste asked.

"Everyone's good, except for Gwen. She picked up strep throat from Chase so their family had to stay home tonight."

"Oh, I'm sorry. I remember how awful you feel with strep."

"Alex said the doctor put them on penicillin to knock it out quickly. They should be better soon."

She smiled at him. "Maybe I'll call and send Gwen some flowers."

"I know she'd like that. Burke and I can kick in on the cost. I imagine your mother and Lila would like to do so, also."

"That will let us send her a big arrangement. I'll call it in to a florist in Port Royal. There's a cute shop on Paris Avenue I know of."

They grew quiet then as they skimmed down the North Edisto River to the island. The serenity of the river, the sandy banks, and lush greenery along the way soothed her emotions. She smiled at some kayakers passing along the shore and enjoyed watching children playing on the beach near St. Christopher's Camp.

After arriving and greeting her mom, who she found working with Novaleigh in the kitchen making dinner, Celeste dumped her bags in her old bedroom in the family apartment, and decided to take a walk up the beach before dinner.

The Deveaux Lighthouse station, with its tall red and white striped lighthouse, its bed-and-breakfast inn created from what was once the old innkeeper's home, plus its multitude of outbuildings, cottages, docks, beaches, and winding trails, covered almost 500 acres on Watch Island. The lighthouse island was part of the larger Edisto Island, separated from the mainland by Hurricane Gracie in 1959. Celeste couldn't even remember a time when Watch Island had been connected to Edisto. She'd always boated in or out for anything—school, shopping, or church. It had simply been her life, and that of her family. Their unique, and somewhat isolated life gave her, Burke, Gwen, and Lila the nickname The Lighthouse Sisters.

Her childhood had been happy, but as she'd grown older, she'd known she wanted more for her life than this quiet, simple paced island. So did Gwen, who now lived in Port Royal below Beaufort. Her sister Burke, however, had always loved the island, and she and her husband, Waylon, and her mother, along with the Bouls and the Georges, ran the island's inn and lighthouse. Celeste's younger sister Lila helped, too, since she'd come back. Lila was a bit of a mystery, and Celeste went looking for her now as she left the inn.

She found Lila sitting on the porch of her cottage, sketching birds at the feeders that she'd hung in the trees nearby.

"Nice work." Celeste paused to look over her shoulder. "Do you want to take a break and walk up the beach with me before dinner?"

Lila glanced down at her bare feet. "Let me get my flip flops. I see you have yours on, and I love that one-piece romper you're wearing. Do you sell them at the store? If so, I want one. But in another color."

"I have an aqua blue one that would be perfect for you."

"Maybe I'll come to the city and pick it up next week." She found her flip flops and sat to slip them on. "Imogene called while you were gone to Nashville and she said they needed more of my note cards and a few more paintings for the store."

"You know I can take them back with me."

"Yes, but I haven't picked up the note cards yet. The business that prints them is near the Citadel Mall in Charleston. I won't be far from you when I go to get them."

They left Lila's cottage and followed the sandy path down to the beach. For a time, they simply walked along together, enjoying the blue skies and sunshine of the day, listening to the ocean waves, the gulls, and watching the sandpipers skuttle across the sand.

"I always get such a sense of peace here," Celeste said after a time. "Walks like this were always a soothing balm to my spirit after I came home from Nashville this spring."

"You've been back to Nashville again. How did that go?"

"The recording session went well. It was a comfort to see old friends, a joy to record again and to create. You know that feeling."

"I do, but creating takes away from you as well as giving to you." She looked at Celeste. "I sense you had some experiences, too."

"I did. An odd mix of memories, good and bad, and an unpleasant encounter with Dillon Barlow."

Lila stopped, turning to look at her face. "Did he hurt you?"

"Fortunately, I didn't see him in person. He came to the studio, lying about having an appointment and trying to get in. It didn't work and he got testy with the security guard who had to call the police."

"Is that all?"

"No," she answered, and she told Lila about the letter as they walked on.

"That man has so much evil and manipulation in him, and he has hurt so many people."

Celeste sighed. "How should I pray about him?"

Lila walked quietly for a few minutes thinking. "You can pray for God to touch and change him, a mercy prayer. But it is also right to pray God will deal with him if he has a hard, reprobate heart not open to change, and to pray God will fight for you and protect you."

When Celeste looked shocked at her last comment, Lila said, "I remember many times in the Bible when God's people were dealing with evil populations and people who would not show mercy or grace. Remember when the Israelites left Egypt, when they had finally gotten away from Pharoah, but then he sent soldiers after them?"

"Was that the Red Sea story?"

"Yes, but I'm remembering God told the people not to fear. He said He would fight for them. Sometimes God finds His own ways to remove problems in our paths. God knows when we need His help, when problems are great. We should always ask for His help and expect with confidence for Him to help and be on our side."

Celeste smiled at her. "Like the scripture that says 'if God is for us, who can be against us?'"

She nodded. "Yes. God is always for us and will step in to help and defend us when needed. I've always believed it's rather nice knowing God is on my side, along with all His legions of angels."

"I just read a scripture about that from the Psalms, 'For God shall give his angels charge over thee, to keep thee in all thy ways'... and it said the angels would bear us up so we wouldn't even dash our foot against a stone.' Isn't that a comfort?"

Lila put an arm around her waist. "Do you want me to stand in faith with you that God will watch out for you and keep you safe from Dillon? I've been praying, but I'll renew and strengthen those prayers now. He is a dark man, Celeste."

"He is, and thank you for understanding my concerns. I don't like to be negative, but someone like Dillon is so unpredictable. Gary told me that some people who work with Dillon's agency said he's drinking and doing drugs again. That can't help."

"No, it can't." Lila shook her head. "They only increase problems. It's a sorrow when people don't know that." She paused, turning. "We'd better start back. It's nearly time for dinner."

Celeste stopped to pick up a shell before following her. "Did Novaleigh or Mother make the cake Burke loves?"

"Yes, a carrot cake. Mother made it, and Novaleigh cooked some of Burke's favorites for supper, that scalloped potatoes and ham casserole she likes, a succotash vegetable dish and a broccoli salad, plus cornbread sticks she makes in those old, black cast iron pans."

Celeste laughed. "It's a good thing we took a long walk. I may need to take another one after dinner!"

"At the Community where I lived, overindulgence in any area was somewhat frowned on," Lila replied. "I admit, I've needed to remind myself of those principles often with Novaleigh's heavy meals."

The birthday dinner for Burke was a happy occasion, even though she bemoaned over turning thirty.

"You're getting better not older," Waylon assured her.

She laughed. "You're only saying that because you're older than me." She gave him a soft look then. "Should we tell them our news?"

Waylon grinned in answer. "Burke and I are going to have a baby, due sometime in March."

Etta immediately got tears in her eyes. "Oh, I'm so happy to learn this. I'm going to have another grandchild, and this one will be living right here on the island where I can spoil him or her."

"No spoiling allowed." Waylon laughed. "But lots of loving and babysitting welcomed."

"That's wonderful news, Burke," Celeste said, going around to hug her sister.

Burke frowned. "You don't think thirty is too old to have a baby, do you, Mother?"

Etta patted her hand. "Well, I think it's a little late to ask me that now, but no I don't think so. And this is the perfect time for you and Waylon to have and love a child."

"Waylon, have you told your mother and father?" Celeste asked.

"No, but we plan to tomorrow. I'm sure they'll be excited, too."

Lila looked thoughtful. "Burke, you always loved our old nursery rhyme book. Maybe I can do some paintings of some of the nursery characters for the baby's room."

"Oh, that's a lovely idea, Lila."

Much of the rest of the dinner meeting revolved around talk of babies, making Celeste a little hungry to know that joy herself. Funny, until now she'd never thought she'd wanted to have children. She always thought it would interfere with her career, not be fair to a child.

She smiled to herself. Maybe all Reid's talk about marriage and babies had tucked a new idea into her thoughts.

After dinner, when Waylon, Burke, and Lila left, Celeste played piano and sang a few songs for the inn's guests in the big living room of the inn. Then she made her way out to the pavilion that looked out over the ocean near the lighthouse. Burke had always climbed up to the top of the lighthouse for privacy, but Celeste loved sitting in one of the old weathered Adirondack chairs in the pavilion.

Her mother came to find her after a time. She settled into a chair beside her. "I hope you don't mind a little company. I remembered this was one of your favorite places to come at night."

"It was always a good place to dream, looking out over the ocean and toward the lights of Seabrook across the river."

"You shared with us about your recording session and about the problem with Dillon before we celebrated Burke's birthday. I admit it troubles me knowing that man is still trying to keep a place in your life, still trying to control you. That is what this is all about with him, don't you think?"

"My therapist, Dr. Conrad, helped me to understand that narcissists, like Dillon, don't go after a weak woman to marry and form attachments with. It's a common misconception that they would, wanting someone weaker to manipulate. But he says all the research shows they prefer to connect with strong-willed, self-assured, talented individuals they admire. They feel stronger, in a sick way, if they can make a conquest of a strong woman and then tear her down."

She crossed her legs, getting more comfortable. "Dr. Conrad said they liked to stay friends with their exes, too, so they can continue to use them to get praise, attention, money, or to get help from them when they need it. He says narcissists always draw on others' strengths, but seldom give in return. They have so many unhealthy issues."

"That therapist has been a good help to you. I'm glad Dean knew him and recommended him to us." She shook her head. "Too bad he can't help Dillon, too."

Celeste rolled her eyes. "A person with a narcissistic personality disorder would never go willingly to see a therapist, Mother, because they can't ever admit there is anything wrong with them that needs change. They live in a fantasy world where they see themselves as superior and all their life problems as someone else's fault."

"Well, the more I learn about this man the happier I am that you've gotten free of him." She cleared her throat. "I worried that all this might make you fearful of ever becoming involved with any man again. In fact, you told me that any man even getting close to you made you anxious and uncomfortable."

Celeste, guessing her mother had something on her mind asked, "And? I can tell you have something else you want to ask or say."

She patted Celeste's arm. "I've never been good at subtlety. It's a disadvantage sometimes."

Celeste waited.

"I heard you've been seeing someone. I overheard Gwen saying something to Alex when she was here, and Novaleigh asked me if I knew the man well that you were seeing." She hesitated. "I assume it is the man who helped you buy Imogene's shop, Reid Beckett. He came down to the island with you once."

Celeste had never been comfortable sharing her private life readily, and she had learned to be even more circumspect and careful to keep her life to herself since becoming a well-known recording artist.

She tried to think how to answer her mother. "Perhaps you made the connection between Reid Beckett and his Uncle Thurman Beckett, who owns Thurman's restaurant where I used to sing as a girl. Reid and I met there many years ago. So the friendship we have renewed goes back to that time. Reid isn't someone new in my life, Mother, which is probably what makes me more comfortable with him."

"He seems like a nice young man, but it's very soon for you to be getting involved with anyone."

Celeste closed her eyes trying to decide how to answer. "I'm probably more aware of that than anyone else, Mother. Be assured I will take my time in getting to know anyone I might grow interested in either now or in the future. Impulsive decisions in relationships can bring unexpectedly disastrous problems."

A little annoyed, Celeste turned to look at her mother. "Surely you should know I will be exceptionally cautious in forming any kind of relationship after all I've walked through."

Her mother put a hand to her mouth, sensing Celeste was getting testy over this issue. "I probably shouldn't have said anything, but I'm glad to hear you say you're being careful," she added. "And I truly hope you don't have any more trouble from Dillon."

"Me, too, and don't hesitate to let me know if he ever calls here to bother you or anyone in the family or if he should ever come here, Mother. He is really dangerous, not just to me."

"I will, Celeste, and believe me when I tell you I'm proud of you and of all your hard work and success with your music. We all look forward to seeing you perform at the Gaillard in Charleston next month. Additionally, I love the shop you bought, and I am already very fond of Imogene Hathaway."

She hesitated and smiled at Celeste. "Actually, I'm very fond of Reid Beckett, too. He seems a strong, good man. Just take your time, honey. Be sure of your heart and be sure of Reid and who he is."

CHAPTER 18

Learning Celeste was going to her family's place for her sister's birthday and to spend the night, Reid gave his friend Benson a call.

"Hey. How are you doing, Ben? Can you get away to come over to my place for dinner tonight?"

"I'd like that. This last week has been rough."

"I know it has. That's why I thought a break might be nice for you." Reid hesitated. "If it's okay, I think I'll just order pizza and salad and pick up some colas."

"That sounds great., but let me call in the order to Giovanni's and pick it up on my way over. You've fed me often enough this week. It's my turn now. I'll get a couple of cannoli pastries, too. I haven't had one of those since I left Charleston."

"Sounds good."

"Hey, do you want me to bring my CD of *Rogue One*, the Star Wars movie, that came out last year?" Ben asked. "I spotted it in my room last night. We can watch it again to get ready for the new release of *The Last Jedi* coming out soon."

"Yeah, that would be great." He and Benson had always been big Star Wars fans since they were kids.

After his call, Reid ran a few Saturday errands, got a little yard work done outside, and then cleaned up before Ben arrived at six with their dinner.

"Glad I called the order in ahead," Ben said, heading in the back door. "I'd forgotten how busy the Pizzeria di Giovanni is on a Saturday night. It's so close to the college, you know. A lot of kids go there."

"We sure loved that place while in school." Reid took the pizza box from Ben, while Ben dumped his other bags on the counter.

"Yeah, those were good times." Ben grinned. "I look forward to seeing Marcus again soon, too."

"I would have invited him to join us tonight but he's taking his new girlfriend to a family dinner at his parents."

"Whoa!" Ben's eyes widened. "No kidding. He must be getting serious."

"It's looking that way." Reid got some plates out of the cabinet.

"Who's the girl? Do you know her?"

"I do. She's a nice girl from Edisto. Works downtown at CeeCee's Place on King Street."

Ben snagged a couple of glasses for their colas. "Isn't that the shop you were telling me Celeste Deveaux bought?"

"Yeah, it's the same place. The girl, Vanessa George, grew up at Edisto like Celeste did. They've been friends since childhood."

"Small world sometimes, isn't it?"

"It is." Reid carried two plates to the table, while Benson brought the pizza and side salads he'd picked up to the table. Then he went back to get their drinks while Reid snagged a handful of napkins and some silverware.

"I got one of those sausage and pepperoni pizzas with mushrooms, green peppers, onions, and black olives added." He opened the pizza box. "It looks great, doesn't it?"

They dug in and then spent some time eating, while a popular music station played in the background.

"I still can't believe Celeste Deveaux came back to South Carolina and bought a shop in Charleston." Ben winked at Reid. "I know that's given you another shot at her. How's that going?"

"Slow but sweet."

"At least it's going." Ben guzzled some cola before adding, "Guess what? Do you remember that girl I used to date in school, Grace Ravenel?"

"The redhead who always had her nose in a book?"

"Yeah, well I ran into her today, walking her dog at White Point Garden. I went there to take a break around lunch, ran into her walking a little Springer Spaniel."

"And?"

"And she's turned into a real good-looking woman. She's living back at home downtown like I am." He stopped to eat some more pizza. "Guess what she does for a living?"

"Works as a librarian?"

"Good guess, but she's an author. No kidding. She writes books—historical novels, each one set at an old historic home around the South Carolina Lowcountry. She goes around and visits the houses, collects research about them, interviews and talks to people about their history, and then weaves a story bringing in truth and fiction."

"Huh. Sounds like the two of you have a lot in common with your interest in historic places and old architecture." Reid grinned. "You planning to pursue her?"

Ben winked at Reid. "She did happen to mention that she walks her dog as a writing break every day at about noon before lunch. I think that sounds like a good time for me to take a walk every day."

Reid laughed out loud. "I'm glad to see something good turning up for you amid all of this family mess with Clarence."

Benson rubbed his neck. "It's been a tough time, especially for Mother."

"I was proud of how your mother handled all that yesterday." Reid paused. "She may just look like a gracious, little Southern belle but she's one tough woman. I came away from that meeting with a new admiration for her."

"Me, too," Benson admitted. "I often saw how Clarence schmoozed and manipulated Mother in past, especially after Dad got killed. You know how Clarence is, oozing charm and compliments, softening people up to get what he wants. Mother was hurting, missing Dad in that time. It vexed me how Clarence always seemed to use her and how she made excuses for him, not seeming to see what he was really like."

"Are you bitter?"

"No, only sad at all the hurt he's caused Mother, and angry that he's been so stupid with his life but is so unrepentant."

"What happened since yesterday morning? Your Mother gave Clarence some strong ultimatums then."

"According to Deanna Leeds, the girl Clarence had working part-time in the realty office," he answered, "Clarence freaked out yesterday afternoon when he found out the guys he'd been working with in the contracting business had loaded up, cleaned out their bank accounts and left town. Evidently, they hadn't bothered to touch base with him. Deanna said she always suspected something wasn't right with their company."

Benson stopped to drink some cola and eat the last of his pizza. "Additionally, someone in the police department came by to talk with Clarence yesterday right after he got back from seeing Mother, saying they were checking into the contractors' background and thought there might be some shady dealings going on. Deanna was in the office, listening in on everything, and they asked her questions, too. They apparently hadn't yet picked up on the fact that Clarence had his fingers in the same dirty dealings in his own way."

"How did you find out all of this?" Reid asked.

"Deanna Leeds called the Pennyman business number in Charleston late yesterday afternoon, and talked to Florence at the appraisal office. She said Clarence told her to call them to write her a paycheck. She also told Florence that Clarence said he was leaving town on business and didn't have time to do it." Ben shook his head. "Deanna evidently rattled on and on, upset, telling Florence that Clarence was in a frenzy, packing up stuff in boxes in the office. She said it made her nervous, and she wanted Florence to know if anything bad was going on she didn't have any part in it."

"All of that come down fast, didn't it?"

"It did, and it obviously motivated Clarence to move fast, too. He closed out his bank account yesterday afternoon, tried again to get monies out of the realty account Gresham Hillard and Mom had frozen. He also cleaned out his personal stuff from the family beach house and left town. Robert drove to the Folly Beach office and to the family house today to check everything out."

"Does anyone know where Clarence has gone?" Reid asked.

"No, and Mother doesn't want to know."

"Where do you think he'll go?"

Benson paused a minute to consider the question. "I honestly don't know, but if I had to make a guess, I'd say to the Dominican Republic."

Reid seemed surprise. "Why there?"

"Well, when we were younger Dad took us there for a vacation. Clarence was in high school then. A friend of Dad's owned a vacation house in Santo Domingo. Dad liked it down there. So did Clarence. They actually looked around at property, which Dad thought reasonable at the time, but he decided a place in the Caribbean too far from the U.S. to keep tabs on."

Benson reached for another piece of pizza. "Anyway, it is a beautiful place and a reasonable place to live. Sometimes when Clarence was being petty and small, and didn't get his way, he'd threaten to leave home. He'd say, 'Maybe I'll just move down to Santo Domingo.' The idea was supposed to wheedle Mom and Dad into giving in to him about something he wanted to buy or do, but the remembrance came to mind when you asked. Clarence is scared, and the Dominican Republic is outside of the United States, and it is a place he knows. Plus, Clarence likes the beach."

"Will you follow up and check on it?"

"No, I won't. Like Mother says, it's best we don't know. I didn't even suggest this idea to her, either, so don't mention it when you're visiting." He paused. "Besides, Clarence could have gone anywhere."

"I won't say anything. Did Clarence take a lot of money with him?"

"Oh, yes. He'd been funneling funds into his new account since Dad died. It was a significant amount. Unless he's stupid, he'll be okay. He could easily pay cash for a small house or condo, find a job of sorts and live rather well."

"On money he stole from your family."

Ben rubbed his arm. "Think of it this way. What if it had been your brother Charlie? Would you and your folks have been happier to see him take off with more family money than his due or go to prison?"

"I do see your point. And your mother did give Clarence the option to choose." Reid thought about it. "I'm not sure what Mom and Dad would do if it was one of us."

Benson shrugged. "I'm glad Mother made the decisions in this. I wouldn't have wanted to."

"Will your mother still want to downsize now?"

"She asked me to tell you that she plans to wait on that for a season. I told her I would stay at the house with her and Justine for now. The business on Broad is close enough for me to walk to, and I'm needed there right now."

"I think that's a good decision, Ben."

"Well, living with those two somewhat formidable women—Mom and Justine—both of them strong-willed and rather set in their ways—will present challenges for a guy used to being on his own. However, I'm going to move into the apartment above the garage and create a little privacy for myself later. That will help."

"How is your mother doing?"

"She's had some emotional times, but she confided in me that she and my dad always had worries about Clarence. They tried really hard to give him the support he needed, even with some of the cognitive problems he had. You may not remember but he always needed to get extra tutoring, had trouble with school. That's why Dad set up the realty business for Clarence to manage at Folly, to give him useful work they felt he could handle but to keep him out of the appraisal business." He laughed. "Florence threatened to quit if Clarence kept coming over there trying to throw his weight around."

"Who will handle the Folly Beach realty office now—or will you close it?"

"We've talked about that. It's not really my thing or my cousin

Robert's thing. You remember he's Aunt Florence's son."

Reid nodded.

"Anyway, Robert and I both like the appraisal business, want to work there, and are needed there. But we have an idea that seems like it might work. Robert's son, John, in his twenties now, has a business degree and has been working for a realty company in Mount Pleasant. We think John could do a good job managing the Folly Beach office. Robert and I will help him, as there are a lot of problems to straighten out, like rentals to get updated, but Mother likes the idea of giving him the job, too, and keeping the business in the family. He's a good young man and smart. And he seems excited about the plan."

Reid pushed his plate back. "Well, this has been a story, Ben, but I'm glad to hear things are working out." Curious he asked, "Will you keep the part-time girl who works at the Folly rental office?"

"No. Mother said if she'd been too stupid to see some of the issues going on at the office, and willing to lie about rentals in poor shape and cover up for Clarence in other matters, that she wasn't someone we wanted to keep on. Florence told her they were closing the office until new management could be found, and that they regretted they would need to let her go. Florence sent her paycheck to her, and we have temporarily closed the office until we can get some of the problems resolved to reopen it."

"What if Clarence comes back?"

"He would be very foolish to do that any time soon. Somehow, I don't think we'll hear from Clarence for a long time at least. Beyond that, who can say. Some things you deal with when you need to, Reid."

Benson got up to start helping them clean up from dinner.

"Are you ready to settle in to watch some Star Wars?" he asked. "I've been reading about the new film *The Last Jedi* that's releasing before Christmas and I checked out the trailer. I think it's going to be a good one, but I thought it would be fun to see *Rogue One* again to get in the mood for it."

Reid finished cleaning and putting food away while they talked.

"I saw *Rogue One* when it first came out," he said. "It goes back in time, almost like a new story, and the plot follows that group of rebels who band together to steal plans of the Death Star." He grinned. "It had a killer third act and a great climax, didn't it?"

"Yeah, the action was riveting, story solid, characters amazing. Some people call it one of the best Star Wars films ever, even when nearly all the good characters got killed before it ended."

The men got another cola from Reid's refrigerator and carried their dessert, a can of peanuts, and a bag of M&M's upstairs to Reid's den where they could settle in for a relaxing evening of watching a good film and enjoying each other's company.

The next day on Sunday, Reid went to church with his family and then home to relax until time for Celeste to come back.

She texted that she was home around five, and Reid suggested again that they drive to Joe Riley Waterfront Park to take a walk before going to dinner at the Fleet Landing Restaurant. After she agreed, he pulled on a pair of tan shorts, a maroon golf shirt, and tucked his feet into a comfortable pair of walking shoes before heading out the door. They'd both agreed to dress casually for time outdoors with temperatures in the seventies today,

A short time later, Reid enjoyed letting his eyes drift over Celeste when he picked her up. She wore a pretty navy top in some sort of soft fabric with skirt-like shorts to match. A long, thin necklace hung around her neck and she had tied her hair back with a scarf.

"You always look like a million dollars," he said to her. "And you must have a million pairs of shoes," he added, noticing her navy tennis shoes exactly matched her outfit, as usual.

She gave him a perky smile. "I do like shoes and I intend to marry a man with a large closet and a lot of shelves for shoes." She looked down to admire her shoes as they got in the car. "I do think shoes can so enhance an outfit."

Reid wisely decided to make no comment.

She chatted about her sister's birthday and her visit to Edisto while he drove to Concord Street to look for a parking space by the park. Street parking was free in Charleston on Sundays, and he luckily found a good spot not far from the restaurant.

They soon headed down the scenic walkway of the Joe Riley Park that stretched along the waterfront. A little breeze blew off the Cooper River, making the day especially pleasant. They strolled down the shaded path, stopping at the Pineapple Fountain, an elaborate, multi-teared water feature popular with tourists and locals. Celeste snapped photos at the fountain and along their way as they continued toward the southern end of the park.

"How long is this walkway trail?" she asked.

"It's a half-mile from end to end, a mile round trip—not hard for most people, especially with benches all along the way where you can stop and talk, and look out across the river."

"It's landscaped so beautifully," she answered, stopping to look at a bed of late flowers. "I always love to come here."

"The park has received several awards for its landscape design."

"Gwen and I brought the children here one day. They loved the children's park at the south end and the splash fountain they could run through to get wet."

"That fountain is at Concord Street near the Rainbow Row block of colorful houses."

She turned her sunny smile toward him. "Don't you love all the colored houses throughout the city? Charleston is such a unique place. I've always loved it here ever since I was a girl."

Reid noticed a few people glanced at Celeste every now and then, as if noting she looked familiar but no one approached her. She kept her focus on talking to him and enjoying the day.

It took only about fifteen minutes to walk to the end of the park, even with stops along the way. On their return, they paused to sit on a bench for a moment.

"My mother asked about you yesterday," Celeste said. "She's worried about me getting involved with anyone so soon."

"You see? It's not only my parents. However, after church today, I asked if I could bring you to meet everyone when we celebrate my granddad's birthday in early October."

She giggled. "I guess that worried them, that you want to bring me to meet the family."

"Maybe, but they seemed pleased at the idea. I hope you'll come. I'm not sure if we'll have the gathering at my parents' place on Legare or at my grandparents' at Seabrook."

"I'll try to come. Families are important. We both want our families to see we're comfortable together."

They strolled back up the pathway, passing the Pineapple Fountain again where children sat on the fountain's walls, splashing their feet in the water.

A little further along, near the big pier, Celeste noticed an odd pedestal foundation in the middle of a walled patio. "What is that?"

"It's Echo Rock." Reid led her closer to the rock structure in the courtyard's center. "There's a dry moat underneath this round pedestal. Climb up on top of it, stand in the middle, and say a few words or sing a few song lines and see what happens. The sound will echo back, after bouncing off the rock's surface."

"No kidding?" Captivated, she climbed on the pedestal to try it, said a few words which echoed back and then began to sing one of her well-known songs. A crowd soon gathered, recognizing her voice and enjoying the free show. Even one of the street performers, with a saxophone, came to add free musical accompaniment.

"Wasn't that fun?" she said after visiting with people and signing some autographs.

"Your sister Gwen was right that you're a ham—and a natural with people. It's so obvious you love what you do."

"I do." She tucked a hand in his arm. "Do we have time to walk out on the pier before dark and before our dinner reservation?"

"Sure," he answered. "It's only six. Our reservation is at six-thirty, and the sun won't set until after seven."

The long, 300-foot fishing pier reached far out into the river to Vendue Wharf and it was lined with open-air pavilions, picnic tables and benches.

As they reached the end of the pier, to lean on the rails looking out over the water at the boats passing by, Celeste asked, "Where do you keep your boat?"

"At the marina on the Ashley River, past Colonial Lake. If we celebrate Grandad's birthday lunch at their place at Seabrook, we can boat down—if it's a nice day."

"I'd like that." They walked back down the pier and then up Concord Street to the restaurant.

"You've been checking your watch." Celeste noticed.

"I made a six-thirty reservation and it looks like we'll be getting there on time and even a few minutes early."

She took his arm again. "That will give me time to pop into the ladies' room and freshen up."

The restaurant sat on the waterfront, across the street from the old Custom House, and a long pier led to the restaurant entrance.

"I made our reservation for a table by the windows, so we could look out over the water as twilight settles in."

"I like that idea." She hugged his arm against her. "This has been a nice afternoon, Reid. Sometimes my life gets so busy and full, I forgot simple pleasures, like the joy of simply walking through a pretty park."

He leaned over to give her a quick kiss on the cheek. "I used to dream of days like this with you in the past, but the reality is far better than any of my old dreams."

"Now, see, there's your romantic side again. I do so love that about you, Reid Beckett."

Seated a short time later, they studied the menu and then ordered. Reid chose flounder, fries and green beans, and Celeste wheedled the waiter into giving her grilled shrimp and a steamed vegetable medley.

"You're still being careful about what you eat," he commented.

"I have to," she answered. "Every pound shows on camera and on stage. I'm blessed to be naturally tall and slim, like my sisters, but weight is something all entertainers have to think about."

Once the waiter brought their iced tea, Celeste said, "Tell me about your visit with Benson now. I want to know everything that happened."

Reid filled her in on all the details Benson shared with him.

"I'd like to meet Annabel Pennyman," Celeste said as he finished. "What a strong woman she must be, and I understand some of the grief she must be feeling. You blame yourself when those you know and love head in a wrong direction, disappoint and shock you. It must be especially hard when it's your own child that you gave your heart and love to. Bless her heart."

"I'm sure she'd like to meet you, too, Celeste." He drank some of his tea. "Benson also wants to meet you. I thought one night soon we might get together with him and an old friend he met again recently, that we both went to school with."

She gave him a considering look. "I can tell from that little smirk of yours the old friend must be a girl."

"Yes, it is, a girl who was in our class, named Grace Ravenel—a bookish girl, a lot like Benson. I think it's nice they reconnected and that a little spark has kicked in. Ben's a good man; he deserves joy."

"Do you think we all deserve joy?" she asked.

"Absolutely, and I think we should hunger for it and seek for it. A Maya Angelou quote I love says: *We need joy as we need air; we need love as we need water.*"

"That's a lovely quote." Celeste smiled at him.

"Didn't the Lord say that He wanted our joy to be full?" Reid asked. "But like many things we have to choose joy every day and keep choosing it. We need to realize we are meant to have it."

"Lila has a quote in calligraphy on her wall. It says: *Joy is the infallible sign of the presence of God.* It's written by Pierre Chardin. He was a French priest, I think."

"I like that thought. I often feel God's presence strongly in times of joy, times of overwhelming awe. Don't you?"

"I'm coming more to that place. I let life and the demands of it pull me away from the closeness I once had with God, but I'm getting that closeness back now. I'm working at getting it back." She hesitated. "We don't always talk about spiritual things, Reid, but I think we may both be seekers, that we both want more of that type of joy."

Their food came then, shifting their thoughts and their conversation. Later when Reid took Celeste home, she said, "I'm not inviting you in tonight, Reid. I feel sort of soft and vulnerable and far too yielding toward you."

He cupped her face and kissed her, gently and sweetly. "I'd like to tell you I'm feeling strong enough in that way for both of us, but it would be a lie. My thoughts right now are far too wayward."

"Then we'll have sweet dreams, won't we?"

He laughed. "Yes, very much so. I hope you know I love you, Celeste Deveaux."

"I think that may be the first time you've said that, Reid. But those words are sweet, too."

He kissed her again and let her slip in the door. And then he walked away with a full heart, even if she wasn't ready to offer the same words of love to him.

CHAPTER 19

A Saturday in mid-October

October arrived, bringing cooler weather to the South Carolina Low Country but the temperature today, on this fine and sunny Saturday, was still in the upper sixties.

"Isn't this a lovely day?" Imogene asked as Celeste returned from Miller's café with lunch.

"It is and I enjoyed simply walking down the street in the sunshine." She set their take-out order on the table beside the checkout counter.

Imogene peeped into her bag to pull out her sandwich. "Isn't Miller's All-Day restaurant a blessing for us, so close to the store? I'll probably take the other half of this chicken salad sandwich home with me for dinner unless Vanessa wants it. I imagine she'll be here soon." She glanced at the iced tea Celeste was pulling out of the bag for herself. "Didn't you get anything to eat, honey?"

"No. I'm going with Reid for a late lunch and birthday celebration for his grandfather today. Remember?"

"I'd forgotten that, but I know you'll enjoy it." She looked across the table with a smile at Celeste. "It looks like you and Reid Beckett are getting a little serious."

Celeste shook her head. "I can't afford to get serious about anyone with all the trouble with Dillon still going on."

Imogene leaned forward. "Has something else happened, honey? I noticed you've been a little quiet all morning, except with the customers. I thought everything was going really well with your new song, already so popular and rising up the charts. Your new album is coming out any day now, too, with pre-orders piling up for it already. I can't wait to get it here at the store."

"The new release is going well and the album looks like it's going to be popular." She hesitated. "But Dillon isn't happy about all this and he's been giving Gary some problems in Nashville."

"It's quiet in here for a minute." Imogene looked around. "Tell me about it."

"You know I told you about Dillon wanting to record a song with me. He went to Gary to push for it when he didn't hear from me. Gary made it clear to Dillon this wouldn't happen. However, Dillon had foolishly already talked to some media people and told them we were releasing a song together. Dillon flew into Gary then, blaming him, saying Gary had turned me against him and a lot of other foolishness."

Celeste sighed before continuing. "Gary had to call security because Dillon was making such a scene. Dillon retaliated by keying and damaging Gary's car one night in the parking lot near his place. Now Gary is having to take a lot of additional safety measures, worrying about what Dillon might do next."

Imogene went to ring up a sale and chat with a customer and then came to sit back down with Celeste. "That Dillon Barlow is such a sick man. Have you gotten any calls or notes from him yourself."

"A few, most pushing for me to follow through and do the song with him, telling me I owe it to him."

Imogene reached out to pat her hand. "Well, I'm so sorry about all this. I know it worries you, but I'm glad you're here safe with us and not over there in Nashville near that man."

Celeste started to say Charleston was hardly an ocean away from Nashville but she decided not to voice the words. So far, Dillon had not been foolish enough to seek her out here.

The store got busy again then, and she and Imogene cleaned up the remains of their lunch so they could talk with and help customers. Vanessa came in a little later to work, too, and then Loretta, allowing Imogene to leave and go home.

Celeste glanced at the clock by the register. "Vanessa, will you and Loretta be all right if I leave now? Reid hoped to leave at one so we could be at his grandparents by two."

Vanessa smiled at her. "Sure, you go on. Marcus said you were going to boat down to Seabrook. That will be fun for both of you. Don't worry about things here. Loretta and I will be fine. She's staying until five and I'll be here until we close at six. You know I'll lock up and text you if there's anything you need to know." She waved at a familiar customer coming in the door. "You go enjoy a good time, and I'll look forward to hearing about it later."

Celeste smoothed the front of her floral sundress she'd chosen to wear today. "Do you think this dress looks nice?"

Vanessa giggled. "For heaven's sake, don't worry about how you look. That's a gorgeous dress, the perfect mix of dressy and casual and very flattering on you. You look beautiful."

"Thanks. I don't usually question how I look, but I haven't met a lot of Reid's family yet."

"They'll love you. Everyone does."

Assured, Celeste went upstairs to text Reid that she was ready, and they soon drove to the marina and headed out into the Ashley River. Reid's boat was a nice one, like many Celeste's family owned, and they soon skimmed past Fort Sumter and into the Atlantic Ocean.

Celeste had tied her hair back in a ponytail and she enjoyed the feeling of the breeze blowing across them as they headed down the coastline, soon passing the Morris Island Lighthouse and Folly Beach.

"It's a great day, isn't it?" Reid asked.

"Yes, I'm glad it was pretty so we could take the boat."

Near the Stono Inlet, further down the coast, Celeste pointed toward Bird Key Heritage on an island near the shore. "Look at all the white egrets there today. Bird Key, like the Deveaux Bank near our lighthouse island, is home and nesting ground to many waterbirds. I'm so glad South Carolina has worked to keep bird sanctuary areas like these protected."

Reid pointed to a couple of dolphins in the ocean beyond them, popping to the surface as they swam.

Despite all the problems niggling in the back of her mind, Celeste began to relax in the beauty of the natural world around her.

"Do you think your grandfather will like the hummingbird feeder we got him and the bird guidebooks?" she asked Reid. "I spent a lot of time the other day in Buxton Books on King Street, near our store, looking at different books, trying to decide on the best ones."

"He'll love the books you found and the bird feeder. He's really getting into bird watching now, and his other hummingbird feeder is getting old and it isn't nearly as nice as this new one. I don't think he has any field guides or books about birds."

She smiled, pleased.

"My grandad and my grandmother like to sit on their back porch and watch the birds at the feeders and in the trees," he told her. "Having lived in the city in downtown Charleston for so long, they're really loving the relaxing, natural pace at Seabrook."

"Do you think they'll like me?" She bit her lip.

He laughed. "I'm surprised to hear a question like that from a poised and confident woman like yourself, Celeste."

She crossed her arms. "These are not fans, Reid; they're your family."

"Well, quit worrying. Everyone will love you." He grinned. "Actually, all my family are fans, too. They're probably more worried about impressing you than you are about impressing them."

"Terrific." Celeste wrinkled her nose. "I'm not sure that thought is reassuring. I suppose knowing your parents' earlier concerns about me hasn't boosted my confidence much."

He leaned over to give her a kiss. "Relax and enjoy the day."

She tried to do so, but somehow the problems with Dillon seemed to have rattled her composure more than usual.

They passed the beach at Kiawah Island and them skimmed past Captain Sam's Inlet and the coast at Seabrook before turning up the North Edisto River.

"There's the Deveaux Lighthouse." Celeste pointed to it. "If we have time after the birthday lunch for your dad maybe we can run across the river to see my family for a few minutes, too."

Reid winked at her. "Now, you're making me nervous."

She waved a hand at him. "You know you've met all my family before. It won't be a new experience."

"Maybe, but they're still deciding if they like me or not and if they think I'm good enough for you."

She leaned closer to where he stood driving the boat to give him a small hug. "That isn't a worry of mine, Reid Beckett."

"That's good to hear."

They passed St. Christopher's Camp, and Privateer Point, and then turned up Bohicket Creek toward the marina where Reid's brother Charlie was meeting them.

"Gosh, you look beautiful, Celeste," Charlie said as he walked out on the dock to meet them. "We're all really excited you could come today to help celebrate Grandad Beckett's eightieth birthday."

Charlie drove them to Seabrook then, stopping to get through the gate, and winding along the resort's shady roads to reach Reid's Grandparents' grey beach home. It sat at the end of a wooded cul-de-sac amid palm trees, pines, and large oaks draped with Spanish moss. The one-level home, not as big or pretentious as Reid's parents' grand home in Charleston, made Celeste smile as they pulled into the driveway. It was the sort of home she was used to as an island girl.

Celeste was soon warmly welcomed by Heywood and Frances Beckett, Reid's parents, and then introduced to Reid's grandparents, Leland and Clarice Beckett, who greeted her with hugs and welcoming words. Reid's sister Lori and her husband John arrived a few minutes later with their young children, Stephen and SueEllen, and the house was soon full of the chatter, laughter, and warmth of a loving family. In the easy atmosphere, it didn't take long for Celeste to relax and get comfortable.

Seabrook, where Reid's grandparents lived, was an ocean front resort community that had developed on Johns Island in the 1970s.

Celeste could still remember standing with her sisters high on top of the lighthouse, and looking across the North Edisto River, to watch more and more properties sprout up on land once only sparsely settled. She knew that in the 1800s, William Seabrook, who had once owned the land where her family's lighthouse stood, had also owned Seabrook and used it for growing cotton and later as hunting grounds. Life had really changed along these coastal areas, as more and more development occurred and as more and more tourists wanted to move to the beach to live.

"This is a beautiful house," she told Reid's grandparents as they showed her around.

The older couple lived inland from the coast on one of Seabrook Island's quieter and more private roads. Their home, which Celeste learned they'd bought for a retirement place, had a big comfortable living area, a lovely kitchen with lots of windows, a large dining room, two bedrooms and baths, and a big screened porch room that reminded Celeste of her family's porch at the inn where they shared their meals together.

Lunch proved fun and relaxing. Reid's grandad loved all his gifts and the fuss everyone made over him. Celeste found herself a little glad the house didn't have a piano so she wasn't asked to sing and perform, but the Becketts all assured her they'd already bought tickets and were looking forward to her show at the Gaillard Center later in the month.

The time sped by, getting acquainted and visiting, and a couple of hours later, as Lori and John rounded up their children to head back home to Summerville, Reid and Celeste left with Charlie, too, who dropped them back at the marina.

"I hope you had a good time, Celeste," Charlie said as she and Reid got out of his car near the dock. "Everybody liked you, and you already feel like one of us."

"Thanks, Charlie," she said, giving him a hug and a kiss on the cheek that made his face flush a little.

Because darkness wouldn't fall at the coast until much later, Reid and Celeste stopped by the island to see her family. It would have been a shame not to stop while so close, if only for a little while. Celeste had texted Burke they were coming, and her family gathered for a short visit at Burke and Waylon's place at the lodge near the marina. Not long after five, Celeste and Reid said their goodbyes, knowing Celeste's family needed to begin getting ready for dinner at the inn.

"This has been an almost perfect Saturday," Celeste said to Reid as they climbed back into his boat. "I know Mother would have liked us to stay for dinner, but I didn't want us to boat back in the dark."

"We would have been all right," he assured her, "but it's more fun to boat in the daytime when you can enjoy the scenery. It is harder, too, to see markers, debris, and other boats at night."

She sent him a mischievous grin. "That's why we still have lighthouses."

"Ha, ha, and be assured I do know from talking with Waylon the problems they still see and the rescues they sometimes have to make at night."

"I can still remember times when Daddy went out in horrible weather to help someone. The lighthouse still serves a good purpose, and I'm glad it's still operational. Many don't operate anymore."

"Have you read about all the efforts going on to save the Morris Island Lighthouse at Folly Beach?" Reid asked as they left the island and started up the coast toward Charleston. "Weather and erosion have almost destroyed it."

"Yes, it sits out in the middle of the water now, but Dad said when it was built that it sat about 2700 feet inland," Celeste said. "They thought they built it in a safe place, but erosion has hurt it. Hurricanes have battered it, too, destroying most of the buildings that once stood around it."

"Folly Beach has receded extensively with shoreline erosion, too. It used to be bigger." He steered the boat around a jet ski coming from the other direction. "Now the land has gradually retreated, leaving the lighthouse stranded out at sea. The sand all around the Morris Lighthouse is eroding, too, and further endangering it. The entire lighthouse structure is beginning to lean. It would be a shame to see it lost, though, so there is a big preservation effort going on to get the funds needed to save it."

"I hope they succeed. I've always been grateful our lighthouse has stayed safe and strong all these years."

They passed Folly Beach and the lighthouse then, heading closer to Charleston.

Reid's cell phone pinged and seeing Marcus's number he answered. "Hey, brother. What's up?"

"Where are you right now?" he asked, his voice anxious. "Is Celeste with you?"

Celeste, sitting beside Reid at the helm, could hear Marcus's words. She leaned toward the phone. "Hi, Marcus. I'm here with Reid. We're in his boat coming back from visiting our families. Is there a problem?"

"Yes, there's been trouble and a bad accident," Marcus said. He hesitated, "It was at the store. Dillon Barlow came and caused trouble as Vanessa was getting ready to close."

"Oh, no." Celeste gasped, tears starting. "Is Vanessa all right?"

"No. She's in the hospital. Barlow got ugly with her. I'm here with her now. Why don't you guys come here, too. We're at the Roper Hospital on Calhoun, and we can fill you both in on the rest when you get here."

"Tell me where to find you, Marcus," Reid said, his voice anxious. "We should be docked and there in about twenty minutes."

Celeste, upset, heard Reid's words in a sort of fog.

"When I got to the hospital, Vanessa was still in the emergency room," Marcus replied. "But she's in a room now." He gave Reid the room number.

"Are there any police or security at the store and at Celeste's apartment?" Reid asked.

"Yes, the officer here at the hospital, who's been talking to me and Vanessa, said they had someone there. I told him I was calling you and he's waiting to talk to you and Celeste."

They heard the officer say something in the background.

"What did he say?" Reid asked.

"He said to keep Celeste with you. Barlow got away. They don't know where he is. He said Celeste shouldn't go back to the store or to her apartment right now."

"Are you sure Vanessa is going to be all right?" Celeste asked, still crying and hugging herself with the shock of it all.

"She got roughed up, Celeste, but she's going to be okay."

They heard Vanessa's muffled voice in the background.

Marcus chuckled. "Vanessa said to tell you, Celeste, that you were right that Dillon Barlow is a real wacko." He paused. "Let me get off this phone now. We'll tell you all the rest when you get here."

CHAPTER 20

After getting off his cell phone, Reid headed up the Ashley River to the marina where he kept his boat. The river was busy on a Saturday and he was forced to slow for boats skimming in and out of other marinas and inlets.

Celeste, still crying, had hunted out a package of tissues from her purse. "This is all my fault."

"No, it's not, Celeste. Don't say that or think that." He reduced his speed further as he reached the marina. "If anyone is at fault it is Dillon Barlow. Surely you know that in your heart."

He steered into the marina and then pulled into his slip. "Get out and help me tie up," he said, thinking Celeste needed something to do.

"Okay." She jumped out of the boat to help.

The marina wasn't far from Roper Hospital on Calhoun, and they soon found a parking space in the hospital garage and headed toward the elevator to Vanessa's room.

"Wait just a minute." Celeste grabbed Reid's arm, spotting the gift shop. "Let me get Vanessa a get-well balloon."

She zipped into the shop, and in typical Celeste fashion, got not one but three colorful balloons tied with pretty ribbons.

"This will cheer her up," she said, joining him again.

"I'm sure it will," he agreed, glad she'd stopped weeping.

Finding Vanessa's room, a short time later, Reid opened the door and looked in. "Ready for a little company?"

Vanessa smiled and waved from the bed.

"Look what I got to cheer you," Celeste said, showing her the balloon bouquet and then tying it onto the end of the bed.

She went to hug Vanessa then, crying again now to see Vanessa's condition, while Reid went to stand by Marcus.

"Oh, Vanessa, I am so sorry about this." Celeste sat down on the end of the bed. "I feel like this is all my fault. I even asked you to come in and work this afternoon."

"No, you didn't. Imogene did. A friend of hers asked her to be the special Story Lady at the library today and to read to the children. I offered to come in and close so she could go."

"Well, I should have filled in instead."

"And maybe gotten yourself shot," Marcus put in.

Reid looked around, interrupting. "I thought you said a policeman was here waiting to see us."

"He got called out, but another guy is coming in a few minutes. A detective, I think," Marcus answered, sitting down in one of the chairs.

"You look really roughed up," Reid said, moving closer to Vanessa to pat her cheek gently. "I see bruises turning some pretty colors and a black eye. You sound good though, but I see a splint on your forearm. What have they said about you?"

She made an effort to smile. "I came out of it pretty well because help came quickly. I'm banged up and sore though. I have a sprained forearm near my wrist, but no concussion and no other external injuries or any internal ones. I'll mend. It could have been a lot worse."

"That's the truth," said Imogene coming into the room carrying a bouquet of flowers. "I got here as soon as I could, Vanessa. The traffic is awful on Saturday." She set the flowers on a side table and then went to give her a gentle hug and look her over.

Then she went to hug Celeste. "That Dillon Barlow is one evil man. Thank goodness you weren't in the store by yourself. Honey, he had a gun and no good intent in his heart."

Reid interrupted. "Why don't one of you tell us what happened. Remember Celeste and I weren't there."

"Well, sure, honey." Imogene patted his arm fondly. "I'll start. You all know Vanessa was working for me this afternoon and that Celeste had gone to Reid's family's place at Seabrook for a birthday party. At about six I called Vanessa at the store to see how everything had gone, to check and see if she'd had a good afternoon. She interrupted me to say she thought she saw a man looking in the window that looked like Dillon Barlow. In another minute she told me she felt sure it was him."

Vanessa interrupted then. "I'd been seeing a man look in the store every now and then during the late afternoon, acting sort of suspicious. I've always been taught that near closing time in a retail store is when robberies often happen, so I was keeping my eye on him. Then I recognized him. He's a handsome man and distinctive with that golden blond hair. I knew it was Dillon Barlow, and I figured he wasn't stopping by to be cordial."

Imogene jumped in again. "I told Vanessa to press our security alarm to notify the police and I told her I was going to call the police, too. We all know Celeste has a restraining order, and a long term one, that is supposed to keep that man away from her. I told Vanessa to act real cool and normal until some officers got there."

"When I got off the phone, I saw him opening the door," Vanessa put in again.

"How did he act?" Reid asked, sitting down in one of the chairs in the room beside Marcus.

"Cool, smooth, charming, smiling at me. I didn't act like I recognized him. I nodded toward him like he was a customer looking around. I sort of hoped if he didn't see Celeste in the store he might just leave."

"What did he do then?" Celeste asked, biting a nail.

"He asked for you, said he was a friend, visiting in town," Vanessa replied. "I told him you weren't in the store today, that you were out of town."

"That's when he started to get nasty," Marcus put in.

Vanessa nodded. "He came right up to the counter and leaned over it and said, 'I know she's around. You're lying. I saw her here in the store earlier. I've been waiting until close to have a little talk with her."

Imogene looked toward Celeste, shaking her head. "I did see a man hanging around the front of the store this morning, Celeste, looking in the window when you were there. I thought it was only a man looking for his wife. I'll bet it was him. We were both real busy this morning if you remember."

"What happened next?" Reid asked Vanessa.

"I was annoyed that he called me a liar. I told him I was telling him the truth, that Celeste was not in the store and that I wanted him to leave as I was getting ready to close. I suggested he could come back another day or call to make an appointment with you." She paused. "I came around from behind the counter to sort of gesture to him to leave, telling him I needed to lock up. Then he went off like a crazy man or something."

She shook her head at the memory. "He grabbed me by the arm and wrenched it behind me, getting right in my face, and said, 'You listen to me, girl. I have business with Celeste Deveaux and I know that you know where she is. I also know she has an apartment upstairs, too, and I think you and I might need to go up there and knock on her door to see her.'" He leered at me then and said, "You know who I am, too, don't you?"

Vanessa shivered, remembering the scene. "I guess he could tell by my expression I did know him and he laughed real mean. Then he pushed me up against the counter, starting to talk nasty-talk to me, telling me what he might do to me if I didn't cooperate. He even started groping me, trying to feel me up right there in the store. I pushed at him and kneed him then, trying to get away so I could run, but he grabbed me and knocked me down to the floor and started to hit and kick on me."

"Right there in our store, can you believe it?" Imogene interjected with shock. "He must have been high as a kite on something to do that in broad daylight in our store where anyone could look in and see him."

Vanessa picked up the story again. "I learned later someone had looked in the window and put in another call to the police, telling them they thought someone was being assaulted at the store." She made a face. "Dillon was hurting me then, kicking and hitting me, asking me over and over where you were, saying he'd stop if I told him."

"Man, I wish I'd been there to beat his ass," Marcus put in.

"A police officer opened the front door of the shop then and seeing him, all but straddling me on the floor," she continued, "he pulled his gun out and told Dillon to get up, saying all that police-stuff officers recite when they intercept a crime in progress."

She took a deep breath before continuing. "Dillon did get up then, but he pulled a gun out, that he had concealed on him somewhere and shot right at the officer. I couldn't believe it. I thought my heart was going to stop. The shot hit the officer in the arm, which knocked him down, but then he fired back from the floor, hitting Dillon."

"Oh, my gosh," Celeste said.

Vanessa paused, thinking. "I think the shot hit Dillon somewhere around his middle because I saw his hand go there and I saw blood. But then he took off out our side door. The officer tried to get up and pursue, but he was bleeding and calling in for backup. Everything got real crazy after that."

Vanessa took another deep breath, wincing at a pain that hit her when she did. "Some other officers showed up then. Two pursued after Dillon and one stayed behind to see about me and the officer that had been shot. I remember that man asked some questions, and I answered as best I could before an ambulance came and transported me and the officer to the hospital here."

Marcus added, "Vanessa asked someone to call me before they loaded her in the ambulance and I got to the hospital not long after she did."

"My phone was in my purse but I wasn't thinking very clearly by that point, really hurting, especially my arm and side where Dillon booted me with his foot." She winced. "One of the officers got my purse though, from behind the counter, so I could bring it with me to the hospital."

"When Vanessa got to the hospital she called me, too," Imogene added. "Merciful heavens, things could really have gone bad if the police hadn't gotten to the shop when they did. That man is deranged for sure and I guess he's still out there somewhere, running around with a bullet in him."

An officer came in the door then. "I'm Bryan Polinski, a detective with the Charleston police. I hope you don't mind, but I've been listening to the last of this story at the door. The other officer filled me in on most of this account, as did Reese Smithfield, the officer who was shot in the altercation."

Detective Polinski came in and walked closer to Vanessa's bed. "I'm really sorry for all that's happened to you, Ms. George. We're doing all we can to find Dillon Barlow, who attacked you so brutally and shot one of our officers. By the time our backup people got to the shop, they weren't sure in what direction Dillon had fled. There are a lot of side streets, little alleys, and garden pathways in downtown Charleston. We didn't know where Barlow might have parked a car to get away in or even what kind of car he might be driving. We do have more information on that now, but Dillon Barlow seems to have fled the downtown area."

He turned to Celeste. "I assume you're Celeste Deveaux, Dillon Barlow's former wife. What can you tell us to help us with this incident, and where do you think Dillon Barlow might go?"

Celeste shook her head. "Detective Polinski, I really don't know. My best guess to offer, unless Dillon is holed up somewhere and plans to come after me next, is that he might try to head back to Nashville, hoping his agency can get him out of any trouble he's brought on himself here."

She sighed. "Dillon doesn't think like other people, Detective, and sometimes when he uses drugs or alcohol, he isn't a sane or sensible person. He's like a Jekyl and Hyde type. You never know which of his personalities you might encounter."

"I'd say amen to that," Vanessa added. "He acted real charming at first with me and then went sort of ballistic. His eyes got all glazed over when he got mad, like a crazy man or a druggie."

When a nurse came in briefly to check on Vanessa's IV, Detective Polinski took a moment to get each of their names, and their contact information, and to clarify how each of them were connected to Vanessa, the store, Celeste, and Dillon Barlow.

After the detective finished, Imogene asked, "If it's okay, Mr. Polinski, I'd like to leave now if I can. I need to check on the store and clean it up." She hesitated. "I don't think, however, that it will be safe for Celeste to stay at her place tonight, do you?"

"No, and I don't think it's safe for any of you to be at the store, even for a short time, until we've apprehended Dillon Barlow or have some idea where he is," he answered. "Ms. Hathaway, you are free to go home if you like, but please don't go to the store. It's not safe, and I still have two officers there in case Barlow comes back."

"Is the store locked to keep everything secure?" Imogene asked.

"Yes, it is, and there's crime scene tape at the store which should deter anyone," he added. "I hope we can resolve things for you to open again soon. Be patient with us."

"We're always closed on Sundays anyway, but I hope we can open again on Monday," Imogene replied.

"I do, too, Ms. Hathaway," he answered.

Imogene went to hug Vanessa and then Celeste before leaving. "Vanessa, you get some rest," she said. "I'll be over to see you again tomorrow."

As she left, Celeste asked the officer, "She'll be all right, won't she? Imogene lives over on James Island and not downtown, but she does live alone."

Detective Polinski considered her words. "I'll call and ask a patrol car to drive over to her house and check on her, maybe keep a watch nearby tonight. Did Barlow know her?"

"No. He didn't know anyone here except for me," Celeste answered. "And possibly my family."

Reid saw the panicked look cross her face then.

He turned to the detective. "Celeste's family lives on Watch Island at Edisto, where the Deveaux Lighthouse is. Do you think

Barlow might go there?"

The detective rubbed his neck, thinking. "That island's only accessible by boat. That wouldn't make it easy for Barlow to get to, wounded as he is. Also, there wouldn't be any medical help he might need there. I don't think he'd go that far, either, but I'll call and let some people at the island police department know he's a fugitive and evading arrest and what the situation is."

Detective Polinski stepped out of the room for a few minutes to make calls and then returned.

"There's still no information on Barlow," he reported.

"Could the officer who was shot tell you anything about where his shot hit Dillon?" Reid asked.

"If you remember, our officer was in the floor, hurt himself, so he couldn't shoot straight. He said it looked like the bullet went into Barlow's abdominal area somewhere, perhaps toward one side. He saw him clutch himself and, like Vanessa, he saw blood."

Detective Polinski propped against the wall. "Without proper medical care Barlow is at risk with that bullet in him." He sighed. "We've contacted all the area hospitals. We've also contacted facilities outside of Charleston, especially those near the interstate headed toward Nashville, in case he checks himself into an emergency room for care. The doctor here told us Barlow is a danger to himself and others on the road, if he's on the road, with that gunshot wound."

Reid looked at Vanessa's eyes drifting shut and turned back to the detective. "I think Vanessa has had enough company and questioning tonight. She needs some rest. Do you need to ask any of us more questions right now?"

He glanced at the clock. "No, I think you can all head home. I know where to reach each of you if I need to."

His eyes moved to Celeste. "Do you have somewhere you can stay tonight or someone you can stay with, Ms Deveaux? It is not safe for you to return to your apartment above the store."

"I often stay at the Elliott House Inn," she started to say.

Reid interrupted. "She can stay at my place. I have a house on

Clifford Street. She doesn't need to be alone tonight."

"That would be a better option," the detective agreed.

Celeste glared at Reid. "I'm not sure that is appropriate, Reid. And I don't have any clothing or toiletries with me." She turned to Detective Polinski. "Can someone at least escort me to my apartment to retrieve those things?"

He considered it. "I'll call to see if I can get you an escort to let you in the apartment to pick up a few things you might need." He smiled. "Actually, I can go with you. I need to stop by and check with the officers there at the store anyway. We're leaving both of them, at the front and back of the shop, for the night, or until we have something more definite on Barlow."

"Celeste, please go and stay with Reid," Vanessa added, anxiously twisting her hand in the sheets. "I don't think it's safe for you to stay anywhere alone, even at a hotel. That man is really crazy."

"If I stay at any man's house alone, I could have some difficult publicity problems," Celeste argued.

Marcus stood from his chair then. "I'll go and stay with Celeste and Reid at his place so everything is proper. I don't think Celeste should be alone tonight either. Also, if there should be trouble, there will be two of us to protect Celeste. That should be safer for her."

Detective Polinski nodded. "That's a good point, Marcus. Tell me where the house is, Reid, and I'll get somebody to watch your place, too," he said. "We're not dealing with a mentally stable person from all I've learned. Barlow's a loose screw for sure, and the sooner we find him and deal with him the better. I don't like the idea of him out in my city here, wounded, crazy, and probably still doped up either."

Celeste went over to get her purse and then said, "Well, Detective, I guess you know what my life was like in the past, living with that man as long as I did."

"It sounds like it was a good thing you severed ties with him," he replied as they all left.

"Where are you people parked?" he asked.

"My car is in the hospital parking garage," Marcus said.

"Mine, too," Reid added. "Celeste came with me."

As they exited the hospital, the detective pointed to where his vehicle was parked not far from the door. "Bring your cars around here, if you would. I want you both to follow me over to King Street. I'll go inside with Ms. Deveaux to pick up a few things she'll need from her apartment, then I'll follow you to your place, Mr. Beckett, and also assign a guard there tonight."

"It seems like you're putting a lot of security on this," Reid commented, puzzled at the additional measures the detective kept mentioning.

He actually grinned then. "If anything happened to Celeste Deveaux in our city, Mr. Beckett, it would be very bad publicity for our department. So, yes, we are taking some additional precautions here. The fugitive is also a well-known entertainer. There will be enough publicity when this all hits without our department being blackened, too. You do understand that, don't you?"

"I certainly do, and thank you," Celeste said. She smiled at him. "Are you married, Detective?"

He looked surprised. "Yes, ma'am. Why?"

"I'll be sure that you and your wife get free tickets to my show later this month at the Gaillard Center as a thank you. This has been a frightening and trying time, and I'm grateful for how you and the department have handled this."

"Thank you," the officer said. "I'll check with my department head to see if that offer would be acceptable."

A short time later, Reid let them into the back door of his home.

"Did you get everything you needed at your place?" Reid asked Celeste.

Her mouth twitched in a grin. "Enough for a pajama party."

Marcus laughed, and Reid was glad for a moment of levity.

As they passed through the kitchen, Marcus stuck his head in the refrigerator to look around. "Man, there's not a lot to eat in here, but there's breakfast food. I'm going to cook us some eggs and bacon. I didn't get any dinner and I know you two didn't."

"What can I do?" Celeste asked.

"Find some dishes and silverware for us and set the table. Reid can make us some coffee." He looked in the refrigerator again. "Hey, you've got some of those fancy cinnamon rolls in here that only need to be baked and then a little icing spread on them. My mama taught me how to make these. I always liked to pop the container to take them out."

Celeste giggled. "My sisters and I used to love to make those, too. I'll help you with them."

Reid found himself glad Marcus had come with them. He would bring some levity into their situation and help to keep Celeste's fears and worries at bay. This time had to bring back bad memories for her and troubling anxiety about what Dillon Barlow might do next.

"Vanessa called her mama before you guys came to the hospital," Marcus said as they sat around the table eating their food hungrily.

"She called Novaleigh?" Celeste asked.

"Yeah, her mama's coming over with her dad first thing in the morning. I thought about staying with Vanessa at the hospital tonight but the doctor said she really needed to rest quietly. He was giving her some major pain pills, too, but if she's better tomorrow and all her tests come back okay, he probably will let her go home." He frowned. "Her mother plans to take her to the island to rest and recover a few days."

He looked across at Celeste. "She's got a sprain in her arm that the doctor said will need to stay in that splint for one or two weeks. And some of her bruises will hurt a lot for a few days. I wish I could take care of her." He shrugged. "But sort of like with you and Reid it isn't my place to stay with her."

Celeste giggled. "No, and I imagine Novaleigh made that point crystal clear if you even suggested it."

"Yes, ma'am, she sure did." Marcus chuckled. "That's another reason why I offered to come over here with you," he added. "I didn't think Celeste wanted her mama or sisters coming up here to fuss and flutter over her." He looked at her. "I'm surprised they haven't been calling you. I figure Vanessa's mama told them there had been trouble. You didn't call them yet either, did you?"

"No, and I should call them. There are probably messages on my phone. I turned it off earlier so I wouldn't get calls. Novaleigh has probably spilled the beans to them about the situation and I'm sure they're worried."

She grew silent for a time. "What in the world got into that man to come down here after me like this? What did he hope to accomplish? To get me to say yes to a recording session he wanted us to do together? To punish me because I dared to say no? I wish I knew how his twisted mind works. I was never able to understand how he saw and interpreted things, how so many things threatened him so easily, how he trumped them up into more drama than they deserved."

Reid reached across the table to put his hand over hers. "You know your therapist told you that you're not responsible for Dillon's problems or for fixing them."

"Yes, I know." She sighed. "But I always feel sorrowful for the problems he inflicts on himself and others, for the irrational ideas he gets in his mind about things."

"Life can be hard to understand sometimes and the people in it even harder," Marcus offered.

"Yes, you're right about that," she answered.

Marcus pulled his cell phone from his pocket then. "I'm going to go up to the spare bedroom where I always stay, Reid, and call and see if Vanessa can talk for a few minutes." He grinned at them. "I want to say a few sweet nothings to her. You two be nice down here while I'm gone." He laughed. "Don't do anything I wouldn't do."

Reid and Celeste cleaned up the kitchen, and then settled on the sofa in the living room. Celeste flipped through a magazine while Reid looked through the newspaper.

"I'm still in shock over all this," she said at last, laying the magazine aside. "What do you think will happen to Dillon?"

"I don't know, but it won't be good. He shot a police officer this time. That's a pretty big criminal charge."

She leaned back against the sofa. "Sometimes I think all this nightmare will never end. I dread calling my mother and my agent, Gary, about this, but I think I should call both." She stood and went to find her purse to get her phone.

Reid got up, too. "I'll walk upstairs for a minute and check on the guestroom where you'll be staying. That will give you some privacy for your calls."

She smiled at him. "Thanks."

He smiled back. "Just don't talk sweet nothings to Gary, okay?"

She laughed and walked over to kiss him before he left the room. "I won't and I'd better sneak a little kiss from you while Marcus is upstairs, too."

Reid kissed her back and wished he could do more to make her heart feel better tonight.

CHAPTER 21

Celeste slept poorly that night, her dreams fitful, often waking her with alarming images and a rapid heartbeat. She did a lot of praying in the night hours, too. She felt sure her family was praying, also. She had called her mother after talking with Gary. He said the story about Dillon would probably hit the news big time this morning, and Celeste knew she didn't want her family reading about it in the newspaper or seeing a blip about it on the internet before she talked to them.

Burke called her, too, after she talked to her mother, offering to drive up to get her. "Waylon and I can come get you and bring you down to the island with us. Isolated like Watch Island is, you would be safer with us, don't you think?"

"No, I need to stay here near the store, Burke, near the police if they need to contact me," she answered. "They have put on extra security for this situation. They know there will be a lot of publicity around the event. Also, the detective working on this case, Detective Polinski, promised to personally keep me informed of any happenings. Thank you so much for your love and prayers, Burke, but I need to stay here until more is known."

She heard Burke hesitate. "Mother said that you're staying at Reid Beckett's home. Don't you think that might create some negative media attention?"

Celeste smiled at her words. "Marcus McClain is here, too. I'm not by myself with Reid. A security officer is outside and, Burke, this is not a time when either Reid Beckett or myself are thinking about a tryst. Even the media should know that. Additionally, the police will back up the fact that this was their recommendation to have me stay with Reid and Marcus rather than alone tonight."

Not surprisingly, Reid's parents expressed similar concerns and suggested she could stay at their home. Reid countered to them that the police didn't want to involve and endanger any more people than necessary right now.

She heard him add, "Dad, if there should be any problems, which is unlikely, the security guard assigned here can quickly get help from the other officers positioned at the shop a few blocks away. Also, Marcus and I are here as a safeguard, too."

Actually, Celeste didn't think Dillon would come back to the store or look for her again right now. When his mind cleared, even a little, he would realize he'd lost control. After he had attacked her in past times, he always acted repentant the day after, bringing her gifts and flowers, trying to set things right again and shifting, amazingly, back into a clear and sane state of mind again.

Thinking of him in the night hours she said to herself, "Dillon Barlow, this time you might have gone a little too far. You stepped over the line of what you can justify easily or lie about this time."

Somehow the night hours passed, and in the morning Celeste took a hot shower to wake herself up and then wandered downstairs to find Reid and Marcus already in the kitchen, working on breakfast.

Marcus grinned at her. "Good morning, pretty thing. We've made coffee and more scrambled eggs and bacon. Reid doesn't have any more of those fancy cinnamon rolls but we made toast."

Reid stood from where he sat at the table. "Let me fix you a plate."

She waved a hand at him. "No, sit back down. I can do it." She got a plate from the cabinet and walked to the stove to get a small helping of eggs, a piece of bacon, and a slice of toast." She carried her plate to the table and then returned to pour a mug of coffee.

"I talked to Vanessa this morning," Marcus put in, around buttering a slice of toast and spreading blackberry jam over it. "She says she's hurting in places she didn't even know she could hurt, but she's doing all right otherwise. Her mama and daddy are there with her now. She said she might get to go home later today after the doctor sees her again. I'll go over later today, too, if I can leave here."

Reid's cell phone pinged and he went to a side table across the room to pick it up, saying a few words to someone, ending the call and then coming back. "That was Detective Polinski. He's outside and wants to come in and talk with us." He glanced at Celeste. "I hope it's okay with you to see him. I told him I'd let him in."

"It's fine," she replied. "I hope he has some news."

Reid let the man in then, stopping to let him get a cup of coffee in the kitchen. Celeste noticed he was in uniform again, with various badges and emblems noting his rank—a tall, fit man, probably in his forties with dark short hair, a bit of a beard and mustache, and serious gray eyes.

"What's your first name, Detective?" she asked him as he came to sit down with them.

"It's Thomas," he answered, taking a long sip of coffee.

"Do you have some news for us, Thomas," she said.

"Yes, a mix of good and bad." He paused.

He seemed to consider how to begin. "Apparently, when Barlow fled the shop, he headed to his car, that we now assume he'd parked obscurely on a side street. It seems probable he thought all this out well, maybe drove around and considered the best place to park so his car wouldn't be recognized. We also know he was staying at The Charleston Place over on Meeting Street. We tracked that through his credit card. He came in late Friday, asked someone at the desk how to get to Thurman's and said he thought he might have dinner there."

"I was playing the piano Friday night at Thurman's but Celeste didn't sing," Marcus put in. "I didn't see the man that night, but I don't know if I would easily recognize him."

Reid added, "He might not have stayed long. He might only have dropped by to look for Celeste's car or to see if she was in the restaurant singing, as she sometimes does."

Celeste shivered. "So, Dillon came specifically looking for me, going to Thurman's, where media had noted I sing sometimes. Then early on Saturday, he came to the shop, found it busy, but probably saw me working. I assume he decided to come back later at close, knowing I'd have more time to talk to him."

"That's probably right," the detective agreed.

"Man, that was calculated, wasn't it?" Marcus put in.

Reid looked thoughtful. "Staying at The Charleston, which isn't far from the Gibbes Museum and Lenhardt Garden behind it, Dillon could easily have cut through the garden walkway directly from Meeting Street to King Street. It's a quiet pathway route, where he wouldn't have been readily seen if he fled on foot, after he attacked Vanessa. He could have parked his car at or near the hotel."

The Detective nodded. "That's possible. We don't know exactly where he parked his car yesterday, but we do know he had already checked out of the hotel. I guess he planned to start back to Nashville after talking with you, Ms. Deveaux."

"It's Celeste," she said.

Reid frowned. "Detective, we seem to be doing a lot of speculating about when Barlow came, where he stayed, how he planned things to have a meeting with Celeste, how he might have fled the scene, but you haven't told us anything more. You did suggest that Dillon probably planned to start back to Nashville. Is that what happened?"

"It is," he answered. "You know Barlow was wounded. We also know he was probably bleeding, doped up, and trying to get far enough away to not get caught. He probably thought, with his mind messed up, that he might make it to Nashville or at least to some place along the way where he could stop at an emergency room, claim someone shot at him while traveling, and get some help."

"Is that what happened?" Celeste asked.

"Not exactly." He took another sit of his coffee. "Remember it was getting dark on the highway and Barlow's ongoing bleeding would have caused him to start going into shock. This would create dizziness, rapid pulse, and possibly nausea. Shock can literally cause your organs to start to fail, too. We think this is what happened to Dillon on the road. Unable to control the car, he missed a curve and ran off the road, not in a good place either."

Detective Polinski hesitated. "By the time someone reported seeing the car down the embankment, and police found Barlow and transported him to the nearest hospital in Orangeburg, it was too late. I'm sorry, Ms. Deveaux, the hospital was unable to save him. In fact, he was declared dead on arrival. There was nothing anyone could do."

Celeste took a deep gulp, hugging herself and beginning to cry. "What a horrible ending to his life. Such a sorrowful waste, too."

"I'm sorry to bring this bad news, but I didn't want to simply call you with this story. I thought you'd want to know what happened." He paused. "Dillon Barlow has a long record of problems and perhaps instability. The hospital found evidence Barlow was also on drugs and drugs were discovered among possessions in his vehicle. The gun was found there, too."

Celeste was aware Reid had moved his chair closer to her and wrapped an arm around her. She leaned against him, grateful, feeling cold and sick with the news.

Marcus blew out a breath. "Gosh, what a waste, like Celeste said. That man had it all and he blew it—talent, looks, fame, and money. You just wonder how people get twisted up like that." He glanced toward the detective. "I guess you see this kind of stuff a lot."

Thomas Polinski nodded. "Yes, more than I'd like to."

He drank the last of his coffee and stood. "I have a lot of reports to do and other follow-up with this, but again, I'm sorry to bring this news. It's hard to learn anyone you once cared for has met such a tragic and unnecessary death."

"There's a sort of justice in it, too, though," Marcus commented, saying what they were all thinking but hated to say.

"Maybe," the detective agreed. "But it's always a tragedy when a life is lost." He paused, hesitating for a moment. "I plan to drop by the hospital and let Ms. George know what has happened, too."

"I'll follow you over," Marcus said. "I don't need to stay here anymore. Celeste can go back to her own place, can't she?"

"She can. There's no danger now." He turned to Celeste. "You and Ms. Hathaway are welcome to open the store on Monday as usual, if you feel up to it. I'm sure Ms. Hathaway can help out with that. She mentioned she had owned the store before you. I believe you can count on her if you need help. We're grateful she contacted the police when she did as soon as Ms. George spotted Dillon Barlow."

Detective Polinski grinned. "One of the officers told me what Ms. Hathaway said when she called. She said we'd better move fast and get over to her shop or we'd get a lot of publicity with the store belonging to Celeste Deveaux. She and Vanessa George acted very smart when they saw Barlow, too, realizing that the man even being in Charleston could only mean trouble."

Celeste wiped the last of the tears off her face, stood, and reached out a hand to the detective. "Thank you for everything you've done, Thomas Polinski. I'm truly grateful."

"Hard things like this are never easy, but it was a pleasure to meet you and your friends."

He left, Marcus following after him, and Celeste went over to Reid's large sofa in the living area, sat down, leaned back, and closed her eyes. "This all seems unreal."

Reid came to sit beside her, wrapping an arm around her, and leaning over to kiss her cheek. "You're safe now, Celeste. That fact will dawn on you as the shock wears off. You won't need to worry any more about what Dillon Barlow might do, what ugly letter or threat he may send your way, or if he might hurt you or any of your friends or family any more. It's over and done now."

She looked across at him, the realization dawning on her, too. "That's true. I feel guilty to feel relieved; it's such a selfish emotion when a man's life has been lost. But he won't be able to hurt any other people now."

A little later Reid dropped Celeste off at her own apartment.

She'd insisted he go on to meet the clients he was scheduled to show properties to today. Imogene had come to the shop to check on things, and after lunch, she and Celeste went to the hospital to visit with Vanessa again before she was released.

Novaleigh and Clifford George, Vanessa's parents, were there, with Marcus, too, and Celeste saw more arrangements of flowers now tucked around the hospital room.

"There's my girl," Novaleigh said, coming to wrap Celeste in a big hug. "Honey, this has been an awful ordeal, but the Lord has taken care of things and brought His own justice."

Vanessa frowned at her words. "Mother, I think Dillon Barlow created his own problems and brought his own justice on himself."

Novaleigh lifted her eyes at her daughter's words. "So he did, but when we step out of a right way of living, we step out of the protection of the Lord, give the enemy a right to attack our lives. That poor man, Dillon Barlow, had been letting the enemy run his life for a long time. It isn't natural for folks to act like he did."

Clifford came to hug Celeste, too. "Well, I'm simply glad both my girls are all right." He went over to kiss Vanessa's cheek.

Imogene spoke to both of them for a few minutes and then went to hug Vanessa, too.

"The doctor is working on getting discharge papers ready so we can take Vanessa home," Novaleigh added. "Clifford and I are going to run over to her apartment to pack some things for her. We should be back shortly."

She found her purse, getting ready to leave, and then turned to Celeste. "Honey, do you want us to take you home to the island with us for a rest after all this?"

"No, I'll be fine," Celeste answered. "But take good care of Vanessa so she can heal, and I don't want her to be in any hurry to get back to work."

"I agree with that," Imogene added, "And Vanessa, don't you be worrying about the store. Celeste and I will take care of things. You just get a nice rest and let your mama cook some of her good food for you."

Vanessa frowned. "The doctor said I'd be fine in about a week," she argued, "And even if I need to wear this splint at the shop for another week, I'll be fine to come back to work."

Marcus leaned forward from where he sat. "I already told Vanessa I could drive her to and from work until her splint is off and she can drive herself." He glanced at Novaleigh and Clifford. "I'll take good care of her whenever she comes back."

Celeste saw Novaleigh give him a thoughtful look.

As they left, Marcus said, "I'm going to run down to the cafeteria and get myself something to eat while you girls visit." He looked at Vanessa. "Do you want me to bring you anything?"

"No. I'm fine, Marcus," she answered. "They brought me lunch."

When he left, Imogene sat down in one of the chairs in the room and said, "My, my. We girls sure have had us a time, haven't we? I'll bet we'll have a lot of traffic in the store wanting to see what they can find out that the newspapers didn't report. There's stuff all over the media already about this."

Celeste winced.

Imogene shook a finger at her. "There may be a lot of coverage out there but it's all sympathetic to you, so don't you be worrying."

"I'm sure some tabloids will try to put their own spin on things though," Celeste said, sitting down in one of the other chairs in the room. "I don't look forward to it, and I hate that it's happened right now as my album is coming out, with my tour starting at the end of the month, too."

Vanessa snorted and held up her arm with the splint on it. "Are you crazy saying stuff like that? Look what that man is capable of? And you should know it better than I do. I don't know what he'd have done to me if that police officer hadn't come when he did. That crazy man needed to be stopped. He's done enough hurt and damage already and he didn't seem to be headed down any road to repentance and change from what I could see. I'm sorry if I sound unkind, Celeste, but hurting as I am with bruises all over, I feel he got his own back, like karma. What goes around comes around."

"She may be right, honey," Imogene agreed. "Justice isn't always pretty but it sometimes sure needs to happen."

Celeste sighed. "I guess I was simply remembering some of the good things about Dillon and maybe a few good times. I feel sorry for his family, too. His dad's gone, but his mother will grieve over this and his sister. They live down in Texas somewhere."

"Were they close to him?" Imogene asked.

"No, I think there were issues in his family, too. I only met his mother and sister once. He never talked about them. He never called or kept up with them, either, or wanted to go visit them. I don't think he even knew where his father was buried." She paused. "I guess Dillon's agency will take care of his burial. Maybe his family will come. I don't even know if Dillon had a will."

"You let his family see to those things and don't give more thought to it," Imogene said. "There may be old issues back there with them, like you said, but his family will see to everything. Family does that. I'm sure some money will come to the family, too, even if there is no will. He had to have accumulated some assets as well-known as he was."

Vanessa smiled at Celeste. "What you need to do now, girl, is not look to the past but get your eyes on the future. You just keep astonishing the world with your talents, enjoying the people that are good to you, that care about you, and love you."

"That's right, honey," Imogene agreed. "Tough times don't last but tough people do. God will strengthen and help you. You'll see."

As Celeste sat visiting and laughing with these two women she loved, she knew they were right. Earlier, resting in her own apartment, a scripture had come to her mind, 'forgetting those things that are behind, reach forth unto those things which are ahead.' She planned to work hard to do just that.

CHAPTER 22

The next weeks were filled with a lot of publicity about Dillon Barlow, how he attacked one of Celeste Deveaux's employees, pulled a gun on an officer, shot him, fled, and later died. The tragedy of Barlow's death quickly splashed across the headlines of newspapers and magazines. Later pictures of Barlow's small family funeral in Nashville trickled into the media, and interviews abounded telling about Barlow and the thoughts of others about his life and death.

Reid decided entertainers received little privacy and he regretted that for Celeste's sake. Some of the tabloids even wrote articles wondering about the pending lawsuits of other women Dillon had abused, and several revived the entire situation of Dillon's attack on Celeste and their subsequent divorce.

Reid was thinking about this today when his brother Charlie came into his office to show him a big write-up in the Charleston newspaper about Celeste's upcoming tour and her Debut Performance at the Gaillard Center.

"Nice to see something positive for a change," Charlie said with a grin. "Look at this great spread about Celeste's *The Come Back* show."

He passed the newspaper to Reid and sat down in one of the chairs across from Reid's desk. "They wrote that her show, which starts at seven, will last about ninety minutes. Mom just told me Thurman's is hosting a private reception after the show for friends and family. She said Uncle Thurman is so excited about it. He's actually closing the restaurant Saturday night so they can get ready."

"I thought it was good of him to offer."

Charlie grinned. "Well, you know Celeste's people are paying for the time, space, and the food, so he won't lose any money. And it will be great publicity for the restaurant."

"I'd say Uncle Thurman can add a few more Celeste Deveaux pictures to his entry display after this, too."

"Yeah." Charlie passed some papers across the desk to Reid. "Here is a little more info about that upcoming sale we've been working on and the updates about the needed work the owners finished after the inspection earlier. They did everything asked."

Reid and his brother talked about business matters they were both involved in then, but as Charlie stuffed all his papers back into a folder to leave, he added, "Hey, Reid, I'm sorry I didn't help things along with your relationship with Celeste at Mom and Dad's that time when I spilled the beans that you were seeing her."

Reid shrugged. "It would have come up at some point that I was seeing a lot of Celeste, so don't worry about it, Charlie. But as payback, tell me what they're saying now. Mom and Dad have been rather discreet in talking to me since the shooting and everything."

Charlie looked a little uncomfortable. "I guess they're just wondering if Celeste will stay around now that Barlow is dead. She still has a place in Nashville. She's getting ready to go on tour again."

He hesitated. "Celeste is a huge star, Reid. When she gets back on tour, around all that glamour and that big life, she might decide staying around Charleston is too small a life for her. It was a place for her to hide out when Barlow was threatening her, if she returned to Nashville. But he's gone now. I guess Mom and Dad wonder, and I have too, what changes this might mean for her."

"I don't know the answers to those questions either, Charlie, but I guess we'll see," Reid decided to say.

Charlie shifted in his seat and then added, "We all know that you're really into her now. I hope you don't get hurt."

Reid sent his brother a smile. "I've always known the odds with

Celeste. I won't regret the time with her, Charlie, no matter which way things go. But thanks for worrying about me."

Charlie leaned forward. "I really like Celeste. You never know what big-name stars will be like. But she's easy to be with. The family likes her, too."

"I've been glad to see that. Like you say, fame changes some people in a negative way, but it doesn't seem to have hurt Celeste."

"Yeah, well, maybe things will work out somehow," Charlie said, standing to leave. "I'll let you know how this house sale with the Gilcrest property goes."

His brother left and Reid got back to work. However, his mind kept drifting to their conversation all day. In honesty, he worried about the same things. He'd always known, realistically, that Celeste might have fun here for a time in Charleston, running a shop, enjoying a different life, but that her old life might draw her back.

As he left the office that evening, Reid walked down the sidewalk by CeeCee's Place and saw her working in the front display window with Vanessa. He knocked on the window and waved.

She climbed out of the window to open the door for him. "Hi. Come on in if you want. Vanessa and I just finished our change out of the front windows. With all that's been going on, we haven't had time to work on it until now. You can see we've gone with a more autumn display, bringing in pumpkins, haybales, scarecrows, and fall leaves. This fall look should last us until it's time to decorate for Christmas when I get back from tour."

He passed her the newspaper Charlie had left with him. "Did you see this nice spread about your performance this weekend at the Gaillard Center?"

Vanessa snatched the paper from him as she climbed out of the window. "Oh, look at this Celeste! It's a great write-up. Marcus and I are so excited about this. We can't wait for Saturday."

Celeste glanced at it, smiling, and then began pushing displays back in place that blocked the entry to the storefront windows.

"Can I keep this article?" Vanessa asked.

"Sure," Reid said, not mentioning he had already picked up an extra of his own, thinking Celeste would want this one.

"Reid's eyes moved over Vanessa then. "You look really good now, Vanessa," he said. "And I'm glad to see you back at work with no after effects."

She laughed. "I'm glad to be back working. I was bored at home." She wiggled her arm that had been hurt. "My sprain is healed now, too. It bothered me for a week or two, and I hated dealing with that splint I had to wear. But Marcus was real sweet. He took good care of me after I came back from mom and dad's." She hesitated. "We're going out to eat tonight. Do you guys want to go with us?"

Reid hesitated, looking to Celeste to answer for them.

Seeing them hesitate, Vanessa added, "You can help us celebrate. We're getting engaged."

Celeste's mouth fell open. "What? You didn't even tell me!"

She looked embarrassed. "Marcus only asked me last night."

Celeste grabbed her hand. "Where's your ring? I would have noticed if you had a ring."

"It was a little too big. Marcus is getting it sized and picking it up this afternoon. Hopefully, I can show it to you tonight."

"Well, then we'll definitely have to come." Celeste clasped her hands. "Are you free tonight, Reid, so we can help them celebrate?"

"Sure." He nodded.

"Where are you and Marcus going to eat to celebrate?" Celeste asked Vanessa. "It needs to be someplace really nice."

Vanessa wrinkled her nose. "I don't think we've decided yet."

"Well, call Marcus and see if he'd like to go to High Cotton on East Bay, and tell him I'm picking up the dinner tab," Reid said, giving Vanessa a hug of his own. "I'm really happy for you guys, and dinner is my treat tonight."

She zipped back to the desk to get her phone from her purse.

"That was nice of you to offer that," Celeste said. "High Cotton is a gorgeous place and it will make a nice memory spot for Marcus and Vanessa. It has a wonderful ambience—old exposed brick walls, beautiful hardwood floors, lovely table settings." She glanced to where Vanessa stood chatting with Marcus on the phone.

"He says that sounds great," Vanessa said, hanging up after a minute and walking back.

Reid glanced at his watch. "It's just after six now. I'll call and make our reservation for seven-thirty if that's all right. That will give us all time to clean up and get over to the restaurant."

"Marcus suggested seven-thirty, too. He's just getting out of the office now himself." She glanced at her own watch. "Celeste, I'm going to head home to shower and get dressed so I'll be ready when Marcus comes to pick me up. You can lock up, can't you?"

"Absolutely," she replied, giving Vanessa another hug before she headed out the door, grabbing her purse before she left.

Looking after her, Celeste said, "I can't believe she went all day without even telling me about this."

"If it makes you feel any better, Marcus didn't call to tell me, either."

She laughed. "Well, we know now, and I'm tickled for them both." She turned toward the door. "Reid, I'll let you out now and then lock up. I need to change clothes, too. What time should I be ready? "

"About six-forty-five." He opened the front door.

She put a hand on his cheek and leaned up to kiss him. "It was really nice of you to offer to pay for dinner and to suggest High Cotton. It's a little pricey for Marcus and Vanessa's budget, but it will make a special memory for them."

"It will," he said, kissing her back lightly. Hesitating, he added, "You seem very calm with this big show coming up Saturday."

"It's just my life, Reid. I'm used to it." She grinned. "Besides, Gary called and said the event is almost sold out. That's the only part we really worry about."

A little later, Reid and Celeste met Marcus and Vanessa at the restaurant on East Bay Street. They were soon settled at a quiet corner table by one of the restaurant's long windows and then ordered dinner after studying their menus. Reid chose High Cotton's lobster with sweet pea risotto, Celeste and Vanessa ordered the restaurant's grilled scallops with asparagus and side salads, while

Marcus, almost always a beef and potatoes guy, opted for ribeye with parmesan fries.

"Let me see your ring now!" Celeste said as the waiter left, spotting it on Vanessa's hand.

After the girls carried on about Vanessa's engagement ring, Reid asked Marcus, "Why didn't you call and tell us about this, Marcus? This is a happy occasion."

He shrugged. "Well, we planned to. Vanessa wanted to wait until she got her ring and I wasn't sure how soon they could resize it. Luckily, the jeweler was there today when I went back to the store on my lunch hour so he was able to do it right then while I waited."

Vanessa smiled at him and at Celeste. "It all worked out. I was planning to come in the store tomorrow and show off my ring and share my news then. But isn't it nice that Reid stopped by and we could get together to celebrate tonight."

"It definitely is," Celeste agreed. "This happy news has made my day, and I feel like I personally helped to bring this romance and marriage about. Afterall, it was because I took Vanessa to Thurman's on her birthday this summer that the two of you even met."

Marcus grinned. "That's why I didn't notice you were even at the restaurant that night at first, Celeste. I was too busy watching Vanessa."

Reid saw how those words pleased Vanessa. "Well, you picked yourself a fine woman to spend your life with."

"I agree," Marcus said, winking at Vanessa across the table.

"Have you made any wedding plans yet?" Celeste asked.

"We haven't even told our families, but we're thinking about a wedding after Christmas. Both our businesses will be in the slower season then in January so we can get away for a honeymoon, too."

"Imogene and I will be delighted to cover for you whenever you two can plan that," Celeste assured her. "Will you get married at the island?"

"Yes, on Edisto Island at the family church." She grinned at Celeste. "Will you sing something at my wedding if you're not traveling then?"

Celeste put a hand to her heart. "I'd be honored."

They talked about wedding and vacation ideas for some time until their food arrived. Marcus shifted the conversation after a time. "Man, I am so stoked and excited about your show coming up on Saturday, Celeste. Our seats that you gave us are really good ones, too, right near the front. I can't wait."

"Do you know what you'll sing?" Vanessa asked.

"Yes, the agenda, or setlist of songs, for all the tour performances gets set way ahead. The scheduled setlist will be basically the same at every show on the tour unless Gary decides I should add a special song, like one linked to a city I'm visiting or at the request of some bigwig. Sometimes, we vary the performance plan slightly but not usually. Things go smoother when everyone is on track together."

"What songs will you sing?" Marcus asked.

"I usually first sing one of the most popular songs on the latest album released, something upbeat to get the audience in a good mood, then more songs from that album, with well-loved past songs mixed in as a nod to fan loyalty. The songs alternate between upbeat, lively ones, that keep me moving around on stage, to some where I can sit on a stool and interact with the audience in a quieter way. My performance time on stage, overall, is usually about an hour and fifteen minutes but introductions and possible encores extend that so the entire show ends up being about ninety minutes total."

"Don't you get nervous?" Vanessa asked. "That Gaillard concert center is huge with balconies all around and everything."

Celeste smiled. "It's what I do all the time, Vanessa. There's always a little buzz of anticipation and nerves right before you go on stage. That's when I pray, asking God to help me give my best, and praying there won't be problems with the sound equipment, lighting or with any of that technical stuff we sometimes encounter at performances. Those things cause more problems than anything else on tour. That and transportation issues and set up problems."

"Who takes care of those aspects?" Reid asked.

"Primarily my tour manager Harry Blackwood. He's the best. He makes sure everything goes well, that everyone is where they need to be. Harry has a big job but he handles it like an art form. I'm really blessed to have Harry. I've worked with him for a long time now."

Marcus asked, "I know you said there would be about twelve stops on your tour. Vanessa said you're leaving after the show on Monday morning. Is that right?"

She smiled. "Yes, the crew will all come in for this show and we'll head out Monday on the road."

Reid felt his heart sink. It wasn't that he hadn't known this was coming, but he knew she would be gone almost six weeks, through November and not coming back until early December.

"I'll miss you," Vanessa said, saying the words Reid wanted to say.

Later when Reid walked Celeste upstairs to her apartment door, she asked, "Do you want to come in for coffee? I even have a box of homemade peanut butter fudge you can get into and take home with you. A fan came by today and brought it to me."

"Well, that's an almost irresistible offer."

"Almost?" she asked.

"Well, I would hope for a sample of the other irresistible sweets in the room, too, like the one in the silky green dress."

Her eyes lit up at his words, her mouth quirking in a smile. "I might see if that could be arranged, too."

"Well, then," he said, following her into the room.

"You know something I've always noticed about you when we're alone," she said, shutting the door behind him. "You're more playful and fun with me then. More romantic and sweet, too."

"I'm glad you like my romantic side." He gathered her in his arms to kiss her.

"You're such a good and giving man," she whispered against his neck after a moment.

"Ah, Juliet," he whispered back. "*My bounty is as boundless as the sea, my love as deep. The more I give to thee, the more I have, for both are infinite.*"

She giggled. "While I'm traveling, I'm going to brush up on lines from Romeo and Juliet so I will have a return response for these sweet and clever lines of yours."

"Actually, the lines I just quoted are ones Juliet said to Romeo and not Romeo to her." He kissed her forehead. "But they were what came to mind." He held her against him tightly for a moment. "I'm going to miss you very much, Celeste."

"I will be back, Reid." She drew away to start across the apartment toward the kitchen to make coffee.

"But will you be the same?" He said the words softly, but she turned at them.

"Why do you think I might be different?"

"You'll be going back to that exciting life, traveling on tour, meeting famous people, going interesting places. It must be heady and I worry it will pull you back into its spell."

She laughed, turning to start the coffee and then coming across the room to sit on the sofa, patting the seat beside her.

He sat down.

"You have a very distorted idea of an entertainer's life on tour. It's work, Reid, and hard work. Yes, it has its exciting aspects and moments, but a lot of it is traveling from town to town, event to event, on a tour bus. We often park our buses and vans in the venue lot where we perform. All of us on crew spend so much time together we get literally sick of each other's company after a while. It's a novelty getting an opportunity to take a long hot shower in a motel room, to sleep there, too, in a spacious, comfortable bed when we can, to do any of the normal little things so many people do every day and take for granted."

She got up to go over and pour them both a cup of coffee, and she brought him back a couple of pieces of fudge on a napkin.

"Want a bite?" he asked, holding out a piece of fudge after he'd sampled it. "It's homemade and wonderful."

"Tempter." She leaned forward. "Let me taste it on your kiss though. I can't afford to touch sweets right now."

He obliged her and enjoyed kissing her longer for a moment,

before letting her go. "So, are you saying that an entertainer's tour isn't something that calls to them? Thrills them? Makes them keep wanting to go back for more?"

She leaned back on the sofa, sipping her coffee. "It has alluring aspects I admit, but it has a dark side, too. At least to me. My manager Harry Blackwood tries to hire a good crew and he tries to insist on moral behavior on the road. But people are people, and some of the crew always seem to be a little rough around the edges. I get tired of hearing the bad language and running across some of the crew engaged in behaviors I'd call indecent, or vulgar and immoral."

He frowned. "Do guys hit on you? Try stuff they shouldn't?"

"Sometimes I get some of that on the road but not usually from our crew. They know to leave me alone, but among themselves it can sometimes be a different story."

"What else is a problem?"

"Eating healthy and right, getting enough exercise, enjoying a good, deep sleep. Everyone thinks touring must be so romantic but it isn't. At least not to me in many ways."

She learned toward him with a tempting look on her face. "This is romantic though, Reid. What we have right here together. This is what I'll be remembering while on the road." She ran her lips over his cheek, around into his hair, down his neck, and back to his mouth.

He knew he groaned. "Don't tempt me too much here, Juliet, unless you want to take this further." He pulled back to look at her. "We could do that."

"No. We've talked about that before." She got up to swap out her coffee cup for a bottle of water from the refrigerator. "Do you want some water?" she asked, holding up another bottle.

He nodded and she brought him one, sitting down this time in the chair across from him.

"I wouldn't have pushed it further than you wanted," he said softly, looking across at her.

"Yes, but I might have." Her voice softened. "Let me just sit across from you and tuck the look of you into my heart and memory."

He closed his eyes and shook his head. "Those words aren't helping. And parting won't be a sweet sorrow but only a sorrow for me. I've grown accustomed to you in my life."

"And I you." She smiled at him. "Lila said this would be a test for us to see how deep our affections lie."

"Do you think that's true?"

"I don't know. Do you?"

He studied her. "I fell in love with this sixteen-year-old incredible young woman who sang at my uncle's restaurant years ago. I didn't understand those feelings then but they were powerful, stronger after I kissed you and indulged in a little more, out in the back garden that night. All these years that old memory has stayed lodged in my heart, subtly dimming any other relationship I tried to take further over these years. When I saw you again that night in Thurman's this summer, my heart soared back to life. So, it seems unlikely to me that my affections will be changed by a six-week space, when they held fast ten years."

She smiled at him. "Those are lovely words."

He considered her. "Perhaps this time will tell you how deep your affections lie. You have known two other men in marriage. Perhaps your heart is not as sure as mine."

"I've been through a lot over these past years that has made me wonder about my judgement in a way I never did before."

"Well, then." He studied her. "Perhaps this time away will tell your heart and mind what it clearly needs to know."

"It seems rather sure right now, Reid Beckett." She sighed. "I read a quote the other day by E.E. Cummings that said: *Distance is just a test of how far love can travel.*"

He grinned. "Then maybe we'll fall more and more in love while you're away on tour. Although I can't imagine anything deeper for me." He stood. "Come kiss me goodnight, Juliet. I'm at my restraint limit for being gentlemanly. I need to head home."

Reid kissed her at the door, getting ready to leave.

She looked at him, her eyes meeting his, and then she sang softly, "Your brown eyes make me beautiful; when I see you watching me; You seem to look within my soul, seeing more than I can see….I want to know you past these nights; To follow you out the door; Inside me sings an aching hope; You make me dream of more.'"

"I remember that song well from long ago," he said.

"I sang it to you, Reid," she said as she ushered him out the door. "And I wrote it for you, too. Listen to it sometime when I'm gone and you'll know my heart."

CHAPTER 23

On Monday, traveling up the highway, Celeste glanced from the magazine she was leafing through to look across the bus to where her agent Gary Feinstein sat.

"You're staring at me," Gary said.

"Yes, why are you traveling with me? You never travel with me. You booted my assistant, Carmen, out, sending her to ride in the girls' van with the dressers and the other women on the crew. She wasn't happy, Gary."

"Carmen Yost will be all right. I told her I needed to talk with you about some things."

"Well, I need to go over several things with Carmen, too, about wardrobe and other issues. She always travels with me, Gary. I don't want her upset and looking for another job. She's a fantastic assistant—detailed, meticulous, smart. She screens out people I don't need to talk to, keeps my life ordered and on schedule, runs errands for me, literally anticipates my needs. She handles my business through the agency in Nashville every day beautifully, and she makes my tour life as smooth and stress free as possible."

He laid his phone down, after checking it a last time. "I said we need to talk about some things."

Celeste watched him fidget when he said it.

"If you keep lying to me, we won't be talking about anything. We could talk business anytime."

"All right. We really do need to talk but I had a call from Reid Beckett. He said I'd better put on extra security and take care of you or he'd come after me."

Celeste couldn't help laughing.

"Don't laugh," Gary frowned at her. "He was serious."

"And why do I need extra security now? Dillon Barlow is no longer a threat."

He rubbed his neck. "Well, some die-hard Dillon Barlow fans have been a little upset about his death. They've made some noise, said some things."

"Let me guess. They decided to fault me for Dillon's death."

"Just some crazy dudes, Celeste. The kind who think men ought to keep women in line and women ought to go along with it. The wacko-kind. We haven't paid any attention to them, but Reid saw a blip on media or something and got his panties in a wad."

"So now you are riding along with me to Raleigh. Is that where the trouble is?"

"Nah, it's some guys out west somewhere. It was only a random interview with a couple of dudes, and it happened weeks ago around the time of Dillon Barlow's funeral. There hasn't been another word about it since. It's not a real problem, it's just …"

She giggled. "It's just that Reid saw it and got worried about it."

"Yeah, and honey you need to talk to him more about this business and how things work."

"I agree," she said. "And he should talk to me about anything he's concerned with and not you. I also need him to understand that you, traveling in my bus, does not give me extra security. I doubt you could do much of anything to protect me in an unexpected situation, but Carmen Yost could. She has a black belt in karate and she has firearms training. I've seen her step in when some guy tries to mess with me before. Believe me, he deeply regretted it."

Gary fidgeted in discomfort. "I sort of promised Reid, though, that I would stick around you."

Celeste shook her head. "I'll talk to him tonight. And at our next stop, get Carmen back in here and you go back to the bus with Harry."

"We do need to talk about a few things, Celeste. Now would

be a good time." He handed her a tour agenda. "These are our performance stops. We added a few mid-week ones, like this event we're heading to now in Raleigh at the Martin Marietta Center downtown. You know that getting started late working on the tour, not following our usual schedule of setting events as far in advance, meant some concert halls were already booked. But we ended up with a good schedule even so. We've had a lot of interest for *The Come Back* tour and album."

She made a face. "I can just hear the thinking. Battered, abused woman, nearly killed by husband, returns to the stage. Yadda, yadda. I hate that my sorrows have created new interest in me. And this new twist with Dillon coming after me again, vengeful, and getting himself killed has added another layer of sensation. People will come out to see me, if only to see if I look different, look traumatized."

Gary frowned. "It's not that bad or morbid. Most people are sympathetic; they want to support you in your comeback."

Celeste gathered her hair up and hooked it in a twist. "I know, and don't worry, I'll do good shows. Didn't I do a good show in Charleston?"

"It was a fabulous show. You were stunning and the reviews went out of the roof. You know that." He paused. "Nolan would have been so proud."

She smiled at Gary then. "I think of him every time I go on stage, and I remember all Nolan did for me. How good to me he was, how blessed I was to have him. I give him a little wave in heaven every time before I walk out on stage."

"I'm glad all that problem with Dillon Barlow is past."

"He came after you, too," Celeste said, shifting to put her feet up on the sofa she sat on. She glanced out the window, glad to see fair weather and no rain. She always hated traveling on tour through harsh storms, bad weather, ice or snow.

Looking ahead, she googled the Martin Marietta Center on her iPad. She turned it around to show Gary a photo after a moment. "Look at this auditorium. The seats are upholstered in an orange red. I need to text Carmen to tell Roxanne I need to wear my green dress and not my red one for this Wednesday show. My red dress will clash with the theatre and these seats."

Celeste frowned at the image and then smiled. "Carmen has probably already checked this out and started the changes. But I'll text her." She did, sending her the link to the theatre photos.

After a few moments of quiet, Gary said, "How do you plan to go forward now, Celeste? Dillon is out of the way. Will you move back to Nashville to your condo?"

Celeste closed her eyes for a moment, gathering her thoughts. "My life took me off in some new directions, due to the unfortunate problems that found me. I had a rough time, but I'm good now, Gary."

She hesitated. "However, I find I really like many of the new directions I've discovered during this hard time. I've found that other things are rewarding, too, besides only performing, singing, writing songs, being on the stage."

Celeste saw his panicked look.

"But be assured, Gary, those things will be a part of my life as long as I can enjoy them," she added.

He sighed. "I'm glad to hear that. You have a great gift."

"Thank you, and I believe the gifts God gives you He expects you to use. But I want to keep many of the new aspects of my life, too. I want to find a balance between those different aspects. It isn't unusual among entertainers. Many of them have their fingers in outside businesses and philanthropic activities, like Dolly Parton, for example. I make very good money from songwriting, too. I want to keep doing that, keep seeing that I have time for that. Artists I admire like Dolly and Carol King have shown me how lucrative that can be."

Gary nodded. "You make more than most other artists just because you do write all your own music."

"I know you've sometimes wanted me to perform some other songs, branch out, but I want to continue to perform my own work, Gary. I can put my heart and passion into doing that in a way I can't in singing other music. My own songs come from within my own heart and soul. They are like a part of me. Also, I like the persona, the image, of being an artist who sings only her own songs. Nolan saw the advantage in that, the branding and the uniqueness of that as part of my public image. You've been with me since my early days. You've seen that work well, Gary."

"I have, and again, the man was a genius." He picked up the cola on the table beside him to drink the last of it and then asked, "How do you want to play this now?"

"I'm on tour right now, a shorter tour than usual, but I like that. I'm open to do performances in between tours that would be beneficial to my career and good for the agency and Capital. I'm all right at this time continuing to do a new album every year or two with a tour to follow. However, I don't think I need to tour every year now to stay in the heart of the public."

"Your reputation is well-established now."

She paused. "We'll think about all this as we go along. Sometimes, if I don't release a new album one year, we might release a single or two, if I write something good, and if the time seems right. You can help make those decisions."

"Thank you. We try to take good care of you and your career at our agency."

She hesitated. "You've seen that I can continue writing songs in South Carolina as well as in Nashville. I've proved that to you. The sales of this album show the new album is as good, or better, than albums I've written before. I don't need to live in Nashville, but I'll keep my condo there so I can come to the city whenever needed."

"Well, that's true I guess, but …"

"Spit it out, Gary. What's worrying you?"

"What if you marry again? What if you decide to have a family?"

She grinned at him. "Do we need to create a list of well-known female artists that we both know who have married, birthed children, and who continue to be loved by the public and are performing and successful? I always thought you more open about things like that."

He fidgeted in his chair again. "But is Reid Beckett open about things like that? He seems to be very traditional in his viewpoints."

She crossed her arms and smiled. "Which goes to show how little you know him. Do you know what he said to me not long ago when I expressed concerns about that? He laid out a scenario to me of how he thought marriage and family shouldn't be any problem for me if we should grow serious and want to marry some day in future. He talked about how he could easily take care of any babies we had when I traveled, with help, telling me he had a good way with children."

Gary laughed. "That doesn't sound like the guy I've spent some time with, but I like hearing that he's that open and flexible."

"I think he really is," she agreed and then sent him a look. "So have we talked out the things that have been worrying you now?"

"Yes, I think so for now. I'm glad you're wanting to continue in the industry and that you've thought out how to handle other things you value with it." He grinned. "Celeste, I do feel confident that if anybody can do it, as you've talked about, you can. I have confidence in you."

"Thank you, Gary. That means a lot."

She looked at the agenda in her lap. "Talk me through where we're touring now, including any changes you've made since we went over this last. I'll sit down with Carmen later and we'll go over everything in more detail, too."

Gary glanced at his agenda copy. "Wednesday, as we've discussed, we'll be in Raleigh at the Martin Marietta Center. It's an easy move in and out there. An accessible place. We have good space for the buses and crew but you can go over to the Hilton nearby if you want. I might, too. Harry and I usually share a big room. I can get one for you and Carmen until we pack out and move on."

"I see Washington DC is next for Friday night. Will we be at the Kennedy Center or at the Lisner?"

"At the Lisner; It seats 1,500. We'll probably pack it out, but that's okay. I have some good interviews and coverage for you there, when we arrive and through Friday before the show. The

Lisner is on the George Washington University campus. Would you be open to talk to some students, maybe in drama? It looks good in the papers and you usually like doing that."

"I can do that. I like to encourage young people."

"We'll be going to Philly on Saturday early and with a show that night. Not much time for media or interviews, but we'll be busy in New York with a lot of interviews and some talk shows, already scheduled, before your show kicks in on Friday."

"Will that show be at the Lincoln Center?"

"No, at the Town Hall downtown, beautiful old theatre, seats 1,479. With a couple of days of press and appearances ahead, and the work and promotions we've already done, we'll pack it out, too."

Celeste groaned as she studied the next tour point on the list. "Then we're going directly from New York to Columbus, Ohio, for a show the next night. How many hours away is that?"

Gary shrugged. "About eight hours, but you can sleep on the road. We'll leave right after the New York show. No time for any meet-and-greet events. Part of the crew will go ahead to set up; part will stay to take down. Sometimes it's the way the schedule works out, Celeste."

She glanced down at the agenda's details. "Well, here's a perk. My show there will be at that incredibly beautiful, old Ohio Theatre Performing Arts Center on State Street downtown." She googled it on her iPad. "I love simply looking at that glorious place, built in 1928 originally and later saved and restored. They don't make theatres like that anymore."

They made their way through the entire schedule as the bus ate up the miles on the road. As usual, Celeste had a show on most every Friday night somewhere, another on Saturday at their next stop, with an occasional show in-between on a Wednesday or Thursday. Occasionally she had a Sunday evening performance, making for a grueling weekend with three nights in a row. But Gary and Capital set few of those multi-show weekends.

As they finished talking through the tour, Gary smiled. "Hey,

I've got a surprise possibility for you. When we're in Hollywood, California, Martina's place isn't far outside the city. I pulled some strings and I can take you out to her place. It's in the Topanga Canyon area. Your friend's property—the one Martina works for--backs up to the park, and Martina's place is just down the road. It's safe for you to go see her now with Dillon gone. She said she and the kids would be really thrilled to see you if it works out."

Celeste put a hand to her heart "How sweet of you to think of that. I'd love to see Martina again, if only to be sure she and the kids are happy." She hesitated. "If Martina wants to come back to Nashville now, I could probably help her move to the area. Does she have family in Nashville? I don't remember her ever mentioning any."

"No. Her people live in Mexico, so California is actually closer." Gary smiled. "Martina told me it feels more like home there. She's happy where she is."

"Well, I hope we can work a visit with her in. I definitely want to see her. And thank you for planning it."

They rode in silence for a time, Gary answering texts and emails, Celeste reading an article in her magazine and looking out the window at the fall colors, now touching the trees with October near its end.

As often happened. as she rode for miles on tour, Celeste found thoughts for new songs drifting through her mind. She began scribbling lyrics and words down on a note pad.

"Hey, Gary," she said after a time, "I've had an idea for a new album." He looked up, his phone forgotten.

"How do you like the album title, *Southern Girl*, with a song with the same title, possibly as the headliner." She smiled at him. "I've already written it, and I have a few more song ideas working, inspired by being in the deep south again. I thought it might be a nice link for my fans to my living in Charleston now. I've even written a Charleston-based song, celebrating the city, the beauty and romance it hides."

"You should know about the romance it hides, since you found a corner of it." He teased.

"Well, blessedly, Reid Beckett is nothing like Dillon Barlow," she said, looking out the window again.

"No, he's a good man, and I admit I like him, even if he gets a little bossy about you sometimes." Gary paused. "He makes me think of Nolan when he does that though. Nolan was always protective of you."

Gary scribbled a few notes on a legal pad beside him. "I like your idea of a *Southern Girl* album. See what you can do with it. I'll talk with some people in Nashville. See what they think."

He wrote a few more notes down. "Send me a song or two later that you think might work for it. That may help me sell the idea."

She smiled at him. "I already have one called 'Sweet Southern Man' you'd probably like."

He laughed. "I bet I'd recognize the man, too."

After a little time, she said, "Gary, have you been watching for that right one for you?"

"Honey, with all that's been going on with you, Dillon Barlow, getting this tour ready, and piles of work with my other artists, I don't think I would have recognized a potential 'right one for me' if she'd bumped into me and knocked me down."

Celeste crossed her arms. "Then maybe you need to get away on a holiday so you'd have a better chance to run into her." She considered her words. "Or I might start looking for someone for you."

He shook a finger at her. "No matchmaking, Celeste Deveaux. If she's out there we'll find each other at the right time. Sometime." He sat back, thinking. "I think when you meet the right someone, you'll just know somehow and maybe smile at each other for no reason."

Celeste put a hand to her heart. "Oh, Gary, I love that thought. I can see those words in a song."

"Well, dedicate it to me if you write it." He looked out the window. "I do think about the idea sometimes."

Celeste got up to look for some lunch in the refrigerator and gave him a kiss on the cheek. "Everyone in their secret heart thinks about romance, Gary, about finding someone to love. It's wired into us from the beginning of time, to yearn for a helpmeet suitable for us. No matter what we say, we hope for love to find us."

Later that evening, settled into the hotel room that Gary found for her in Raleigh, with a quiet time to herself, she texted Reid: "*Romeo, Romeo, wherefore art thou, Romeo?* If you can, give Juliet a call."

Less than five minutes later, her phone rang. She glanced at the number coming in and smiled.

"Hi," she answered. "I was thinking of you."

"Hi, back. I was thinking of you, too. Where are you now? On the road or settled in somewhere?"

"We're here in Raleigh. It's only about four hours from Charleston. Gary had a late afternoon TV spot scheduled for me after we got in, dinner out afterward with some people associated with the performance center, but I'm finally settled into a hotel room Gary got for Carmen and myself. He usually gets us suites when he can for more privacy." She paused. "Carmen had some meetings with the crew and errands to do, so I had a few minutes to myself. How was your day?"

"Busy meetings. A couple of new listings." He chuckled and Celeste loved the sound of it. "I've also started looking for a house for Marcus and Vanessa."

"Really? How did you get involved in that?"

"Marcus has been living in a small apartment above his family's business, on the third-floor, since college. It's not the ritz, but he's been saving his money so he could buy a place downtown eventually. He can't move Vanessa into that apartment where he lives, and her rental is small. So, I'm trying to help Marcus find something he can afford."

"I'd love to help with that if I can, maybe with the down payment."

"I'm looking around. I'll let you know. I know they both want to stay downtown if they can, maybe live close enough to walk to work. Marcus's family business is on Beaufain off of King Street so I'm focusing on that area."

They chatted about a few other things, and then Celeste said, "Reid, when you have concerns related to my professional life you need to bring them directly to me and not to Gary. I know you mean well, calling Gary, but there's so much you don't know about the business and the industry I work in—just as there is a lot I don't know about the realty and brokerage business you work in. The appropriate thing to do, when you have any concerns or questions, is to talk directly to me. I hope you can see why that would work best."

Reid cleared his throat. "Gary and I sort of had an agreement we'd look out for you, touch base with each other about security concerns."

"I can understand why you both discussed that when Dillon Barlow was such a problem, but that isn't the case anymore."

"Well, there was an issue related to that about…"

Celeste interrupted. "I know about that. It's no longer an issue. You need to remember that every little issue related to entertainers, no matter how trivial, tends to find its way into the news, usually inflated, aggrandized, and added to in some way."

"Did I create a problem?"

She laughed. "Only a small one for me. Gary joined me in my bus on the trip to Raleigh. He never does that. My assistant Carmen Yost travels with me. She handles things for me. As well as being an extremely efficient and organized woman, who handles my business with expertise, she holds a blackbelt in karate and has firearms training. Reid, I'm in much better hands with Carmen any day if I need protection than with Gary, as fond as I am of him."

"I guess I got a little macho and over-protective."

"Well, the thought is sweet, but let's handle it in a different way in future, all right?"

"Yeah, I'll do that."

She heard him chuckle again.

"I guess that's my old Southern gentleman blood rising up too much."

"I know, and it touches my woman's heart that you care that much, but you need to remember I've become pretty tough and resilient out here on my own. I have an entire agency and a tour crew watching out for me, too. You might think of it like my own little army on the road."

He laughed. "Maybe I can play superhero and Southern gentleman a little though when you're home with me. Okay?"

"Okay, especially if you tuck in a little romance with it."

CHAPTER 24

The weeks moved along slowly with Celeste away traveling. Reid knew she was working, that her tour was going well, but he missed her. She called him many nights, when she wasn't in a show and had a few minutes to talk, but it wasn't the same as having her here. Seeing her. Being with her. Touching her. He knew he was feeling lovesick, and it ticked him off a little, even though he could do nothing about it.

Tonight, to stave off the loneliness, Reid had invited Benson and Marcus over for dinner, hungering for some company. He'd picked up steaks to grill, put some potatoes in the oven to bake, and made a salad for a side. They usually grilled steaks, chicken, fish, burgers, or ribs when they got together because it was easy. Reid knew his way around the kitchen, but he liked cooking outside best.

Benson soon found him on the patio behind his house, working at the grill. "Hey, brother. Thanks for asking us over." He sat a bag on the table. "I brought a couple of bottles of wine for dinner. I hope that's okay. I picked them up at the Wine & Company on Meeting Street on my way over."

"And I brought dessert," Marcus added, coming around the corner to join them. "I zipped over to Kaminsky's Dessert Café near the Market and snagged one of their famous pecan pies. I think they're even better than my mama's, but don't tell her I said that."

Marcus sat his bakery box on the table. "Are we going to eat out here or in the house?"

"Probably in the house," Reid answered. "Everything's already in there and we won't have to haul stuff out here, but we can take our dessert and coffee out to the porch later."

"Good plan," Benson said, walking over to check the steaks on the grill. "It looks like those are about ready. Marcus and I will take this stuff inside we brought with us and get everything else out we'll need."

Reid turned the steaks on the grill a last time. "Salad and bottles of dressings are in the refrigerator, along with butter and sour cream, for the potatoes. I'll be there in a minute if you can't find anything."

"We're on it, man," Marcus said, heading up the steps into the back door. "I know your kitchen like my own."

A short time later they were all settled around the table, enjoying their dinner.

"How does it feel to be an engaged man?" Benson asked Marcus.

"Don't be ribbing me about getting married," Marcus replied. "The time comes for all of us. Seems like both of you are nosing around and getting pretty serious yourselves right now."

"Do you remember Grace Ravenel?" Benson asked. "I dated her when we were in school."

Marcus paused from eating to think. "Skinny girl, carrot red hair, glasses? The one always reading?"

"She's morphed into a beauty." Reid laughed. "Still red-haired but the skinny has filled out in all the right places."

Benson, always the more serious in their threesome, looked a little embarrassed. "Grace is a real nice girl, good family, smart—she's a well-known author now, too. Did you know that?"

"No, what does she write?"

"Historical fiction, each story based around a Lowcountry historical property."

Marcus grinned. "Hey, that's a good fit for you. You've always loved historic properties. You even went to England to learn more about preserving them and that sort of thing. It's also linked to your family's appraisals business."

Benson filled Marcus in more about his studies at Cambridge, shared stories about some of the places he'd visited. "England is an old country compared to ours. Some of its architecture was created before the United States even developed. We can learn a lot from the British about taking care of and restoring old properties."

"Well, the six of us all need to get together sometime," Marcus put in. "It will be a treat to see Grace again and laugh about old times. You tell her I said hello the next time you see her."

"I will," Benson answered. "She's asked about you and Reid. She remembers both of you."

"Well, we all hung out together a lot in those college years. Had some fine times together," Marcus said.

Reid got up to top off their wine glasses. "Anybody need anything else while I'm up?"

"No, I'm getting stuffed," Marcus answered. "You grilled some great steaks, Reid. Good dinner."

"Everything was good," Benson added.

"Hey, I was sorry to hear about all that mess with your brother, Ben," Marcus put in. "That must have been tough, especially for your mother. How's she doing now?"

"A lot better, and thank you for asking," Ben replied. He filled them in on how the new management at Folly Beach was working out and talked about being back, working and doing appraisals again at the family business. "I'm going to teach a class or two this winter, too, at the College of Charleston."

"You'll enjoy that," Reid said, sitting back, his dinner finished.

"How's Celeste's tour going?" Marcus asked.

"Good. The reviews and media have all been positive that I've heard about."

"I've seen some great stuff, too," Marcus added. "I bet she's having a blast. It must be a big high getting out on stage like that, having all those people coming to see you. It's got to be cool. I wonder if a lot of guys hit on her?"

"You could have left that last comment out," Reid said with annoyance.

"Oh, don't get yourself in a huff," Marcus said. "You're just missing her and feeling jealous of all those men wishing that they could spend time with her. It's just the way it is in the entertainment world."

Still annoyed, Reid started clearing off the table. "Let's get this food cleared away and the dishes put in the dishwasher, and then we'll take some pie out on the porch. I think I'll make coffee, too."

"Good idea. I'd like coffee," Ben said, getting up to help him carry plates and glasses back to the kitchen.

Marcus quit ribbing him, and the rest of the evening went well, just three guys having a good time talking about work, sports, politics, happenings around town, and any other subject that came up.

That night, Reid got to talk to Celeste again. His heart lifted when he saw his cell phone ping at nearly midnight.

He grabbed his phone to read her text: "I know it's late but call me if you're still up."

"I'm still up," he said when he called her back. "Still up and thinking about you. Are you all right?"

"I am. Just tired."

"Where do you head next?" he asked.

"We're leaving Vegas tomorrow," she answered. "Thank goodness. It's not one of my favorite places, not the kind of crowd I like best. Tomorrow, we travel to Texas for shows in Dallas and Houston, then to New Orleans, Birmingham, and on to Atlanta, then finally back to Nashville." She sighed.

"And then home to Charleston," he added.

"Yes, and home to you," she whispered. "I think about you more than I imagined I would, Reid."

"Sweet words to hear. Benson and Marcus came over to dinner tonight and I got testy with Marcus because he suggested how many guys were probably hitting on you."

She giggled softly. "I like that you're feeling a little jealous. But Carmen and the crew keep a good watch on me. I haven't had any problems, more than the usual overzealous devotees."

"When do you come home?"

"I fly back Monday after my show at the Opry on Saturday night. I actually look forward to that one and sleeping at my own place for a couple of nights when we get back to Nashville."

"Tell me your flight time and I'll come get you at the airport."

"No, let me take an Uber from the airport. I'll text you when I get in and you can come over then." Her voice dropped. "I'd like it better seeing you without a crowd all around."

Somehow the weeks dragged by, but a plan began to form in Reid's mind while he waited. Friar Lawrence had counseled Romeo: *Wisely and slowly; they stumble that run fast.* But he and Celeste weren't Romeo and Juliet, star-crossed lovers who would come to a tragic end and die. They were sweet lovers who deserved happiness.

Reid felt certain in his heart they belonged together, that the fates had brought them together a second time for a purpose. He saw no reason any longer for pretending otherwise. As December arrived and Celeste returned to the Opry for her final celebratory performance in her tour, Reid began to plan for his performance, too.

On Monday, the day Celeste would be flying back to Charleston, Reid left work smiling, knowing he'd soon be seeing Celeste again. Her flight was a late one, not arriving in Charleston until around eight. He knew she had meetings in Nashville she needed to attend and an early dinner with Gary before he put her on her flight.

She texted him shortly after eight, "My flight is pulling in to the airport. I'll text you when I get to my apartment."

"See you soon," he texted back.

Not waiting, he drove over to CeeCee's apartment, parking his car behind his office instead of her shop, and then waited out of sight for her.

She soon arrived, waving at the Uber driver as he left. Then she picked up her bags to carry them to the door, unlocking it and letting herself in. Reid moved to the spot he'd picked out then. He knew she'd see the note on her door that read: Come Out to The Balcony.

A few minutes later, he saw her peek out the back door and walk out on the long piazza porch, looking around.

"*Ah, it is Juliet, my love,*" he called out, moving into the light where she could see him. "*How fair and beautiful you are.*"

"Reid Beckett, you idiot. What are you doing down there? I haven't seen you in over a month, and I hardly want to simply look over my balcony at you."

"Fair one, I will come to you soon," he persisted in his role, "But first seek out the precious gift I left for you—a golden heart, not as lovely as you in this light, but I hope it will please you. You will find it hanging by a thread if you seek around you."

She gave him an exasperated look but then began to search the porch. Reid watched her spot the heart then, hanging from one of the potted plants.

"I have found it Romeo." Celeste grinned, reaching to untie it from its yarn thread. "And, oh, it is lovely."

He'd hunted through several of Charleston's antique shops, until he found the perfect gold, heart-shaped box with European crystals and intricate filigree work on it. He could see it glittering in the porch's light. It looked like something Romeo might have offered Juliet.

"You can come up now." She leaned over the balcony to smile down at him.

He dropped to one knee. "*Did my heart love till now? Forswear it, sight, For I ne'er saw true beauty till this night ... And with love's heavy burden do I sink.*" He paused. "In the box is my heart and my hope."

She opened the heart box and peeped inside, her eyes widening.

"My heart and my life are yours, Celeste," he said in his own words now. "I am hoping you will marry me and spend your life with me. I believe we are star-crossed for joy and happiness not sorrow. I love you with all my being. Could you say yes? Does your heart love me now, too? Lila said this time would be a test for how deep our affections lie. I know mine well. Do you know yours?"

He saw tears on her cheeks.

"I will not give you that answer over the balcony, Reid. Come up here. My door is open."

He sprinted around to the back door and up the stairs to her apartment. The door was open, and she stood across the room looking at him.

She wiped some tears away. "So many lonely nights I pictured how you looked in my mind, but nothing is so handsome as you are. Come kiss me."

He did, his heart thrilled to hold her close again, to catch that subtle jasmine scent of her cologne she always wore and the special scent that was all hers. Reid kissed her cheek, her neck, then moved his mouth back to hers. Such a sweet moment.

"Will you say yes, Celeste?" he asked again, drawing back enough to look into her eyes. "Have you had the time you need to be sure?"

She gave him a misty smile. "How can I not say yes when even the ring is the perfect size and fit?" She pulled her hand from behind him to display it.

The ring was set in 14K gold, like the heart box he'd found to put it in—a lovely oval diamond ring with small diamonds in the band on either side. Reid had known any ring had to be something rather stunning to please Celeste. And it was.

"I do love you, Reid Beckett, and I do say yes."

Thrilled, he kissed her again and then whirled her around. "We're going to have a happy life, Celeste."

She laughed. "Well, put me down before, as you said, under love's heavy burden you sink."

She wrapped her arms around him again when he did. "You are truly the most romantic man. I will always remember I had a Romeo and Juliet proposal under my balcony."

Reid smiled at her, pulling her snug against him and enjoying the feel of it. "With a woman whose life is filled with memorable performances, I had to try to create a special moment to propose."

"You did it beautifully. Come sit down now and talk to me. I am tired from the tour and all the travel."

They moved to sit on the couch together, Celeste leaning her head against his shoulder. "This is so nice, coming home to you."

"It could be nicer." He winked at her. "And it will be nicer when we marry."

She smiled at him. "When do you want to get married?"

"Tomorrow." He grinned.

She laughed and swatted at him. "You know I've only been divorced since June, not even a full year now. Dillon's death and all that media is barely two months behind me, too." She paused. "The media would have a field day with the news that I am remarrying again so soon."

He gave her time to think.

"My family will be shocked enough that we're already engaged," she added. "I can only imagine what your family will say. They're not even totally sure they approve of me as a future daughter-in-law yet."

"And your point is?"

"There will be a lot of talk. That's my point."

Reid thought about her words. "Let me ask you this. Won't there be talk anytime we choose to marry, in part simply because you're a well-known singer? Won't there be talk if we wait or if we marry sooner? Would it matter when?"

He saw her thinking about it.

"Personally, I think we've waited since you were a girl to find each other, to love each other. I know Nolan took you away before I could pursue you and that he was good to you, good and kind from all you've told me. He made you happy and handled your career as your manager. I know he helped you become who you are. Perhaps that was a part of the destiny you needed to walk. But we have a destiny, too. A good and happy one, I think."

"Maybe."

He leaned closer and put his hands on either side of her face, leaning over to kiss her lightly again. "So many times, while you were gone, I thought to myself, 'I could get on a plane and fly over there this weekend—to wherever you were—to see you, hold you, spend a little time with you. But I knew from your cautions it would cause talk, that the media would pick up on it, that it might cause negative repercussions. Even when you flew in to Nashville, I wanted to come more than I can say, to be with you, to see you perform again. But I couldn't because there would be talk."

"I thought of that often, too," she admitted. "It seemed silly some nights when I was missing you so much that you couldn't fly over to be with me, especially when I had a few days between performances. Or, actually, any time would have been a joy."

He stroked a hand down her face. "Would there have been talk if I'd visited and we were married?"

She shook her head. "Probably for a time, but then probably not as much so. The media can't speculate about what a husband and wife are up to like they might lovers."

He leaned in to kiss the skin in the vee-neck in her sweater. "I'd like to be your lover."

She fanned herself. "My mind just formed some tantalizing pictures, Reid Beckett."

"Mine, too." He laughed. "You know, I just thought of something." He pulled out his cell phone, typed in some words in his search engine and then opened an old YouTube song by Bonnie Raitt. He clicked to let it play and grinned at Celeste as the words rolled out.

She giggled. "Gracious, I haven't heard that song 'Let's Give Them Something To Talk About' in a long time. Bonnie Raitt released it back in 1991 on her album *Luck of the Draw*. It's a great song."

"It is, and I say they're going to talk anyway, Celeste, your agent and the agency, the media, the tabloids, your fans, our friends, my family, your family, so let's give them something to talk about, honey. Let's just get married and be happy."

"You're getting to me, Reid Beckett, with your crazy reasoning."

"It's not crazy. It's the truth. Don't we deserve happiness regardless of what people are saying? Do they know our hearts and what is best for us? Or do we?"

She stroked her hand down his cheek and neck, letting her hand drift between the buttons of his shirt. "I'd like to be married to you, Reid Beckett. I learned a new line from Romeo and Juliet for you: *This bud of love ... may prove a beauteous flower when next we meet.* It has been lovely already, hasn't it? And I can easily envision more."

Reid looked into her beautiful eyes and said, "Let's do it, Celeste. And soon. Let's give them something to talk about. Why not? It can't hurt you or anyone to learn you've honorably married, that you fell in love and chose to be happy."

"Do you have a time in mind for this crazy idea of yours?"

He opened his phone to a calendar page. How about this Sunday afternoon if we can work it out at St Michael's where we both attend? If we wait longer, we'll be pushing into the Christmas holidays and the media might catch wind of it and show up." He grinned at her. "I have in mind just getting the rector to marry us quietly on Sunday afternoon, with our families there and a few friends, and then having a little celebration afterward at Thurman's. Uncle Thurman wouldn't mind opening up the restaurant on Sunday for a family get-together. What do you think?"

"I'm stunned. I don't know what to say."

"Say yes unless you are hungering for a big, lavish wedding with lots of media coverage."

Celeste closed her eyes. "Let's sit here for a minute and let me think about it."

Reid leaned back, found the Bonnie Raitt YouTube and let the song play again while she sat thinking.

"It's hard to think sensibly with that song playing and seducing me, Reid Becket."

He gave her an innocent look. "I can't imagine what you mean, but I do think about you every day and dream about you at night. Aren't those sweet words?"

She pushed at him. "Okay, Mr. Planner, tell me how this can work. Convince me."

"A visit to see the rector tomorrow at St. Andrews would be first, to set the date, and to help him see the need for something quiet and private. I think he will easily understand that. Then we'll need to make a visit to both families to let them know our plans, to invite them to celebrate the day with us. I'll need to talk with Uncle Thurman to set up the reception after. We'll let our closest friends know but ask everyone for secrecy. You'll need to buy a dress, something lovely you like. I already have a nice black tux. A few flowers would be nice if we could manage that discreetly, maybe get Imogene to handle that. I'm sure Marcus would play the piano so we'd have a little music."

He shrugged. "Then we show up, happy with smiles, and get married, pledging to love and cherish each other forever through sickness and health until death do us part. I have no problem with those words and vows, do you?"

"Is it that simple?"

"It can be, and it should be." He smiled at her.

She looked around. "I guess I would need to move in with you since you have a house."

"That sounds sensible," he said, trying not to grin. "As we settle in, I'd be happy for you to make changes at my place, to make it feel more like 'our' home, rather than only 'mine.'"

"Well," she said. "It is something to think about."

He turned off his phone and kissed her again, admittedly with more passion than before. "Loved one, don't let me pressure you though. If you would rather wait until spring or until summer, we will. This isn't an ultimatum, only an invitation."

She sat back, her breathing a little escalated, like his.

"I will have to keep my name for the stage, and we will have a lot of money matters to work out."

"Your wealth and your name are yours to keep. I only want your heart and your love, Celeste."

She sighed. "Oh, gentle Romeo, my true love's passion, how can I say no to you." She laughed. "And why say no when it is what we both want and when we are both sure? Here is my answer, if you can arrange it, we will do it. And, quickly, before the press gets wind of it."

And so it was that on Sunday afternoon at four pm in the afternoon, Celeste Deveaux walked down the old historic aisle of

St. Michael's Church on Broad Street, the same church in which she'd prayed to God about whether to buy CeeCee's Place, the same place where she'd prayed over many other weighty matters and found rest and answer. They did not have attendants for their wedding, but all their family and friends sat in the beautiful old pews to see them wed. Imogene had, indeed, taken care of the flowers, with two lush bouquets of roses, in deep burgundy, ivory white, and peach, at the front of the church, Celeste's bouquet echoed them in the same colors.

Celeste wore a long, ivory wedding dress, rich with old lace, discreet in design, its skirts sweeping the floor and trailing behind her. A lacy veil draped over her hair but didn't cover her face, which Reid saw, to his joy, wreathed in smiles as she walked down the aisle to him. He wore his best tux with a burgundy rosebud as a boutonniere.

It had been amazing how quickly everything had come together. The families had been shocked of course, tried to "talk them out of it" as they'd expected. But he and Celeste only passed each other grins over their talk and objections. And now, as the time was here, Reid saw only happy faces, happy with them and happy for them.

As they finished their vows and the rector called them man and wife at last, he added with a wink to Reid, "*And may this alliance happy prove for this pair of star-crossed lovers.*"

RECIPES from *Light in the Dark*

Novaleigh's Peach Muffins

1 ½ c. all purpose flour	1/3 cup vegetable oil
¾ cup sugar	1 large egg
2 tsp baking powder	½ cup milk
1 tsp ginger	1 ½ tsps. vanilla extract
1 tsp ground cinnamon	½ tsp kosher salt
1 ¼ cups chopped ripe peaches	1/3 cup vegetable oil

Directions:
Heat oven to 400 degrees. Line 8 muffin cups with paper liners and put 2 tsp water in empty cups. Whisk flour, sugar, baking powder, ginger, cinnamon and salt until well blended. In large measuring cup, add oil and egg, then add milk to the 1-cup line. Add vanilla and whisk until blended. Pour into bowl with dry ingredients; fold in the peaches. Pour evenly into the 8 muffin cups. In a side dish, mix 1 Tablespoon sugar, 1/8 teaspoon of both ginger and cinnamon to make a spiced topping. Sprinkle over muffin batter. Bake 15-20 min til golden brown.

Novaleigh's Cheesy Potato and Ham Casserole

- 1 (30oz) pkg frozen hash brown potatoes, thawed
- 1 8-oz container sour cream
- 1 (12oz) pkg pre-cooked ham steak, diced
- ½ cup butter, melted
- 2 cups shredded cheddar cheese
- 1 (10.5 oz) can cream of chicken soup
- Sprinkle of black pepper and garlic salt

Directions:
Heat oven to 350 degrees. Grease long baking dish, like 9x13. In large bowl mix hash browns, ham, cheese, onion, soup, sour cream, butter and seasonings. Transfer to prepared baking dish and cover with aluminum foil. Bake until bubbly and cheese is melted. Remove, sprinkle with toasted bread crumbs and more cheese if desired. Return to oven without foil for 15 minutes

Annabel's Half Moon Cookies

1 cup butter
½ cup sugar
2 cups flour

1 teaspoon vanilla
6 oz chocolate chips, melted
6 oz white vanilla chips, melted

Directions:
Cream butter and sugar, add flour and vanilla. Make ½ inch balls of dough, roll in sugar and place on cookie sheet. Flatten cookies with spatula. Bake at 350 degrees for 12-15 minutes. Remove and cool 10-15 minutes. Dip one side of cookie into melted dark chocolate; cool on waxed paper or chill to set the chocolate. Then dip other side of each cookie into white chocolate. Leave thin line between chocolates as you dip them. Cool on waxed paper sheet. Chill to set the chocolate.

Frances' Peas and Mushrooms

2 T. olive oil
1 T. unsalted butter
¾ chopped onion
2 cloves garlic minced

1 lb frozen peas
1 c. sliced baby mushrooms
½ cup chicken broth
½ tsp Italian seasoning

Directions:
Heat olive oil and butter in large skillet. Saute onion and garlic until translucent. Add sliced mushrooms and saute until fragrant. Add broth, peas, seasoning and a little salt and pepper if desired. Cover pan with lid and cook until peas are tender, about 5 minutes.

Etta's Carrot Poke Cake

1 15.25-oz box Duncan Hines Carrot Cake Mix
(plus eggs, oil, and water to prepare)
16-oz carton whipped cream
1 cup pecans, chopped well
2 3.4-oz boxes instant cheesecake pudding mix
2 cups whole milk

Directions:
Make carrot cake per instructions on box in a 9x13 inch pan. Remove from oven and immediately poke holes all over the cake. Whip cold milk and cheesecake pudding mix well and pour over the cake and into the holes. Chill 10-15 minutes until pudding sets. Then spread whipped topping over cake. When ready to serve, sprinkle pecans over the top and drizzle caramel sauce over all.

A Reading Group Guide

LIGHT IN THE DARK

Lin Stepp

About This Guide

The questions on the following pages are included to enhance your group's reading of Lin Stepp's *Light In The Dark*.

DISCUSSSION QUESTIONS

1. As this book opens, you learn quickly that Celeste is still being threatened by her ex-husband Dillon Barlow. What happened in her marriage with Dillon Barlow that caused her sisters to come bring her home to heal? Although Celeste is now divorced, and has legal restraining orders on her life for protection, why is Dillon Barlow still angry with her and pursuing her with threats? Would you be frightened to receive calls and letters like Celeste has been receiving?

2. Celeste has been seeing a counselor to help with the troubling issues in her life. What has Dalton Conrad, Celeste's counselor, helped her to know about Dillon Barlow? Have you ever known anyone with narcissistic problems like Dillon's? Why is living with a narcissist or interacting with them particularly difficult? A quote on Dr. Conrad's wall reads: You're always one decision away from a totally different life. When Celeste asks if he really believes those words, he answers that he hopes to help his clients realize that "no one is locked in to any particular life role, that change is always possible." Do you think that is true? How are these understandings helping Celeste?

3. Celeste has a sweet, longtime friendship with Vanessa George, who is Novaleigh and Clifford George's daughter. Vanessa is working in a retail store in Charleston, so when Celeste goes to Charleston to see her counselor, she takes Vanessa out to dinner for her birthday. Where does Celeste take Vanessa to dinner? What problems do you learn that Vanessa is having in her job? Why is Thurman's a special place for Celeste? What happens at Thurman's that causes Celeste to sing there?

Discussion Questions

4. Reid Beckett's uncle owns Thurman's Restaurant in Charleston, and he stops by after work to take his uncle some papers to sign. What business do you learn that Reid Beckett is in? He stays to have dinner at the restaurant and to visit with his friend Marcus who plays the piano there. How does he react when Celeste goes to sing with Marcus impromptu? What do you learn about how they were acquainted in past? Although Reid was attracted to Celeste then, why didn't he pursue a relationship with her? What does Marcus tell Reid about Celeste that he didn't know?

5. After meeting with Dr. Conrad in Charleston, Celeste goes shopping, an activity she loves. Have you ever been to Charleston, South Carolina? Do you enjoy shopping and exploring downtown there? Why is Celeste attracted to Imogene Hathaway's store on King Street? What is it called and what is it like? What problem is Imogene having that she confides about to Celeste? What idea does this give Celeste as she looks around? Where does she go to help her know if the decision that she is considering is a right one? What happens there that helps Celeste know what she should do?

6. At work on Thursday morning, the day after he saw Celeste again, he looks up to see her standing in his doorway. Why is she there? As Imogene Hathaway's broker and real estate agent, what questions does Reid ask her about buying Imogene's store? How does he advise her? How does Imogene feel about the idea of Celeste buying her business when Reid goes to see her later with the contract proposal? Is CeeCee's Place a store you would like to visit?

7. How does Celeste's family react to her decision to buy CeeCee's Place in Charleston? What concerns do they have and how does she answer their questions? Charleston is about forty-five minutes from Edisto Island. Where does Celeste plan to live

Discussion Questions 273

in Charleston? How does Celeste's decision also help her friend Vanessa with her problem situation? What does Celeste hope Vanessa will do in her new business? What gifts does Celeste bring to her new business and why is it a good fit for her as a side venture?

8. When the sale of CeeCee's Place finalizes, Reid Beckett begins to consider the possibility of renewing a relationship with Celeste? How does Celeste's need for a piano and her acquaintance with Marcus open an opportunity for seeing Celeste more? How does Marcus react to possibly helping Celeste with her music? What further ideas does he have for them both when he learns Vanessa George will be working at CeeCee's Place? What do you like about Reid's friend Marcus?

9. Gary Feinstein is Celeste's agent. How long has she been working with him? What was Gary's connection to Celeste's first husband Nolan Culver? When Gary comes to meet with Celeste in September, he isn't happy with how long she has been distanced from the music scene?. How does he feel about her buying a retail store in Charleston? As he says, "People are wondering what's going on with no new songs or new album even being talked about." How does she help him see that this change has been positive for her? What new album does she tell him about that especially makes him happy?

10. Reid worries about Celeste's meeting with her agent. Why? What counsel does Marcus give him about that? When Reid and Gary Feinstein meet later at Thurman's how do they get along? How do you see in their meeting that both care for and are concerned about Celeste and want her to be safe and happy? Later in the story, how does Gary show in other ways he cares for Celeste? What did you learn about Gary and the entertainment business he and Celeste work in?

11. Reid and Celeste's relationship moves up a notch when she has a scare at Thurman's one night, seeing a man in the dark around her car. Reid takes her home and what happens then? What do you learn about their past encounter when Celeste was younger? As their relationship advances, Reid shows a playful, romantic side, often quoting Romeo and Juliet lines to Celeste. Did you enjoy seeing this new side of Reid, as Celeste did? How do their feelings begin to change for one another? What are the ongoing problems that keep their relationship from advancing more?

12. While Celeste is shuffling her new life at CeeCee's Place, her music career, and her growing feelings for Reid Beckett, Reid is dealing with his own business and family concerns. Who are the Pennymans and how does Reid get involved with Annabel Pennyman in trying to help her sell her home? What unexpected problems does Reid run into and how do he, his father, Annabel's son Benson, and the Pennyman's lawyer handle them? Who is the individual trying to cheat and defraud Annabel Pennyman? What did you think of Clarence Pennyman? Have you ever known of a situation where a family member tries to cheat another family member out of money? Did you admire how Annabel Pennyman handles the matter? What would you have done?

13. As the fall moves along, Celeste goes to Nashville to record her new record. What concerns does she have about returning to Nashville, even for a short time? How is Gary Feinstein and her recording company working to keep her safe while she is in the city? What did you learn about how a record is recorded and the work it takes from a large team of people? What problems did Dillon Barlow cause while Celeste was there? What was he pushing for Celeste to do with him and why? What was her response? Did you enjoy hearing snatches of some of Celeste's new songs?

14. With a new album coming out, Gary and her recording company have also planned her fall tour to come after its release. How long will she be on tour and where will she be traveling to perform? The first scheduled performance, to highlight the changes in her life, is planned for Charleston at the Gaillard Center. Later, when Celeste is on tour, what do you learn about an entertainer's life on the road? What are some of the problems and pleasures in being on tour?

15. Romance isn't only in the air for Celeste and Reid. Vanessa and Marcus soon grow serious as the book progresses, too. When they get engaged, where do Reid and Celeste take them for dinner? What do you like about this couple? In addition, Reid's friend Benson Pennyman, back in town now, starts a new relationship, too. Who does he meet and where? How has he known Grace Ravenel before and what does she do for a living? Why, amid all this, is Reid so worried about Celeste going on tour and how that might affect their relationship?

16. After a trip to help celebrate Reid's grandfather's birthday, Reid gets a call from Marcus that Vanessa has been attacked by Dillon Barlow at the store and hospitalized with injuries. At the hospital, what story does Vanessa, and Imogene, tell Reid and Celeste about what has happened? With Dillon still at large, the detective on the case, Bryan Polinski, does not want Celeste to return to her apartment above the store or stay alone. What does Reid suggest? How does Marcus help out with this to make it less media-provocative for Celeste to stay over at Reid's?

17. The following morning Bryan Polinski comes to Reid's home to update them on the case. What do they learn happened to Dillon Barlow? How does Celeste respond to the news? Marcus comments: "Gosh, what a waste… that man had it all and he blew it—talent, looks, fame, and money." After a time, Celeste

says, "I feel guilty to feel relieved; it's such a selfish emotion when a man's life has been lost. But he won't be able to hurt any other people now." How did you feel to learn about Dillon Barlow's death? Isn't it a sorrow when people allow their lives to go to ruin. Have you ever been a part of a situation like or similar to this when ongoing problems cost another person their life? How did it affect you and others you knew?

18. As the blook closes, Celeste is finishing up her lengthy tour and Reid is back in Charleston worried that she will be different, and feel differently about him, when she gets back. Lila has suggested that their separation will help them both know the real depth of their relationship. Reid, sure of his own heart, decides to propose when Celeste comes back. How does he do that in a romantic way? How does Celeste respond? When they discuss the idea of when to marry, what does Reid suggest and how does he persuade Celeste to go along with his idea? When did they marry and how did you like the ending of this third book in the Lighthouse Sisters series? What did the rector say after pronouncing them man and wife?

Books by J.L. and Lin Stepp

The Afternoon Hiker
Discovering Tennessee State Parks
Exploring South Carolina State Parks
Visiting North Carolina State Parks
Coming next -- *Traveling Georgia State Parks*

Books by Lin Stepp

The Smoky Mountain Series

The Foster Girls	*Tell Me About Orchard Hollow*
For Six Good Reasons	*Delia's Place*
Second Hand Rose	*Down by the River*
Makin' Miracles	*Saving Laurel Springs*
Welcome Back	*Daddy's Girl*
Lost Inheritance	*The Interlude*

The Mountain Home Books

Happy Valley
Downsizing
Eight at the Lake
Seeking Ayita
Shop on the Corner
Coming Next --- *The Red Mill Bookstore*

Christmas Novella

A Smoky Mountain Gift
In When the Snow Falls

The Edisto Trilogy

Claire at Edisto
Return to Edisto
Edisto Song

The Lighthouse Sisters Series

Light the Way
Lighten My Heart
Light in the Dark
Coming Next
The Light Continues

About The Author
Lin Stepp

Lin Stepp is a native Tennessean, businesswoman and educator. A *New York Times*, *USA Today*, *Publishers Weekly*, and Amazon best-selling international author, Lin has twenty-four published novels out, including her twelve beloved Smoky Mountain novels, all set in different Tennessee and North Carolina locations, five Mountain Home books, a novella in one of Kensington's Christmas anthologies, and six South Carolina coastal novels, including her three Edisto Trilogy books and her third release in the new Lighthouse Sisters series.

Lin and her husband J.L. also write regional guidebooks, including a published Smoky Mountain hiking guide and TN, SC, and NC state parks guidebooks, all filled with hundreds of color photos. Writing and adventuring are her joys and more new novels set in the Smokies and at the beach are on the way, as well as more colorful regional guidebooks. Lin's title *Claire At Edisto* was the *2019 Best Book Award Winner in Fiction: Romance*, sponsored by American Book Fest and her novel *Welcome Back* a finalist in the 2017 Selah Awards. Lin enjoys speaking for events, festivals, libraries, and book clubs. And she loves reading, hiking, exploring out of doors, and keeping up with her readers. Look for her pages on Facebook and Twitter and follow her monthly blog and newsletter, too, that you will find on her author's website at: *www.linstepp.com*.

Milton Keynes UK
Ingram Content Group UK Ltd.
UKHW010654080324
439098UK00001B/40